CLIVE CUSSLER'S
GHOST SOLDIER

Clive Cussler was the author and co-author of a great number of international bestsellers. His series include the famous Dirk Pitt® adventures, such as *The Corsican Shadow*; the NUMA® Files adventures, most recently *Condor's Fury*; the *Oregon* Files, such as *Fire Strike*; the Fargo Adventures, which began with *Spartan Gold* and the Isaac Bell historical thrillers, which lastly included *The Heist*. Cussler passed away in 2020.

Mike Maden is the author of *Clive Cussler's Hellburner* and *Fire Strike*, the critically acclaimed Drone series, and four novels in Tom Clancy's #1 *New York Times* bestselling Jack Ryan Jr. series. He holds both a master's and Ph.D. in political science from the University of California at Davis, specializing in international relations and comparative politics. He has lectured and consulted on the topics of war and the Middle East, among others. Maden has served as a political consultant and campaign manager in state and national elections, and hosted his own local weekly radio show.

TITLES BY CLIVE CUSSLER

DIRK PITT ADVENTURES*

Clive Cussler's The Corsican Shadow (by Dirk Cussler)
Clive Cussler's The Devil's Sea (by Dirk Cussler)
Celtic Empire (with Dirk Cussler)
Odessa Sea (with Dirk Cussler)
Havana Storm (with Dirk Cussler)
Poseidon's Arrow (with Dirk Cussler)
Crescent Dawn (with Dirk Cussler)
Arctic Drift (with Dirk Cussler)
Treasure of Khan (with Dirk Cussler)
Black Wind (with Dirk Cussler)
Trojan Odyssey
Valhalla Rising
Atlantis Found
Flood Tide
Shock Wave
Inca Gold
Sahara
Dragon
Treasure
Cyclops
Deep Six
Pacific Vortex!
Night Probe!
Vixen 03
Raise the Titanic!
Iceberg
The Mediterranean Caper

SAM AND REMI FARGO ADVENTURES*

Wrath of Poseidon (with Robin Burcell)
The Oracle (with Robin Burcell)

The Gray Ghost (with Robin Burcell)
The Romanov Ransom (with Robin Burcell)
Pirate (with Robin Burcell)
The Solomon Curse (with Russell Blake)
The Eye of Heaven (with Russell Blake)
The Mayan Secrets (with Thomas Perry)
The Tombs (with Thomas Perry)
The Kingdom (with Grant Blackwood)
Lost Empire (with Grant Blackwood)
Spartan Gold (with Grant Blackwood)

ISAAC BELL ADVENTURES*

Clive Cussler's The Heist (by Jack Du Brul)
Clive Cussler's The Sea Wolves (by Jack Du Brul)
The Saboteurs (with Jack Du Brul)
The Titanic *Secret* (with Jack Du Brul)
The Cutthroat (with Justin Scott)
The Gangster (with Justin Scott)
The Assassin (with Justin Scott)
The Bootlegger (with Justin Scott)
The Striker (with Justin Scott)
The Thief (with Justin Scott)
The Race (with Justin Scott)
The Spy (with Justin Scott)
The Wrecker (with Justin Scott)
The Chase

KURT AUSTIN ADVENTURES®

Novels from the NUMA Files®

Clive Cussler's Condor's Fury (by Graham Brown)

Clive Cussler's Dark Vector (by Graham Brown)

Fast Ice (with Graham Brown)

Journey of the Pharaohs (with Graham Brown)

Sea of Greed (with Graham Brown)

The Rising Sea (with Graham Brown)

Nighthawk (with Graham Brown)

The Pharaoh's Secret (with Graham Brown)

Ghost Ship (with Graham Brown)

Zero Hour (with Graham Brown)

The Storm (with Graham Brown)

Devil's Gate (with Graham Brown)

Medusa (with Paul Kemprecos)

The Navigator (with Paul Kemprecos)

Polar Shift (with Paul Kemprecos)

Lost City (with Paul Kemprecos)

White Death (with Paul Kemprecos)

Fire Ice (with Paul Kemprecos)

Blue Gold (with Paul Kemprecos)

Serpent (with Paul Kemprecos)

OREGON FILES®

Clive Cussler's Ghost Soldier (by Mike Maden)

Clive Cussler's Fire Strike (by Mike Maden)

Clive Cussler's Hellburner (by Mike Maden)

Marauder (with Boyd Morrison)

Final Option (with Boyd Morrison)

Shadow Tyrants (with Boyd Morrison)

Typhoon Fury (with Boyd Morrison)

The Emperor's Revenge (with Boyd Morrison)

Piranha (with Boyd Morrison)

Mirage (with Jack Du Brul)

The Jungle (with Jack Du Brul)

The Silent Sea (with Jack Du Brul)

Corsair (with Jack Du Brul)

Plague Ship (with Jack Du Brul)

Skeleton Coast (with Jack Du Brul)

Dark Watch (with Jack Du Brul)

Sacred Stone (with Craig Dirgo)

Golden Buddha (with Craig Dirgo)

NON-FICTION

Built for Adventure: The Classic Automobiles of Clive Cussler and Dirk Pitt

Built to Thrill: More Classic Automobiles from Clive Cussler and Dirk Pitt

The Sea Hunters (with Craig Dirgo)

The Sea Hunters II (with Craig Dirgo)

Clive Cussler and Dirk Pitt Revealed (with Craig Dirgo)

CHILDREN'S BOOKS

The Adventures of Vin Fiz

The Adventures of Hotsy Totsy

CLIVE CUSSLER'S
GHOST SOLDIER

MIKE MADEN

MICHAEL  JOSEPH

PENGUIN MICHAEL JOSEPH

UK I USA I Canada I Ireland I Australia
India I New Zealand I South Africa

Penguin Michael Joseph is part of the Penguin Random House group of companies
whose addresses can be found at global.penguinrandomhouse.com

First published in the United States of America by G. P. Putnam's Sons,
an imprint of Penguin Random House LLC 2024
First published in Great Britain by Penguin Michael Joseph 2024

001

Printed and bound in Australia by Griffin Press

The authorized representative in the EEA is Penguin Random House Ireland,
Morrison Chambers, 32 Nassau Street, Dublin DO2 YH68

A CIP catalogue record for this book is available from the British Library

HARDBACK ISBN: 978–0–241–70433–2
TRADE PAPERBACK ISBN: 978–0–241–70434–9

www.greenpenguin.co.uk

CAST OF CHARACTERS

THE CORPORATION

Juan Cabrillo—Chairman, and captain of the *Oregon*. Former CIA non-official cover.

Max Hanley—President, Juan's second-in-command, and the *Oregon*'s chief engineer. Former U.S. Navy swift boat veteran.

Linda Ross—Vice President, Operations. Retired U.S. Navy intelligence officer.

Eddie Seng—Director, Shore Operations. Former CIA agent.

Franklin "Linc" Lincoln—Operations. Former U.S. Navy SEAL sniper.

Marion MacDougal "MacD" Lawless—Operations. Former U.S. Army Ranger.

Raven Malloy—Operations. Former U.S. Army Military Police investigator.

Eric Stone—Chief helmsman on the *Oregon*. Former U.S. Navy officer, weapons research and development.

Dr. Mark "Murph" Murphy—Chief weapons officer on the *Oregon*. Former civilian weapons designer.

George "Gomez" Adams—Helicopter pilot and chief aerial drone operator on the *Oregon*. Former U.S. Army helicopter pilot.

Dr. Julia Huxley—Chief medical officer on the *Oregon*. Former U.S. Navy surgeon.

Hali Kasim—Chief communications officer on the *Oregon*.

Kevin Nixon—Chief of the *Oregon*'s Magic Shop.

Maurice—Chief steward on the *Oregon*. British Royal Navy veteran.

Russ Kefauver—Intelligence analyst. Former CIA forensic accountant.

Mike Lavin—Chief armorer on the *Oregon*. Retired U.S. Army armament/fire control maintenance supervisor.

Amy Forrester—Physician assistant on the *Oregon*. Former U.S. Navy combat medic.

Steve Gilreath—Helmsman on the *Oregon*. Former U.S. Navy veteran.

Jesse Benson—Team leader of the firefighting unit on the *Oregon*. Former U.S. Navy veteran.

UNITED STATES

Callie Cosima—Underwater robotics and marine engineer.

Langston Overholt IV—CIA liaison to the *Oregon*.

Erin Banfield—CIA senior intelligence analyst.

USAF Major Brian "Hawkeye" Joslin—F-35 Lightning II fighter pilot.

USAF Captain Will "Mad Dog" McGhee—F-35 Lightning II fighter pilot.

USAF Captain Peter Stallabrass—Commander of the E-3 Sentry mission crew.

ITALY

Colonel Mattia Piccinini, Italian Carabinieri "KFOR MSU"—Kosovo Force Multinational Specialized Unit. Arma dei Carabinieri.

Lieutenant Salvio Bonucci, Italian Carabinieri "KFOR MSU"—Kosovo Force Multinational Specialized Unit. Arma dei Carabinieri.

THE ISLAND OF SORROWS

Rahul Tripathi—Indian national. Professional video gamer and weapons designer.

Captain Gustavo Plata—Former Guatemalan special forces unit, the Kaibiles.

Sergeant Major Florin Drăguș—Former member of the Romanian 1st Special Operations Battalion.

Lieutenant Sergei Osipenko—Former member of the Wagner Private Military Company.

Sergeant Abdul Al-Mawas—Former member of the Syrian Army's 25th Special Mission Forces Division (aka "Tiger Forces").

Sergeant Conor McGuire—Former member of the British Army's 22nd Special Air Service Regiment.

Senior Corporals Jakub and Pawel Warschawski—Former members of the Polish special forces unit GROM.

When you're wounded and left on Afghanistan's plains,

And the women come out to cut up what remains,

Jest roll to your rifle and blow out your brains

An' go to your Gawd like a soldier.

—RUDYARD KIPLING,

"THE YOUNG BRITISH SOLDIER"

PROLOGUE

1945

NORTH FIELD, GUAM

The *Moonshiner* was the eighty-seventh aircraft in a line of 145 B-29B Superfortress bombers rolling down the tarmac. Their primary target was an aircraft factory near Tokyo, 1,500 miles away— about the distance from Canada to Mexico, and most of it over shark-infested waters.

Normally stationed by the "putt-putt" auxiliary motor during takeoff, the claustrophobic twenty-two-year-old tail gunner, Technical Sergeant Carl Jansen, had been given permission to stand near the cockpit so he could watch the takeoff through the big glass canopy.

The pilot mashed the brakes to the floorboard, his eyes fixed on the bomb-laden plane ahead of him wobbling uneasily into the sky.

Jansen mopped the sweat from his forehead, but it wasn't from the heat. He'd seen enough fatal crashes during takeoff to know this part of the flight was as dangerous as the flak and fighters waiting to ambush them along the way. This would be his fourth mission over Japan. Not so long ago, he was riding a Farmall F-20 tractor in his father's cornfields near Manteca, California. Over his mother's protests, he waived his occupational service exemption to join the war before it was too late.

Finally cleared by the tower, the pilot advanced the four throttles, rattling the airframe as they powered up. He released the brakes, and the *Moonshiner* rolled forward with its crew of eight and twenty tons of munitions.

Moments later, the sixty-seven-ton war wagon was aloft.

★

IN THE AIR OVER TOKYO

Jansen stood in the cramped tail section compartment, his head on a swivel and his hands on the radar-assisted pedestal gunsight. Japanese interceptors preferred nighttime attacks and they especially favored hitting the big American bombers from the rear.

That put Jansen squarely in the crosshairs. It didn't matter. He had a job to do. Built for speed and increased range, the B-29B had only one gunnery station—his. If Japanese fighters closed in on his vulnerable position it just meant he had a better chance of swatting them out of the sky with his three .50-caliber Browning machine guns.

He told his mother that his body armor and helmet protected him from Japanese bullets, but it wasn't true. He put more faith in his parachute despite the fact he had never gone through actual jump training.

The tail section roared with engine noise as the young gunner glanced through the large armored-glass windows. The night sky was filled with the shadows of bombers in formation—and, more ominously, hundreds of small black clouds of flak thumping all around them.

The first planes were already dropping their loads. Clouds covered the city far below, their undersides lit up by the flickering lights of exploding ordnance.

"Bombs away," the bombardier said. His voice over the interphone was clear and measured despite the thundering flak. The *Moonshiner* shuddered as the thousand-pound bombs released from their bay.

Jansen had once sat in the bombardier's tiny, unarmored compartment in the glass nose during a training flight in Texas. "Best seat in the house," the mustachioed lieutenant had joked with him. Jansen wasn't so sure back then. But now, standing here, with their P-51

Mustang fighter escorts far behind them, Jansen wondered if the bombardier wasn't right after all.

A sudden, blinding explosion tore through Jansen's compartment. Searing pain clawed at his back, shredding his parachute. With the distant shouts of "Bail out!" screaming in his headphones, the gunner turned and reached for the emergency door only to see the *Moonshiner*'s flaming fuselage streaking high and away as the tail section separated from the rest of the plane.

The tail section helicoptered down like a falling maple seed. Even if Jansen wanted to jump, he couldn't. Too shocked to scream, he hardly registered the ice-cold wind scouring his face and whistling beneath his helmet.

His narrowing eyesight fixed on the maelstrom of light erupting beneath the hellish clouds far below.

Jansen's mind reeled in terror, his death certain.

★

UNIT 731 COMPLEX
JAPANESE-OCCUPIED MANCHURIA
Four days later

Dr. Yoshio Mitomo stood in the doorway of his clinic, shivering in the biting wind as the Japanese army truck screeched to a halt. Neither his thin lab coat nor well-trimmed beard offered any protection against the subzero temperature.

A burly sergeant jumped out of the cab, his boots sinking into the snowdrift. He barked orders as he approached the canvas-topped rear.

The truck gate slammed open and the large body of an American was tossed out. He lay in the snow, groaning as two soldiers leaped out of the back and began hitting him with the butts of their rifles, shouting for him to get up. The big American cried out in pain as he curled up in a fetal position to protect himself.

"Stop this!" Dr. Mitomo shouted as he stumbled through the snow. "I order you—stop this, now!"

The sergeant barked another order and the two privates stopped their assault.

The doctor stooped close to the American. The flyer was only dressed in a ragged flight suit stained with blood, some of it fresh. His left leg appeared to be broken.

"Help me get him inside before he freezes."

"Yes, sir!" the sergeant barked.

The two privates grabbed the American roughly and yanked him to his feet.

"Careful! This man is injured—"

"So what? This man is a war criminal," the sergeant said. "He bombs innocent civilians."

"Do as I say, Sergeant—or else."

The sergeant's snow-flecked face reddened from the bitter cold and his barely contained rage. He studied the doctor's implacable gaze before finally giving a curt nod and uttering a guttural "*Hai.*" He barked more orders to his men. They gently lifted the flyer to his feet.

Barely conscious, the tall American draped his arms around the necks of his diminutive guards and used them like crutches to steady himself. He turned to the doctor and whispered in a barely audible voice, "*Thank you.*"

Mindful of the still raging sergeant, Dr. Mitomo fought back a smile, but nodded an acknowledgment. His eyes caught the name tag printed on the flyer's chest:

TSGT. JANSEN

★

Jansen sat tall in a chair in Dr. Mitomo's office. His Chinese-made cotton pants and shirt were several sizes too small for the big-boned Dutchman, but clean and warm. Over the past two weeks, his broken leg had been properly set and cast, his infected wounds stitched and dressed, and a steady diet of healthy food, water, and tea had proven as restorative as the antibiotics and vitamin supplements Dr. Mitomo had provided. A pair of crutches leaned against the wall.

Jansen was certain he was being sent to a death camp after his capture and abuse by Japanese home guards. His initial prison stay on the outskirts of Tokyo had been a living nightmare, and his transport into the frozen north was itself nearly a death sentence. Guilt haunted him, convinced the rest of the *Moonshiner* crew were all dead.

His only consolation was to witness firsthand the utter devastation the U.S. Army Air Corps had wrought upon the enemy.

Sitting here in a sterile, well-lit room with Dr. Mitomo was strangely calming as the doctor read through a thick file on his desk.

"According to my records, you seem to be on a rapid road to recovery," Mitomo said. His English was faultless, having studied biochemistry at UCLA for three years before the war.

"I feel pretty good. And if I haven't said it before, I'll say it now. Thank you for your kindness."

"Of course. I'm a medical professional."

"We were told that American prisoners were not well treated."

"Unfortunately, that is often true, as you yourself experienced before arriving here."

"So tell me, Doc, why am I here?"

Mitomo shut the file folder.

"Your American air corps has destroyed most of our medical facilities on the mainland. Here in China we have escaped your wrath. It is one of the few places where any kind of decent medical care is possible for American POWs."

"When do I get shipped outta here?"

Mitomo pulled open a drawer and pulled out a pack of cigarettes. "Smoke?"

Jansen waved a big paw. "Nah, thanks. Never liked 'em. But you go ahead."

Mitomo flicked a lighter, and lit up. After taking a few puffs, he continued.

"I'm still working on finding a camp that will be less harsh than the one you are bound to be sent to."

Jansen arched his brow. "I appreciate that."

Mitomo smiled. "We're not all monsters, you know." He blew a cloud of smoke. "I would like to ask you a few questions, if you don't mind."

Jansen frowned. "You know, the Geneva Convention only requires me to give you my name, rank, and serial number."

"Which you have kindly provided. We have also determined that you belong to the 314th Wing based out of Guam, and that your aircraft was named *Moonshiner*, if I'm not mistaken."

"My name is Carl Jansen, my rank is technical sergeant, my serial number is—"

Mitomo waved a hand. "No need for all of that. You don't have to confirm or deny anything. All of that information was taken from the tail section of the plane you arrived in." The doctor laughed and shook his head. "It's a miracle, you know? How did you survive such a thing!"

The doctor's infectious laughter caught Jansen off guard. He couldn't help but smile himself.

"God himself must have set me down in those trees. Momma prays a lot."

"I am very pleased that you didn't die. You must have been in prime physical condition just to survive the mental stress of the ordeal."

"We ate pretty good back on the farm. Dad always said, 'Food is medicine.'"

"A wise man. Now, the questions I wanted to ask you were simply about your medical history, such as whether or not you ever had smallpox. That sort of thing."

Jansen's eyes narrowed.

Mitomo smiled again. "I'm not trying to pry out of you any military secrets about smallpox or the quality of American medical care. No offense, but I'm probably already better versed in such matters than you are."

"Then why do you want my medical history?"

"I said that you are on the road to recovery, but you're not quite out of the woods. I need all the information you can give me so that I can be sure I'm treating you properly. For example, are you allergic to sulfa drugs?"

"I don't think so."

Mitomo took his response as a good sign. He opened the file back up and made a notation. He asked several more questions about childhood diseases, previous injuries, and his military vaccination record. Fifteen minutes later, he shut the file again.

"So, overall, how do you feel at the moment?"

Jansen rubbed his scruffy chin. "I could use a shave."

Mitomo stroked his well-groomed face. "I bet you could grow a fine beard."

Jansen grinned. "My mother made me promise not to. No tattoos, either."

"Ah, yes. Mothers." Mitomo stabbed out his cigarette. "Perhaps I can arrange something. In the meantime, I have one other favor to ask."

"Sure."

"I'd like to run a series of tests. Hearing, eyes, breathing. I want to make sure that we're not missing anything that might prove harmful or even fatal later on. I can't promise you quality health care once you leave this place. Is that acceptable to you?"

Jansen shrugged. "Yeah, that's fine."

"And then I can get you that shave."

★

Jansen sat in a small, enclosed glass booth with a headset perched over his ears. It almost felt like the tail gunner's compartment.

"Can you hear me?" Dr. Mitomo asked on the other side of the glass. He sat at a small desk with a control station and spoke into a microphone.

"Loud and clear, Doc."

"Good. The test will begin momentarily. You will hear a series of tones, sometimes in the left ear, sometimes in the right, sometimes in both. If you hear a tone in your left ear, lift your left hand; if the right ear, the right; and, of course, both hands if the tone rings in both ears. Understood?"

"Understood."

"Let's try it. Ready?"

"Ready."

Mitomo pressed a button on the control station.

A moment later, Jansen raised his left index finger.

"Very good, Carl. It looks like we're all set. Ready to begin the test?"

Jansen nodded. "Ready."

"Then let's begin."

Mitomo adjusted several dials and knobs for a few moments, then pressed the first tone button. Jansen lifted his right hand. Two seconds later, he lifted the left.

Jansen's face paled, his breathing shallow.

"Is something wrong?"

"Doc . . . I don't feel so good."

"Tell me what you're feeling."

Jansen bolted out of his chair, but his splinted leg gave way. He fell back, gasping for air, his panicked eyes pleading with Mitomo. He screamed for help, but the sound caught in his mouth. He clutched at his throat as his eyes rolled into the back of his head.

The big American airman crashed against the glass and crumbled to the floor.

★

Dr. Mitomo held the cigarette in his lips as he examined Jansen's open chest cavity. The corpse lay on a steel dissecting table.

Lieutenant General Ishi stormed into the autopsy room. He was the commander of Unit 731, officially known as the Epidemic Prevention and Water Purification Department of the Kwantung Army. In reality, it was Japan's testing center for chemical and biological warfare.

"What have you discovered, Mitomo?" the mustachioed surgeon asked.

"My aerosolized botulinum has worked perfectly on the American specimen."

He poked at the musculature around Jansen's lungs with his scalpel.

"The diaphragm, abdominals, intercostals, scalenes—even the sternocleidomastoid. All hard as vulcanized rubber. Total paralysis, and nearly instantaneous."

Jansen had been selected because he was considered a prime example of American biology.

Mitomo had put out an urgent request to the army for any captured Americans. Jansen had arrived in such terrible shape, however, that Mitomo was compelled to restore his health so that the test could be properly administered.

"And how many specimens have you tested?" Ishi asked.

"This is the fifth American. He's a perfect specimen with an excellent health record and no comorbidities. He showed no resistance to the botulinum whatsoever."

"Then we can proceed with Operation Black Chrysanthemum?"

"As soon as we produce sufficient quantities of the neurotoxin."

"Excellent. I will inform our superiors. Well done, Mitomo."

"Thank you, sir."

"When you have finished your examination, burn the body, as you have all the others."

"Of course."

Ishi clapped Mitomo on the shoulder.

"Thanks to you, we shall yet win this war."

1

The long convoy of armed Toyota pickups loaded with Nigerian troops raced north in a line through the desert on a hardpacked road bracketed by thick stands of gnarled acacia trees. A howling wind clouded the air with fine powdery sand, red as rust in the late-afternoon sun.

The column was still three hours away from the village where the regional commander of the Islamic State faction was reportedly hiding. The Nigerian soldiers were far beyond the safety of their fortified base, but they were coming in force. The local fighters were armed with little more than AKs and rode air-cooled motorcycles. Their preferred targets were unarmed villagers and helpless farmers, not soldiers.

"*C'est comme la surface de Mars*," said the driver, a first sergeant. He wore the scorpion patch of the 1st Expeditionary Force of Niger (EFoN). His American military surplus camouflaged uniform was covered in dust.

Lieutenant Wonkoye, the mission leader, grinned at the sergeant's comment.

"So you have been to the Martian surface, Sergeant?"

The sergeant flashed a blindingly white smile beneath his oversized helmet and shook his head.

"It's what the Americans used to say."

"Americans used to say a lot of things."

Wonkoye instantly regretted his comment. He actually liked the Americans, especially the operators he trained with. But American soldiers were mostly gone, thanks to the military junta that now ruled his nation. The only Yanks left occupied the massive American-built drone base in Agadez, but its personnel were forbidden to leave it.

The American Special Forces trainers were fearsome warriors with great knowledge and combat experience, yet they were humble, unlike the French *paras* who had fought alongside them over the years. Wonkoye remembered the big Americans training them hard, but still coming down to the Nigerian camp and playing *le football* with them—unlike the swaggering French who, despite their easy smiles and common *langue*, held the Nigerians in quiet contempt.

No matter, Wonkoye thought to himself. Those days are long past. The Americans and the French had been expelled on the orders of Niger's new president, himself an Army general. Wonkoye, a fervent patriot, quite agreed with that decision, perilous as it was.

The Islamist plague was exploding across the region. Over the years, both the Americans and French had spent a great deal of money to fight the jihadis in Africa. Their efforts were nationalistic, not humanitarian. They fought the terrorists in Africa so that the war would not be brought to their own homelands.

Both Western countries had partnered with Niger, one of the poorest nations in the world, in the long, bloody struggle. It might have been better if the West had sent aid instead of guns, Wonkoye had often thought, but those were matters for his superiors. He was a warrior and his only duty was taking the fight to the Islamist enemy, whose numbers grew daily.

Rumors of a grand alliance between competing Al Qaeda and Islamic State factions swirled in the capital, Niamey. Guinea, Burkina Faso, and Gabon had all fallen to military juntas in recent years, all driven to act by the corrupt and incompetent governments supported by Western powers in the name of security. Other African governments were on the brink of toppling as well, including mighty Nigeria. The jihadists were poised to exploit the pending chaos.

So were the Russians.

Now the precarious future of all of Africa lay increasingly in the hands of Africans. Even Mali—now also led by military men—had expelled the fifteen thousand UN peacekeepers based there. Niger's fate would be determined by Nigerians, and the EfoN was the tip of his nation's spear in the war on jihadi terror. The proud young lieutenant well understood the risks. He was a professional soldier.

Wonkoye turned around and peered at the young faces on the other side of the pickup's small rear window getting jostled around in the truck bed. Their eyes were shut tight against the choking dust, their bare faces raw from the sting of the whirling sand. The back of every other pickup was crowded the same way save for the one hauling spare tires and ammo. Each man clutched an AK-47 or RPG launcher. With their free hands they held on to whatever they could, including the bed-mounted Russian machine guns, as they bounced along.

"Do you hear that, Lieutenant?" the sergeant asked.

Wonkoye paused. Over the roar of the Toyota's diesel four-cylinder engine he could barely make out the familiar sound of helicopter blades beating the air. He had put in a request for air cover, but it had been denied due to the shortage of aircraft.

Wonkoye stuck his head out the window. The stinging sand scoured his face and watered his eyes, but he could still make out the form of a helicopter in the distance to the east, high above the tree line. It was heading north, but circling back around.

"That's a Black Hawk."

"Americans!" The sergeant laughed. "I thought they were all gone."

"They must have seen my request." Wonkoye brimmed with pride. He had been a star pupil of the American operators. Perhaps his reputation was even greater than he knew and his old friends had decided to join the fight after all, even against their orders.

The lieutenant's radio crackled with a message from the lead vehicle.

"Sir, a Humvee is up ahead."

Wonkoye and his sergeant shared a confident look. With the Americans at their side the jihadis stood no chance whatsoever.

Capturing the bloodthirsty enemy commander might even earn Wonkoye a promotion.

The lieutenant raised the handset to his mouth.

"Attention convoy. This is Wonkoye. Everybody come to a halt. The Americans are here. We will break for ten minutes. Food, water— whatever you need. I will confer with the American commander. Wonkoye out."

The lieutenant pointed up ahead. The brake lights of the lead vehicle flared as soon as Wonkoye had given his order and skidded to a stop in the road. The vehicles behind Wonkoye had done the same.

"Go around him," the lieutenant ordered. "I want to parlay with that Humvee."

"Yes, sir."

Just as the sergeant eased the wheel left to leave the road, the lead scout truck erupted in a ball of flame and shredded steel. A burning body leaped from the bed and dashed blindly toward the tree line to the west.

Before Wonkoye could process the fiery image, the same stand of trees erupted in a stream of streaking rocket and machine-gun fire.

Instantly, half the vehicles in his convoy were shattered. Heavy 7.62mm rounds thudded into Wonkoye's truck. Blood splattered the rear window, his soldiers' screams muffled by the adrenaline flooding his system.

The sergeant jerked the steering wheel hard right and headed for the opposite tree line for cover as Wonkoye shouted orders into his radio.

"Head east for the trees. Get to the trees!"

But it was too late. More anti-tank missiles mounted on Humvees hidden in the western tree line had already turned nine of the eleven trucks into burning hulks. The other two were riddled with gunfire and stood dead in the sand, their tires shredded as badly as the thin steel of their doors. The few men who survived the initial attack were cut down in their tracks as they ran for cover.

The sergeant's boot mashed the throttle to the floorboard. His skillful driving avoided hitting the flaming wreck in front of them, and the shattered truck behind them blocked the rocket targeting their vehicle. Wonkoye turned around to see the bloody face of a young private now pressed against the window glass, his lifeless eyes accusing him of utter failure.

Wonkoye watched a corporal in a blood-soaked uniform rack the Toyota's Kord 12.7mm heavy machine gun with its T-shaped handle and open fire just as their pickup dove into the tree line.

Wonkoye shoved the door open and dashed for the trees just as the bleeding corporal was tossed from the truck by a burst of well-aimed machine-gun fire. The lieutenant caught a quick glance of the six lifeless bodies heaped in the truck bed like canvas sacks of butchered meat. He bolted away, his face streaked with tears of shame and rage, his sergeant hot on his heels.

Fifty feet above the treetops the hovering Black Hawk's deafening rotor blades threw blinding clouds of choking sand. Wonkoye screamed as machine-gun bullets stitched into his spine, but it was a skull-shattering round that killed him, plowing his corpse into the sand at a dead run.

2

Juan Cabrillo stood on the *Oregon*'s deck, his clear blue eyes fixed on the distant speck in the achingly bright cobalt sky, one hand upraised to shade his face from the searing sunlight. The *Oregon*'s thundering tilt-rotor aircraft, an AgustaWestland AW609, had begun its descent.

A gusting wind suddenly nudged his strapping six-foot-one-inch swimmer's frame. The blast of wind ran its fingers through his closely cropped sun-bleached hair and his vintage 1950s Hawaiian shirt snapped like a flag in a hurricane.

"Where's that wind coming from? No storm in the forecast," Linda Ross said in her high-pitched voice. Her green, almond-shaped eyes were hidden behind a pair of oversized aviator glasses and a black ball cap. Though strong and lean, she was battered so hard by the breeze she had to grab on to Juan's thick bicep for stability.

"Came out of nowhere," Juan said. "I don't like it."

★

Callie Cosima's tall, athletic frame sat comfortably in the tilt-rotor's copilot seat. Her shoulder-length honey-blond hair was pulled into a ponytail to accommodate the tilt-rotor's headphones and Oakley wraparound sunglasses protected her eyes from the sun's harsh glare. She wore her natural beauty with an unadorned and easy grace and her toned body bore the healthy glow of a woman who had spent a life outdoors, especially on the water.

George "Gomez" Adams piloted the AW609 tilt-rotor, currently configured in helicopter mode. The three touchscreen cockpit displays were straight out of a video game and provided anyone in the dual-control pilot seats complete situational awareness. They'd been in the air nearly two hours.

Gomez had picked Callie up at the private jet terminal at Dubai World Central airport—one of several with which the Corporation had long-standing, discreet arrangements. With piercing brown eyes and a stylized gunfighter's mustache, Gomez was roguishly handsome, but it was his charming cocksureness that cut most women to the quick.

Callie frowned as she pointed through her side windscreen. The Gulf of Oman was dotted with cargo vessels and oil tankers.

"Hey, Gomez. Is that the *Oregon*?"

A pale blue freighter with a white stern superstructure was anchored several hundred feet below. She saw a 590-foot break-bulk carrier with four pairs of yellow cranes towering over five large green cargo hold doors. She'd seen dozens of such vessels over the years. It wasn't at all what she was expecting.

"Yup. That's the *Oregon*." Despite the electronic microphone, Gomez's voice was deep and smoky as a plate of West Texas barbecue brisket.

"Doesn't look like much."

"That's kinda the point." He flashed a leather-soft grin as he eased the aircraft into a gentle descent.

"Hate to ask but . . . Where are you gonna land this thing?" Callie asked.

Gomez opened his mouth to answer, but alarms suddenly screamed in their headphones.

Callie's eyes widened like dinner plates. Her blood pressure spiked into her skull as her stomach puddled in her boots.

They were plummeting out of the sky.

"Wind shear," Gomez whispered calmly in his mic as he simultaneously advanced throttles, mashed rotor pedals, and worked the cyclic and collective to generate massive lift without stalling—and yet, still maintaining control. The twin Pratt & Whitney turbines screamed as the tachometers crashed into the red zone.

The sudden burst of power pinned Callie into her seat as the AW's nose launched skyward. Skeins of high clouds sped across the windscreen.

The aircraft yawed and bucked in the turbulence, but Gomez never broke a sweat. His deft handling of the controls was deceptively fast.

The wind shear alarms suddenly cut off as the tilt-rotor stabilized. Gomez eased the big bird back into a landing approach. Callie sat upright in her seat, a little green around the gills.

"You good, miss?"

"Been in worse situations. Just not up in the air."

Gomez smiled. From what he'd heard about her, that was true enough.

★

The tilt-rotor's three small wheels touched down on the disguised cargo hold door that served as the *Oregon*'s helipad as gently as a feather on a velvet blanket. The whining turboprops cycled down as two aircraft technicians—"hangar apes" in *Oregon* parlance—scurried to secure the vehicle before it descended belowdecks on the elevator.

Juan pulled the cabin door open and Callie descended with a large waterproof duffel in hand. The two had never met, but there was an instant affinity between them, like twins separated at birth.

And maybe something more.

Cabrillo noted the copper tan of her skin, like the Hawaiian surfer girl she was—at least in her spare time. Cabrillo had the same kind of tan when he surfed the beaches up and down Orange County, California, years ago. He still got a lot of outdoor sun, but surfing wasn't the reason.

He extended his hand. "Welcome aboard. Juan Cabrillo."

Callie took it. "Callie Cosima."

Juan felt heat pass between them—and it wasn't from the warm weather.

"I see you bought the e-ticket up there," Juan said. "Heck of a ride."

"We hit a downdraft—or it hit us. By the way, your pilot was truly amazing."

"Gomez is a decorated combat flier. He flew AH-6M Little Birds with the U.S. Army's Night Stalkers—the 160th Special Operations Aviation Regiment—before he came to us. He's the best of the best."

Callie frowned quizzically. "I know his name is Gomez, but the tag on his flight suit read 'Adams.'"

"Gomez is his nickname," Juan said. "He has a certain effect on the ladies. Well, one of the many ladies unable to resist his considerable charms was the courtesan of a Peruvian drug lord who looked a lot like Morticia from *The Addams Family* TV show—"

"And Gomez Addams was her husband." Callie grinned. "Got it. Better than getting called 'Lurch.'"

"True that." Juan gestured toward Linda. "This is Linda Ross, my Vice President of operations, and third in command on the *Oregon*."

"It's a real honor to finally meet you," Linda said. She and Callie shook hands.

Callie noted Linda's shockingly bright mane spilling out beneath her ball cap. "Love the neon hair."

Linda pulled off her sunglasses, revealing a spray of freckles across her petite nose.

"Kinda crazy, I know. I change my hair color as often as I change my socks. Can't break the habit."

"Linda was a Pentagon staffer and blue-water naval intelligence officer before she came to work for me," Juan said. "I think she's trying to color away all of those Navy regulations she used to keep."

"Thanks, Dr. Freud," Linda said, pulling on her aviators.

"I might have to borrow a bottle," Callie said. "I understand you're a sub driver as well?"

"Best on the boat—except for the Chairman." Linda nodded at Juan. She caught the eye of one of the hangar apes, a barrel-chested fireplug in blue utilities. He jogged over.

"Ma'am?"

Linda pointed at Callie's enormous duffel.

"Please take Ms. Cosima's luggage to her guest suite. It's number 311, two doors down from mine."

"That's not necessary," Callie protested. "It's rather heavy. Gear, mostly."

"Happy to, ma'am." The deckhand snatched up the heavy bag as if it were filled with cotton candy and turned on his heels.

By the time she said, "Thank you" he was already speeding off toward the superstructure.

Callie turned back to Juan and flashed a curious look.

"So why do they call you 'Chairman'?"

The big hydraulic motors of the aircraft elevator whined as the tilt-rotor disappeared belowdecks.

"We run the *Oregon* and its operations like a Wall Street company, not a military organization. In fact, our business operation is called 'The Corporation.'"

"You need a better marketing department."

"I don't disagree," Juan said, chuckling, "because I am the marketing department. I'm the Chairman of the Corporation, Linda is Vice President, and Max Hanley is the President. You'll meet him later."

"I've Skyped with him several times. Supersmart guy."

"He helped build the *Oregon*," Juan said. "He's one of the best engineers I've ever known."

"But the *Oregon* was Juan's idea," Linda said, "and he was the original designer."

Callie nodded. "Impressive."

"That's quite a compliment coming from someone like you," Cabrillo said. "I'll take it and run. I bet you want to see your baby."

"Sure do."

"Then follow me to the janitor's closet."

3

A hard rain lashed the entire region. Thick drops pelted the temporary metal shelter like ball bearings poured into an empty steel drum. The sound was deafening.

Captain Song-hyok looked around at his tiny command. Like his men, he was dressed in blue pixelated camouflage. He checked his watch. Thirty seconds to go.

The weather was perfect to shield tonight's rendezvous from the prying eyes of American satellites. The metal shelter hanging over the pier was just an extra precaution as per the Vendor's instructions.

Song-hyok, a seasoned naval officer, surveyed the scene again, running through a mental checklist. The area had been ordered entirely cleared of nonessential personnel. Standing next to him was a naval intelligence officer—a lower-ranking lieutenant commander—and his adjutant, an anxious lieutenant, junior grade.

The dutiful truck driver sat quietly in his cab farther down the pier, as did the lift driver. Both vehicles were parked under portable tarps. Each driver was secretly employed by the Reconnaissance General Bureau (RGB), North Korea's far-more-terrifying version of the KGB.

A half dozen trusted enlisted men stood ramrod straight in the downpour, soaked to the bone and shivering. A portable gangplank lay nearby.

"There," the high-strung lieutenant said, pointing excitedly at the roiling water.

Song-hyok checked his watch. Exactly on time. Moments later, the submarine gently broke the rain-spattering surface of the dark water. Strangely, it had no "sail." The lack of a superstructure gave the appearance of a huge torpedo instead of a sub.

The intelligence officer pulled a small Sony digital camera from his pocket and snapped photos of the hull, angled like the fuselage of a stealth aircraft.

Song-hyok, a surface warfare officer, was no expert on submarines. But in his estimation the vehicle's skin appeared to be something other than steel; possibly carbon fiber. It also seemed to be wrapped in some sort of anechoic sound-absorbing material. If powered by an air-independent fuel cell propulsion system, it would indeed be nearly impossible to detect.

The fact it was completely automated and AI-driven made the machine even more wondrous and terrifying.

Song-hyok and the senior intelligence officer exchanged a glance. Both had been in contact with coastal command over the last two hours. Sonar, radar, and underwater detection units were on full alert and yet nothing had been triggered by the submarine.

Incredible.

Both men shared the same thought. An undetectable drone submarine was worth as much if not more than the valuable cargo it carried on board. But their instructions were clear. Do not board the submarine to effect transfer until instructed to do so, and under no conditions attempt to enter the submarine.

Once the vessel's deck cleared the surface, the bubbling discharge from the ballast tanks stopped and a red LED warning light on the deck began flashing. The sub had surfaced exactly next to the large rubber fenders protecting the pier. Its automated navigational sensors must have been accurate to within millimeters. Song-hyok shook his head in silent amazement.

The boat sat in the water motionless save for the blinking red LED light. Mechanical noises hummed and clanged beneath its decks. Several minutes passed.

"What do we do now?" the young lieutenant asked. He had to shout over the noise of the rain pounding against the sheet metal above their heads.

"We wait," his commander said.

"How do we know this isn't an enemy vessel? An explosive device? It looks just like a torpedo."

The senior intelligence officer's expressionless face panicked his young subordinate. The lieutenant had put himself out on a limb. There was no turning back from his position without losing face. Tonight's mission was historic and the young officer was determined to rise to the occasion.

"Sir, perhaps there's been a malfunction. What if it sinks? What if it leaves without delivering its payload to us? We'll look like fools if we just stand here all night."

The senior intelligence officer squinted at Song-hyok, then turned to the lieutenant. "What do you suggest?"

"A closer inspection."

"We should follow instructions," Song-hyok said. But in truth, he was intensely curious about the strange vessel.

Five more minutes passed. The mechanical sounds suddenly stopped.

The three men shared a worried countenance.

The two senior officers exchanged a few whispered words.

The lieutenant strained to hear them. He caught a few of the terrible words that haunted every North Korean citizen and soldier. "*Our responsibility . . . our fate . . . we will be blamed . . .* " These words had been echoing in the lieutenant's own fevered mind.

The young officer was unsurprised and, in fact, relieved when his supervisor turned to him and said, "You have permission to board and inspect the vessel. Perhaps there has been a malfunction. But you must exercise extreme caution."

"Understood."

The eager young lieutenant threw a snapping salute and dashed to the pier. It was an easy leap to the deck. His boots landed with a nearly silent thud on the sound-absorbing material. He began searching the deck area with his flashlight.

"What do you see?" the intelligence officer shouted.

"Nothing, sir." The lieutenant's eyes swept over the seamless surface like a tenacious terrier sniffing for a fox's scent. He suddenly knelt down. The red LED light flashed against his smooth young face.

"A hatch!"

"Don't touch it," Song-hyok called out.

Too late.

The lieutenant's fingers sought purchase beneath what appeared to be a small latch. A trigger activated.

Instantly, an electric current coursed through his body, sparking a massive tetanic contraction that seized all of the muscles of his body—including his heart. Three seconds later he collapsed to the deck in a tightly wound coil of stiffened flesh.

Dead.

The enlisted men observing the spectacle didn't move. If any of them gasped in horror it was masked by the noise of the torrential deluge.

The sub's flashing red LED light turned green. Whining electric motors opened two large doors in the forward section of the boat. Immediately after they opened, three twenty-seven-foot-long torpedoes were lifted into view on a horizontal rack.

Song-hyok's heart raced at the sight. His career was staked to that rack of torpedoes. He was gambling his life—and the lives of his family—on the success of this mission, all based on a relationship with the Vendor, a man he had never met.

It was a risk worth taking both for his nation and his career. The new cold war was heating up and the Asian seas would soon be brought to full boil as the great powers rushed more and more naval assets to the region.

In the last several months, the Russians had increased their long-range missile exports to North Korea hoping to distract the Americans from events unfolding in Europe and elsewhere. But their Russian comrades wouldn't sell the tactical naval weapons the North Korean Navy needed to protect itself, especially the *Shkval,* their vaunted supercavitating torpedo, capable of underwater speeds exceeding two hundred miles per hour. Originally designed in the 1970s and perfected over the years, no navy in the world had accomplished a similar feat.

And yet, the Vendor had promised to supply something even better—his own advanced copy of the *Khishchnik.* Supposedly still only in the Russian design stages, the *Khishchnik* torpedo—really, an underwater rocket that traveled inside of its own self-generating vacuum bubble—was supposedly capable of ten times the speed of the *Shkval.* And unlike its predecessor, the stealthy *Khishchnik* was highly maneuverable, self-guided, and carried a next-generation targeting package. Compared to the great-power navies, North Korea's possession of this *Wunderwaffe* would give it incomparable advantages, like driving a V12 Lamborghini Revuelto at Le Mans against a fleet of rusted Yugos.

Captain Song-hyok barked an order. The enlisted men hesitated, fearful of the mysterious but deadly boat. But they all knew a North Korean firing squad was even deadlier, especially the ones that featured flamethrowers.

They dashed for the gangplank, lifted it as one, and set it in place. The lift driver eased his vehicle into position opposite the torpedo rack. He extended the long forks horizontally into place as the enlisted men secured the first sling over the top torpedo.

Over the course of the next twenty minutes, all three special torpedoes were loaded onto the waiting transport truck. As soon as the last torpedo had been lifted, the submarine's empty rack began retracting into the hull. The green LED light now flashed yellow in the downpour.

Song-hyok issued another order as he watched the empty torpedo rack disappear belowdecks and the automated doors shut tightly again. The enlisted men retrieved the coiled corpse of the dead lieutenant and rushed it across the gangplank. They carefully set the body down beneath the metal shelter at a respectful distance from the two scowling officers. They then rushed back to retrieve the gangplank just seconds before the submarine's yellow light shut off and the sub slipped beneath the churning water.

Song-hyok stared at the corpse of the eager young officer. It was an unfortunate occurrence. Thankfully, the man was under the lieutenant commander's authority. No doubt he would find a clever way to explain away his own responsibility for the boy's death.

"Congratulations on a successful assignment, Captain," the intelligence officer said. "With these new torpedoes in hand our beloved fatherland can assert its rightful dominance of the sea-lanes."

"As soon as my technical office confirms their readiness status, we'll launch our first real-world test."

"My office will be monitoring your progress with great anticipation." The intelligence officer's smile betrayed the menace in his eyes.

Song-hyok nodded at the lieutenant's fetal-positioned corpse.

"Ah, yes. Tragic, isn't it?" the wily intelligence man said. "Another act of cowardly suicide, so prevalent among our undisciplined youth these days. I imagine his secret access to TikTok spawned a mental illness. Don't you agree?"

Song-hyok offered a noncommittal grunt, turned on his booted heels, and marched toward the waiting truck.

If all went according to plan, the world as he had known it for the last five decades would soon change forever.

4

ABOARD THE *OREGON*

What are we doing standing in a janitor's closet?" Callie asked, still wearing her Oakleys.

She, Juan, and Linda stood in the cramped little room. Shelves were stocked with cleaning supplies and a rolling mop bucket stood in one corner. A whiteboard hung next to a worn utility sink.

The three of them had made their way across the hot steel deck to the stern. They passed into the superstructure, down a linoleum-tiled corridor, and through a modest mess hall with stainless steel picnic benches, a serving window, and a corkboard littered with "for sale" items, typed notices, and U.S. Coast Guard regulations.

They finally reached the far end of the mess hall, where the janitor's closet was located, and where they now stood.

Juan explained to her that everything above decks was fully functional and the *Oregon* was, in fact, a fully licensed and operational cargo freighter.

"But what we're really all about is on the other side of this door— and belowdecks."

"I'm not clear about what it is you actually do here," Callie said. "Mr. Hanley was a little vague."

"According to our records search, you've secured several previous government contracts requiring top secret clearance," Juan said. "Including two with the Navy's WARCOM."

"Spying on me, Mr. Cabrillo?"

"Not as often as Facebook, Alexa, or Instagram. And at least I'm not trying to sell you organic toothpaste or aluminum siding."

"What Juan is suggesting is that your discretion is greatly appreciated," Linda said. Her almond eyes narrowed. "In fact, it's a matter of national security."

Callie nodded. "Understood."

Juan placed his wide swimmer's paw on the whiteboard, activating a handprint scanner. An electronic lock clicked audibly, and the rear wall of the janitor's closet swung open.

Juan gestured toward the plush-carpeted corridor just beyond his hand.

"Welcome to our own private rabbit hole."

★

As they marched through the corridor, Juan pointed out a couple of his favorite masterpieces hanging on the walls, one of several art displays around the ship. The three of them crowded into the small elevator and Juan punched the button to the lowest level.

"Hope you're not claustrophobic," Linda said in the tight space.

"In my line of work, I can't afford to be," Callie said. "But then again, I do like a big window." She finally pulled off her sunglasses and pocketed them.

The elevator descended farther into the belly of the steel beast.

"I assumed you were some kind of government research vessel," Callie said. "But now I'm guessing you're with one of the national intelligence or security agencies."

"Not exactly," Linda said. "We're independent contractors. Most of the time we're doing jobs for the federal government—the ones they can't or won't do on their own."

"By 'independent contractors' you mean mercenaries," Callie said. She eyed Juan up and down. "Where are all your tats?"

"We're not guns for hire," Juan said. "Most of what we do is intelligence gathering. And as far as tats go, we don't like to advertise."

"Not all of our jobs are with the federal government, but we never do anything that would harm the interests of the American people," Linda said. "Our crew is comprised almost entirely of former military veterans or, like Juan, former intelligence community personnel. We're as American as apple pie and Chevrolet."

"More like protein bars and Smith & Wesson," Juan said.

The elevator finally dinged. They had reached the lowest level of the ship. The polished brass door slid open.

Callie sniffed the air as she followed Juan out of the elevator. It smelled of salt water and cold steel.

Juan pointed at the large waterline door. A steep ramp stood next to it.

"We launch our Zodiacs, Jet Skis, and RHIBs through that door. The ramp is Teflon-coated for faster egress."

"Sounds like you're operating the world's biggest party barge," Callie said. "A couple of wakeboards and some fruity drinks and you'd be all set."

Linda laughed. "You're going to fit right in with this crew of pirates."

The muffled reports of large-caliber pistols thumped in the distance.

"Gun range," Linda said. "Right across from our armory department."

Juan gestured expansively. "On the lower decks we have world-class machine shops, a fully functional aircraft maintenance hangar, weapons storage, additional crew's quarters and, of course, our engine compartment."

"I don't smell any bunker fuel," Callie said. "Where do you keep it?"

"We don't have any," Juan said.

"Then how are you powering the boat?"

Linda grinned. "Seawater."

"Excuse me?"

"We deploy magnetohydrodynamic engines," Juan said. "Liquid helium cryogenically cools the seawater and powerful magnets strip away the free electrons. We never run out of fuel so long as we're at sea."

"I thought that technology was still under development," Callie said.

"For everyone else, it is. We just happen to actually use it."

"How fast can this ship travel?"

"Over sixty knots."

"Impossible! This ship must be at least eleven thousand tons."

"Closer to thirteen."

"What kind of props are you using?"

"We don't. Four massive pump jets are directed through two Venturi nozzles with three-hundred-sixty-degree turning radius."

Callie laughed. "The world's biggest party boat is also the world's biggest Jet Ski."

"We can turn on a dime—but when we do, better hold on to your britches," Linda said.

"I'd love to get a tour of the entire boat sometime," Callie said.

"Soon as we get through your field tests," Juan said. "Speaking of which, here we are." He gestured at the cavernous expanse in front of them.

"Welcome to the moon pool."

★

Callie gazed in wonder at the voluminous space lit by floodlights. They were standing in the very center of the deepest part of the ship. The brackish tang of salt water and metal were heavy in the air.

Deckhands had pulled the steel grates above the two massive keel doors. The bottom of the ship, at least in this part of the keel, was now opened to the sea. And because this part of the open hull was level with the sea, the *Oregon* didn't sink.

Underwater floodlights illumined the dark waters below. Beyond the reach of the powerful beams were the vast depths of the Gulf of Oman, reaching nearly twelve thousand feet into the abyssal dark.

Callie glanced up. Overhead cranes on the far side of the compartment cradled the *Oregon*'s two mini subs.

"The one that looks like something out of *The Jetsons* is the *Gator*," Linda said. "That's *my* baby." She was referring to the *Gator*'s sleek, flat forty-foot deck and pilot's cupola of slim, angled windows that barely broke the surface when operating in stealth mode. "She has a depth limit of a hundred feet, but she's got a thousand horses under the hood. She can carry ten fully kitted-out operatives and still do over fifty knots on the surface."

"A stealthy insertion vehicle," Callie said. "Nice design."

Linda pointed at the other craned submarine, long and white like a German *Weisswurst* sausage. Its sixty-five-foot hull was fixed with ballast tanks, battery packs, and thrusters arranged almost as an afterthought. Its blunt-nosed bow featured three viewing portals, powerful xenon lamps, and a pair of articulating mechanical arms.

"That larger one is the *Nomad*. She's capable of a thousand feet, but she can carry a crew of two and a complement of eight divers in full gear—more if we pull out the storage lockers. She has an air lock for egress and a decompression chamber on board as well."

Callie pointed at a third cradle. It was covered in shadows. "And that's my *Spook Fish*."

Juan smashed a light switch on a nearby support beam. A pair of spotlights lit up the mini submarine. Callie's smile radiated like a Coleman lantern.

The *Spook Fish 5000* sported a bulbous, optically perfect acrylic cockpit—like a fishbowl perched on top of a pair of blue pontoons. It could accommodate one pilot and two passengers and featured a single mechanical arm for the pilot to maneuver.

But what set this particular unit apart was the large sealed yellow pod attached beneath the submersible's hull. Callie's deepwater breakthrough lay inside of it and was the reason for Cabrillo's enthusiasm for her project. Its potential could prove a real game changer for future *Oregon* operations.

"Did you name her after an actual fish?" Linda asked.

"Yes. The spook fish is more commonly known as a barreleye.

They're engineering marvels, really. They inhabit deep water, up to three thousand feet."

Callie then gestured with her hands and fingers to demonstrate what she was describing. "The top half of their skulls are transparent, like the cockpit glass on an F-35 Lightning. Their eyes are poised mid-skull and point upward toward the surface, though they can articulate forward as needed. I suppose I picked the name mostly because my submersible sorta looks like one."

The brilliant young engineer turned back to Juan.

"Your entire operation is really quite impressive, Mr. Cabrillo. Given the depth limitations of your two submersibles, I can see why my *Spook Fish* would be an excellent addition to your operations. I want to get started right away prepping for tomorrow's demonstration dive. Is there anything holding us up?"

"A really fantastic lunch, actually," Juan said. "Let's eat first and then we'll get to work. Deal?"

Callie smiled. "Well, I am kinda hungry."

5

Juan, Linda, and Callie rode the elevator back up to the dining level. Linda waved off lunch. She had a scheduled brown bag in the ship's biophysical laboratory to discuss equipment upgrades. She promised to catch up with them back at the moon pool after lunch. Shepherding such mundane details was the least glamorous aspect of her job, but vitally important for the efficient operation of the *Oregon*.

Juan led Callie into the dining room. She couldn't stifle a small gasp.

"This is . . . amazing."

Like everything else on the *Oregon*—save for the crew's individual quarters—Juan had designed the dining room down to the smallest detail.

He modeled the sumptuous mess hall after a classic English gentlemen's club. The dining room featured dark walnut paneling, polished brass fixtures, and coffered ceilings. Along the far wall beyond the main dining room were chesterfield sofas and club chairs arranged near the floor-to-ceiling bookcases featuring a number of first-edition Herman Melville and C. S. Forester seafaring classics.

"We can order from the table or just grab something from the lunch line," Juan offered. "They always put up a couple of good choices to keep things moving faster."

"The lunch line works for me."

Juan and Callie headed for the serving window. They grabbed a couple of trays along with plates and silverware and shuffled into the cafeteria-style line.

A squadron of chefs in pristinely white, double-breasted cloth jackets maneuvered with cheerful military precision around the flaming stoves with bubbling saucepans and sizzling skillets. A senior chef called out orders even as she inspected the finished plates at the pass.

Callie stepped up to the serving window. A smiling, befreckled young sous-chef greeted her.

"Your protein, ma'am?" she said.

"Let's surf and turf our guest," Juan said.

"Aye, Chairman," the young woman said as she plated the meal. "And for yourself?"

"The same."

Callie and Juan proceeded down the line and helped themselves to bacon-wrapped asparagus, smoked corn on the cob, and stacks of *khubz ragag*—paper-thin sheets of local Omani bread. Juan then led the way to an unoccupied booth in the far corner.

The two of them tucked into their food before a server took their order for drinks. Both chose fruit-infused Tahitian waters.

"I'm stunned at the quality of this food," Callie said between bites. "I can practically cut this steak with a spoon."

"We employ Cordon Bleu–trained chefs who hand-select the finest ingredients they can find in our ports of call or, when needed, fly them in from their favorite sources." Juan dipped a pillowy soft bite of lobster into his butter dish and plopped it into his mouth.

"Why so extravagant, if you don't mind my asking?"

"A boat is only as good as its crew, and I've got the best crew in the business. Most of them are separated from their families for months at a time, and the job comes with a few risks. They deserve the best."

"You're a good boss." Callie forked a piece of rib eye into her mouth.

Juan studied her face. She really was a lovely woman in the most natural kind of way. No makeup, no pretense. She had an athlete's poise, but a feminine demeanor. There was also something uncanny about the way the light played in her hazel eyes.

"It's just good business, that's all," Juan said. "We have workout facilities, an Olympic-sized pool, a sauna, a climbing wall—you name it. Peak physical conditioning is important for the job, but it's also great for morale."

"Are your people all on contract?"

"A top-shelf operator doesn't need a contract, and a bum won't live up to one. We're mostly a handshake operation."

"Isn't that risky in your line of work?"

"Not the way we do business. We have a very selective hiring process. Essentially, if we don't know you, you can't be on the team. But once you're on the team, you stay on for as long as you're an asset. We all know when it's time to hang up one's hat."

"I imagine the pay is pretty good."

"Every crew member owns a piece of the Corporation's profits. Their percentage of ownership depends on their rank and time of service. The more profit we make, the more coin in everyone's pocket. The result is that everybody takes extreme ownership of every mission. Even the lowest deckhand can expect to retire a millionaire after enough time in service with us."

Callie finished chewing her steak as she pointed a silver fork at the surrounding room. "All of this costs a pretty penny. I don't think even John D. Rockefeller could've written a check for a luxury liner like this."

"The first *Oregon* was funded from the Cayman Islands account of an assassin-for-hire who, shall we say, no longer needed the money. Since then, we've earned that 'pretty penny' the old-fashioned way— through a lot of blood, sweat, and tears."

"There's been more than one *Oregon*?"

"Yes, as a matter of fact. The very first *Oregon* was a converted lumber hauler heading for the scrapyard—almost half the size of the current vessel. We built another one from scratch, but we lost her in combat a while back." Cabrillo sighed. "We've had brothers-in-arms fall along the way, too."

"I'm sorry."

"It's the high price we're all willing to pay so that others can sleep at night."

Callie nodded her appreciation as she took the last few bites of her meal.

Juan finished his in short order. "Coffee?"

"Please."

"How do you like it?"

"Black as tar."

Juan grinned. "A Navy brat?"

"Couldn't be any prouder."

"How about we take this conversation over to the lounge?"

6

Juan and Callie took up a couple of overstuffed leather chairs beneath a massive oil painting, Crepin's majestic *Battle of Trafalgar 1805*.

Callie gestured at the naval masterpiece above their heads. "My father would have loved that."

"I'm so sorry you lost him."

"You would have liked him."

"I bet."

"He was a senior chief master diver."

Juan whistled. "That's some achievement. He must have had the brains of an astronaut and the skill of a surgeon."

A young steward in a crisp white shirt and sharply creased slacks wheeled a cart and a silver coffee service over to Juan and Callie.

"How's Maurice?" Juan asked.

"He's still recovering from the croup, I'm sorry to say." There was a faint Irish lilt in his voice.

"Still wheezing like a squeeze box?"

"Dr. Huxley suggested that if we could acquire a washboard and a fiddle we could start a zydeco band down there."

"Tell her to check with MacD. He's probably got one of each in his gun locker."

"Coffee, sir?"

"Please."

The steward filled two bone china coffee cups in saucers and set them on the side tables next to their chairs.

"Cigar, Chairman?" the steward asked.

Juan turned to Callie. "Do you mind?"

"Not at all."

The steward offered a leathered box of cigars featuring a wide selection. Juan chose an Arturo Fuente Don Carlos. The steward fired up a Zippo and Juan puffed the luxurious cigar into life before blowing his first cloud of blue smoke toward the vented coffered ceiling.

Callie enjoyed the hint of espresso beans, chestnuts, and earth filling the air as she sipped her coffee.

"Reminds me of my father. He always had a stogie in hand."

Juan took another satisfying puff before setting the Arturo down in the crystal ashtray perched beneath a ventilating device. He picked up his cup.

"What did your father do after he retired from the Navy?"

"Dad started an underwater marine salvage and repair operation. He was based out of Honolulu—that's where I grew up. My mother died when I was born. We had a wonderful life, and he was my world. I grew up on the beach—learned how to surf before I could ride a bike. I was dive certified at the age of sixteen. Even helped Dad out on a couple of projects for the Navy."

"I can see why you decided to follow in your father's footsteps."

Callie's face darkened with a memory. Juan sat in silence, letting her process.

"He was two hundred and fifty feet down, servicing a rig in the Gulf of Mexico when it partially collapsed. The coroner said he died instantly, but I have my doubts. I was nineteen when it happened."

"That's rough for a kid. Anybody, really."

"At first, I couldn't make any sense of it. It seemed so . . . random. He was very methodical, very careful. That's probably why I became an engineer. I see the world as a function of a balance of forces. If the water pressure is too great for a submarine hull, it collapses, and people die. Life is symmetrical. Death is chaotic. And for a while there, I let the chaos get inside of me."

"So how did you process all of that?"

A smile creased her full mouth.

"I knew Dad would have kicked my butt if I quit. So, I didn't. Seven years ago, we managed to rescue three demolition divers at a job in the North Sea. There have been others since. That's when it started to make sense."

"You balanced his tragic death by building a company that saves lives. I know your dad is smiling down on you for that."

"I'd like to think so."

"So you got out of the fins and neoprene part of the business and acquired advanced degrees in Marine and Maritime Intelligent Robotics from the Norwegian University of Science and Technology in Trondheim."

"You've done your research."

"Then you started building underwater vehicles."

"My company can do more work in more places and at greater depths for less risk than a regular operation."

"And that makes you more profitable."

"Which allows me to plow more money back into research and development."

"My people have looked at your work. They were impressed—and trust me, that's no small accomplishment."

Callie smiled. "Thank you."

"My people also tell me you once owned the world record for no-limits free diving."

"I was twenty-two years old. Unfortunately, I blacked out on the way back up and suffered an aneurysm. Nearly died."

Now Juan understood what he had been sensing about her appearance all along.

"Is that how you lost your left eye?"

Juan had noticed earlier the way the dining room lights had played in her eyes. She also had the habit of subtly turning her head so that the right side of her face was always closest to whomever she was speaking with. The more he searched her face the more he realized that the glass left eye was a near-perfect reproduction of her right eye. In fact, it was almost too perfect.

Callie flushed with embarrassment.

"I suppose it's my vanity that won't let me wear an eye patch."

"Like Linda said, you'd fit in perfectly with this pirate crew. They'd elect you captain of the ship if you wore it."

"I'm grateful, actually. It could've been worse. I haven't attempted another world record since."

"Can't say that I blame you."

"Ironically, I've traveled a hundred times deeper in submersibles since then. Only now, I don't have to hold my breath."

"It's still plenty dangerous." Juan was thinking of a fatal accident with a commercial submersible that had been in the news recently.

"It's a calculated risk. But survival is largely a function of good engineering and a clear understanding of hydrostatics."

"It still takes a lot of guts."

"Whatever I've got, I got it from my dad." She took another sip of coffee. "This is so good."

"Fresh-ground Cuban dark roast pour-over. My personal favorite."

"So what about you? How did you wind up in this line of work? My guess is former CIA."

"I was a NOC for longer than I can remember."

"Non-official cover. A spook out in the cold."

"More like in the hot, most of the time."

"Why'd you quit?"

"The American intelligence community has largely become just an-other government bureaucracy, as sluggish and dysfunctional as your local DMV. Red tape, executive orders, legal opinions, and too many white-shoed political appointees more interested in the D.C. cocktail circuit than the national interest. I couldn't take it anymore."

"But you're still in the same game." Callie gestured at the ceiling. "So why do all of this?"

"Same arena, different game. Now we play by our own rules. And we're still playing, because there are still monsters out in the world that mean to do us harm. I'm beholden to only one voice now and that's the one in my head. My mission is the safety of my country and my crew. There isn't anything I won't do to secure both."

Juan picked his cigar back up and took another satisfying drag. If it had been after dinner he would have ordered a couple of fingers of twenty-three-year-old Pappy Van Winkle bourbon, but a full workday was still ahead of them, including a test dive with Callie's *Spook Fish*.

"Dessert?" Juan asked. "Chef makes a tiramisu that will sing in your mouth like a Puccini aria."

"I'm already stuffed to the gills. Maybe I can have a rain check?"

"Of course." Juan checked his watch. "There's one more department I want to show you before I cut you loose to get to work. You game?"

Callie's eyebrows bounced.

"Always."

7

This looks like a spaceship."

Callie's smile beamed as she surveyed the chilled room bathed in the blue glow of LED lights. Multiple touchscreen workstations were arranged in tiered semicircles of steel and glass. Two of the stations were occupied by a couple of young techs, who didn't turn around when she came in.

The entire room was encircled by floor-to-ceiling wraparound 4K high-definition LCD screens providing a bridge-eye, three-hundred-sixty-degree view of the ocean all around them.

"Welcome to the op center," Juan said. "If the engines are the beating heart of the ship, this is the brain."

"Are you referring to the Cray supercomputer or to me?"

Max Hanley sprang up from the command chair centered in the top tier overlooking the room. It was also known as the Kirk Chair, named after the fabled captain of the starship *Enterprise*. Every aspect of the *Oregon*'s operations, from engines to weapons to navigation to comms, could be controlled from it by a single person.

Hanley was one of the older members of the *Oregon*. The fringe of auburn hair circumnavigating his balding dome was silvering. His hard belly strained the buttons on his Tommy Bahama shirt despite Dr. Huxley's mandated daily torture sessions on the Peloton. But the sparkle in his eyes, the flush of his taut skin, his oversized forearms, and a pair of sledgehammer-sized hands told Callie he was still in fighting form. She shook his calloused hand.

"Glad to finally meet you in person, Ms. Cosima," Max said. His infectious enthusiasm was infused with a rakish charm.

"Callie, please."

Juan clapped the slightly shorter man on his broad shoulder.

"Max is my number two and the *Oregon*'s chief engineer. Not only does he baby the engines, he also manages our day-to-day operations. He was also one heck of a swift boat captain back in the day, and he does a fair job of handling the *Oregon*."

"Can't wait to get my paws on the *Spook Fish*'s controls and take her for a spin," Max said.

"Get in line, bub," Linda said as she marched into the room. "Ladies first." Linda turned to Callie. "How was your lunch?"

"Are you kidding me? I'm afraid anything I ever order again from one of those swanky restaurants will taste like cat food." She turned to Max. "No problems securing the *Spook Fish* and my support equipment?"

"Everything arrived on time and was inventoried at the dock before I took possession, as per your instructions," Max said.

Callie surveyed the huge wall displays again. A Panamax oil tanker was steaming south a few miles to port. She turned around, her eyes wide with amazement. Astern she caught a glimpse of the contrails of a high-flying airliner streaking north.

"I feel like I'm standing on the *Oregon*'s bridge even though we're belowdecks."

"We run everything from down here in the op center because we're protected by armor plating. The bridge in the superstructure you saw when you boarded is fully functional. We use it when the operation calls for it."

Max pointed a thick finger at each of the workstations as he called them out. "We have comms, navigation, sonar, radar, weapons—"

"Weapons? I thought you were an intelligence-gathering operation," Callie said.

"That's our primary function," Juan said. "But not everybody appreciates us snooping around in their dirty laundry. We have to be able to defend ourselves when the need arises."

"I'm surprised. I didn't see any guns when I came aboard."

"We keep them under wraps. Besides, our best defense is anonymity. By appearing to be just another ordinary cargo ship, we can slip in and out of ports all over the world without attracting attention."

"Sort of like the old Q-ships from the world wars," Max added.

"That helps explain your need for the *Oregon*'s incredible speed," Callie said. She turned to Max. "Your engines are a miracle of engineering. I'd love a personal tour sometime before I leave."

Max beamed with pride. "I'd be happy to." His attention was snatched away by a flashing light on the arm of the Kirk Chair. The voice of Hali Kasim, the *Oregon*'s chief communications officer, reverberated in the armrest speaker. He was in the hangar assisting a comms upgrade on the AW tilt-rotor.

"What is it, Hali?"

"Langston Overholt IV, on a secure line."

Juan frowned. It wasn't like his former CIA handler to call him out of the blue unless something was up.

"Tell him to hold." Juan turned to Callie. "This sounds urgent. If you don't mind . . ."

"No, of course not."

"Linda, would you please show Callie to her quarters while I get this? I'll brief you later."

"Aye, Chairman." Linda tugged on Callie's elbow and they headed for the exit. When they were clear, Juan fell into the Kirk Chair, fingered the touchscreen, and took the call.

8

Juan, my dear boy. I was growing concerned. Everything copacetic on your end?"

Overholt's concern was genuine. He had been Juan's trusted field handler when Cabrillo was a CIA agent. In fact, he had recruited Juan straight out of the Caltech ROTC program, where the young Cabrillo was double-majoring in political science and mechanical engineering. Despite his age, Overholt's octogenarian voice rang clear and true on the overhead speakers.

"About to test some new equipment. What can I do for you, Lang? By the way, Max Hanley is on the call."

"Mr. Hanley, I trust you are hale and hearty?"

"Fit as a fiddle," Max said. "Yourself?"

"I'll be defending my title as senior club champion again at next week's handball tournament. Thank you for asking. Now, all pleasantries aside, gentlemen, I have an urgent mission I'd like you to consider undertaking."

"Shoot," Juan said.

"As I'm sure you're well aware, this morning's presidential daily brief reported that a few days ago an elite Nigerian Army unit, the 1st Expeditionary Force of Niger, was ambushed, presumably by jihadis. Over ninety officers and men were slaughtered."

The briefing was only distributed to the President, the Vice President, the Director of National Intelligence, and a select handful of top security and intelligence executives with "need-to-know" credentials, including Langston Overholt IV. Cabrillo maintained his top secret clearances, which allowed Langston to provide him access to the briefing and any number of other security documents and emergency alerts.

"I saw that," Juan said. "The details were sketchy. Why do you say 'presumably' ambushed by jihadis?"

"We just received further information on the attack a few hours ago. It turns out there was a lone survivor, a Nigerian Army sergeant who was sheltering in a nearby village while recovering from his wounds. He claims that his unit was attacked by Americans."

Max and Juan exchanged a confused look.

"That doesn't make any sense," Max said. "I thought the Nigerians had already ordered us out of the country after the military coup."

"They did, though technically, we're still in negotiations to maintain our drone base there. But obviously no American units were ordered to attack the Nigerians who, until very recently, were among our best allies in the region in the war against Islamic extremism."

"Did the sergeant offer any proof?"

"He reported the presence of several Humvees with heavy machine guns and anti-tank guided missiles, along with at least one Black Hawk helicopter."

"Since when did we start selling our equipment to African jihadis?" Max asked.

"I assure you that we don't. The latest report also states that when the Nigerians recovered the bodies of their fallen comrades, they also found an expended M72 LAW rocket launcher and a jammed M4 rifle. We ran the serial numbers on those weapons. Their last known location was in an Afghan Army arsenal near Bagram Air Force base."

Juan ran a hand through his brush-cut hair, processing the information. This smelled like trouble, big time.

When American forces withdrew in haste from Afghanistan, massive numbers of American weapons had been left behind. Worse, the vaunted army of three hundred thousand Afghan soldiers the Pentagon had supposedly trained and equipped had evaporated from the field of combat the instant the Taliban began its dash for Kabul. It was later learned that most of those three hundred thousand bought-and-paid-for Afghani soldiers never really existed. They were a "ghost" army of fake names, ranks, and serial numbers that corrupt Afghani politicians and warlords created to bilk the American taxpayer for billions of payroll dollars. Equally important, those nonexistent ghost soldiers had been armed to the teeth with expensive American military equipment.

All told, analysts estimated the Taliban was now in possession of at least eighty billion dollars' worth of weapons and supplies including forty-five UH-60 Black Hawk helicopters, twenty-five hundred armored Humvees, and sixteen thousand pairs of night vision goggles, along with tens of millions of rounds of ammunition for all those abandoned weapons systems.

"I've heard of some rifles and grenades getting over the border into Pakistan and into Kashmir," Juan said. "That makes sense, given the geographical proximity. But Niger?"

"Unfortunately, the Nigerian ambush is just the latest incident. A Filipino special forces unit was slaughtered in a night assault by New People's Army rebels using American night vision goggles two weeks ago."

"Also with American serial numbers located in Afghanistan, I take it."

"Correct. And there have been similar incidents in Colombia and Libya. These arms shipments are tilting the balance of power in these regional conflicts. The U.S. government is deeply concerned with the strategic implications that regime changes incur, not to mention the fact we're embarrassed that it's our arms supply that's causing it."

"Something isn't adding up," Juan said. "The Taliban might have all of our abandoned gear, but they don't have the means for global transport."

"We know it's not the Pipeline," Max said. With the help of a brave Turkish journalist, the *Oregon* crew had successfully dismantled the infamous criminal smuggling ring a few years back.

"Any clues as to who's running the new U-Haul service for them?" Juan asked.

"As of this moment, none."

"Not even the usual suspects? North Korea, Russia, or Quds Force?"

"We've eliminated the Chinese, Russian, and Iranian security forces, as well as the North Koreans."

"Criminals, like Nature, abhor a vacuum," Max said. "It's gotta be one of the mafias."

"Our Interpol friends assure us it's all quiet on those fronts."

"How do we figure into this?" Juan asked.

"I have two assignments for you while you're in Afghanistan."

"Does that mean I get to bill you twice?"

Overholt chuckled. "I'd be disappointed if you didn't try."

"I'm all ears."

"First, I need you to determine how many American weapons are still remaining in the Afghani caches so we know what we're dealing with."

"Can't the Pentagon give you those numbers?"

"You're speaking of the same DoD that can't account for trillions of dollars missing from its accounts. What's a paltry few billion in missing weapons to them?"

"What you need is an auditor, not an operator."

"Second, I need you to figure out how the Taliban is managing to transport these weapons. If we can determine that, we just might have a way to identify and eradicate their 'U-Haul' service."

"You wouldn't be calling me if you had any human assets left on the ground," Juan said. "A run into the Ghan won't be easy."

The Pentagon chiefs not only abandoned weapons and gear, they left behind thousands of loyal Afghanis—the people who fought for the Americans and often died in service to them.

Overholt's voice dropped an octave. "The ones that couldn't flee on their own have either been killed or gone underground. You'd be entirely on our own."

"Excuse me, Mr. Overholt," Max said. "But did Uncle Sam run out of satellites? Why can't you just monitor Afghani air and ground traffic?"

"Excellent question, Mr. Hanley. We've re-tasked multiple birds over the area for just that reason, and we're monitoring all commercial air traffic in and out of Afghanistan. The bottom line is that we don't see how or when or where these weapons systems are being transported. Frankly, I think the transport issue is a bigger concern than the weapons themselves."

"Agreed," Juan said. "I'm surprised the DoD hasn't sent in a Delta team to sniff this all out."

"They did. Two days ago . . ." Overholt's voice trailed off. "They were spotted by Black Hawk helicopters piloted by the Taliban and cut down with Vulcan rotary guns. No survivors."

"And now it's our turn to go in."

"I'm afraid so. That is, if you're willing to take the assignment."

"Who else is there to do the job?"

"Indeed, whom? Good hunting, my boy. And Godspeed."

9

THE ISLAND OF SORROWS
THE CELEBES SEA

The privately owned island sat seventeen miles southeast of the south-ernmost tip of Mindanao in a part of the world some people consider to be a tropical Eden. But the miserable rock looming out of the sea had well earned the name "Island of Sorrows."

The eight high-speed electric motors of the octocopter chirred like an armored insect from a hellish dream as it hovered over the open pit, a mini chain gun slung beneath its frame.

The drone's optical and heat sensors scanned the tangle of bloated uniformed corpses below for signs of life as its targeting reticle raked a red laser slowly over each pale, unblinking face.

Onboard infrared sensors detected the wavelength emissions of carbon dioxide, methane, and hydrogen sulfide—proof of postmortem decomposition, which proceeded rapidly in the island's high heat and humidity.

Chang! A single bullet from the mini gun plowed into the chest of a bearded soldier. The corpse had shuddered slightly as fermenting gases inside the body suddenly expanded and released. The drone's onboard AI sensors mistook that movement as a sign of life and acted to terminate it immediately as per the Vendor's algorithm. The additional release of decompositional gases resulting from the new bullet wound plumed in the drone's infrared sensors.

The drone hovered for a few moments more. Sensing neither increasing body heat nor movement, its targeting algorithms sent the octocopter racing off in a burst of speed in another direction in search of the final, elusive target. In moments, the din of its screaming electric motors gave way to the sound of the pounding surf a hundred meters away.

The corpse that had been shot stirred again. So did the bald one next to it. A third wriggled awkwardly before its blood-matted chest tumbled over.

A fourth form arose from beneath the pile.

Like all of the other soldiers in the pit, Guevara wore a generic camouflage uniform without unit patches or national identity. His shirt and pants were smeared with blood and gore—but not his own. Unlike the others, his uniform had no bullet holes in it.

Confident he had eluded the hunter-killer drone, Guevara climbed out of the pit, stepping on the bodies to reach the top until he could finally scramble over the rocky lip. He didn't bother looking back. These men had been comrades only in death, not life—all of them strangers thrown together in a nightmare of slaughter.

He was the lone survivor.

Finally topside, Guevara raced in a crouch beneath the jungle's heavy fronds and spreading leaves, hoping to evade whatever surveillance devices might be deployed. He finally reached the end of the embankment and leaped into the water, his combat boots splashing in the brackish lagoon fronting the cave. He ripped away the fronds covering the rubber boat tied up inside, climbed into it, and yanked on the starter cord.

Nothing.

He yanked again. It stuttered, but didn't start. In his panic he had forgotten to open up the gas valve and to prime the engine. He did both, and yanked the cord again. The motor coughed into life. He gunned the throttle and the small boat charged forward into the surf.

The rubber dinghy braved the crashing waves, its flat, wide bottom slewing sideways in the frothing white surf, but still scuttling forward until he finally cleared the breakers. As the boat raced down the back of the last roller, Guevara laughed for the first time in what seemed like years, sensing he had finally escaped the gravitational pull of the island of death. He turned his dripping-wet face to a warm and forgiving sun, cleansing him of his unspoken sins, or so it felt, as relief washed over him in a wave of delirious joy.

His eyes didn't catch sight of the flock of seagulls hovering high overhead, nor of the single gull whose unblinking gaze had fixed on the small black boat far below in the crystal-blue waters.

The gull retracted its wings to its sides, increasing its aerodynamic profile and thus its speed. It flew like a god-thrown spear toward the little boat in an unforgiving arc that ended in Guevara's fiery death.

★

ABOARD THE *IZANAMI*
THE INDIAN OCEAN

A thousand miles away from the Island of Sorrows, the Vendor studied the shattered wreck of the burning rubber boat on a single view screen. It was one of an entire bank of monitors tracking his other activities around the world.

A separate bank of monitors displayed the operational departments on his largely automated manufacturing vessel—one of several in his fleet—allowing him to run it from his command center.

The Vendor's long finger brushed a touchscreen control panel, shutting the island view screen off. He sighed, deeply dissatisfied.

He leaned back in his chair, contemplating his next move. The big diesel engines thrumming belowdecks drummed a tattoo inside of his aching skull. He rubbed his throbbing temples for relief, but got none.

Guevara's death was a foregone conclusion even before the gull drone snuffed out his pathetic life. He gave the man credit for his ability to elude a wide variety of fixed and aerial sensors for a few days, but he never had any hope of escape. It was bad enough that Guevara and the other men recruited for this test failed to put up a credible defense. But their inability to mount a viable offense was catastrophic for both them and the test. An effective offense could have provided them a slim hope of survival. It also would have proven the combat effectiveness of his new weapon system.

Despite the fact his new technologies had achieved the desired outcome, the Vendor knew his clients were unimpressed. After all, remote killing had been going on since the first human had discovered how to bash another man's skull with a thrown rock.

His clients were seeking an entirely new class of weapons technology. If the Vendor offered a new demonstration with a similar group of guinea pigs, the same outcome would result and his clients would no doubt accuse him of stacking the deck in favor of his drone-based systems.

What could he do?

The Vendor needed a more robust test to thoroughly convince his clients that a genuine "revolution in military affairs"—the jargon du jour—was at hand. Nothing short of a revolution could hope to unseat the United States as the world's premiere military power. And until that power was wrested from the hated Americans, Washington, D.C., would continue to dictate the world political and financial order under which his brooding clients were subject. That was why they paid him so very well.

The Vendor swiveled his large frame around in his chair, tugging on his silvering beard. His dark hooded eyes stared into the bulkhead with a deep intensity. How could he improve the test?

It seemed obvious now. He needed to provide a genuine combat team, not just warm bodies with guns.

To be combat effective, such a team would require a brief period of training. And he needed to recruit something better than the riffraff he'd hustled off the streets.

What he needed was a group of the world's best warriors—ex–special forces operators. But they had to be men without countries; men who would neither be missed nor mourned and all highly skilled in the arms that he would supply.

But how to find such men?

The edges of the Vendor's dark eyes crinkled as he grinned to himself.

Of course. Something his grandfather had once told him.

The sweetest jar of honey attracts the angriest hornets.

10

Erin Banfield's dark green eyes were blurry after hours of scrolling through computer databases on her monitor. Her small, cramped desk was littered with hard printouts and bankers boxes stacked like Jenga bricks. She looked like a hoarder rather than a gifted CIA senior analyst. She was located in the basement of one of the older annexes on the campus.

Banfield had attended all of the technical conferences and training seminars required for the job, but she still had a hard time trusting the latest artificial intelligence search programs. Over the years she had caught a few mistakes that the supposedly more efficient—some even said "faultless"—machines had committed. In her line of work, the hardest cases were usually broken open upon discovery of the smallest of details—including the ones missed by the witless computer chips.

"Jeez, Erin. Any chance you can pick up a phone?"

Banfield glanced up. Trevor Das, her immediate supervisor, draped an athletic arm over the cubicle barrier. He wore a stylishly cut dress shirt and designer-label suit slacks. She knew from her few visits to his corner office in the main building that the matching suit coat was freshly pressed, tailored to fit his broad shoulders, and studiously draped on a hanger.

"I'm sorry?" Banfield said. She pulled a hank of her flame-red hair behind a freckled ear.

"Your phone?"

She glanced down at her cluttered desk in search of her phone, finally finding it under a stack of bulging file folders.

"What about it?"

Das held up the unplugged phone cord. Cell phones were forbidden in the annex.

"Again?"

Banfield rolled her eyes and grimaced.

"Sorry, Chief. You know I can't handle the distraction."

"It wouldn't have hurt my feelings if you had kept your office near mine."

"I like it down here. Nice and quiet. Lets me focus."

Das couldn't help but grin. Banfield was her own person. He put up with her eccentricities because she got the job done. She was relentless to a fault and had proven her analytical skills were second to none in her nearly thirty years with the Company. He glanced around the office. Or more accurately, the oversized storage room with Banfield's desk thrown into the mix.

"Actually, I don't mind coming all the way down here. I'm training for a triathlon and I need to improve my endurance."

"Funny." Banfield smiled. Das was pleasant enough, and a decent administrator of the interagency arms-trafficking task force they both served. She had applied for the head position and had made it to the final round of interviews—par for the course. Early in her career she had won dozens of commendations for her superlative analytical work. She had single-handedly thwarted terror plots, uncovered spy networks, and ferreted out enemy battle plans. She thought after all her years of faithful service it would finally have been her turn.

And yet she wasn't entirely surprised when Das was handed the brass ring instead of her. It was a management position requiring the necessary people skills to navigate interagency coffee klatches, closed-door subcommittee hearings, and departmental briefings. Exactly the kinds of things she wasn't good at. Still, it would have been a nice cherry on top of her long career that would soon be coming to a close.

But Das? He was so young. Just two years out of grad school. But he was the latest chosen one. The son of a venture capitalist, Das bragged that his childhood playground was his father's Gulfstream as the two of them jet-setted around the globe sniffing out cutting-edge tech opportunities. The privileged upbringing partly explained why the handsome young man was fluent in four languages, including Hindi, his parents' native tongue.

He was also the product of an Ivy League education, a scratch golfer, and a consummate ladies' man according to the office gossip she overheard in the cafeteria.

"So what can I do for you, Trevor?"

Das flashed a beguiling smile.

"You did something with your hair."

In fact, she had just colored her hair yesterday to tame the gray. She absentmindedly ran her fingers through the length of it, an old nervous habit.

"Thank you for noticing. But I'm guessing my hair isn't the reason for your visit."

"I know I've interrupted you, but I need to ask you a question."

"Of course."

Das checked his Rolex. "Look, I gotta run. There's a meeting on the Hill I have to sit in on. I'll keep it short."

"Shoot."

"Tell me more about this Langston Overholt character. You used to work for him, didn't you?"

"Years ago."

"And what's your opinion of him?"

"A legendary field officer, a first-rate intellect, and an old-fashioned, dyed-in-the-wool patriot."

"What's his current status?"

"Technically, Mr. Overholt is retired from active service, but he has an 'emeritus' role with the Agency. He consults regularly with POTUS, committee chairmen, and even allied foreign governments. He still maintains his portfolio and has been given a great deal of latitude."

"Is that why he runs his own black budget?"

"I had no idea. Is there a problem?"

Das darkened. "The old fart is stepping on my toes."

"How do you mean?"

"That dinosaur is running a black op into Afghanistan even as we speak. He's tracking illegal arms shipments. That's *my* turf."

That's interesting, Banfield thought. "Mr. Overholt has an impeccable service record. I'm sure he knows what he's doing."

"I'm sure he does, which is why he also knows he's crowding into my lane. Arms trafficking is my portfolio. He didn't so much as drop me a courtesy note, let alone consult with me on this."

"He must have his reasons."

"Yeah. He's an old fossil who does things his way. I don't like it."

"I understand."

Only, she didn't. Overholt was trading shots with Stasi killers in the backstreets of East Berlin before this kid was a seed in his father's pod. Banfield thought Das should have more respect for his elders—especially one as accomplished as Langston Overholt.

Das read the expression on her face. "You really admire the old T. rex, don't you?"

"Of course."

"Fossils belong to the past. They're museum pieces. The world is evolving, progressing."

"I'm not sure it's evolving for the better, are you?"

Das straightened his back. "'Survival of the fittest' is the name of the game and 'Wild Bill' Donovan died a long time ago. There are more progressive ways of doing the job. Until guys like Overholt finally step aside, we won't be seeing any serious advances in the way things get done around here." His eyes briefly darted to the stacks of paper printouts on her desk.

"I'm sure you know what's best," Banfield said.

"If he messes things up, there will be a price to pay."

"For him or for you?"

Das's dark eyes narrowed for a second, then he flashed a smile, brilliant as a sunrise parting a storm cloud.

Banfield felt its warmth wash over her. A ladies' man, indeed.

"Well, thanks again for your time. Sorry to bother you." He winked. "Keep up the good work." Das turned on his polished Italian loafers and sped away for his meeting.

Banfield sighed. Twenty years earlier she would have given him a run for his money—and maybe even put another notch in her bedpost. But Das was right. Time marches on.

She fished around on her desk for a mechanical pencil and pad, scratched out the letters *L.O.*, and slipped it into her purse.

Overholt was a bit of a dinosaur. The thing was, she loved fossils.

11

AFGHANISTAN

The surly Afghan teenager driving the white Land Rover Defender couldn't have been more than seventeen years old judging by the scraggly beard he was trying to grow. Unfortunately for the boy, most of his hair growth was spurting between his eyes. He had a unibrow that would have made Frida Kahlo blush with envy. A traditional Afghani *pakol* sat on top of his narrow head like a mushroom cap.

The Afghani didn't speak any Russian and his passenger spoke no Pashto or any other tribal language. It didn't matter to the boy's Russian passenger. It was clear from the barely hidden contempt on the Afghani's face he had no desire to speak to a filthy Russian infidel anyway. The jagged red scar on the Russian's face and the blinded milky-white eye beneath it didn't endear him to the boy, either. Built like a fighter and bearing the marks of one, the Russian did a poor job of disguising his military bearing. He wore plain work trousers, a baggy collared shirt, and carried a hiker's plain canvas rucksack.

The Russian's jarring teeth and twisting spine told him the kid was aiming the British four-wheel drive at every pothole he could find. It felt like they were bouncing on a trampoline inside of a clothes dryer. The boy was driving because he was the son of the village chief and local tribal warlord and was therefore trusted with his father's prized guest. Without the warlord, the Russian would never have secured today's meeting.

Trailing a cloud of choking dust, the white Defender climbed the final steep trail and blew past a herd of goats prodded along by a knot of snot-nosed children no older than eight or nine.

Rocketing through the mud-walled village, locals knew to stand aside for the familiar vehicle, apparently a prize seized along with so many others at Bagram Airfield when the British, like all of the other Western powers, fled in a panic.

The Land Rover finally skidded to a stop in front of a walled compound. Two scowling, black-turbaned guards stood outside, AKs at low ready. The boy said nothing, but only stared out of the dusty windshield in a barely contained rage.

Spasibo—thanks—the Russian grunted as he crawled out of the 4×4 truck. It sped away almost the second his booted feet hit the dirt, nearly running him over.

"Stepan! Is that you?" The gray-bearded Afghan chieftain marched out his front door, his hands upraised in a welcoming gesture, his leathered face beaming with a pumpkin's smile of mostly missing teeth. "Come inside. Please."

The milky-eyed Russian glanced around the village. A few Afghanis in traditional garb hurried along the dusty road or stood in mud-brick doorways, all of them pretending not to notice the war-scarred, blond-haired stranger in their midst. The Russian knew that behind every one of those doors was at least one loaded rifle, most likely an AK-47 lifted from the corpse of one of his fellow countrymen years before.

The Russian shrugged away whatever misfortune awaited him inside the chieftain's home, shouldered his rucksack, and limped toward his fate.

★

The Russian grunted as he struggled to take the place on the floor offered by the chieftain, who sat opposite him. A robed servant brought a teapot of hammered brass patinaed with age and battered with use. The servant poured the tea into chipped porcelain cups, then departed the brightly carpeted room. They were all alone.

The two men sipped their steaming-hot tea in silence for a few minutes.

"My son is good driver?" the chieftain asked in broken Russian.

"I've had worse," the Russian grunted. "And better." He took another sip. "How long until your contact arrives?"

"Soon."

The Afghan chief leaned in close and whispered.

"Are you sure about this, my friend? You play a dangerous game."

The Russian shrugged. "*Inshallah.*" As God wills.

Fifteen minutes later the tea service was cleared away just as honking horns blared in the distance. It wasn't long before thick, knobby truck tires crunched to a halt outside the compound.

The chieftain raced outside and shouted a friendly Pashto greeting as the Russian stood by the low table. Moments later the chieftain ushered in a tall Pashtun—six foot six if he was an inch. The man's thick, shoulder-length hair was streaked with gray. Unlike his host, the ginormous Taliban fighter was kitted out like an American Special Forces operator, including digital camouflage, a chest rig with armor plates, and a holstered Glock 17 pistol. The only thing missing was a bump helmet. He yanked off his Oakley wraparound sunglasses.

The Taliban fighter's large black eyes narrowed like a falcon's as he caught sight of the burly Russian.

"Is this the Ivan?" he asked the chieftain in Pashto.

"His name is Stepan Saponov."

"Does he have a phone?" The Taliban feared the Americans might somehow track the Russian's phone signal and lead them to this meeting.

"My son tossed it in the garbage at the airport."

The Russian held out his hand and said in Russian, "You must be Commander Yaqoob."

The glowering Afghani fighter ignored it.

The Russian's eyes flared. "My hand not good enough for you?"

"Russians kill my father, my uncles," Yaqoob said in faltering Russian. He pulled back the collar of his camouflaged jacket, revealing a mass of scar tissue wrapping around his neck like a sleeve of melted plastic. "And a buried Russian mine did this five years ago. I hate Russians. Russians are a plague."

"War is a plague on Russians, too," Stepan said. He pulled up his pant leg, revealing a mechanical limb. "Syria." He then touched his blinded eye. "Bakhmut." The Russian fixed his good eye on Yaqoob. "Shall we two men cry like women over our sorrows or get to business?"

Yaqoob snorted a grudging appreciation for the wounded Russian fighter.

The chieftain quickly ushered the two men to their cushions on the floor and barked an order.

Stepan and Yaqoob never stopped staring at each other; two scorpions in a carpeted, mud-brick bottle. In short order, servants raced in and set before the three men a large stack of freshly baked flatbread, steaming dishes of lamb, eggplant dumplings, sticky rice, and a bowl of dried fruit along with fresh cups of hot tea. The servants dashed out of the room, leaving the three men alone.

Stepan devoured his food, obviously hungry after his long journey, his lips glistening with lamb fat. Yaqoob ate more deliberately, exchanging glances with the chieftain, who took only measured bites.

"He has no manners," Yaqoob said to the chieftain, confident the Russian didn't speak his language. "He eats like a starved wolf."

The chieftain wagged his head. "The Prophet Muhammad, peace be upon him, said, 'Whoever believes in Allah and the Last Day, let him be generous to his guest.'"

"And you vouch for this infidel?"

"I vouch for his money. Besides, only a madman or an arms broker would dare show his face around here."

"Which is he?"

"Perhaps both," the chieftain said, laughing. "I have a nephew in Kabul. He works for the General Directorate of Intelligence. He checked the Wagner rosters. Our friend 'Ivan' here was with Wagner

all right, and before that was a sergeant with the 104th Guards Airborne Division. Arrested for acts of criminality and treason, but escaped. According to FSB records, he is presumed dead."

"He looks at least half alive to me."

"And you would prefer both halves dead?" the old chief asked.

Yaqoob grinned. "Business before pleasure."

12

The Vendor ducked and twisted, blocking every strike of the furious attack. He moved with a grace and fluidity that belied his size. At six foot three and two hundred fifty pounds, he was far taller and muscular than most men, especially those of his nationality.

His father, a strict disciplinarian, raised him to be stronger than the wisest man in any room or wiser than the strongest man. Since childhood, he could never remember not being both at once. The resulting social isolation his lessers imposed upon him meant nothing and only freed him to pursue his passions without hindrance.

The Vendor's sweat-burned eyes searched desperately for an opening inside the blur of arms and legs swinging at him like a threshing machine.

The Vendor was battling his robotic *mook jong*—a high-tech version of a traditional Chinese fighting trainer. But in place of the fixed center post and wooden arms, the Vendor put the AI-powered device— which he called a *makiwara*—on a three-hundred-sixty-degree turntable. He gave it articulating arms and legs that struck in nearly every direction. It was far more dangerous than any human sparring partner—faster, smarter, and programmed to deliver killing blows.

After achieving a ninth *dan* black belt in karate, and mastering several other martial arts forms including Muay Thai, the Vendor had proven himself unequaled in unarmed combat, killing several highly ranked opponents in secret underground fights over the years. Unable to find willing opponents with suicidal tendencies, he invented his mechanical *makiwara* to keep his skills sharp.

Spotting his split-second opening, the Vendor shouted a guttural "*Kiai!*" as he launched a high kick into the robot's padded face. A horn blasted and lights flashed, "killing" the robot, robbing it of power and freezing it in position as if dead.

The Vendor nodded with satisfaction. He turned around and faced the dojo's giant wall screen. The OLED panel camera accurately depicted the Vendor in his black, salt-stained *gi*, drinking in great draughts of air where he stood.

But the robotic *makiwara* was depicted as a hulking American fighter rather than a machine. The "deep fake" American opponent was perfectly rendered, including a white *gi* stained in blood and a badly bruised, clean-shaven Anglo face.

The Vendor's hatred of Americans ran deep in his veins. As a child he drank in the horror stories told by his elderly relatives about the mass bombings of Japanese cities during the war. They recalled in ghastly detail how hundreds of thousands of Japanese civilians were burned alive in the carefully engineered firestorms delivered by American long-range bombers.

The Vendor gestured at the screen with his large left hand, which rewound the digital recording of the fight to the beginning of the match. He gestured again and the fight began. Even the Vendor was impressed with his speedy attacks and impenetrable defenses. When the final, fatal kick was delivered, the digital American's ugly head snapped backward like a Pez dispenser with a sickening crack. IKKEN HISSATSU in Japanese kanji flashed on the screen. *One Punch Kill*.

It was the Vendor's fifth victory of today's workout session in his private dojo. He flexed his powerful hands, strengthened by years of training with the heaviest *nigiri game*—traditional Okinawan lifting jars. He was considering another sparring session, but decided against it.

What he really needed was a long, hot sauna for muscle recovery, but there were pressing delivery issues that demanded his immediate attention. He headed for the shower, his mind already focused on delivering a blow far more deadly than the one inflicted on the robot.

13

Though the Russian spoke no Pashto, he picked up a word or two, his ears keen to the tones in their voices as he tore off another piece of flatbread to mop up the juices on his plate. He stole furtive glances at the two Afghanis. The giant was obviously hostile and the more dangerous of the two. It was the chieftain that concerned him, though. Chances were the two men were related. They spoke in hushed, conspiratorial tones, and Stepan's life hung in the balance of their words.

Thing was, Stepan's Russian hadn't always been much better than his Pashto was now.

Juan's backstory as "Sergeant Stepan Saponov" was unimpeachable. The *Oregon* team had successfully broken into the Wagner database and planted his false identification. To solidify the ruse, Overholt had instructed the chieftain to vet Stepan Saponov with the Afghan intelligence service for confirmation. In fact, the chieftain believed Juan really was an ex-Wagner fighter, not a mercenary secretly working for the Americans.

Cabrillo's undercover getup was equally bulletproof. The *Oregon*'s Magic Shop had worked its miracle wonders again, and Kevin Nixon's Academy Award–winning special effects skills were on full display. Juan's puckering facial scar and blinded eye were so realistic that he almost felt as if he had suffered permanent damage. Not that he minded. His terrifying visage acted like a force field, causing even the surliest Afghanis to avert their eyes and slink away.

The special effects also helped him to get into character. Because Cabrillo was a child with an overactive imagination, his mother had always told him he should go into acting. She never knew that he actually followed her advice. The covert training he got from the CIA was more "method" than anything he would have gotten in UCLA acting classes. For him, every performance was a matter of life or death, and Cabrillo valued the ability to breathe more than any stupid Hollywood trophy.

Juan's only real concern at the moment was the chieftain's reliability. He had never met the man, let alone worked with him. But beggars can't be choosers. Overholt had recruited the chieftain decades earlier during the Russian occupation, but the old man had since gone dormant. In fact, the chieftain had been on a dozen prior CIA watch lists of "known terrorists" and "Taliban collaborators" in recent years. But Overholt found a point of leverage, though it was tenuous at best.

Exploiting the notoriously porous American southern border, the wily old Afghani had arranged for his fourth and youngest wife to "immigrate" to the United States with his three children begat by her. The oldest child was currently in his first year at Stanford medical school.

In exchange for arranging today's meeting with the Taliban, Overholt promised not to contact the Department of Homeland Security and have the chieftain's family deported. But sensing Overholt's desperation, the chief extracted a further promise from him. After the mission was accomplished, Overholt would arrange for the chief's three other wives to be issued legal visas as his "sisters" and his herd of grown children as "nieces and nephews." With proceeds from the vast poppy fields under his control, the chief had already purchased a large family compound outside of Roseville, California, where he planned to retire with his clan.

Cabrillo hoped the chieftain's family loyalties were stronger than his ideological ones. Juan's life was hanging by a precariously frayed thread.

He plopped another piece of spicy roasted lamb into his mouth. If he was going to die today, he couldn't think of a more savory last meal than this.

★

Cabrillo took his last bite and wiped his face with the back of his hand.

"I am grateful for your kind hospitality and excellent food," he said to the chieftain in Russian. "But I think Commander Yaqoob and I have some business to attend to."

"Yes, of course," the chieftain said. A mischievous spark danced in the old man's weathered eyes. "I shall leave the two of you alone to discuss matters." He stood, placed a hand on his chest, and bowed slightly before heading for the back rooms.

"Thank you for coming, Commander Yaqoob," the Russian began.

"I don't speak Russian very well," Yaqoob said in English. "You speak English. Correct?"

"Yes, of course."

"Then we shall speak in English, Ivan," Yaqoob said. "I learned most of it from the Americans when they hired me as a scout." He laughed. "Gullible idiots."

"No wonder they call your country the 'graveyard of empires,'" Juan said.

"Theirs *and* yours." A malicious pride flashed in Yaqoob's eyes.

Juan suddenly wasn't sure if the Afghani was referring to him as a Russian or an American. He swallowed his momentary concern with a casual sip of tea.

Yaqoob's broad hands rested in his lap. He turned his palms toward the low ceiling. "What is it that you want?"

"I serve with a private military unit in the Central African Republic. Mostly ex-Wagner, like me. Russia no longer supplies our weapons or ammunition. I am hunting for both. We pay well."

"What exactly do you need?"

"More than you can supply."

"Try me, Ivan."

Cabrillo rolled his shoulders, working out the kinks in his back from sitting on the floor so long.

"All right. I need seventy-five armored Humvees equipped with either anti-tank guided missiles or M60 machine guns."

The Taliban's eyes softened thoughtfully and his posture relaxed.

"Not a problem. I have equal numbers of both."

"Two hundred pairs of night vision goggles with batteries and cases."

"Also not a problem."

"Five hundred M16A4 assault rifles."

"The ones with the under-mount grenade launchers?"

"Yes. You can do this?"

"No problem." The ferocious Pashtun was now as friendly as a jewelry store salesclerk.

"A million rounds of 5.56 ammunition for the M16s, two hundred thousand rounds of 7.62 for the M60s, and five hundred anti-tank missiles."

The Pashtun shrugged his shoulders nonchalantly.

"This can all be easily arranged—for the right price. What else do you need?"

"LAW rockets, grenades, mortars, and Claymores."

"Medical supplies? MREs?"

"If you have them."

"Trust me, we do."

Cabrillo eyed him up and down with his one good eye.

"I have my doubts."

Yaqoob scowled with disappointment.

"Without trust, my friend, we cannot do business."

"Ah, yes. Trust—but verify."

Yaqoob let loose a belly laugh.

"You quote Ronald Reagan?"

Juan smiled. "Why not? Cowboys and Cossacks—all the same! Besides, Reagan was quoting an old Russian proverb."

Cabrillo leaned over and laid a hand on his rucksack. Out of the corner of his eye he saw the big Pashtun stiffen and his hand slip down to his pistol grip.

"Relax, my friend." Juan reached into his rucksack and pulled out a solid bar of gold and handed it to the Pashtun giant.

Yaqoob weighed the nearly twenty-eight-pound brick of shiny metal in his massive hand. The smile that broke across his face gleamed brighter than the gold.

"For you, personally," Cabrillo said. "A token of our friendship."

"Will the payment for your order be in gold as well?"

"Of course, unless you prefer something else. But what currency is worth anything more than the paper it's printed on these days?"

Yaqoob's eyes fell back onto the gold bar. He'd never held so much wealth in his own hands.

"So, now it's your turn to earn some trust," Juan said.

Yaqoob nodded eagerly.

"Surely, my friend. Surely."

14

Juan Cabrillo, still playing the role of ex-Wagner sergeant Stepan
Saponov, limped his way over to the waiting MD-530 scout attack
helicopter a hundred yards beyond the village. He climbed into the
cramped passenger compartment while Yaqoob slid into the copilot's
seat. The Afghan air force pilot, one of Yaqoob's nephews, throttled
up the single Rolls-Royce turboshaft engine and they lifted off in a
swirl of dust.

Fifteen minutes later, the chopper set down near a rugged plateau.
Yaqoob led Juan into a nearby subterranean cave complex guarded by
two heavy machine-gun emplacements providing crossfire against anyone approaching without permission.

Yaqoob gestured at the vast expanse of the cave. Stacks of crates
and pallets of steel ammo boxes extended far into the darkest recesses.
They approached the nearest pallet. Everything was stenciled in English.

"There, you see? Grenades, mortars, ammunition of various
calibers—over five million rounds in this cave alone. Everything you
need and more. Satisfied?"

"Somewhat."

"Then follow me."

As Juan shadowed him out of the cave he ground his right heel into the dirt, hardly missing a step as he limped behind the tall Pashtun toward the waiting helicopter.

★

Another short hop on the American helo whisked them over to the outskirts of Ghazni, a former Soviet garrison from decades earlier.

They passed through a collection of abandoned mud huts, where sharp-eyed, well-armed uniformed guards kept vigil, hidden away from the prying eyes in the sky. They marched into one hut with an underground passageway and entered a vast subterranean concrete bunker built by the Russians. Acres of crated rifles, machine guns, pistols, and even sniper rifles were carefully organized.

Yaqoob marched over to one crate and popped the latches. He handed the rifle over to Cabrillo. He shouldered the weapon as Yaqoob spoke.

"M16A4. Never fired. Perfect working condition. I can deliver one thousand of these from this one storage facility alone. There are several more such facilities at my disposal."

"Very good."

"Convinced yet? Do we have a deal?"

"Ammo, guns. All good. But it's the Humvees I really want to see."

Yaqoob gestured with his big head. "Let's go."

Juan limped up the steps back to the ground floor of the abandoned hut. Yaqoob didn't see him grind his right heel into the dirt just outside the doorway as they exited the building on their way to the idling helicopter.

★

"The Chinese built that for us," Yaqoob whispered in his headphone, pointing at a giant hospital in the middle of Kabul. "It even has a pediatric oncology ward. The Chinese have done many good things for my people."

Just wait until they call in their chits, Juan wanted to say.

Afghanistan had massive lithium deposits, one of the most strategically significant minerals on the planet. The Chinese government would gobble them up and everything else of value thanks to goodwill projects like this one.

Cabrillo was surprised when the pilot nosed the helicopter down toward the hospital and even more so when he set the skids gently into the center of the circle-H on the rooftop helipad.

Juan followed Yaqoob to an elevator that whisked them down to the lowest level of the underground garage directly beneath the hospital. An armed guard opened a heavy steel door and the Pashtun led Cabrillo into the storage facility. There were dozens of crates of anti-tank and anti-aircraft weapons, including AGM-114 Hellfire missiles and Hydra 70 rockets.

"Hiding these beneath a hospital is brilliant," Juan said. In fact, he was sickened by the callousness of the act.

"Everything you asked for and more—right here. If you like, I can take you to a doctor for that scar. It looks nasty. Maybe he can fix it up."

"No need." Juan dragged a hand over it. "My mother likes it."

Yaqoob laughed and clapped Cabrillo on the shoulder.

"Funny man. Anything else you need to see?"

"What I really need are those Humvees you promised."

"No problem. Let's go."

★

The final stop on their whirlwind tour took them to Bagram Airfield, the scene of the humiliating American evacuation from the country.

The giant facility had originally been a Soviet air base, but the U.S. government took it over, enlarging and improving it over the decades. The longest runways could accommodate the world's largest cargo aircraft including the American C-5M Super Galaxy capable of carrying a quarter-million pounds of cargo nearly five thousand miles.

But with the U.S. Air Force and its vast fleet of aircraft now gone, the Kabul government had provided incentives for commercial aviation to use the facility. Military trainers from China were among the first to arrive.

The MD-530 pilot cleared with the tower and landed Yaqoob's helicopter a safe distance from the main runway, near one of the largest hangars in the facility. Yaqoob and Juan exited just as a gas truck approached the helicopter for a refill.

The heat radiated up from the tarmac as Juan limped along. The high-pitched whine of jet turbines rang in his ears and his nostrils filled with the stench of jet exhaust from a large Air Astana commercial airliner that had just landed. Its tail bore the national flag of Kazakhstan.

The two men approached what appeared to be a fortified hangar. The large doors were closed, but the Pashtun directed Juan toward a small exterior door on the side. An armed guard opened it and in they went.

It clearly wasn't a hangar. It was some kind of storage facility, as large as a football field.

"More vehicles than a Los Angeles CarMax," Yaqoob said.

He was probably right, Juan thought. There must have been at least nine hundred Humvees parked with military precision inside the thick cement walls.

"There are three more such storage facilities scattered around the country. For you? Five hundred Humvees, no problem. A thousand. We also have pickups, passenger cars, ambulances, even an ice cream truck. Whatever you need."

Juan shook his head in disbelief. "You are a man of your word, Commander."

He needed to drop another GPS homing beacon from his boot heel outside the entrance to be read by satellites later or, better still, by Tomahawk cruise missiles. He'd planted beacons at each of the facilities they'd visited so far—but skipped the hospital. He wasn't willing to gamble the lives of sick children against the fatigue of an overworked targeting analyst who might inadvertently screw up.

Juan was racking his brain trying to figure out how to get Yaqoob to show him all of the other warehouses and storage depots the

Taliban had scattered around the country, but he didn't dare make the killer suspicious. The targets he had already identified would have to be good enough for now.

"Are you ready to deal, then?" Yaqoob asked hopefully. Juan saw the dollar signs spinning in his black eyes like reels in a Vegas slot machine.

"Like you said before, if the price is right. What do you propose?"

"For this priceless American equipment?"

"Name it."

The Pashtun did.

Juan haggled with him over the exorbitant price. If he didn't, the Afghani would become suspicious. They both knew his quoted fee was outrageous. A few moments later, Juan got the number down by nearly half. It was still an enormous sum of money.

"You drive a hard bargain, Ivan. But I want to do further business with you, so I will accept your poor offer."

"There is still one issue. How do you plan on transporting all of this?"

"What is the destination?"

"The Central African Republic. Air transport is required."

"It will all be arranged."

"The deliveries must be on time. They must be guaranteed."

"We have the means."

"'We'? No offense, friend, but unless the Americans left behind a couple of C-5 Galaxies, there's no way you can transport all of this equipment."

The Taliban frowned. "The deliveries will be made. You have my word."

"How? The Americans monitor everything flying in and out of here."

"We have a source."

"What source? Who?"

"That is our secret."

"How can I trust this 'source' of yours? What if he is working for the CIA? I must know his name or the deal is off."

The threat of the loss of so much money nearly snatched away the Pashtun's breath. His eyebrows furrowed as he weighed his options.

"I tell you the truth, I don't know his name. I have never met the man. But he has never failed us. Not once."

"You expect me to believe that?"

"He accepts our payments. He makes our deliveries."

"You pay him?"

"No. Someone higher up in my clan does the transfer." The Taliban darkened, growing more suspicious. He leaned over and lowered his voice.

"The man is a genius, or perhaps even a devil. But I trust him— more than I trust you, Ivan."

Who is this "devil"?

Overholt was right. Discovering how this gear was being transported without detection was more important than locating the weapons themselves. Juan needed to find this character.

Cabrillo knew he had one last chance to set the hook—or lose the biggest fish of all.

"My superiors will not accept this. You said it yourself. Without trust we cannot do business. If you can't trust me with the name, you don't have trust in me. I will find another source of weapons for my unit."

Cabrillo turned on his heel, but the Pashtun's frying pan–sized hand seized him by the bicep.

"He calls himself the 'Vendor.'"

"Is he European? Chinese? Mafia?"

"I don't know what he is. Like I said, I never met him. Never spoke to him. All text."

"How did you find him?"

The giant Pashtun shook his head. "He found us."

The "Vendor" isn't much to go on, Juan told himself. At least it was a start. But he needed more.

"So this Vendor. He has the same problem transporting all of this equipment. How does *he* avoid American detection?"

Yaqoob flashed his big white teeth.

"I will show you."

★

Yaqoob commandeered an open-cab baggage cart and drove Juan over to a large hangar complex several hundred yards away. The wide doors were open. The baggage cart tires squealed on the slick hangar floor when he hit the brakes.

"There." The Pashtun pointed from the seat of the vehicle.

An Airbus A320 passenger airliner bearing the blue and white paint scheme and logo of Somali Airlines stood in the center of the building.

"A plane," Juan said with a shrug. "So what?"

"Watch!"

Suddenly doors opened up in the belly of the airliner just as a driverless flatbed vehicle slid under the fuselage. Moments later, a block of passenger seats lowered onto the flatbed and it sped off to a far corner. Another took its place and repeated the process. Within minutes at least three hundred seats had been removed and stacked along a far wall.

Mesmerized by the vision of the automated flatbeds, Juan's attention turned to the fuselage itself as it turned from the Somali Airlines blue and white scheme to all white. A new green, white, and red Tajik Air logo appeared on the tail.

"Electrically charged paint that can change color. Have you even seen such a miracle?" Yaqoob asked.

Juan bit his tongue. *Well, yeah, on the* Oregon.

"So this 'Vendor' has a fleet of airplanes that can automatically change their color schemes and logos. I take it he also changes IFF signals?" Juan knew well enough that "identification, friend or foe" transponders identified aircraft primarily for air traffic control. But he also knew they were easy enough to spoof.

"What do I know of this 'IFF'? The planes come with passengers, the planes go with cargo, the planes come back again with more passengers, or sometimes not. No problems."

"How long have you been doing this?"

"Six months. Twelve, fourteen trips so far. All good."

Juan motioned toward the aircraft. The two fuselage bay doors had converted themselves into a large loading ramp that stretched from the aircraft to the hangar floor.

"Where is this one going to?"

"That is none of your affair. Operational security."

"Can you at least confirm you are capable of long-distance delivery?"

"Would you want me telling strangers about your cargo and destination?"

"Obviously not."

"Then you understand my position." Yaqoob pointed at the aircraft. "Just take a look at that airplane. Do you think it is just a . . . Wait, how do the Americans say it? Oh, yes. A 'puddle jumper'?"

"Understood."

Juan pondered his options. On the far side of the hangar he watched two uniformed Taliban stacking long crates on a pallet. The pallet was already loaded onto the forks of a driverless forklift.

Another Taliban jihadi was wrapping a fully stacked pallet with a roll of heavy clear plastic for load stability. A dozen more stacked and wrapped pallets lined the far wall, but Juan couldn't make out what they carried.

Juan needed more information about the Vendor and his operations, but clearly Yaqoob didn't know any more. He wasn't handling the financial transactions, so there wasn't any chance to steal bank transfer information from him. Right now, Juan's only play seemed to be getting on that plane and planting one of his homing beacons on board. Then the *Oregon* could track the plane to its next destination and perhaps there he could find out more about this Vendor character, his operation's networks, and maybe even more about his clients—buyers and sellers.

"I want to see inside the plane," Juan said. He barked it like an order. No point in giving the big man a chance to refuse his request.

Yaqoob unfolded his long legs out of the cramped little trolley and strode toward the plane.

Juan knew there was always a moment in an undercover operation where the agent knew he was on the verge of scoring big. That moment was usually more dangerous than most because it was the easiest way for an agent to accidentally tip his hand. The trick was to keep a cool head and not get too excited and give away the game. Cabrillo had done this long enough to know that he was just moments away from success. All he had to do was take a few deep breaths, look around the aircraft, drop off the homing beacon, and then get the heck out of Dodge.

Juan watched as a speeding automated forklift heading for the back wall skidded to a halt just feet from Yaqoob, its collision sensors signaling a crash warning to its automatic brakes before it could hit the Pashtun.

Yaqoob hardly noticed. Just as he was about to step onto the ramp of the newly transformed cargo aircraft, his phone buzzed in his camouflaged pocket and he stopped. He pulled the phone out and pressed it against his massive head, and answered it by barking his name.

His voice lowered and he turned his broad back to Cabrillo, his words becoming more heated the longer he spoke. Suddenly he quieted, and listened. Cabrillo couldn't make out the words on the other end or even the language. Finally, Yaqoob sighed. He turned around toward Juan, his face a welter of conflicting emotions.

"It's for you, Stepan." He tossed the phone to Juan in a high little arc.

Caught off guard, Juan reached up with both hands and snagged the phone out of the air—taking his eyes off Yaqoob just long enough for the big Afghani to throw a spine-shattering haymaker, cracking the side of Juan's skull with his anvil-sized fist, and knocking him out cold.

15

Captain Pak's wary eyes were glued to the periscope, its Chinese glass clear and bright. He felt a surge of adrenaline course through his veins as he tracked the South Korean destroyer knifing through the water and growing larger by the minute. The *King Jeongjo the Great* was the bandit nation's latest and most powerful ship, manufactured in Ulsan, Hyundai Heavy Industries' shipyard.

A lusty urge rose up in him, like a hunter drawing a bead on a prized stag bolting through the forest. He shuddered with the thrill of the coming kill.

Pak's submarine was a twenty-seven-year-old Romeo-class diesel-electric boat. It had been built in a North Korean shipyard, a copy of a Chinese variant of a 1950s Soviet design. Despite its age, his boat was in excellent working order and the pride of North Korea's submarine fleet. Its primary advantage was its range and relative quiet.

Thanks to superior Chinese battery technology, Pak had no need to fire up his diesel engines in the last four days, and he also put his boat in ultra-quiet condition. This enabled him to lurk in absolute silence in his target's known patrol lane and wait for his quarry to come to him. His hunter's patience had finally paid off when his passive sonar detectors picked up the noise of the destroyer's high-speed, twin-shafted prop wash.

North Korea's navy had never received its due respect despite the fact it was the third largest in the world, deploying more ships than even the vaunted fleets of the imperialist Americans. What Pak's navy lacked in technological prowess was more than made up for in revolutionary zeal, self-sacrifice, and devotion to *Juche*.

As powerful as these national attributes were, even the Respected Comrade Supreme Commander of the nation understood the advantages that technology conferred in the modern battle space. North Korea's acquisition of the modified *Khishchnik* torpedo from the Vendor was about to change the strategic equation in the waters of East Asia and perhaps even the world.

According to the admiral, the modified *Khishchnik* far surpassed the abilities of the infamous *Shkval*, the world's first operational supercavitating torpedo. By creating its own encapsulating bubble of air, a supercavitating torpedo was no longer subject to the drag and friction of water, allowing it to attain exponentially higher speeds than conventional torpedoes.

Incredibly, the modified *Khishchnik* was capable of mind-shattering speeds and its new fuel system extended its range to over one hundred miles. As the admiral explained, this made the *Khishchnik* the functional equivalent of a hypersonic underwater missile.

Pak's heart nearly burst with excitement as he thought of the honor bestowed upon him. His submarine carried one of the newly acquired *Khishchnik*s. Today, the South Korean Navy would be exposed as an impotent dog and its craven master, the cowardly Americans, as a toothless wolf.

It was time to put his finger on the trigger. But he knew he must be patient lest he startle his sensitive quarry.

★

Captain Cho stood on the bridgewing of the *King Jeongjo the Great*, the pride of South Korea's fleet, smoking a cigarette. The air battered his silver-flecked hair beneath his cap as his eyes fell on the far horizon. A churning slate-gray sky crashed into the frothing wine-dark sea. He smiled at his good fortune.

Long a commercial shipbuilding power, South Korea had entered the ranks of the great seafaring nations with the construction of this world-class destroyer, larger and more deadly than anything else of its type. Bristling with the latest weapons and linked to the omniscient six-megawatt radar of the Aegis Combat System, Cho's vessel could sink or destroy almost any ship or aircraft within a hundred miles.

The *King Jeongjo* was the next step in his nation's long march toward independence from American security promises. His nation was grateful for America's decades-long defense of South Korea. But it was clear China's rapid rise and America's overextended global commitments meant his nation had to shoulder more of the burden for its own defense on land, in the air, and particularly at sea.

The crazed North Korean fanatics were merely an armed extension of China's hegemonic ambitions. Their fleet of ships, though numerous, were generations behind in combat technologies. Most North Korean submarines were little more than refurbished Soviet-era subs, more fit for the scrapyards than modern combat. It was the aging fleet of North Korea's "boomer" subs and their nuclear missiles that still posed the greatest threat. Modern vessels like *King Jeongjo the Great* were his nation's mighty shield against the North Korean submarine terror.

Cho brought his binoculars to his blearing eyes, dried out by the whistling wind singing in the rigging above. Fleet headquarters had informed all patrol ships to be particularly vigilant. Reports of both Chinese aggression against American vessels farther south and of North Korean provocations along the DMZ had put everyone on edge. But so far Cho had encountered nothing of any concern.

"Captain!"

Cho turned around. His tactical operations officer, a lieutenant, stood in the bridge doorway.

"CIC reports possible sonar contact."

16

Captain Cho was out of breath from his mad dash to the air-conditioned CIC belowdecks, his lungs exhaling the rank air of tobacco.

"Captain's in Combat," the tactical operations officer barked.

"I have the conn," Cho replied.

"Captain has the conn," the lieutenant repeated. That meant Cho was running the show.

The captain stood hovering over the shoulder of the sonar supervisor, his best sonar technician, a chief petty officer hand-selected for this billet by Cho himself. The CIC was the tactical nerve center of Cho's ship, where his sensor operations were located. If combat was at hand, this is where he needed to be—not up on the bridge.

The two men stared at the large passive sonar display. Several types of sonar screens were pulled up. The chief pointed at the spectrograph display.

"The algorithm detected a likely torpedo tube door opening two minutes ago."

"You concur?" Cho asked.

"Could be an anomaly." The chief laid a finger on the screen. "But this? It sure looks like it to me."

"Did we get an audio recording?"

"Nothing that I could make out." The CPO grunted. "The algorithm must be smarter than my ears."

"Not likely," Cho said, clapping his old friend on the shoulder.

The chief had served with Cho on other boats for several years patrolling hostile waters. With or without audio confirmation, the chief knew what a torpedo door opening looked like on a spectrograph.

Equally important, his sonar computer had access to the U.S. Navy database storing tens of thousands of previously recorded audio and electromagnetic signatures of combatant vessels, including the sound of torpedo doors opening on every variety of North Korean submarines. No doubt the sonar's computer matched up the spectrograph reading with a similar signature in the database.

In some cases, the specific submarine could be detected by the unique sound of its own particular doors. However, in this instance, no submarine was identified because not enough of the sound signature had been captured by the sonar computer.

"Where is it?" the captain asked.

The sonar tech then dragged the B-scan display forward, showing both the range and bearing of an object relative to their destroyer.

"Eleven thousand two hundred meters, bearing oh-eight-seven degrees."

"No other signatures?"

"None."

The captain breathed a sigh of relief. No other signatures meant no submarines in the water—or any of their "fish" racing toward them. Cho wondered if his sonar arrays had picked up the clanking of lost shipping containers colliding in the water or the industrial noise of a commercial fishing trawler instead of a torpedo door.

He turned to the radar technician.

"Anything?"

"No, sir."

"Anything on the cameras?" Cho asked. A sub running at periscope depth would leave a thin, feathering wake on the surface.

The watch stander monitoring the optronic mast shook his head. "Nothing, sir."

Cho and his chief exchanged a relieved look.

"Log it in the computer as an anomaly."

"Aye, sir."

Captain Cho stood and stretched, and cracked his neck. He was still on his break. Time enough to go topside and finish his smoke.

"Keep me posted if anything else pops up. I'll be back in fifteen."

"Sir."

Cho turned for the exit.

Alarms suddenly blared, and warning lights flashed.

Another sonar tech shouted, "Fish in the water!"

Cho whipped around and barked orders at his crew.

"Evasive maneuvers! Sound battle stations! Reports! Bearing, speed, range!"

The chief shouted back. "Torpedo bearing oh-eight-seven degrees relative. Speed . . . Wait . . . That can't be right."

Klaxon alarms blared throughout the ship signaling general quarters.

An electronic voice shouted in the ship-wide speakers, "General Quarters! General Quarters! All hands man your battle stations! All hands man your battle stations!"

"Speed!" Cho shouted over the keening Klaxon.

"Computer says . . . 1,911 knots."

"Impossible."

"Eleven seconds to impact."

Cho bellowed at his combat team, the finest in the fleet.

"Helm! Get me flank speed! Emergency power! Fire Control— torpedo decoys, now!"

The destroyer lunged forward like a panther, ducking its steel shoulder deep into a steep turn as the ship's four big turbo-diesels roared belowdecks. Techs grabbed their station desks or risked getting thrown out of their chairs.

"Eight seconds to impact."

"Decoys away!"

"Sonar, get me a target fix on that tango," Cho said. "Fire Control, put three Red Sharks on that tango—now!"

The chief's gaze was fixed on his screen. Even across the room, Cho could see the speeding torpedo track racing toward his boat, blazing a curving red trail across the black screen as it tracked his fleeing ship.

Rage washed over Cho. The Klaxon roared overhead.

"Somebody kill that alarm!"

The instantaneous silence was immediately interrupted by the roar of three vertical launch tubes firing in succession, sending three Red Shark anti-sub rockets into the air. Within moments, the Red Shark rockets would release their homing torpedoes into the water.

"Can't shake his track, Captain!" the chief shouted.

The fire control station reported dutifully, "Decoys failing."

Cho cursed. *None of this was possible!*

He snatched up the mic for the ship's intercom and punched a button.

"All hands, prepare for impact! Prepare for impact! Prepare—"

★

"Impact!" The North Korean sailor grinned ear to ear, his hands still clutching his headphones. "Sonar indicates a large explosion, sir."

Captain Pak nodded, his own sly smile curling his thin mouth. There was no way the *King Jeongjo the Great* could have survived such a strike. Even if the warhead hadn't detonated, the kinetic energy of a nearly six-thousand-pound torpedo traveling at over nineteen hundred knots would have ripped through the destroyer's hull like a railroad spike through a wet cocktail napkin.

All faces turned to their captain.

"Today we have made history. Today we have scalded the whimpering dogs," Pak said. "And the Great Leader will wave our banner of glorious victory over our enemies."

The bright young faces burned with pride.

And just as quickly, that pride was slapped away.

"Sonar reports one . . . two . . . three splashes, sir!"

Pak stiffened, fearing the worst.

"Sonar reports high-speed screws. Torpedoes!"

The tactical officer shouted his orders.

"Launch decoys! Flank speed! Evasive maneuvers!"

Captain Pak heard his words, but they sounded distant, as if shouted through thick glass. The ship's active sonar pinged over the crackling loudspeakers, tracking the speeding torpedoes as they closed.

A calm washed over Pak as the sub angled nose-down in a desperate run. It was all in vain. His boat could barely make thirteen knots underwater; the torpedoes homing in on them traveled four times that speed.

Only moments now, Pak thought as the sonar pings rang faster and faster in their ears.

All eyes turned to him again, their desperate faces paled with doom.

What could he say to comfort them?

"We have done our duty, comrades," Pak said. "What better death than that?"

A few heartbeats later, the hull shattered and they were all snatched away into the shadowless gloom of the sea.

17

The Vendor watched the articulating robot hand deftly insert the computer board inside the command module.

Originally developed for the video gaming industry, the board's advanced microarchitecture and central processing units were built for machine learning. In fact, it was the gaming industry that had always pushed some of the most important advances in chip design for artificial intelligence. After all, they were chasing the incredibly lucrative market of dopamine addiction. Billions of people were hooked on first-person sport and shooter games, world-building fantasies, and simulated porn.

Bound by the inefficiencies of government waste, bureaucracy, and intervention, national defense industries had long lagged behind the free market free-for-all of billion-dollar gaming enterprises. But not all defense bureaucrats were morons. There was a decades-long relationship between the military industrial complex and video games involving transfers of talent and technology. Training, combat, and flight simulations, strategy games, and even virtual reality were all line items in national defense budgets. But it was the mighty computer chips the gaming industry was developing that powered it all.

Ironically, these same computing boards powering games of war were also driving the next generation of actual, blood-shedding war.

With the "brain" insertion of his Yari kamikaze drone complete, the automated assembly line moved the command module to the next level of drone construction. The Vendor's management software had indicated that three of the four storage holds belowdecks were already full to capacity with Yaris stored in their quad-configured launch pods.

The Yari was his own variant of the infamous Russian Lancet drone, though his was far superior to the game-changing weapon. Cheaper than the average American car, the Yari was powered by a simple electric motor and capable of carrying a wide variety of mission-specific warheads. But the Yari's true genius was its AI-driven ability to select its own targets for destruction as it loitered over the battle-field. With no need for ground or satellite communications, the Yari was also immune to anti-drone electronic countermeasures.

Additionally, the Vendor had built into the Yari a swarm capacity, allowing one drone to locate a target and instantly communicate with other Yaris on the ground or in the air in order to assemble a coordinated mass assault. Each four-winged drone was fitted with collapsible wings and loaded into a four-drone launcher. No taller than the average man, launchers could be placed on the ground, in the back of truck beds, on rooftops and shipping containers. A nearly infinite number of launchers and their Yaris could be linked and synced, and operated both manually and remotely.

The Yari was just one of several new weapon systems being developed and manufactured by his organization. No longer hampered by the petty bureaucratic politics and narrow-minded herd moralities of his former employers in the Japanese defense industry, the Vendor's genius for destruction was finally unleashed when he disappeared mysteriously several years ago, secretly stealing petabytes of advanced weapons designs in the process.

Shunned by the lesser minds who governed him, the Vendor had long since abandoned primitive notions of patriotism. Stealing weapons secrets wasn't an act of treason or even greed. The most important parts of those plans came from his own highly advanced mind, which meant they were his after all, despite the petty legalisms he'd agreed to early in his career when he was less confident and easily exploited.

Those stolen plans formed the basis for his first forays into private weapons manufacturing, which had proven wildly successful. The money came hot and fast and he quickly expanded his capabilities. His ultimate goal wasn't greed but chaos—and the chance to prove his genius to the bureaucratic midwits that had rejected him.

Chaos was the key.

The Vendor viewed chaos as the prime virtue from which all others emerged. Even the gods couldn't create the universe without chaos first being present. In turn, chaos birthed its angry progeny, crisis. These two ideas stalked humanity like tigers in the jungle. The greatest leaps in human invention came when chaos threatened human extinction. Without chaos, true genius was impossible.

Chaos was also the precursor to profits. The more chaos in the political order, the greater the need for machines of destruction. Defense budgets swelled; money flowed. The font of government-printed currencies continuously filled the Vendor's coffers and funded his never-ending expansion.

That prodigious cash flow along with his legendary status in the international design community allowed the Vendor to build a clandestine network of current and former weapons designers from around the world.

He also built and operated a flotilla of ship-based automated manufacturing facilities along with a fleet of transportation vessels and aircraft.

This transportation network had become a surprising source of revenue. There was an insatiable demand for smuggling existing weapons stocks including the horde of American arms the Taliban now possessed.

His entire organization was under enormous pressure from his clamoring clients. The demand for his new and improved variants of the latest weapons systems was far outstripping his ability to supply them. He couldn't build automated manufacturing vessels fast enough, though crewing them certainly wasn't as much of a problem. The advantages of floating industrial complexes far out at sea and beyond the territorial jurisdictions of hostile governments were obvious, but there were also challenges—and not a few perils.

Just as the next quad launcher was being filled with its fourth Yari, the Vendor's digital watch dinged on his wrist.

"Excellent," he said to himself.

The third applicant for the "VIP security" assignment posted on the dark web had cleared his records check and accepted the job offer. Of course, none of the applicants would know that the true mission was a battle to the death with the Vendor's new weapons systems on a remote island until it was too late.

The dark web advertisement promised a twenty-five percent up-front payment of an extravagant salary upon such acceptance. The Vendor tapped his watch and transferred Bitcoin into the applicant's account. At this rate of recruitment, he would be traveling to the Island of Sorrows sooner than he planned.

18

Juan's eyes flittered open, but his mind was fogged by a brutal migraine headache and a throbbing pain on the side of his skull. A high-pitched roar filled his ears and his face was pressed against cold metal, cold as the air around him. He suddenly remembered Yaqoob's hammering blow against the side of his face and his lights snapping out. The burning pain in his cheek made him think it might be broken.

He shook his head to clear a few more cobwebs, but it felt like his brain was hitting the sides of his skull like a tennis ball in a can, so he stopped. But it was enough to get his bearings.

The roaring noise was the whine of jet turbines. He glanced around, still lying on the floor. His vision was blocked by pallets stacked with metal cases and wooden crates. Everything was shrink-wrapped in plastic and then covered with cargo straps. Glancing a few inches in the other direction showed the base of the pallet nearest him. It was constructed of plywood sheets with seven-inch-thick honeycombed cardboard sandwiched between them. He'd seen this kind of setup before on humanitarian aid drops over Africa. No doubt each pallet had a parachute packed on top.

He tried to raise his hands to rub his eyes, but his arms couldn't move. In fact, his wrists were zip-tied behind his back. Worse, he was wrapped up like a mummy in plastic from his shoulders to his thighs—just like the pallets. He was lying on the metal deck of the aircraft, tossed there like a sack of wet cement.

No doubt about it. He was cinched up tighter than one of his *abuelita*'s spicy tamales.

Adrenaline kicked in. If there was anything that Cabrillo couldn't abide, it was the loss of freedom of movement. That angry endocrine surge cleared his mind enough to get to work.

He leveraged his legs to roll onto his back. His shoulders ached and now he was crushing his bound wrists, but he had a better view of his situation. At least his ankles weren't tied up. Either they ran out of zip ties or they felt sorry for him with his prosthetic leg.

Cabrillo noticed that the ragged end of the plastic wrap ran down his front. That gave him an idea.

He looked around until he found what he was hoping for—the head of a nail sticking out of the corner of a nearby pallet. He flopped and wriggled like a catfish in the bottom of a johnboat until he was able to scooch his way up against it.

It took him ten minutes of careful twisting and turning against the nailhead for him to finally peel back the edge of the plastic several inches along his torso.

It took him several more exhausting minutes of micro-movements to get the exposed plastic edge secured to the nailhead.

He took a deep breath to replenish his reserves, then gently rolled himself over. The sibilant whisper of the unwrapping plastic lifted his spirits, but he ran into the bulkhead before he was free. He wriggled his way carefully back to the pallet without tearing the plastic, resecured the plastic to the nailhead, then rolled away again. He repeated the process several more times until he was finally free of the sheeting, emerging from the cocoon of plastic film like a crippled snake shedding its translucent skin.

Drenched in sweat despite the cold and fighting through the burn of lactic acid eating into every muscle fiber in his body, Juan rolled onto his back once again. Planting his boots on the deck he thrust his hips upward, forming a high-angled bridge from the top of his knees down to his shoulders now pressing against the floor.

He then angled his thighs closer to his twisting arms until his fingers were finally able to reach the first of three buckles securing his prosthetic leg. Since he'd already shown the Taliban his artificial limb they had no reason to be surprised by it as they were securing him—let alone suspect anything of it.

By now Juan's hands ached as if they had been crushed in a hydraulic press because of the blood flow restricted by the zip ties. But with the grace of an arthritic yoga instructor, he managed to manipulate his numbing fingers enough to unlatch the buckles beneath his trousers and pop them open.

He then lowered himself and used his left boot to leverage against his right boot until he finally inched the prosthetic free from his pant leg. With his hands still tied behind his back, he couldn't see the leg itself, so he had to open the secret compartment with his stiffening fingers like a blind safecracker.

Once opened, Juan found the razor-sharp Benchmade Infidel double-action switchblade, flipped it upside down, and flicked it open. Suffering a few cuts along the way, he finally managed to saw his way through the hard plastic zip tie.

His wrists now free, it felt like fire ants were biting the skin beneath his hands as the blood rushed back into his fingers.

Exhausted from the Houdini-like escape, Juan quickly reattached his leg and climbed unsteadily to his feet. His head was still throbbing from his beating, but all of his exertions had cleared his mind, flooding it with questions, the most important of which was *Who had ratted him out?*

The only people who knew about his mission were the *Oregon* crew and Overholt. Cabrillo would have bet his life on their discretion and loyalty and, in fact, had done so on numerous occasions. No, it was somebody else. That was a leak that needed to be found and plugged as soon as possible.

Juan also didn't understand why Yaqoob hadn't killed him outright or at least tortured him for information about his identity and mission.

Apparently whoever was on the other end of that phone call had told the murderous Pashtun to save those pleasures for himself when Cabrillo would arrive on his doorstep trussed up like a Christmas goose.

He might have been better off with the bloodthirsty Taliban giant.

As bad as things had gone so far, they could have been a whole lot worse if a guard had been posted in the plane's cargo bay. Cabrillo scanned the area. He saw several CCTV cameras posted up high, but apparently no one was monitoring them since no armed crewman was appearing.

Cabrillo did a quick inventory of the aircraft. He estimated at least five hundred thousand rounds of 7.62x39 ammo, along with five hundred crated AK-47s, several pallets of cased M67 fragmentation grenades, and a hundred boxes of Kevlar body armor. It was enough gear to equip a small insurgent army.

The question was, where was it all going?

Juan ducked down behind one of the pallets and fished around in the compartment of his combat leg, pulled out his Thuraya X5-Touch, the world's smallest satellite smartphone, and powered it up. The screen indicated several missed incoming calls from the *Oregon*. He punched a saved number and after a series of electronic squawks and beeps an encrypted voice came on the line.

"You had us worried there, buddy," Max said. "We've been watching your tracker flying through the air for the last two hours. Wasn't sure if that was you or Superman. You good? By the way, you're on speakerphone."

Every member of the *Oregon* crew including Juan had a GPS tracker embedded in their hip or thigh for just this kind of scenario.

"Got my clock cleaned pretty good, but I'm still in it to win it. My Taliban friends tossed me into the back of a flying milk wagon, only it ain't milk I'm staring at."

"You just crossed over the Pakistani coast. You're about fifteen thousand feet above the Gulf of Oman."

"Not far from where I started."

"Fortune favors the bold, or so I've heard."

"What's my flight path?"

"You skirted south to avoid Iranian airspace. Could still be headed for the Saudi peninsula or maybe Africa on the other side. No telling just yet."

"Have Eric pull up flight logs for a Tajik Air flight out of Kabul. Takeoff would have been, what did you say? Two hours ago, give or take."

"On it," Eric Stone said.

"What's your situation?" Max asked.

"They bundled me up pretty good, so they must not think I'm a threat back here in the cargo bay. Neither the pilots nor the crew have come back to check on me."

"No indication of any Tajik Air flights out of Kabul yesterday or today," Eric said.

"What's our radar show?" Juan asked.

"No IFF, if that's what you're getting at. We married up an aircraft blip with your tracking GPS, so we've got a pretty good fix on you. The cross section on our screen is a little fuzzy. We're guessing there's some kind of radar-absorbing coating on the plane's skin, but it looks something like an Airbus A320."

"That's correct, but trust me, it's no ordinary Airbus. I wish I knew where this rig was headed."

"It will be out of our radar range pretty soon," Max said. "Maybe we can hack into local ground radar and track it as it moves."

"Unless it decides to fly below or around ground radar range," Eric added over the speaker. "African air traffic control isn't exactly up to speed in that regard."

"Mark, any chance you can hack into this thing's computer?"

Juan had read enough security briefs to know that the National Security Agency had developed sophisticated hacking tools to break into enemy aircraft avionics in order to either crash or hijack them in times of war. Most militaries had taken defensive precautions against such cyberattacks, but this was a civilian plane. If Mark could breach the system, he could rifle through the plane's avionics to determine its flight path and final destination.

"That's a long shot, Chairman. If I can find its GPS guidance signal, I might be able to sneak in through the back door, depending on the chipset. Give me a sec."

What seemed like an eternity to Juan abruptly ended as Mark Murphy came back on the line. "Looks like your plane isn't using GPS."

Juan was surprised. "Inertial guidance? That's pretty old-school."

"Yeah, but it prevents exactly the kind of shenanigans we just tried to pull off."

Juan blew out a long breath. He really needed to find out where this flight was headed. Without any electronic means he only had one other option.

"Gentlemen, the service on this airline is the pits. I'm gonna have to file a complaint with the captain. I'll be in touch."

19

Cabrillo killed the call, pulled his Benchmade knife and pried open one of the AK-47 crates. He kept checking the cockpit door to see if any armed crew members were charging out to check on him, but so far, so good.

He next opened up an ammo crate, peeled open one of the ammo cans, and loaded in ten rounds of 7.62x39 into the thirty-round banana mag. That was plenty. If he needed more than ten rounds to do the job, an extra twenty or even two hundred wouldn't get it done, either.

Juan dashed for the cockpit door. If anybody knew where this plane was going it was the pilots. He held his weapon low in case someone was watching on the CCTV or through the peephole in the door.

Ever since 9/11, commercial aircraft featured steel-reinforced, triple-locked bulletproof cockpit doors to prevent terrorists from hijacking flights. But after the Germanwings Flight 9525 pilot's suicide flight in 2015, extra precautions were taken so that authorized flight crew could access a locked cockpit door if necessary. One of those precautions was an emergency keypad used to open the door in case of pilot incapacitation.

Juan glanced at the emergency keypad. The only problem was that if the pilots were actually alert they could easily override the keypad bypass—not that Juan had any idea what that bypass code might be. If he could pry the pad away from the wall he could attach Murphy's virtual lock-picking device—if he had loaded one into his combat leg. Unfortunately, such was not the case.

He considered contacting the *Oregon*, but there was nothing they could do from their end. He could try a bunch of different combinations, but there was a nearly infinite number of possible permutations for the emergency bypass and getting that number wrong even once would lock the digital system down permanently.

He thought about shooting the door open for half of a nanosecond before deciding that the risk of accidentally killing the pilots was greater than the slim probability of successfully blasting open a bulletproof door.

The other option was rigging a grenade or two to the door and using Kevlar armor plates to keep the shrapnel from slicing into a vital system like the sensitive turbines and crashing the plane.

But the same problem of force presented itself. A blast strong enough to blow the door open would probably kill the pilots as well.

That really left only one possibility.

Cabrillo picked up the cabin phone. A moment later he heard a muffled ringing on the other side of the door. He waited for one of the pilots to pick up.

If he couldn't blast his way in, he might be able to sweet-talk his way through the door—a skill his late wife had blamed for his ability to charm his way into her reluctant heart so many years ago.

As a CIA NOC he had used his natural gift of gab to break into and get out of more sticky situations than he ever did with a gun. Juan possessed the heartfelt empathy of an FBI crisis negotiator and the sale-closing skill of a boiler room telemarketer.

And if all of that didn't work, he would thunder the kind of ominous threats that would cause a blood-sworn yakuza to rat out his own saintly grandmother. Cabrillo put together several talking scripts in his head as the phone continued to ring.

And ring.

And ring.

Clearly nobody was picking up. Why?

Cabrillo had one last ace up his sleeve. He fished out his Thuraya X5-Touch and pulled up one of Mark Murphy's newest apps. He activated the video camera and placed it against the fish-eye peephole in the door. Like every other peephole, the lens was designed to look outward, but its fish-eye distortion prevented anyone from looking inward. The screen on Juan's phone verified this optical reality. He couldn't see a darned thing. He rotated the lens gently against the peephole, imagining he was trying to look around the cockpit interior.

Satisfied he had enough imagery recorded, he tapped on the app's CONVERT button and watched the progress bar race through to its completion. When it finished, it opened a new file called "Converted. mp4." Juan hit the play button. Thanks to algorithmic wizardry, Murph's software analyzed the patterns of light propagation and image formation caused by the lens distortions and made calculations to compensate for them in reverse. In short, Juan was now looking at an algorithm-generated fish-eye view *into* the cockpit so that he could see what was going on with the pilots.

The only problem was that there were no pilots.

In fact, there weren't any seats, either.

Or yokes, pedals, switches, gauges, mics, or toggles. The entire cockpit was as slick as a Bosch stainless steel refrigerator door— without the ice maker.

It was a completely automated cockpit.

Without any digital or analogue readouts, it was impossible to determine where the plane was headed.

Now what?

20

Since there was no way to determine the plane's destination, Cabrillo had to figure out another way to track it. He remembered the small GPS targeting beacons he was planting at the Afghan ammo dumps with his boot.

He pressed his boot heel into the deck and applied enough pressure for it to release the next tracker. He bent down to pick it up so he could hide it somewhere—but there wasn't one. The depositing mechanism must have jammed. He tried again. Nothing. Either the mechanism was failing to deploy the trackers or he had accidentally deployed several trackers at a time. The delivery device was effective but imprecise. He couldn't just leave his boot behind. Even if there were still trackers stuck in the mechanism, they only activated after they were deployed.

What were his other options?

He knew the *Oregon*'s radar was tracking the plane now, but its range was limited. There was only one last possibility.

After pocketing his phone, Cabrillo dropped his trousers.

He snicked open the switchblade and gritted his teeth as he began to slit open the sensitive skin on his hip. But at that moment the plane hit a pocket of turbulence, driving the blade deeper than Juan intended. Blood spurted over the knife as Cabrillo dug out his personal

Oregon tracker. His blood-slicked fingers nearly dropped the miniature device before he pocketed it.

He then cut a piece of his shirt off for a bandage and jammed it into
the bleeding wound before pulling up his pants and cinching the belt
tightly to hold the bandage in place.

He wiped his bloody hand against his shirt and pulled his sat phone
back out of his pocket.

"Max, the satellite still reading my tracker?"

"Like NORAD tracking Santa's sleigh on Christmas Eve."

"Good. Keep it locked. I'm planting my tracker on the plane so we
can keep eyes on."

"You pulled your tracker? Ouch. What's next?"

"The plane is all automated. Lemme think about it. Don't go anywhere."

"Standing by."

Juan killed the call. He spied a nook on the bulkhead behind a
junction box and secured his tracker there, careful to wipe away any
traces of blood he smeared on the panel.

Now he had to find a way to get off the plane.

He began searching for anything that looked like a storage locker
where he might find an emergency parachute. Ten minutes later he
gave up the search, his headache still pounding on his skull like a rendition of "Babalú" on a Cuban conga drum.

He leaned against a nearby pallet considering his dwindling options when suddenly the obvious solution hit him like, well, an angry
Pashtun.

Juan examined the parachute deployment bag secured to the top of
the pallet he had been leaning against. It was comprised of two parts.
The first was a small drogue chute designed to catch the initial gusts
of wind in a free fall. The opened drogue chute would then pull out
and deploy a much larger cargo chute located inside of the deployment bag.

Juan snicked open his knife and cut away the straps holding the
deployment bag and drogue chute. He looked around the compartment. He didn't see any static lines.

Normally there would be static lines attached to the drogue chute, but he didn't see one on his pallet or on any of the others. Those static lines would have been fixed to the aircraft so that when the pallet shot out the back, the static line would tug on the drogue chute and deploy it.

That meant these chutes were opened either by an altitude sensor or a timer. He examined the drogue chute and spotted the altitude sensor. He decided to remove it. He wasn't going to risk his life on the possibility that the Vendor's automated system could somehow force a malfunction of his unit. Better to rely on the old-fashioned method.

Juan then cut off several long pieces of the polyethylene cargo webbing securing the load to the pallet via buckles. Minutes later he pieced it all together with the deployment bag, heavy as sin owing to what was no doubt at least a half dozen fifty-foot-long suspension lines and a big cargo chute. He detached the drogue chute and gripped it tightly in one hand, careful not to let the drogue chute lines get tangled up with anything. After he leaped out of the plane he'd release the drogue and it would pull the bigger cargo chute out of his jerry-rigged pack.

He scanned the dissected ammo pallet with his engineer's eye. He estimated it weighed at least four thousand pounds, maybe even five. That was twenty to twenty-five times his own lean muscular body weight of two hundred pounds. The cargo parachute was designed to carry the much heavier weight. Cabrillo knew the drogue chute couldn't do the job for him, but he wasn't sure if he weighed enough for the big chute to fully deploy its canopy.

Well, he'd find out soon enough.

Cabrillo secured the makeshift parachute rig to his back, cinching it tightly to his shoulders and around his thighs with the buckles that had secured the cargo straps to the pallet. The contraption wasn't pretty and it sure as heck wasn't going to feel good when that chute popped open and yanked him skyward, but it should do the trick.

He pulled his phone out and called Max.

"My Uber app isn't working, so if you don't mind, I could really use a ride."

"You found a chute?"

"In a manner of speaking."

"Air's gonna be a bit thin at your altitude," Max said. "And I hope you brought your long johns. Murphy estimates the ambient air temp is around twenty degrees."

"I love a good cold plunge—even if it is at a hundred twenty miles per hour. Question: After I make the jump, how long will it take for you to reach me?"

"Eric's calculating that," Max said. There was silence on the other end for a few moments.

Eric's voice finally chimed in. "At full speed, no more than thirty-seven minutes. Water temperature is around eighty-four degrees."

"Practically a hot tub. I'll see you in thirty-seven minutes then," Juan said as he headed for the exit door.

21

Juan grabbed the red door handle and prepared to lift it to the OPEN position, but he stopped in his tracks.

He turned around and stared at the cargo bay brimming with weapons and ammunition. It was all headed somewhere, no doubt a conflict zone. But in Cabrillo's experience, such weapons of war were only nominally used in combat against enemy forces. Most often, they were used to brutalize and kill the unarmed civilians caught in the middle. Judging by the size of this cargo of death, that meant a lot of innocents were going to suffer.

But it couldn't be helped. Cabrillo had the option of calling the *Oregon* and ordering them to shoot down the airliner after he jumped out. That would spare whatever civilians were waiting on the other end of this ratline. But it also meant he and his crew would never find the network of this so-called Vendor character. And who knew how many more lives might be at risk if the Vendor network was allowed to continue its operations?

It was a classic moral dilemma—the kind of thing that operatives like him weren't supposed to concern themselves with as they carried out their orders.

Save the few? Or sacrifice the few for the good of the many?

Juan looked at the manual door latch in his hand. His anger flared.

He refused to sacrifice anybody.

He would fight to save them all or die trying.

He scanned the automated plane's bulkhead. He didn't have access to the cockpit or the onboard computer. But the whole system couldn't be only automated. After all, the exit door could be manually opened. Why couldn't the cargo bay?

His eyes tracked along the floor until he spotted a run of electrical conduit that snaked its way into a hole in the cargo floor. He then traced the conduit's path in reverse until he spotted a locked electrical panel higher up on the bulkhead.

Juan raced over to it and tried to pry it open. No luck. He fished around in his combat leg and pulled out his lock picks. He seldom used American Express these days, but he never left home without his picks.

He slipped the torsion wrench and pick into the lock and with a couple of surgically precise twists popped the panel door wide open.

Pocketing his pick set, he scanned the control panel and flipped the MANUAL BYPASS toggle to ON. He then mashed the CARGO BAY DOOR button. Hydraulic motors spun up and moments later the bottom of the plane opened like bomb bay doors. The cargo bay was now filled with the roar of the big turbofan engines screaming beneath the wings and the howling ice-cold wind careening inside the space. The parachute deployment bags on top of their cargo pallets shuddered in the tornadic wind. The temperature plunged with each passing second.

Juan then pressed the LAUNCH button. The rollers embedded in the ramp began spinning and the first row of two pallets lurched forward. The next row of pallets advanced behind them and so on all the way to the back of the cargo bay, including the pallet he had plundered.

The first row of pallets tipped off the edge of the ramp and tumbled into the air. Cabrillo smiled knowing that all of these weapons and the carnage they represented would soon find a home at the bottom of the Gulf of Oman.

The second row of pallets were the next to fall, and shortly after that, the third. Each subsequent row continued marching into the airy abyss like square lemmings off a cliff.

While he was waiting for the last two rows of pallets to drop off the ramp, he reexamined his drogue chute one last time, then gripped it tightly in his hand. If he deployed it too quickly there was a danger the jet exhaust could tangle it up as it unfurled. He needed to clear the plane for at least a few seconds before releasing it.

Juan watched the last row of pallets, the twentieth, fall into the sky. The cargo bay was now empty.

That was his cue.

He charged down the ramp like a Viking berserker, shouting, "*Valhalla!*" as he leaped spread-eagle into the void.

★

Cabrillo wasn't sure if he jumped into the air so much as the plane vomited him out, speeding away from him at over seven hundred feet per second.

Whichever it was, the effect was the same. He felt as if he'd jumped into a frozen lake of air. Without benefit of goggles or oxygen mask, the force of wind rabbit-punched his face, robbing him of breath and stinging his eyes.

Three seconds after clearing the plane Juan deployed his chute. The ripstop nylon canopy deployed perfectly. Seconds later, the drogue pulled the big cargo chute out of his pack, dragging its suspension lines behind it. The enormous canopy snapped fully open with a familiar *pop!* The pack's jerry-rigged straps cut sharply into Juan's inner thighs and shoulders like tourniquets yanked down by a circus strongman.

Suddenly the problem of the too-large cargo chute for too-little weight presented itself.

At first, Juan's downward progress stopped and then he shot up like a slingshot. Way up.

But without the downward force of heavy cargo weight, the fully deployed chute began losing its inflation. Worse, the flaccid canopy collided with the violent turbulence pummeling the air behind the jet's powerful turbofan engines, threatening to collapse the chute entirely.

Juan jerked on the suspension lines—this kind of cargo rig didn't have steering lines—hoping to keep the chute from collapsing on itself.

He needn't have worried.

The cargo jet erupted in a massive ball of flame, throwing pieces of the fuselage, wings, and tail section tumbling toward the sea, and shooting shrapnel across the sky.

A giant piece of red-hot aluminum sliced through Juan's fragile canopy like a drunken samurai's katana through a rice-paper wall, shredding his chute.

And plummeting Cabrillo to his doom.

22

Juan's canopy collapsed as quickly as it had filled. His subconscious lizard brain told him there was nowhere to go from here but down. Way down.

Cabrillo had long ago learned the art of detachment, especially when facing fatal catastrophes. Improvisation was one of his superpowers, but detachment was his impenetrable shield against the fiery darts of chaos. Emotions clouded the mind in a crisis, hampering decision-making. But panic was a mind-killer—and always fatal.

His Caltech-trained brain began running calculations. He knew the typical parachutist fell at an average speed of 120 miles per hour. That meant he had already covered over a thousand feet, give or take. The math all pointed to a simple question:

How long was it going to take him to die?

There was no way he could survive a fall of fourteen thousand feet without a working parachute.

Since down was the only direction he was capable of at the moment, he turned his gaze in that direction. With no small delight he spotted the blooming black mushroom caps of at least seven pallets far below him, falling away in stair steps, with more opening as the seconds passed. If he had to guess, the altitude sensors had been set to automatically deploy at five thousand feet.

The only problem was that pallets with deployed chutes were now falling at a leisurely rate of around fifteen feet per second, while he was knifing through the air at closer to one hundred seventy feet per second. He needed to make some adjustments—fast.

One of the advantages of fighting and surviving innumerable gunfights was that Cabrillo had developed superlative muscle memory in regard to quick reaction, aiming, and eye-hand coordination. Instinctively he spread his limbs wide to create as much drag as possible to slow his descent, and used his arms and legs to control his direction.

He was falling too fast to catch the nearest deployed parachute. He blew past it like a Ferrari on a straightaway, so he aimed for the next one.

Juan braced for the impact, uncertain as to what to expect. The fully deployed canopy was stretched to its max by the massive weight of its cargo below, its inflated fabric taut as a backyard trampoline.

Thanks to Newton, Cabrillo knew that force was a function of mass times acceleration. At the moment he was two hundred pounds of meat hurtling ever faster through the air at thirty-two feet per second.

With that kind of force he would either hit the canopy and bounce off it like a golf ball hitting the sidewalk—or punch through it like a Buick through a pool cover.

Cabrillo crashed into the crown of the big canopy. To his surprise he neither bounced nor penetrated.

Instead, the force with which Juan hit the chute collapsed it.

The chute folded in on itself, and closed in around Cabrillo like a bug in a Venus flytrap. He twisted his body as if rolling off the world's flimsiest mattress and escaped the chute's feathery death grip before his own lines got tangled with the others.

Out of the frying pan, Juan thought as he found himself once again plummeting toward the unforgiving sea.

What he felt, however, was that his rate of speed had slowed considerably thanks to the collision with the chute. He took aim at the next parachute some five hundred feet below him and twenty feet to the right, his twisting body and limbs mimicking the ailerons and flaps of the world's least aerodynamic plane.

His exertions paid off and he found himself crashing into the next canopy at half the speed with which he'd hit the previous one. With any luck he'd be able to ride this one down without collapsing it.

But as an engineer, he knew that neither physics nor aerodynamics had anything to do with luck.

The chute fluttered for several seconds before collapsing in on itself. But that gave Juan enough time to pick his next target—and change his tactics.

Unfortunately, he had sped past nearly all of the other floating pallets. The last ones available to him were the first three pallets pushed out the cargo bay door. As near as he could tell they were about three thousand feet above the sea—and less than three minutes away from impact.

Picking his next and last target, Juan didn't aim for the one nearest him, floating almost directly below. Instead he picked the lowest of the bunch, which was also some distance away on the horizontal. It was the pallet he had the greatest chance of missing.

And it was also his best shot at survival.

Cabrillo stretched himself out to create as much drag as possible and slow his descent, stiffening his limbs against the upward force to keep from tumbling keister over teakettle. Once stabilized, he angled his arms and legs to alter his aerodynamic profile and targeted the last chute. But this time, instead of shooting for the canopy, he aimed for the pallet.

Juan crashed smack-dab into the center of the stack—and hit it like a speeding hockey forward cross-checking a parked Zamboni. Every bone in his body rattled.

But because the free-floating pallet wasn't fixed to the ground, it gave way under Juan's impact, lessening the blow. He snagged the cargo support straps with his nearly frozen fingers, halting a bounce from the pallet that would have sent him plummeting to his death.

Juan's weight and impact swayed the load back and forth, but the giant parachute held its shape. Cabrillo climbed hand over hand up the cargo straps until he reached the top of the pallet. He used the suspension lines to pull himself up and then to steady his stance as he stood on top of the stack.

The dark blue waters of the Gulf of Oman were rushing up fast. Standing on top of the speeding pallet that was still dropping at fifteen feet per second felt like riding a free-falling elevator to the bottom of the shaft.

Cabrillo's only hope of survival was to crawl up into the chute rigging as high as he could without collapsing the canopy. He inched his way up, careful to distribute his weight as evenly as possible in the lines. With any luck, the pallet would crash into the sea and temporarily relieve the downward pressure on the parachute, while he remained in the rigging safely above the crash, and just long enough to leap beyond the pallet below.

But, of course, Cabrillo didn't believe in luck.

The two-ton pallet hit the water with a thundering splash like a World War II depth charge, blasting a geyser of water high into the sky—and straight into the parachute canopy above.

But the blast of water was a boon. It blew Cabrillo out of the rigging into a high, cartwheeling arc that dropped him twenty feet away in a splashing, high diver's belly flop. The crash landing hurt like the dickens and drove him under the surface. He crawled his way back up, coughing up seawater that burned his sinuses like a soldering iron—a painful proof of life.

All things being equal, it was better than being dead.

A sudden jerk yanked him backward, hard. Survival instincts kicked in. Cabrillo gulped down a mouthful of air just as he was dragged beneath the surface. His shocked brain instantly understood that the fifty-foot-long lines of his own failed chute must have become entangled with the pallet chute lines. The two-ton pallet was dragging him down headfirst to the seabed thousands of feet below.

Cabrillo's fingers clawed at the buckles securing his improvised parachute harness. Every passing second dragged him deeper into the abyss, the rising pain stabbing in his ears like knitting needles.

Panic's icy fingers began gripping Cabrillo's heart, but he soldiered on, loosening the last buckles and stripping away the harness as fast as he could. All of that exertion burned out the last of the oxygen in his lungs.

All Cabrillo could do was exhale away the noxious fumes in a stream of trailing bubbles as he clawed his way back up until he finally broke the surface, gulping in air as fast as his bellowing lungs would allow.

Another geysering splash thundered just a few yards away from him. He was still in harm's way. He glanced up and saw the sky filled with parachuting pallets. Some were falling away from him in scattered ranks into the sea, but surface winds were swinging some of them back around.

Mustering the last of his energy reserves, he leaned into the water and swam away, his long, smooth strokes conditioned by the hundreds of miles he'd put in over the years in the *Oregon*'s swimming pool. He didn't stop until he felt clear of the probable landing zone some hundred yards from where he began. Once stopped, he caught his breath again and then stripped off his boots, utterly exhausted.

Juan lay on his back to gather more energy. Water erupted in distant thundering splashes in his peripheral vision as pallets hit the water. But his eyes were focused on the trailing cloud of black smoke pointing a crooked finger to where the airplane had exploded.

Cabrillo was certain the *Oregon* wouldn't have shot it down without his express orders. *So who did?*

He knew he'd have at least thirty minutes to think about it as he waited for his ship to arrive.

Juan's practiced fingers found the compartment in his combat leg and he reached for his smartphone to contact the *Oregon*, but the phone wasn't there. Then he remembered he'd pocketed it and he pulled it out. Not surprisingly, the fall from the sky or the seawater— or both—had killed it.

Cabrillo treaded water. No telling if his bleeding had stopped or if it was sending out a "Hot Donuts Now!" signal to every patrolling shark in the region. He was too tired to care.

After surviving the elevator ride from hell he decided he'd had enough aerobic conditioning for one day.

He stretched out his aching limbs, floated on his back, and fixed his eyes on the sky. His heart rate slowed with the sound of his own labored breathing ringing in his ears as his mind embraced the terrifying reality of the last few minutes.

What would he tell his crew? Would they even believe it?

Did he?

Cabrillo roared with laughter.

He closed his eyes and felt the heat of the sun on his face and the warm embrace of the sea. The caressing waves upheld him as if God himself bore him in the palm of his hand, a gesture of grace against the terrors he had just suffered.

Cabrillo was grateful for the respite, however long it might last.

23

Juan's eyes had been tracking the horizon when he finally caught sight of a speck in the shimmering distance. In what seemed like mere moments the speck became a white shape, and the shape became a ship, and in short order the *Oregon*'s familiar hull and cargo cranes roared into view, skimming along the surface like a speedboat.

There were few pleasures in life as satisfying as standing on the upper bridge of the *Oregon* running at flank speed. But now, with a duck's-eye view from the surface, he gained a whole new appreciation for the physics-defying spectacle of nearly six hundred feet of steel racing along at over sixty knots throwing a surging wake behind it big enough for Laird Hamilton to surf.

Eric Stone's skill at the helm came into full display. The *Oregon*'s engines slowed as the ship made an effortless ninety-degree turn and came to a stop a mere hundred yards from Juan's position. The resulting waves bobbed Juan up and down a dozen feet at a time, but he was no worse for the experience. Juan knew that Eric probably could have parked the boat six feet away if he had chosen to, but safety protocols forbade it.

Juan caught sight of Max's beefy arms semaphoring from the main deck high above the water and he returned his own jaunty salute from down below. The *Oregon* didn't bother dropping anchor; it held its position with its array of thrusters, its purring engines quietly sucking in the free electricity offered by the sea.

The sound of the boat garage door rolling open rippled across the water. Seconds later, two roaring Jet Skis came flying off the interior ramp. They hit the water with a splash, their high-revving engines rooster-tailing water behind them as they raced toward Juan's position.

Cabrillo recognized the golden-blond hair of Marion MacDougal "MacD" Lawless waving in the breeze on the lead Jet Ski. Juan chuckled. MacD would make riding a lawn mower look cool. The former Army Ranger could have parlayed his devastating good looks into a career as a Hollywood hunk. Instead, he chose to serve his country as one of the nation's elite Special Forces operators before joining the *Oregon* crew. Few women could turn their eyes away from the sculptured Adonis and his honeyed Creole accent could melt a block of chromium.

Racing right behind him was Eddie Seng. In contrast to the beefy Cajun with his flowing golden mane, the wiry Chinese American wore his hair "high and tight" Marine Corps style. Eddie was a former CIA undercover operative like Juan who had served in Marine Recon before joining the Corporation. The New York City native was a martial arts master, but Eddie's primary skill set was combat team leadership, which was why Juan named him director of shore operations.

Both Jet Skis slowed to a stop before their engines had even reached maximum rpms.

"You gave us the *frissons, mon ami*," MacD yelled over his rumbling engine. "You good to go?"

Juan tossed him a weary smile. "Could use a hand."

Eddie reached down with his cabled arm and hauled Cabrillo out of the water. Significantly smaller than the other two men, Eddie was preternaturally strong. Anyone foolish enough to call him Bruce Lee to his face quickly found themselves on their backs in a choke hold and taking a sudden nap that ended in a skull-pounding headache when they finally awoke.

"Ready, boss?" Eddie asked.

"*Avanti*," Juan said.

Eddie gunned the throttle and off they flew.

★

ABOARD THE *OREGON*

Callie stood in the boat garage doorway next to Linda Ross and Dr. Julia Huxley. At five foot three, "Hux" was one of the more diminutive women on board the *Oregon* and also one of the most attractive.

The crew of the *Oregon* was entirely professional in that regard, but Hux had never cared for the unwanted attention she often got from men during her Navy career. The former chief medical officer of the San Diego Naval Base wore her thick dark hair in a perpetual ponytail, flattened her soft brown eyes with government-issue glasses, and hid her curvaceous figure beneath her daily uniform of baggy hospital scrubs and a lab coat.

A senior deckhand swung the lift arm out of the boat garage and over the sea as the two Jet Skis thundered to a halt just inches from the hull. The deckhand lowered the lifting cables for MacD to attach to the eyebolts on either end of his Jet Ski as Juan climbed up the ladder.

"I didn't know you made house calls, Doc," Juan said as he steadied himself on the deck.

"I don't. I just came down here to fetch you back to the clinic." Huxley frowned. "By the looks of you, I'd better call for a stretcher."

Juan waved a dismissive hand. "I'm fine. A trip to the galley would suit me better."

"You gave us another start," Linda said. "When the plane broke apart we assumed the worst."

"Somebody blew that plane out of the sky," Cabrillo said as he fished his busted phone out of his shirt pocket and handed it to Ross. Water poured out of its cracked case.

"I hope it blew up *after* you jumped," Callie said.

Juan grinned. "Technically, yes. Speaking of which, you obviously met Hux." He had to raise his voice over the surging electric winch lifting MacD's Jet Ski out of the water.

"Deflection is the highest form of childishness," Hux said. "Let's get you to the clinic."

"I really like her," Callie said, smiling at Huxley. "She doesn't mess around."

"That's her angry-mommy voice," Juan said. "She normally saves that for the clinic."

Hux stepped closer to Cabrillo and lightly held his chin in her fingers. She gently turned his head and studied the massive bruise on the side of his face.

"Nasty contusion. Slight edema. You crash into a brick wall?"

"The other way around."

"Let me see your eyes."

Juan faced Hux, but spoke to Linda.

"I need you to get Murph and Eric on a search for an arms dealer that goes by the name of 'the Vendor.'"

"'The Vendor'? Sounds like a Bond villain. Any details? Age, race, nationality . . . zodiac sign?"

"That's all I've got. It's up to them to figure out the rest."

Hux frowned. "Juan, your eyes are slightly dilated. I need you to come back to the clinic for an examination."

"Not a good time, Doc." He said to Linda, "I need one more thing."

"Name it."

"When that plane broke apart, were you able to track any of the debris?"

Linda nodded. "The big stuff, sure, until it hit the water."

"Think you can plot a track to the center of the debris field?"

"Sure. What do you have in mind?"

Juan turned to Callie. "You ready to test your vehicle?"

"Heck ya. Let's get after it."

"Not an option," Huxley said, stepping back. "Getting you to the clinic wasn't a suggestion. It's an order from your ship's doctor."

Juan raised an eyebrow. "An order, is it?"

"Ten minutes in my clinic so I can clear you for concussion. Otherwise I'm declaring you unfit for duty."

Juan fought back a laugh despite the pain. The diminutive doctor was tough as nails when it came to the health of her crew. He glanced over her shoulder. MacD and Eddie were helping the deckhand wrestle the Jet Skis into the garage.

"Sounds like mutiny to me, Dr. Huxley."

"Just following what my contract says. By the way, you wrote it, not me."

"How about a couple of naproxen and a shot of Four Roses Single Barrel and we'll call it a day?"

Huxley ignored him. "And then there's that Hippocratic-oath thingy I keep reminding you about from time to time. Even if I do clear you, you need to get some rest."

"Like my old priest used to say," Juan said, "'There's no rest for the wicked and the righteous don't need any.'"

Hux threw a thumb at the elevator door.

"Your choice: the clinic or the clink."

Cabrillo raised his hands in surrender. "Okay, Doc. Let's go."

Hux guided Juan by the elbow toward the elevator. He called over his shoulder at Linda and Callie.

"Linda, get that radar fix as soon as you can and plot a course. Callie, get your boat ready."

"What's the plan, boss?" Linda asked.

"We lost all of our leads on that plane when it exploded. I think I know a way to get at least one of them back."

"Hux, call me when you know something," Linda said.

"Will do." Hux pushed the elevator button.

"How about that shot of Four Roses, Doc?" Juan asked. "I know you've got a bottle in your file cabinet."

"You're still on duty. But Lord knows I'll need two fingers as soon as I get rid of you."

24

Ten minutes in Huxley's clinic turned into almost an hour as she hooked Juan up to a cocktail of intravenous fluids and painkillers and began her examination. Expert at medical triage, the trained Navy surgeon did a brief but thorough physical before rolling the Chairman into an MRI machine.

Huxley read his MRI imagery while Juan devoured a skillet-toasted Reuben sandwich dripping with tangy sauerkraut, homemade Thousand Island dressing, and melting Swiss cheese he'd ordered from the galley.

Huxley could only shake her head at the scan results. Though he wouldn't admit it, she could tell he'd been through the ringer. And though he was clearly battered, bruised, and swollen, Cabrillo's supreme physical conditioning had prevented any serious injuries. The only surgical intervention he needed was a couple of stitches for the knife wound in his hip he inflicted upon himself.

For a moment during the physical, Huxley was convinced he had suffered some kind of traumatic brain injury. He hadn't been able to clearly explain to her how he managed to parachute down beneath a cargo canopy ill-designed to carry the weight of a man.

But what appeared to be temporary memory loss gave way to a familiar twinkle in Cabrillo's clear blue eyes. She suddenly realized it wasn't a brain injury or even a faulty memory at work, but an act of willful obfuscation. She wasn't sure why Cabrillo didn't want to tell her the truth about what happened at altitude, but she'd find out eventually. Since the MRI came out completely clear and the *DSM-5* didn't list either fibbing or dissembling as diagnosed mental disorders, she couldn't justify deactivating him from service.

"Anything else, Doc?"

"Not that you ever listen to me, but I highly recommend you take a few days off. Give yourself a chance to recover."

"I'm good to go."

Huxley wrinkled her nose.

"Well, at least take a shower. You smell like old bait."

★

Cabrillo was more than happy to take Huxley's recommendation to heart. He made his way straight to his cabin and headed for the green-marble-tiled shower.

Like every other member of the *Oregon*, Cabrillo was given an allowance to decorate his private quarters according to his own taste. With the help of Kevin Nixon's Magic Shop, his suite was transformed into a stylized version of his favorite movie, *Casablanca*. The pièce de résistance was a working copy of Sam's upright piano, upon which Juan belted out his own soulful rendition of "As Time Goes By" when properly lubricated with strong drink.

Stripping off his clothes and prosthetic leg, Juan headed for the shower, grabbing the support bar as he blasted himself with hot water from the multidirectional showerheads. He let the nearly scalding hot water work its magic deep into his muscles as he sucked in great draughts of steaming air to clear his lungs. Finally, he snapped the faucet controls in the opposite direction and blasted himself with ice-cold water until his hot pink skin was numbed to the bone.

Clean as a newborn babe and fully refreshed, Cabrillo pulled on a pair of skivvies, spiked his hair with a dab of hair putty, and hit the intercom to call for a meeting in the conference room in ten minutes.

★

Cabrillo marched into the walnut-paneled conference room, clearly energized and ready to rock and roll. He, Linda, and Callie were dressed in *Oregon*-branded blue coveralls.

The *Oregon*'s conference room design was inspired by the White House Situation Room. The *Oregon*'s version featured big-screen monitors on the walls and a long mahogany table surrounded by high-backed leather chairs with each position fronted by a small videoconferencing station.

Max, Linda, and Callie were already seated at the table. So were best friends Eric Stone and Mark Murphy.

Eric Stone, the *Oregon*'s chief helmsman, was dressed like a refugee from an accounting firm in his pressed chinos, oxford shirt, and Warby Parker glasses.

On the other hand, the *Oregon*'s chief weapons officer, Mark Murphy, looked like he'd just fallen out of a Mexican wedding hammock at the Bonnaroo music festival. His head was crowned with a dandelion's mane of unkempt hair and his chin was dusted with what looked like dryer lint. He wore black skater pants and black Doc Martens combat boots. His psychedelic concert T-shirt announced:

THE UNCERTAINTY OF PUNK TOUR
Featuring:
Johnny Heisenberg and the Double Slits
MELBOURNE, AUSTRALIA
TBD

Juan took his customary seat at the head of the table.

"I trust you all read my report," Cabrillo said. He had dictated a brief summary of the events in Afghanistan in between bites of his Reuben sandwich while still in the clinic. It provided details on the vast numbers of weapons in Taliban hands and Juan's concern regarding the mysterious Vendor.

"Those fanatics have more distribution centers than Amazon Prime," Max said. "But it's this Vendor character we need to chase down. Too bad about the plane."

"Any idea who shot it down?" Juan asked.

"No missile track was recorded," Murph said.

Juan frowned with confusion. "Are you suggesting a catastrophic failure? Or did it self-destruct?"

"My guess is the latter," Eric said. "Murph and I think that you must have initiated a self-destruct sequence when you overrode the automated system and manually dropped the ramp and launched his pallets."

"Kinda makes sense," Max said. "Automated aircraft and forklifts and whatnot means this Vendor either has a severe aversion to union labor or he's trying to maximize his anonymity. Blowing that plane out of the sky was a costly but effective way to cover his tracks."

"Hard to believe a pilotless cargo plane was also operating as a commercial airliner," Linda said. "How did he pull that off?"

"Maybe that was all a ruse. Could be a transport network for smuggling terrorists, illegals—people who don't care about planes and pilots, just destinations." Juan turned to Linda.

"Did you locate the crash site?"

"The debris field was distributed over two miles." Linda checked her watch. "As of six minutes ago, the *Oregon* was stationed smack-dab in the center of it."

"You know what I'm looking for," Juan said.

Linda nodded. "The flight data recorder."

"Bingo. That'll tell us where it was headed, and if we're lucky, everywhere it's been in the past thirty days."

"Unfortunately, where we're anchored is exactly 9,207 feet above the seafloor. You're looking for the head of a needle at the bottom of a nearly infinite haystack."

Cabrillo noted the wry smile curling her mouth.

"And?"

"Tell him, Murph," she said.

Murph pressed a remote control. One of the big monitors popped on, displaying a sonar field. A red dot flashed in the four o'clock position.

"We either got lucky or he got lazy, but either way our friend with the automation fetish forgot to disable the plane's underwater locator beacon. As soon as the tail section hit the water, the underwater locator beam began firing a signal at thirty-seven point five kilohertz."

"That's a pretty typical locator frequency," Eric said, turning to Callie. Annapolis had drilled into him the need for analytical specificity, but he was also trying to impress the stunning engineer. "And the locator beam tells us exactly where the flight data recorder is."

Murph leaned in close to Eric and whispered loudly, "*Well said . . . Captain Obvious.*"

Eric ignored him, and turned toward the Chairman.

"Our hydrophones picked up the locator pings and, as you can see, the tail section—"

Murph hit another button on his remote, overlaying a digitized image of an intact tail section resting precariously on a ledge.

"—where the flight data recorder is located, is perched on this ledge just 7,214 feet down."

"Just?" Max asked.

"Just," Callie said with a smile.

Juan swiveled his chair in her direction.

"Is the *Spook Fish* prepped?"

"Prepped and ready."

Juan stood. "Good. Then let's see what your little deuce coupe can do."

25

pproaching maximum test depth. Estimated time: thirty seconds."

A soft chime accompanied the automated feminine voice as it repeated the message. The warning display panel flashed 4,000 FEET the *Spook Fish*'s maximum test depth, an engineering euphemism for crush depth.

Callie silenced the alarm.

The *Spook Fish*'s cockpit was incredibly quiet in part because it was well insulated against the frigid temperatures and hull-crushing pressure of the sea. The low hum of the electrical motors was barely noticeable even when the thrusters spun up their revolutions for small maneuvers. Comms weren't necessary. The cabin was so small and quiet that passengers only whispered to be heard. The intense quiet magnified the startling creaks and thuds of the pressurized hull equalizing itself as the *Spook Fish* descended into the depths.

Their only communication with the surface was through short text messages via low-frequency acoustic modems and a buoy relay.

"Isn't the name of your boat the *Spook Fish 5000*?" Linda asked.

"Yep."

"I assumed the '5000' stood for a five-thousand-foot operational depth. But we just alarmed at four thousand feet."

"Yep."

"So why is it named the *Spook Fish 5000?*"

Callie shrugged. "The *Spook Fish 4000* just didn't sound as good in the marketing materials."

"Next time bring your marketing department down here. They might rethink that."

"I am the marketing department," Callie said. She shot a wink at Juan just as a thundering "pop" hit the hull.

Juan chuckled. "Reminds me of *Das Boot*, but without the depth charges."

Linda and Juan weren't terribly bothered by the descent into the stygian dark, though neither of them had even been close to this depth. Both of them were expert sub handlers. The *Nomad* was capable of diving to one thousand feet, though they rarely took her down that far.

They had, however, exchanged a couple of sidelong glances along the way down. Their mutual unspoken concern during the descent was Callie's complete reliance on her AI-powered piloting and navigation system.

To Callie's credit, the AI navigation worked perfectly. Its specialized sensors instantly acquired and honed in on the flight data recorder's underwater locator beacon pinging at 37.5 kHz once per second. The beacon had thirty days of battery life, so there was no danger in losing the signal anytime soon.

So far, so good.

Juan's fingers twitched occasionally, his subconscious mind craving the security of human hands on a yoke. He knew that numerous studies had shown that humans were far more dangerous behind the wheel of a car than any self-driven system. He also knew that the most common reason for airplane crashes was pilot error.

But Cabrillo was old-school. As impressed as he was with the performance of Callie's automated vehicle, he felt more human in the analogue world. It seemed as if machines were taking over nearly every human activity, and in so doing were taking control of human destiny.

Callie sat in the middle seat between Juan and Linda in front of the pilot's touchscreen station, her primary interface with the *Spook Fish*. For backup there was also a pilot's yoke and throttles. There was also a pair of joystick controls for the drone.

All three had a front-row seat to the view outside—not that there was much to see. No sunlight penetrated down this far. They had passed into the lightless bathypelagic zone some eighteen minutes earlier. Linda thought it looked like they were driving through a midnight blizzard in Montana. The *Spook Fish*'s bright, high-intensity LED lights illuminated a wall of constantly falling "marine snow" comprised of clumps of dead microscopic organisms, sand particles, and even fish feces originating in the water layers above.

Linda noted the digital clock. They had been descending for an hour and three minutes. The *Spook Fish* was zeroing in on both the sonar imagery of the tail section and the underwater location beacon signal. Callie used their descent for training time for Linda, who would be the submersible's primary operator when it was eventually turned over to the *Oregon*, though Juan was paying close attention. They had trained on the simulator software Callie provided several days before her arrival, but in truth the navigational computer did all of the work. The only role a human pilot had was to set up the mission parameters, communicate with the surface, and provide emergency backup if needed.

The softly thrumming engine motors ceased their operations just as the computer voice announced, "*Warning. You are at maximum test depth of four thousand feet. Do not proceed further. Do not proceed further.*"

Callie killed the verbal alarm, but the text warning still flashed on the navigation console in bright red letters.

The marine snow fell beyond the optically perfect acrylic bubble surrounding them. The *Spook Fish*'s thrusters fought to maintain its position in the slow-moving currents.

"Well, we're at the end of the line," Callie said. "Now the fun begins."

★

Today was as much a test for Juan and Linda as it was for Callie's submersible. They would be the ones to pilot the *Spook Fish* on the deepwater adventures Cabrillo planned for her. He often thought of his need for a vessel with the combined automated features and extreme depth capabilities that Callie's vehicle possessed. Until now, none had existed. The *Oregon* mostly sailed in deep waters, and on more than one occasion his people had nearly died in dangerous underwater operations.

Juan's interest in the *Spook Fish* was accelerated when he came across the rumor of the sinking of an old Cold War–era Soviet fishing trawler decades ago. A cover for a Soviet electronic eavesdropping vessel, this particular trawler was secretly ferrying a key component in the Soviet "Perimeter" system, also known as "Dead Hand." In effect, Perimeter was a semiautonomous nuclear launch program.

During the Cold War, the threat of mutual assured destruction (MAD) promised that if America attacked Russia with nuclear weapons, the Russians would have sufficient nuclear arsenals to retaliate and destroy the Americans. Therefore, it was suicidal for the Americans to ever launch a first strike.

But American technological advances in the 1980s suggested the United States could launch a devastating first strike—preventing any kind of Soviet retaliation. This made the prospect of nuclear war more likely. Thus, the Soviets developed Perimeter. In the event the U.S. decapitated Soviet leadership in a nuclear first strike, the "dead hand" of Perimeter would still be able to launch a retaliatory strike from the grave. Perimeter restored the MAD calculus and, logically, deterred any American decision to launch a first strike.

America's current interest in the old Soviet Perimeter system was that apparently it was still operational and deployed by the current Russian government. Acquiring the sunken trawler's Perimeter cargo would be a massive intelligence coup that would undermine Russian strategic security.

And for such a coup, Overholt would pay handsomely.

As of this moment, only Juan knew the location of the trawler—his source having revealed it in the moments before her death. Even the venerable St. Julien Perlmutter, the world's foremost marine historian and archivist, was unaware of the trawler's whereabouts, though he was able to confirm its mysterious disappearance.

Now Juan was trying to determine if the *Spook Fish* could give him the ability to retrieve it—and quickly. The clock was ticking. Recovering the Vendor's flight data recorder was as good a test as he could imagine.

If it succeeded today, Callie's submersible would open up a whole new line of revenue for the Corporation. The CIA hadn't possessed deepwater capabilities since the *Glomar Explorer* decades ago on which, ironically, Max had been the chief engineer. But today's global security issues were increasingly located in the crushing depths of the world's oceans. The *Spook Fish* was an ideal vessel for that kind of work—if it performed according to expectations.

They were about to find out.

★

Callie pressed a button on the touchscreen and a new monitor lit up displaying a bright light illuminating the marine snow.

"That's the first-person-view camera on the drone," Callie said. She tapped another button that disengaged the drone from the underside of the *Spook Fish* hull and sent it on its way toward the flight data recorder and the tail section.

"Specs on the drone cable said three thousand feet," Juan said. "Can't wait to see how this works." He wasn't exaggerating. Ever since he found out about Callie's invention he had been chomping at the bit to get a real-world demonstration.

Of course, Callie hadn't invented the first deepwater submersible— there were several others in operation with many thousands of hours logged by underwater scientists, videographers, and the like.

Callie's unique contribution was both the drone itself and, more importantly, the three-thousand-foot-long graphene navigation and power cable that she had developed.

The problem with previous remotely operated tethered drones, otherwise referred to as ROVs—remotely operated vehicles—was the cabling. Conventional cables had to be short because they were thick and heavy. If the cable was too long, it would weigh down the ROV and impede progress.

Callie had solved that problem by developing a new manufacturing process that made graphene cable possible. Graphene was a "miracle" substance that still hadn't quite fulfilled its promise in practical engineering applications.

Graphene was comprised of a single, two-dimensional layer of carbon atoms. The resulting material was two hundred times stronger than steel, highly conductive, extremely flexible, and waterproof.

Her other invention was even more practical. Because her father had been killed in an underwater demolition accident, Callie applied her incredible skill sets to building a drone capable of doing the same work, fitted with the necessary tools for automated welding, cutting, fastening, and unfastening. She had also developed other specialized ROVs.

What was even more incredible was that her demolition drone deployed an AI program to carry out its tasks without human assistance. In deepwater environments, humans became quickly fatigued, cold, disoriented, and even frightened as they attempted to carry out difficult or complex tasks. Drones suffered none of these ills, nor did they require oxygen or get the bends. The worst thing that could happen was the drone would be destroyed.

Better still, it would leave no grieving daughters behind.

By combining the graphene cabling with the highly capable work vehicle, Callie was providing the underwater community a vastly safer, cheaper, and more capable system than any single human could deploy.

Juan saw the value of her new system immediately and already it was paying off—or at least, was about to. All three of them stared at the drone's first-person-view monitor. Within a few minutes, the shadow of the airplane's tail section appeared far below in the gloom like a broken, Gothic mansion precariously perched on a dark, snowy mountain crag—upside down.

A yellow alarm light flashed on the drone video monitor as the drone slowed and then stopped at three thousand feet. The END OF CABLE message flashed on-screen. With the *Spook*'s depth at four thousand feet and the drone down a farther three thousand feet, the total extended reach was at seven thousand feet.

But the tail section was located at 7,214 feet, and still out of reach.

"How important is it to get that flight data recorder?" Callie asked.

"If we don't get it, people will die," Juan said.

"Then I'll have to lower the *Spook* down another 214 feet just to reach it. And another hundred feet just to be sure we have enough to maneuver around down there."

"I take it you've never taken her down that far before," Juan said.

"To tell you the truth, I've never been down *this* far before. I doubt another 314 feet will make that big of a difference. But if we go for it, I can't promise we'll make it back up."

"This is our mission, not yours. I can't ask you to risk your life."

"Would you go for it if I wasn't here?"

"I'd have to try," Juan said.

Linda nodded. "It's what we do."

Callie smiled. "You're my kind of people."

"What kind is that?" Juan asked. "Crazy?"

"Yeah. But in a good way."

She tapped the override keys on the navigational console, confirming and reconfirming that she wanted to proceed beyond the *Spook Fish*'s maximum limit depth, all the way down to 4,314 feet.

The automated system engaged and the electric thrusters whirred to life. The *Spook Fish* edged downward. Thirty seconds passed, when the hull suddenly clanged like someone hit it with a ball-peen hammer.

Linda jumped.

"Yikes."

"No worries," Callie said. "She's a sturdy girl, just a little noisy."

Juan's eyes were glued to the depth gauge. The warning lights and digital readouts flashed faster and faster the deeper they pushed beyond the safety limit. When they hit 4,314 feet, the thrusters stopped.

"Let's try the drone one more time," Callie said. "Only this time, I'll take it in myself."

Before the descent, Eric had forwarded a downloaded schematic showing the location of the flight data recorder near the cone of the tail section. The schematic indicated that there was an access door marked FLIGHT DATA RECORDER INSIDE. That was Callie's target.

Callie gently maneuvered the drone's piloting joystick with one hand and worked the thruster control with the other. It was no simple task. The drone was over a half mile away.

The drone inched through the shower of falling debris that swept across their field of view at a hard angle. The current was moving faster near the ledge, the same way wind speed picks up next to the face of a mountain. Callie fought to keep the drone steady despite the AI-piloting assist as the shaking drone image closed in on the broken fuselage. The drone's bright LED light swept along the aluminum skin near the tail cone, but no words appeared.

The three of them exchanged a worried glance.

"Here we go," Callie said as she crept the drone between the fuselage and the silted ledge beneath it. The camera screen filled with swirling debris as the drone's thrusters kicked up silt when the vehicle passed through the gap.

Unable to see anything in the view screen, Callie could only "feel" her way forward through the muddy blizzard, though she felt nothing in the joystick—there was no haptic feedback. It was all instinct.

Moments later the camera vision cleared enough to allow Callie to execute her next maneuver. She rotated the vehicle one hundred eighty degrees so she could read the other side of the fuselage.

"There," Linda said pointing at the monitor. In upside-down letters half submerged in silt they all read:

ɟ⅃IƆHꓕ DⱯꓕⱯ ꓤƎƆOꓤDƎꓤ IИƧIDƎ

Callie blew air through her teeth.

"That access door is going to be a problem." Like the letters, the door was partially covered by the silt.

"How big of a problem?" Juan asked.

Callie shrugged. "If I can't get to the bolts directly I can use the cutting torch. But that torch is a real battery drain. We might cut our way through but run out of air in here if I'm not careful."

"I vote for careful," Linda said.

"It's just going to take a little bit of time," Callie said. "I've seen worse."

"We've got all the time in the world," Juan said. "Or at least eleven hours, if I'm reading your gauges right."

"Easy peasy." Callie smiled.

Juan smiled back. That was something his Gundog Linc always said.

Usually before all hell broke loose.

26

The Vendor pulled away from the microscope on his lab desk. He yawned and stretched his tall, muscular frame to work out the kinks in his back from sitting too long. He'd been so deep into his mental "flow state" that he'd lost all track of time. The ability to concentrate his brilliant mind entirely on a single problem for hours on end was his ultimate superpower. It allowed him to make incredible breakthroughs over the years, and ultimately, to build the vast organization he now controlled.

His primary challenge with getting into such a flow state was losing the ability to stay abreast of other events needing his immediate attention. His solution to that challenge was a heavy reliance on automated systems to track and execute decisions quickly and reliably without his input.

The Vendor's bleary eyes suddenly popped open when the overhead alarm sounded. He called out in a loud voice to his AI assistant, Keiko, available to him in every department throughout the ship.

"Keiko, why the alarm?"

"Flight number 252 out of Kabul self-destructed three hours ago."

The Vendor swore. That could only mean something went terribly wrong.

"Why am I only hearing about this now?"

"The nature of the alarm was not a Priority One threat. Also, you silenced the audible alarm when you came into the lab to work. I have been sending visual alarms, but you have not responded to them. As per my protocols, I overrode the audible prohibition after the allotted time."

The Vendor glanced over at the nearby station. A warning light was, indeed, blinking.

He swore again. Keiko was still too "programmed" in her thinking. He was still trying to work out the algorithms that would allow her to take more initiative in threat assessments. But that was a problem for another day.

He hobbled over to the computer station.

"Keiko, pull up the last fifteen minutes of 252's internal video feeds and put it on my screen."

"Certainly."

A moment later, the video screen was filled with a dozen separate CCTV images.

"Keiko, edit these video files so that they produce a single narrative organized chronologically."

"Just a moment, please."

Seconds later, the twelve small screens merged into a single large one.

The Vendor scrubbed through the newly assembled movie. He stopped when the bound figure—an American undercover operative, according to Banfield—began to move. He leaned in close to watch the squirming American work his way out of his bondage. Impressive.

Especially the part with his prosthetic leg.

"Those idiots," the Vendor said. The Taliban had done a poor job of securing the American. They should have known better.

When he had received the warning from Banfield about an American agent attempting to infiltrate his arms network in Kabul, the Vendor's first instinct was to turn him over to the medieval savages for torture and information extraction. But the Afghani methods for such procedures were far too crude. Their insensitivities to suffering—particularly American suffering—meant they couldn't be trusted not to kill him before they extracted useful information about his identity and other necessary details.

But clearly the decision to hand the American over to his contact in Bangui for a chemical interrogation was a mistake. That mistake cost him a valuable shipment and an even more valuable aircraft.

Banfield's scant information about the American was enough to convince the Vendor to capture him. But now he understood this was clearly no ordinary undercover agent. The man was skilled enough in his black arts to fool Yaqoob, his deeply suspicious Taliban operative, and to penetrate into the most sensitive part of his Afghan operation. All previous American attempts had been easily discovered and defeated.

He wanted to know who this man was, who sent him and, more importantly, what he may have actually discovered. But there were so many moving parts to his master plan that he didn't dare engage with this particular distraction. No doubt his ego had been wounded by this enterprising fellow, but this was no time to indulge in schoolboy emotions.

No, what he really needed to do now was kill the man before he could pass along his information. The question was, what did he actually know?

The Vendor studied the rest of the digital images up until the moment the man leaped from the plane with his cleverly improvised parachute harness. Seconds later, the aircraft exploded, destroying all onboard cameras, rendering the collated image on his monitor into a blizzard of digital snow.

The Vendor rewound the tape and played it again, searching for clues. He saw several things that piqued his curiosity.

"Keiko, show me where the plane self-destructed."

Another monitor winked into life and a Google-styled map appeared. A flashing red dot indicated the approximate location of the crash over the Gulf of Oman beyond the border of Pakistan.

"Keiko, plot a probable landing location of a man, say, ninety to ninety-five kilos in weight parachuting from the plane's last known location. Include prevailing wind and weather information, along with last known aircraft speed and altitude in your calculations."

"Calculating."

Moments later, a small light blue circle appeared on the water far from shore. Keiko added, *"Probable landing location is within this zero-point-three-square-kilometer zone."*

The Vendor estimated it would take the agent hours to swim to land from that location—assuming he could make the journey at all.

"Do we have any air or sea assets near that zone?" The Vendor possessed an eidetic memory and he was certain there were none, but he had learned long ago that humility was a far more reliable asset than perfect recall.

"None."

The Vendor noticed the American had made a phone call to someone. That would only be possible with a satellite phone—there were no cell towers in the Gulf of Oman. The phone appeared to be a commercially available device.

"Keiko, search the video and identify the brand of device the intruder used to make the satellite call."

The Vendor watched Keiko rewind the video and then scrub it forward at blinding speed until the video froze on a single frame showing the American holding the satellite phone.

Keiko put an image box around the man's hand, which held the phone a few inches from his face. Keiko enlarged the box image by a factor of six hundred percent, which pixelated it, smudging it out of all recognition.

"Keiko, upscale the image."

"Already in process." Even as she spoke, the smudged image filled in until a crystal clear picture appeared. The satellite phone could be easily seen in Juan's hand. The Vendor read the brand before Keiko even spoke.

"I believe that is a Thuraya X5-Touch phone," Keiko said.

"Is that the same UAE company that provides mobile-satellite service to the region?"

"*Yes. One and the same.*"

Keiko pulled up the Thuraya website and began reading from it.

"'*The Thuraya X5-Touch is the world's first Android-based satellite and GSM phone offering unparalleled flexibility—*'"

"Keiko, stop reading. How many satellites does Thuraya operate?"

"*Thuraya operates two geosynchronous satellites.*"

"Do we have access to both?"

"*We compromised both in prelaunch construction via one of our network associates.*"

"Keiko, I want you to determine which of those two satellites the phone in question utilized to make its call. Second, I want you to access that satellite and acquire the metadata from that call. Third, from that metadata I want you to determine the location of the receiver of that call. Am I clear?"

"*Perfectly. Please give me one moment.*"

The Vendor twitched with agitation. Something wasn't adding up.

"*The call was received,*" Keiko said, "*by a vessel currently located approximately seventeen point seven kilometers west of the center of the estimated parachute landing zone.*"

"Pull up an AIS information screen for the Gulf of Oman. Overlay and center it onto the landing zone. Display every ship within one hundred kilometers of the landing zone."

According to international maritime law, every passenger ship no matter its size and every cargo vessel displacing over three hundred tons was required to broadcast an automated identification system signal for maritime traffic control and safety. Almost as quickly as the Vendor had given his AI assistant the order, a cluttered array of over forty ship icons appeared on the screen. The icons were various shapes and colors corresponding to the types of vessels.

"Keiko, eliminate all of the ships except the one receiving the sat call."

Instantly, all of the vessels disappeared save a yellow triangle.

Several more screens quickly followed. The surly weapons designer grunted with satisfaction. Keiko had anticipated his next command

and cycled through the data until a picture of the vessel, its dimensions, destination, and name all appeared.

"The *Norego* . . . Iranian-flagged," the Vendor read aloud.

"*The* Norego *is still located approximately seventeen point seven kilometers west of the center of the parachute landing zone. It appears to be holding its position.*"

"That's still too far for a swim," the Vendor said aloud. And then it hit him. "Wait! You said the alarm sounded three hours ago. Go back to the AIS screen. Show me the *Norego*'s position three hours ago."

The yellow triangle instantly appeared sixty kilometers southwest of its current position.

The Vendor frowned. "Play forward at five-times speed to the current time."

"*Playing forward.*"

Keiko did precisely as instructed. The Vendor was surprised to see the *Norego* race to the center of the parachute landing zone.

"Keiko, freeze the image.

"That doesn't make any sense," the Vendor said as he compared the elapsed time to the distance traveled. "Keiko, how fast was the *Norego* traveling in that sixty-kilometer stretch?"

"*Approximately 110.01 kilometers per hour.*"

"A ship that size? Impossible!"

"*Apparently 'knots,'*" Keiko said. She giggled at her own pun.

"Stop your nonsense," the Vendor growled. "And disable your humor function."

"*Humor function disabled.*"

The Vendor stared at the flashing yellow icon. That was no ordinary ship. It was a spy vessel of some sort with incredibly advanced engine technology.

And given the fact it had anchored at the parachute landing site, it no doubt had picked up the agent. *What happened next?*

"Play forward at two-times speed."

The *Norego* tracked west away from the parachute landing zone until it came to a stop exactly where they had first identified it a few moments ago.

The Vendor checked the time on the monitor and confirmed it was the current hour and minute. Why was the *Norego* anchoring there right now? Hadn't it already picked up the agent?

"Keiko, on this same map, plot the probable debris field of Flight 252 under prevailing weather conditions at the time of the explosion."

"This will take a moment."

"Don't dawdle."

"Wouldn't think of it."

The Vendor's eyes were fixed on the screen. Moments later, a proposed debris field appeared, marked in green.

And the *Norego* was parked right in the middle of it.

"That ship is trying to recover my cargo!"

"That is my estimation as well."

That didn't make any sense. The Gulf of Oman was too deep. *Unless . . .*

"Keiko! Lock on to that vessel with a targeting package and send that data to missile launchers one and two."

"Task completed."

"Keiko . . . *Launch!*"

27

Using the view screen and controls inside the *Spook Fish*, Callie maneuvered the drone so that its prop faced the silt pile partially covering the flight data recorder's access door. Within moments the prop blew away the silt, providing clear access.

"This is one of the reasons why I haven't deployed a fully automated drone system yet," Callie said. "Sometimes there are problems that still require a human to figure out."

"That graphene cable is a real breakthrough," Juan said. "It lets you keep control and provides extra power to your unit."

"Unless you get all tangled up, then you might lose both. But that's an operator error, isn't it?" Callie said.

Linda nodded. "The combination of automated and manual control makes a lot of sense to me."

"You're about to see why I like both."

Callie accessed the drone's socket tool and affixed it to the first of ten bolts. Thanks to Eric's download of the Airbus's schematics, she knew all of the bolt sizes they would encounter on this trip. It was nice to have, but wasn't really necessary. The drone's self-adjusting socket tool was designed to automatically fit any bolt within standard parameters.

Callie then put the socket function into auto mode. Juan and Linda watched with fascination as the drone's socket ratcheted out the first bolt, then located the next nine and removed them as well. Once they were all removed, Callie retook manual control of the drone and manipulated its gripper arm to pull open the flight data recorder access door.

She then guided the drone inside. She used its bright LED lamp to find the recorder bolted to a bulkhead bracket that was now hanging upside down. The bright orange metal box was ten inches long, six inches tall, and five inches wide. It was marked in inverted black letters: FLIGHT RECORDER DO NOT OPEN.

According to the downloaded spec sheet, it weighed only ten pounds—no problem for Callie's drone, especially given the buoyancy of salt water. She maneuvered the drone to the two multi-pin connectors fixed to the box. One was connected to a power supply, and the other communicated with the data terminal. Both were easily disengaged by Callie's deft handling of the controls. Within moments, she was working on the bracket bolts to free the box.

A text message from the *Oregon* suddenly flashed on the *Spook Fish*'s main monitor.

"Be advised . . . we are under attack."

"Get me comms," Juan said.

Linda tapped a virtual toggle switch on the monitor. A virtual keyboard appeared under the flash warning.

Juan used his index fingers to type out, "SITREP."

There was no response.

"SITREP!"

Nothing.

"You want me to surface?" Callie asked.

"You have that box secured yet?"

"Need another minute."

"Take it. We need that box."

"You sure?"

"The *Oregon* can handle herself," Juan said. He meant it. And Max was a fine commander.

But at that moment Cabrillo would have given his other leg to be in the Kirk Chair taking the fight to the enemy. The *Oregon* was his lady, and there was nothing he wouldn't do to protect her.

But down here, thousands of feet below her keel, he was useless.

★

ABOARD THE *OREGON*

Alarms sounded on Murph's early-warning screen.

"Air defense is tracking two high-speed missiles heading our way. They have radar lock on our position."

Max turned in the Kirk Chair.

"Hali, sound general quarters."

"Aye, Max." Hali Kasim punched the alarm button. An old-school Klaxon shrieked throughout the vessel as red GQ lights flashed.

"Wepps, distance and speed?"

"Approximately five miles out, one hundred eighty-two degrees relative. Closing at Mach Eight. Estimated impact: twenty-seven seconds and counting." Murphy put up a giant digital clock counting down the impact.

Max wanted to make the *Oregon* a smaller target.

"Helm, hard about. I want bow-on to those things. Wepps, activate automated air defense weapons."

"Aye," Eric said, his hands on the helm controls.

"Roger that," Murph said as he punched a button on his weapons station.

The *Oregon*'s electric engines spun up at nearly the speed of light as the vector thrusters rotated into position. The big 590-foot vessel turned on a dime. Everyone in the op center grabbed their station desks. Belowdecks, plates crashed, books flew, and heaven help any poor slob stuck in the head.

Before the *Oregon* completed her turn, the two air defense systems immediately engaged, and both displayed on separate wall screens for everyone in the op center to see.

"Wepps, put your missile radar tracking screen on one of the wall monitors."

"Done." Murph tapped a few keys and one of the wall screens showed his radar tracking display. Now everybody could watch the action as the two missiles sped toward the bull's-eye at the center of the screen—the *Oregon*.

The first air defense system to deploy was the Laser Weapon System (LaWS) emerging out of the top of the *Oregon*'s fake smokestack. The telescope-looking device rotated instantly to the direction of the missile attack.

The second was the Kashtan combat module, a close-in weapons system. A steel sleeve lowered at the top of the forward crane tower revealing the twin thirty-millimeter rotary six-barrel cannons spinning up, designed to deliver ten thousand rounds per minute of explosive-tipped tungsten projectiles. The Kashtan also featured anti-aircraft missiles that upon explosion projected an impenetrable fifteen-foot-diameter wall of fragmented steel, destroying anything in its path.

"LaWS is locked on. Kashtan is prepared to fire." Murph waited for permission to engage.

"Release fire controls."

"LaWS firing."

All eyes fixed on the laser. Nothing could be seen or heard. The laser light was invisible and silent, though the superheated air rippled like a mirage.

Six seconds passed. It felt like an eternity.

Nothing happened.

The digital clock sped past 17.6 seconds.

"What about the LaWS?" Max asked.

"No effect," Eric said. "Maybe they have some kind of reflective coating?"

"Missiles now at four miles—"

Murph's voice was cut off by the roar of two of the Kashtan's missiles auto-launching. The system was programmed to launch at targets reaching within four miles of the ship.

"Kashtans should impact in five point four seconds," Murph reported.

Two heavy thuds like mortar rounds sounded high overhead.

"Chaff deployed," Eric said.

"Kill the Klaxon," Max said as he did the math in his head. If those Kashtan missiles missed their marks, the incoming rockets would hit the *Oregon* in just over twelve seconds.

Five seconds passed like five hours.

"Incoming missiles breaking up," Murph shouted.

The op center broke out in cheers.

"Sonar detects two splashes," Eric said, breaking the celebration.

"Debris?" Max asked.

"No. Two high-speed screws detected—tangos one and two coming in hot."

Murph tapped his screen. "Estimated time of impact . . . thirty seconds."

"Activate automated anti-torpedo systems," Max said.

"Paket activated," Murph said. The Russian-built anti-torpedo system featured ten-foot-long mini torpedoes. Another wall monitor camera pulled up the Paket launchers. Two Paket torps burst out of their tubes and hit the water.

"Pakets away," Murph said.

"Manual override, Wepps. Put two more fish in the water."

Murph grinned. "I was hoping you'd say that." He smashed two firing buttons on his panel and two more Paket torpedoes launched into the water.

"Helm—evasive maneuvers, now!"

Eric slammed the throttles. The giant freighter's deep-V monohull reared like a racehorse out of the gate and charged forward through the dark blue water, its massive frame stabilized by T-foils and fins fixed to the keel.

A mirror image of Murph's monitor popped up on another wall screen. Four virtual Pakets depicted in green raced toward two incoming red icons.

The clock counted down. At just over fourteen seconds the first Paket collided with the first incoming torpedo.

"Tango one destroyed," Murph announced.

But the second Paket missed its target.

Max leaned forward in his chair.

All eyes were fixed on the remaining two Pakets honing in on the last speeding torpedo—just heartbeats away from slamming into the *Oregon*'s hull.

★

"Got it," Callie said, her hands deftly working the drone controls.

A distant, low-frequency thud echoed inside the *Spook Fish*.

Juan and Linda exchanged a worried glance.

"What was that noise?" Callie asked. She didn't move her eyes from the drone's view screen as she maneuvered back under the plane's tail.

A few seconds later, a second thud sounded.

"Incoming message," Linda said.

The main monitor flashed a new text from the *Oregon*. She read it aloud with a smile.

"All clear."

28

Callie and Linda helped the deckhands secure the *Spook Fish* as Cabrillo and Hanley made their way to the elevator. Murph and Eric were already in the lab with the dripping-wet flight data recorder and prepping it for examination.

Juan punched the elevator button. "Too bad we couldn't find the attack vehicle trying to kill my ship."

"Eric hacked into a French military satellite over the region. We tried to triangulate the missile launch location by reverse-tracking the missiles, but a hundred thousand square miles of cloud cover over the area blinded us."

"What about our radar?"

The elevator door opened and the two men stepped inside. Juan hit the floor button.

"Too far away to pinpoint anything."

That worried Juan. The *Oregon* had Aegis-class equivalent radar capabilities. "So more than one hundred nautical miles."

"Looks like it. Judging by their speed, size, and payload, Wepps thinks those missiles were likely powered by mini turbojets—the same kind found on cruise missiles."

Juan nodded, pulling up data from his prodigious memory files. "If they were cruise missiles, we could be looking at a three-hundred-mile range. Maybe more. And who knows the range of the torps they put in the water. Did you say they came in on a low trajectory?"

"Yeah. And that suggests a ship-based launch, but there's no telling. Eric says we have Mark 54 torpedoes fixed with glide wings that launch from P-8s at thirty thousand feet. And most low-flying Storm Shadows are plane-launched first."

"And nothing from the Sniffer?" Cabrillo was referring to the *Oregon*'s automated surveillance array capable of picking up and decrypting virtually any kind of signal in the electromagnetic spectrum. The Sniffer helped make the *Oregon* one of the most powerful spy ships afloat.

"Hali said there wasn't anything useful or actionable," Max said.

"Let's table the search for now. I suspect at this point it's a dead end." Cabrillo checked his Doxa watch. "We'll head to the lab and see what the boys have found under the hood of that box. But first I need to make a quick port of call at the little submariners' room."

"Ditto that, Chief. I've got ten cups of coffee sloshing around in my eight-cup thermos with a stopper that ain't as snug as it used to be."

★

Juan, Max, Eric, and Murph stood in the electronics lab around a large worktable. Linda had the conn now, and Callie was still in the moon pool securing the *Spook Fish*.

Murph and Eric hovered over the orange flight recorder box as they attached the retrofitted power supply and data cables with surgical caution. An open laptop stood next to the recorder.

"Lucky we had a couple of spare mil-spec D38999 connectors lying around," Murphy said. "Perfect fit."

"So glad you retrieved this bad boy," Eric said in a whisper as he tightened the power fitting. He flipped a switch on the box. "We're powered up."

"Excellent." Murph connected the flight recorder to his laptop with a USB adapter cable and began tapping keys. "Now we're going to find out every airstrip that plane ever landed on, every flight path it ever took, and every—"

Murphy frowned.

"Problem?" Juan asked.

"This thing's encrypted. Doesn't make any sense."

"Sure it does, if you're trying to hide something," Juan said.

"Well, we'll just see about that."

"You need any help?" Eric asked.

"Nah, this looks pretty easy. I'll fire up my magic decoder ring and—"

Snap. Murphy's screen flared like a supernova.

Eric dashed over. "What happened?"

"What do you think happened? Someone put a dead man's switch on that thing—along with the software equivalent of an IED. It not only wiped its own hard drive clean, it zapped my machine."

"What about the Cray?" Juan asked, referring to the *Oregon*'s supercomputer.

"Good thing I wasn't connected to the mainframe. No telling what might have happened."

Murph tugged at his wispy chin beard. "We're dealing with some seriously sinister genius here—the automated plane, the missile-torpedoes, and this level of cybersecurity? Somehow my machine got reverse-hacked—and that's something even the NSA hasn't been able to do."

"You mean this Vendor character?" Max asked. "It can't just be one guy."

Murph shook his head. "If it is just him, it means this dude is a one-man DARPA."

"It has to be a national government," Eric said. "Who else would have those kinds of resources?"

Juan frowned. "The usual suspects?"

Eric and Murph exchanged a look. "Yeah, we've been talking about that. None of them have deployed these kinds of capabilities before."

"So maybe it's not one of the usual suspects," Max said.

Juan folded his arms. "Or maybe it's all of them."

Max raised one of his graying eyebrows. "A consortium?"

"Like the Legion of Doom," Eric said.

"No way. Not DC. Think Marvel. Sinister Six, all day long. Dr. Octopus? Hello?"

"Yeah, you're right. I wasn't thinking."

Juan and Max exchanged a confused look just as Callie stepped to the table.

"Comic book references. Cool," she said. "Wasn't quite expecting that in a flight data recorder debrief."

Eric and Murph couldn't hide their delight at her appearance. Both were obviously smitten.

Juan couldn't help but chuckle.

"Okay, gents. Cartoon stories aside, tell me more about what you two observed," he said. "What kind of weapons system are we talking about?"

"Never saw anything exactly like it before," Eric said. "The only missile-launched anti-submarine system I know of is our RUM-139 vertical launch anti-submarine rocket. But that missile only has a range of around twelve nautical miles."

Murphy nodded. "This was an anti-sub rocket on steroids."

Juan frowned with curiosity. "What did you mean when you said you've never seen anything 'exactly' like it before?"

"It's almost as if they slapped Mark 54 torpedoes on Storm Shadows. A hybrid. Taking two existing systems and putting them together."

Juan turned to Murph. "What about the torpedo signature? Something off the shelf?"

"It wasn't a perfect match, but they sure sounded like Mark 54s."

"And the missiles? Did our radar database recognize the profile?"

"No, not exactly. But then again, the radar profile was pretty close to a Storm Shadow. Maybe a modified version of it. And it moved at the same speed a TR60-30 turbojet would."

"That's the engine a Storm Shadow uses," Eric said to Callie.

Callie smiled. "I kinda figured."

"Whoever is designing this stuff is moving fast, almost improvising," Eric said.

"And it's definitely an automated operation," Murphy said, "given that airplane of his."

"Design or construction?" Max asked.

"Some combination of the two is my bet."

"The bottom line is that we still don't know who actually did this and we don't really know what weapons they used," Max said. "Where does that leave us?"

Juan rubbed his face, exasperated.

"What we do know for sure is that we had a lead on this Vendor character, and after I breached his drone airplane it exploded. And when we located his airplane wreckage in the water, the *Oregon* was attacked. If there is a consortium, the Vendor is the point man. And he's deploying extremely sophisticated weapons. That means he's even more dangerous than we suspected. Speaking of which, did Overholt light up those Afghani weapons caches?"

Max shook his head. "He contacted us when you were black box hunting. Those trackers you laid down? All of them stopped transmitting."

"Malfunctioned?" Juan asked.

"No way. Tested them myself," Murph said. "They got zapped. Either by the Afghanis—"

"—or the Vendor," Juan said. He blew a blast of air through his nose, frustrated.

"We are way up a tall tree, gentlemen, and somebody keeps stealing our ladder."

29

Looks like it's time to get out and take a little walk," the lieutenant said to the sergeant driving the vehicle. The old logging road trailing through the forests north of Mitrovica had finally dead-ended at the foot of a steep mountain thick with trees. The air was heavy with the smell of pine and diesel exhaust.

The Iveco VM 90T Torpedo, an Italian version of a Humvee, pulled to a stop. The driver radioed back to the trailing Torpedo. Within minutes, the lieutenant and twenty of his Italian carabinieri had dismounted. One man remained stationed behind the machine gun affixed to each Torpedo while the others did weapons and gear checks. They wore camouflaged uniforms and large red armbands marked KFOR MSU—Kosovo Force Multinational Specialized Unit.

The MSU, part of NATO's ongoing peacekeeping efforts in the turbulent region, had been stationed in Kosovo since 1999. They were well known and largely respected by the locals on both sides of the conflict.

Lieutenant Salvio Bonucci's unit normally policed Mitrovica, where it was stationed. No easy task. The city itself was a microcosm of the larger regional conflict.

Muslim-majority Kosovo had broken away from Christian Serbia after Yugoslavia dissolved in 1992. Serbia opposed it. Though the UN refused to authorize it, NATO both initiated a deadly bombing campaign against Serbia to force the issue and recognized Kosovo's independence.

Tensions were still high all these years later. In Mitrovica, the MSU provided a buffering function between the hostile Christian Serb majority in the north part of town and the restive Muslim minority in the south.

But today Bonucci's specialized platoon had been sent out of the city and into the forested mountains. Their mission was to arrest two Salafist jihadis accused of an attempted assassination of a Serbian politician in Mitrovica and seize any weapons in their possession. A confidential informant reported he knew of their location and the possible existence of a weapons cache at the top of this particular mountain. Both jihadis had violent criminal records and had only recently converted to the religion of peace.

Though it was little more than a routine arrest, the lieutenant knew it was an urgent mission; hence the sudden reassignment of duties. Armed attacks on Christian Serb and secular Muslim politicians by the radical jihadis had increased exponentially in the last several weeks. The result was an escalating number of deaths and subsequent revenge murders.

According to Bonucci's commander, finding these two jihadi criminals and bringing them to justice was key to preventing an all-out civil war in Kosovo, and Bonucci had been tasked with doing so. Each of Bonucci's military policemen carried M4 carbines and the abomination of a pistol known as the Glock 17 instead of the unit's retired Beretta 92FS semi-autos—works of art in steel.

"Check your photos," Bonucci told his men. Attached to each man's forearm was a photo sleeve with pictures of the two Salafists wanted for arrest, Amir Muriqi and Ibrahim Hajrizi. Both in their late twenties, they were former members of the Albanian mafia who were radicalized in the same mosque, one of eight hundred in tiny Kosovo. Both Salafists wore the characteristically long beards without mustaches favored by many of the traditionalist Muslims in the region, but had the look of violence in their eyes.

★

Despite his senior rank, Bonucci rotated into the exposed point position. He believed in leading his men from the front and sharing their risks.

Drenched in sweat from the steep climb, he raised his hand and signaled a stop with a clenched fist. According to his GPS, this was the location where the confidential informant had requested for a meeting. From this point, the informant would lead them directly to the caves where the Salafist criminals were supposedly hiding.

Several meters back, Bonucci's sergeant repeated the same command. The rest of the unit, marching uphill in a ragged triangle behind the sergeant, halted. They all stood on a steep, uneven slope surrounded by thick trees. Most were gasping for breath and sweating like their commanding officer. They weren't used to the rugged terrain after so many months of city work.

"*Tenente*," the sergeant said, jogging up. "I don't have a good feeling about this place."

"These are the coordinates. The men are tired. We'll wait a few minutes to see if this guy shows up. Tell the men to take a water break."

"And if this informant doesn't show up?"

"We press on up the mountain and see what we can find. Besides, I suspect this might be a treasure hunt without a treasure. You know how it is with informants." The young lieutenant clapped the burly sergeant on his broad shoulders.

The older noncom had served two tours in Iraq in the Italian Army before transferring to the carabinieri. His instincts told him they were in danger but, he reminded himself, his therapist said that his PTSD had made him paranoid and that he should not give in to it. Perhaps his lieutenant was correct.

The sergeant nodded. "A few minutes rest will do them good."

The lieutenant smiled—just as the tree above his head exploded.

The 40mm grenade shattered the wood, throwing giant splinters like shrapnel as roaring M4 carbines hammered the air with 5.56mm jacketed rounds.

Bonucci screamed in agony as he crumbled to the ground, clutching his bloody face.

The sergeant grabbed the lieutenant's collar with one hand as he fired blindly into the woods with his carbine in the other. He dragged Bonucci behind a gnarled pine for cover and propped himself against it for a firing platform. Supersonic rounds thudded into the other side of the trunk as he fired his weapon. He sensed more than saw that gunfire was erupting in a near-perfect circle around them.

The sergeant barked orders directing his men where to fire. Thirty meters away, his lance corporal hit the dirt with a scream, clutching a bloody arm, and a third man was cut down by a spray of gunfire that stitched across his legs. Their comrades bravely grabbed them up and hauled them out of harm's way despite the rounds kicking up dirt all around them and the grenades smashing the trees above their heads. Shouts of "*Allahu Akbar*" echoed beyond the tree line.

"Retreat! Back to the vehicles!" the sergeant shouted. He ordered half the men to direct their fire downslope to clear a path toward the road. The sergeant and half a dozen others fought a rearguard action to slow the enemy's advance, dragging their wounded comrades along with them.

Fifteen minutes and thirteen casualties later, the Italians reached the Ivecos and piled in after the wounded as the heavy machine guns in the trucks above them roared with covering fire.

The two Torpedoes slammed into reverse and gunned their engines in a wobbling retreat back down the road.

A camouflaged jihadi leaped out of the trees and fired an RPG at the lead vehicle. The streaking rocket exploded beneath it, flipping it over, but not destroying it.

The sergeant jumped out of the second Iveco and led the charge to rescue his comrades. He put a half dozen rounds into the chest of the jihadi before he could reload his RPG.

Now enraged, the surviving carabinieri charged back uphill, pouring withering gunfire into the trees. The machine gun from the second truck offered covering fire as they advanced. But it was to no avail.

The jihadis shouted for victory as they melted back up the mountain.

30

Juan hung by his fingertips, his feet dangling some thirty feet above the deck. A fall from this height would kill him.

And that was the point.

Cabrillo had no natural fear of heights, but his recent adventure without a working parachute was still a splinter in his mind— something that needed to be extracted before it had the chance to fester and possibly affect future performance. Peak mental conditioning was the sine qua non for everything he did.

Equally important, wall climbing was one of Cabrillo's new favorite pastimes. Staying in top physical condition was the second leg of his performance stool. Nothing was better for large and small motor muscle development, endurance, and overall strength than a perilous climb up a sheer rock face even if it was only attached to the *Oregon*'s hull.

At the moment, he faced a particular challenge. The next handhold was technically out of reach. To get to it required a herculean effort to release one secure grip in hopes of acquiring the distant one. The likelihood of failure was nearly certain, but failing to make the attempt guaranteed no further upward progress. It was a classic rock-climbing zugzwang dreamed up by Russ Kefauver, the *Oregon* fitness maniac who constantly redesigned the climbing wall he originally installed.

"How's it going up there?" Linda shouted from below.

Juan tightened his grip on the one secure handhold and reached into his chalk bag with his other hand. The chalk would strip the sweat off of his fingers and increase his grip in preparation for his leap.

Before Juan could answer her, Hali Kasim's voice rang overhead in the gym. "Chairman, call for you. Langston Overholt."

"I'll take it over the speakers, Hali. Thanks."

Cabrillo glanced down at Linda Ross on the floor holding the safety rope wrapped around her waist and strapped to Juan's harness. "You hear that?"

"How could I miss it? I've got ya."

Juan kicked away from the wall and began his assisted descent as Overholt came on the line.

"Juan, my boy. Catch you at a good time?"

"Good as any, Lang. Linda Ross is with me."

"Delightful. Ms. Ross, always good to speak with you. I hope this call finds you well."

"Fit . . . as a fiddle," Linda grunted as she eased Juan's two-hundred-pound frame toward the ground, letting the rope slip through her gloved hands.

"Are you in some distress, Ms. Ross? Your breath sounds labored."

"Nothing out of the ordinary."

Juan's feet finally touched down on the rubber mat. "She's just pulling her weight around here—and mine. We're in the gym."

"I was calling to find out if you heard the latest news about the sinking of the South Korean destroyer?"

Juan unhooked himself from his harness.

"Only the headline. I've been out of the loop over the last twenty-four hours. Fill me in."

"The Office of Naval Intelligence has done an analysis of the attack studying sonar, radar, and radio transmissions. The bottom line is that it was sunk by a high-speed torpedo of unknown design."

"How 'high-speed'?" Linda asked.

"In excess of nineteen hundred knots, I'm afraid."

Juan whistled. "Is that even possible?"

"The U.S. Navy Lab once fired an underwater projectile in excess of twenty-nine hundred knots," Linda said. "And there are rumors of a new Russian system, the *Khishchnik*, supposedly capable of that kind of speed. But as far as actual torpedoes go, the Russian *Shkval* only tested at two hundred knots—and the Iranian *Hoot* topped out at 194."

"The sensors don't lie," Overholt said. "Neither do the three-hundred dead and wounded Korean sailors who suffered the catastrophe."

"I'm guessing we've ruled the Norks out," Linda said.

"Our analysts are confident this technology is well out of their reach," Overholt said. "It's clear the North Koreans fired it, but they certainly didn't build it."

"Which means they bought it," Linda said.

"The question is, from whom? The Russians? Or this Vendor menace? And if the latter, where did he acquire it from?"

"We think he's more than a broker," Juan said.

"How so?"

Juan gave him a rundown of the events over the last several hours, particularly the Vendor's missile-torpedo attack on the *Oregon* and the technological sophistication of the weapons. He also shared the consensus opinion that the Vendor was involved with some kind of network with access to advanced technology and automated manufacturing capabilities.

"That makes him both an arms broker and an arms maker," Overholt said. "Brokering existing arms was bad enough. But if he's also manufacturing them, especially advanced systems, then he is truly a strategic threat. I can't urge you strongly enough. Find the Vendor and destroy his network as quickly as you can."

"We've been trying. The man's a ghost. So far, it's all been a dead end."

"Press on, my boy. If anyone can do it, it's you and your team."

"You know we don't quit. Ever."

"Indeed, I do. That's why I gave you the assignment. Good hunting."

31

Juan pushed through the steel door into Murphy's darkly lit customized cabin, modeled after the hovercraft *Nebuchadnezzar* from *The Matrix*, Murph's all-time favorite movie.

Murph sat at one of the *Nebuchadnezzar*'s control stations, tapping away at a keyboard, totally engrossed in his work. Callie and Eric hovered over his shoulders, equally enthralled.

They were surrounded by a dozen other monitors waterfalling the iconic matrix language as screen savers, all arranged just like the movie. Empty beef jerky wrappers and crushed Red Bull cans overflowed the trash bin near Murph's station.

Juan fought back a sting of irritation, hoping he wasn't being invited to a Fortnite championship round or some other nonsense they didn't have time for. The soles of his boots clanged on the floor's steel grates as he approached the trio absorbed in Murphy's screen.

"You called for me?" Juan asked.

The three looked up, surprised by his entrance.

"You gotta see this, Chairman." Murph waved him over with a hand.

Cabrillo strode to his station, noting the odors of stale sweat, Cheez-Its, and Axe body spray. It smelled like every men's college dorm room Juan had ever been in. Murph's and Eric's clothes were wrinkled, their hair disheveled, and both men needed a shave, though with Murph that wasn't so obvious.

Callie on the other hand was fresh as a daisy, like she'd just emerged from the water at Maui's North Shore.

Cabrillo leaned over. "What am I looking at?"

"After we left the lab yesterday, Callie came by and started poking around the flight data recorder's fried hard drive," Eric began. "And what she found was this." He tapped a key on Murph's board. It displayed a piece of software code.

"And that is . . . ?"

"It's a fragment of a line of code pointing to the dark web," Callie said.

"Why would the dark web be on the flight recorder?"

"Probably a link to a geolocation or some other kind of address for delivery," she offered.

Juan nodded, intrigued. "The dark web is the perfect place to transact illegal business."

"Buying *and* selling," Murphy added.

"Were you able to track down somebody with that snippet of code? An address for delivery?"

"No," Murph said. "But it was enough to give us a few ideas."

"Basically, we asked ourselves, if we were trying to find qualified customers online and not give away our identities, what would we do?" Eric said.

"In other words, these two geniuses cobbled together a search engine optimization profile, using AI to refine the parameters," Callie said.

"Meaning?" Juan asked.

"In short, what kind of ad would the Vendor run on the dark web?" Callie said. "What was the most likely approach to sell tech-related weapons to qualified buyers with big money, preserve anonymity, avoid U.S. and NATO detection—that kind of thing. Their AI-assisted coder generated some really interesting algorithms."

"We then reverse engineered all of that and built an AI bot to go out and find dark web pages that fit those algos," Murph said. "Our search came back with over fifty hits and we've spent the last several hours sorting through those—with Callie's help, of course, since she was the one that found the code in the first place."

"I only just got here an hour ago," Callie said. "They've been at this all night."

Juan sniffed the air. "Yeah, I can tell. So show me what you've found."

Murph sat up and noticed the potato chip crumbs littering his Brave Parakeets concert shirt. He brushed them off and then pulled up a new screen. It was published in five languages including English.

"This posted just a couple of days ago."

Eric read the English ad aloud.

"'Urgently seeking twelve combat-experienced special operations warfighters for a VIP security event. Need one-plus sniper. Close-quarters combat experience a must. Non-Americans preferred. English-language *fluency* required. Minimum pay is fifty thousand U.S. per week, two-week minimum guaranteed in Bitcoin (BTC). Immediate twenty-five thousand U.S. transferred to your account upon acceptance. If interested, contact . . .'" Eric didn't bother reading the rest.

"Sounds like an old gun-for-hire ad in *Soldier of Fortune*," Juan said. "Why do you think this is a Vendor ad?"

"My AI program is ninety-seven point three percent certain it is given the parameters we loaded in. I happen to agree. The non-U.S. preference is a real giveaway."

"If you're confident, that's good enough for me." Juan rubbed his chin, thinking. "Okay, let's take advantage of this."

He turned to Eric. "Stoney, we'll start by grabbing the undercover mission protocols checklist."

"Will do." Stoney stepped over to the nearest monitor and started tapping keys.

"Murph, contact the Magic Shop and our special records division."

"Who's going in?"

"Me and Linc."

Murph grinned. "Linc has the sniper cred for sure. They won't have to make anything up about his record. Do you want a new legend or pull one from the archive?"

"Let's hit the archive. I'll do 'El Sicario.' Saves time trying to memorize new material."

"Gotcha."

"As soon as Stoney downloads that checklist, I want the two of you to quarterback everything through all departments. We can't afford to have anything fall through the cracks. This Vendor cat has his act together."

"Will do."

"You guys know the drill. We'll need DoD and Mexican military records, used passports with visa stamps, social media histories, fake girlfriends, pocket litter, vacation videos. The whole enchilada. Put a fire under everybody's tail. With the kind of money this guy is offering, he'll fill up with applications *tout de suite*."

"We won't let you down," Eric said as the shared document checklist popped up on both his phone and Murphy's.

"We're on it," Murph said. He knew the special records division employed AI systems to create all of the official and personal documentation in record time with utmost precision and attention to detail. And the Magic Shop had perfected both the art and science of physical deception with its 3D-printing tools. But no AI programmer on the planet had cracked the code for intuition or instinct. Murph agreed with Cabrillo that human eyes overseeing the project were vital, and two pairs of eyes were better than one. They had to ensure that the entire package "felt" right and passed their own tests of believability. Juan's and Linc's lives depended on it.

"Aren't you missing something?" Callie asked.

"What's that?" Juan asked.

"While the computer calculated a small chance this could be a wild-goose chase, I think it's quite probable this murderous genius has set a trap for you—some kind of 4D chess master maneuver."

"She's right, boss," Eric said. "This would be the perfect play for that sort of thing."

"Or . . . the contract is really just a contract," Murph said. "Except that you and Linc could be on a one-way trip to an unexpected Custer's Last Stand."

Eric crossed his arms. "Or you walk into a police ambush that gets you thrown into a Third World dungeon with a life sentence, squat toilets, and no windows."

"Believe me, I can think of even worse outcomes," Juan said. "But what's the alternative? This is the only lead we have and our mission is to stop the Vendor—or die trying.

"I appreciate your concerns, but our business, gentlemen, is risk. Calculated, anticipated, and minimized to the best of our ability. But at the end of the day, none of us gets out of this *carnicería* alive. And on that day there is a judgment we all face. We won't be rewarded for the risks we avoided but for the hazards we braved to do good in the world as best we could, even if we failed in the attempt. Isn't that what we all signed up for?"

Murph and Eric nodded in solemn agreement.

Callie's eyes radiated with admiration. "Amen to that."

32

Juan and Linc were already on their way to Malaysia, having been accepted by the dark web advertiser for the VIP security assignment. The impeccably produced fake military service documents, IDs, and legends generated by the *Oregon*'s crack teams had worked perfectly.

As soon as Juan and Linc received their respective initial payments, the mysterious employer provided two airline tickets. To avoid suspicion, the two operators began their separate journeys from different starting locations that took them on circuitous routes that both ended at different times in Kuala Lumpur, Malaysia's capital city. That seemed a logical destination. "KL" was a large and busy international business and transportation center as well as a melting pot of cultures, races, and religions. A collection of multinational mercenaries would draw little if any attention in a city like that.

Though it was doubtful KL was the final destination, it was no doubt closer to wherever the actual mission was going to take place. Otherwise, why bother sending them there? Juan, Max, and Linda agreed that taking the *Oregon* down to Malaysia made sense. They would at least be closer to the action and available for backup should the need arise.

It was on the second day of transit that Max received a call from Langston Overholt. Hali explained that Juan was unavailable and

Max was in command. Max took the call while sitting in the Kirk Chair.

"Thank you for taking my call, Mr. Hanley. I trust Juan is in good health?"

"He and Linc are chasing a lead on the Vendor."

"As it so happens, I might have a lead for you as well."

"Fire away."

"A detachment of Italian carabinieri was recently ambushed by a mob of Salafists in Kosovo. NATO-KFOR believes a new source of weapons is flowing into the Kosovo region and falling into the hands of the local jihadis."

"The Vendor's Afghanistan stash?"

"That would fit his pattern. What's particularly worrying is that many of these radicals have combat experience in Iraq and Afghanistan and have now cycled back to the European continent."

"Combat trained and newly armed. That's not good."

"Now you know why I'd like you to send in a team to investigate. With any luck, we might get a lead on the Vendor's transport network or perhaps even his actual location."

"Kosovo isn't exactly a vacation spot these days."

"Indeed, it is not. The entire region is a tinderbox. A rising faction of Islamic extremists is calling for a new European holy war—one begun in Bosnia-Herzegovina in 1992 by Al Qaeda and other mujahideen against the Christian Serbs. The Christian Slavs in the region are in an uproar. I'm sure I don't have to remind you that World War I began when a young Serbian nationalist assassinated Archduke Ferdinand in Sarajevo."

"If memory serves, the Austrians then declared war on Serbia, Russia declared war on Austria, Germany on Russia, England and France on Germany—"

"—and so on in a series of bloody dominoes that decimated a generation of Europeans. Like Bismarck said twenty years before it happened, it would be some 'damn foolish thing in the Balkans' that would lead to a great European war. I'm afraid we're not far away from a similar scenario today."

"And our friend the Vendor is providing the matches to set the place on fire all over again."

"Precisely."

"I'm just not sure how we can pull it off," Max said.

"What's the problem?"

"We're on our way to Kuala Lumpur to back up Juan and Linc."

"Don't you have other operators at your disposal?"

Max rubbed his chin. He fully understood the strategic significance of the Vendor's operations, but his first responsibility was to the *Oregon* and its crew and especially to Juan, his best friend. He couldn't abandon Juan and Linc for the sake of the *possibility* of uncovering the Vendor's operation in Kosovo. Juan and Linc were on a mission to do precisely that.

But what if their trip to KL really was a wild-goose chase?

Equally important, Max hated to dilute the spec ops team. Peeling off more of them to Kosovo meant the remaining fighters might have to do more with less in a gunfight to save Linc and Juan.

What would Juan do?

"Tell you what, Lang. I'll ask for two volunteers for the mission."

"Fair enough. I'll forward all the intel I have. Please keep me posted."

"Will do."

★

The *Oregon*'s team room was an eclectic mix of couches, blackboards, unit flags, and wall monitors. It was the place the ship's special operators congregated for mission briefings and debriefings—or just to hang out. All of the *Oregon*'s crew were hand-selected specialists in their respective fields, but the pipe hitters were a breed apart—a fraternity of violence executed up close and personal. Max always supposed that was the reason the team room looked more like a frat house media den than an actual office space.

He had called them all together to brief the mission. Eddie Seng, the director of shore operations, was there. So was MacD, Linda Ross, and Raven Malloy, the newest member of the Gundogs. A West Point graduate, Malloy's mixed Native American heritage and facility in both Farsi and Arabic served her well on two tours of combat-decorated duty in Afghanistan as a U.S. Army investigator.

Gomez Adams was draped over one of the couches like an abandoned beach towel.

Max stood at the head of the room. A map of Kosovo displayed on the monitor. He explained the situation on the ground and what was at stake. He also laid that against the mission Juan and Linc were on and the need to back them up.

"I need to add that Overholt doesn't want us pouring gasoline on the fire over there. It's black in, black out. We're just looking for intel, not a body count. That means guns are secured unless fired upon. Clear?"

Heads nodded.

"So, I'm looking for two volunteers. If you don't feel it, don't sweat it."

"Where in Kosovo, exactly?" Linda asked.

Max drew a red circle around a city with the tip of his finger.

"Up north. Above this place called Mitrovica."

Raven's hand shot up.

"You served with KFOR before Afghanistan, didn't you?" Eddie asked.

"That's right," she replied. Her lustrous black hair was pulled into a French braid thick as a hawser. "I served with the MSU based in Mitrovica years ago. I know the place and some of the players pretty well."

"Excellent. Anybody else?"

MacD raised his hand. "I'll tag along. Always wanted to see that part of the world."

"Then we have our team," Max said. "Eddie, let's the four of us have a sit-down and lay out the particulars. The rest of you are dismissed."

The others shuffled out of the room as the four sat down around a desk shoved into the corner. Eddie pulled up a map on the desk monitor and they all got to work planning out the mission. Raven's experience in the area provided critical input, but in truth it was all a shot in the dark without more intel on the ground.

As always, the *Oregon*'s Gundogs would have to improvise. That wasn't a problem. It was their most formidable weapon, taught to them by the master of the art himself, Juan Cabrillo.

33

The smallish, two-story building at the Film City base for the Kosovo Force was very modest by NATO standards. The camp's odd name was a leftover from an aborted intent to establish a Yugoslavian version of Hollywood at the site. MacD eyed the unremarkable building and supposed its occupants tried to make up for its diminutive stature with the Trump Tower–styled gold letters announcement over the entrance: HEADQUARTERS KOSOVO FORCE. A light rain filled the air with the musty, mineral smell of wet pavement.

After checking in at the security desk, Raven and MacD were directed to the second floor and the door marked COL. MATTIA PICCININI. TRAINING OFFICER.

The colonel was cast straight out of a Fellini film—a well-built, handsome Italian man with a cleft chin, wavy dark hair, and dark brown, mischievous eyes. He greeted Raven with a warm smile that melted into an even warmer hug.

"It's been so long!" the colonel began. "I was so happy when I got your email."

"How are Sofia and the kids?"

"My wife is more beautiful than ever and the twins are both in college now. Thank you for asking."

While the two of them were reacquainting, MacD took in the colonel's office. One wood-paneled wall featured a large topographical
map of Kosovo as well as a geographical map of the region including
the surrounding countries of Albania, Montenegro, Serbia, and North
Macedonia.

A second, "ego" wall was covered with framed photos of Piccinini
saluting or shaking hands with flag officers and dignitaries from
around the world. There were also unit and personal commendations
along with his professional and weapons certifications.

An impressive career, MacD thought.

"Colonel Piccinini, this is my partner MacD." Raven had already
explained to him in an email she and MacD worked for a private con-
tracting firm.

The two men recognized the warrior in each other and shook hands
firmly.

"*Piacere di conoscerti*," MacD said. It's a pleasure to meet you.

Piccinini was impressed with the formal address. He responded in
kind. "*Il piacere è mio.*" The pleasure is mine.

He added, "Your Italian is excellent."

"Uncle Google taught me everything I know, and that ain't much."

The colonel chuckled. "Has Raven told you of her service here in
Kosovo?"

"No, as a matter of fact."

"She was an excellent young officer. We were her first assignment
as a military investigator. The Albanian mafia was running a drug-
smuggling ring into NATO bases in Europe. She helped break it up.
Unfortunately, she also broke the hearts of a few of my men."

Raven fought back a blush.

Piccinini waved them both into chairs before he sat behind his
desk. "Please, be seated. How may I be of service?"

"First of all, we read the brief about the attack on your men above
Mitrovica," Raven said. "I'm sorry for your loss."

The cheerful Italian's mood darkened. "Thank you. It was a bad
day, and a rushed operation. No one killed, thank God, though many
were wounded and a young lieutenant blinded."

"If I read the report correctly, the weapons cache wasn't found and no arrests were made."

"Unfortunately, that is correct. One bandit was confirmed killed."

"What weapon did he carry?"

"A Chinese-made RPG launcher."

"The report stated that some of your men thought that NATO-standard weapons were used. M4 carbines, especially."

"Also correct. Why is that of interest to you?"

"It's actually the reason why we're here. We think we know who's supplying those weapons to the Salafists."

"Excellent. Who is it?"

"He goes by the name of 'the Vendor.' Have you heard of him?"

Piccinini shook his head. "No. What can you tell me about him?"

"Not much. We don't know his identity, or his location, or really much of anything. That's what we've come to find out. We want to go to the ambush site and look around. We're hoping we can find a clue from the weapons cache stored up there. Any chance you can show us the way?"

Piccinini shook his head. "I would gladly take you there myself, but the brass is embarrassed and wants to pretend the ambush didn't really happen. We don't have the manpower to punish the offenders, let alone drive them off that mountain. So instead, the authorities have designated that area a no-go zone for all KFOR personnel."

"Can you at least show us where it is on a map?"

"Only approximately."

The colonel stepped over to the topographical map and traced a path on it with his finger as he spoke.

"The logging road ends here. From there you'll have to proceed by foot up steep terrain with heavy trees. It's located up high on the mountain, somewhere in this two-kilometer radius."

"And where did the ambush take place?" MacD asked.

"Exactly here, farther down." The colonel touched the map, then stepped away so the rugged Cajun could examine it more closely.

"They were scheduled to meet with your informant, right?" Raven asked.

"The team stopped at the meeting point, but found themselves in the middle of a firefight."

"What happened to the informant?"

"I've tried to reach him. He's not answering my texts."

"I don't mean to be obvious, but . . . isn't it possible he betrayed your squad?"

Piccinini shrugged in the most Italian of ways. "Of course, anything is possible. But I doubt it. He turned his back on the radicals and now is mostly a hermit."

"What do you mean, 'turned his back'?" MacD asked.

"He fought with ISIS for several years overseas, but had a change of heart after he saw what animals they were. He returned home to live in peace. But when he saw the radicals coming back to the area, he reached out to me."

"Is there really such a thing as a 'former' ISIS member?" Raven asked.

"If you met him, you'd understand. He's quite cautious. He trusts almost no one except me and the people I recommend to him. His name is Nedim Ramadani."

"If you think he hasn't turned, and he's not answering your texts . . . ?" Raven didn't want to finish the thought.

"I know. He's likely dead."

"Can you tell us where he lives up there?" MacD asked.

Piccinini pointed at another location. "The last time I met him, he was living here. But that was a year ago. If you can find him, he will be your best chance of finding the Salafists and their weapons cache."

"And if we can't?"

"Then you are on your own. And God help you up on that mountain. My hands are tied. I can't back you up."

Raven nodded. "We understand."

"If you trust this Ramadani fella, that's good enough for us," MacD said. "We'll go take a look-see." He pulled out his cell phone and snapped close-up photos of the topo map.

"We could use a few supplies," Raven said. "Any chance you could point us in the right direction?"

"As a KFOR officer I can't officially help you."

Piccinini reached into his pocket and handed Raven a set of keys. "But my personal vehicle is parked out back. I believe you'll find everything you need in it."

"*Grazie mille*, Mattia," Raven said with a faultless accent.

"*Prego.*"

34

That's gotta be him," McGuire muttered as he angled for the curb, pounding the horn on his Daihatsu van with the flat of his big hand.

The traffic around Kuala Lumpur's international airport was always crowded with colorful taxis, ride shares, buses, and passenger vehicles, but today was a real logjam. He laughed at the cursing faces screaming at him from behind their windshields in God knows what languages as he bulled his way over to the curb.

McGuire hit the button to open the sliding door of the unmarked white van. The former SAS operator was bearded and his arms covered in sleeve tats—standard operator chic. But the Black man standing at the curb was dressed in business casual and gripping a well-worn, deep-pocket leather duffel. His bald head was smooth as a trailer hitch, and his eyes were covered by a pair of wraparound sunglasses. With his massive physique straining the fabric of his shirt and slacks he looked more like a professional bodybuilder than a stone-cold killer.

But McGuire, a former operator himself, easily recognized a fellow apex predator just by the way he stood.

"Davis?"

"You got it."

"McGuire."

McGuire stuck out his hand. Davis's long fingers wrapped around McGuire's like a child taking hold of a doll's hand.

"Thanks for the ride, brother." Davis tossed his leather duffel onto the bench seat, then climbed in after it.

McGuire pulled open a silvered Faraday bag, designed to keep signal radiation out—and in. "OPSEC, my boyo. Need your phone."

Davis grunted with the effort and annoyance of fishing his phone out of his pocket and tossing it into the bag.

"You'll get it back after the mission." McGuire punched the button to close the sliding door as he glanced into his side-view mirror.

"You're the last one to arrive. Where'd you fly in from?"

"Started in Benghazi," Davis said. "Routed through Cairo, then Saudi. A couple of overnight layovers. Could've walked here faster." His deep basso profundo voice rumbled like an idling Chevy small-block V8 engine.

"Yeah, well, sorry about that, mate. I didn't make the travel arrangements." McGuire punched the gas and leaped out into the river of honking cars.

"No worries, man. Just sayin'."

"I get it. Might as well settle in. We've got a wee bit of a ride."

As soon as McGuire cleared the airport's bumper car traffic, he hit the hands-free call button on his steering wheel. A heavily accented voice picked up on the other end.

"You have him?"

"On our way. Don't start without us."

The phone clicked off. McGuire glanced at Davis in the rearview mirror.

"I read your jacket. CIA paramilitary."

"Eight years, six months, twenty-four days."

"I'm surprised we never met. You and I were in theater together about the same time."

"We had a saying in special ops. If you knew I was there, I wasn't doing my job."

McGuire chuckled. "You must've been good at your job, then. You stick out pretty good. You're built like the Michelin Man."

"Like I've never heard that one before."

"I hear Libya is crazy."

"Heart of darkness, man. But good money." Davis turned his gaze toward the window, ending the conversation. McGuire was being too nosy, and the truth was that Davis's story was a bit thin because he didn't exist.

Unlike Cabrillo, Franklin "Linc" Lincoln didn't live and breathe this kind of undercover work. Linc was a special warfare operator. His job was to hurt people and break things, not playact, and his expertise was the business end of any sniper rifle he could wrap his big hands around. Unable to speak any other languages or push into the deep psychology of undercover personality changes, Linc had to basically be himself.

But because of the Vendor's technical prowess, Linc needed some kind of cover lest he be discovered—which would not only have led to the rejection of his application but also would have alerted the Vendor they were on to him. The easiest thing to do was to put Linc in a completely different and utterly covert service branch. No need for language skills, and the likelihood of another CIA special ops fighter in the mix was practically nil.

The dark web ad specifically stated it preferred non-Americans but also needed a sniper. They gambled on Linc's incredible sniper "legend," which was actually based on his real service record. Apparently, the gamble paid off. With any luck, they were one step closer to finding the Vendor.

If this really is a Vendor op, Linc reminded himself. There was still a fifty-fifty chance it wasn't.

★

Two hours later, McGuire turned off the two-lane asphalt road and onto a rutted dirt track, splattering the white Daihatsu van with a thin coat of mud. Fifteen minutes after that, he pulled to a stop beside a large lean-to that stood on the edge of a wide jungle airstrip.

The covered lean-to featured several picnic benches, where a dozen operators from multiple nationalities sat or stood, all drinking Tiger Lager beer. Tats, beards, scars—and lots of attitude. Some were telling war stories, while others told jokes for men who laughed too loud.

It looked chummier than it was, Linc knew. Like the first day of football camp, or enlistment day at the intake center. Everybody yaks it up because they're nervous, but also because they're sizing each other up, trying to establish dominance hierarchies. Linc laughed to himself.

If they were dogs, they'd all be sniffing each other's butts.

On the far end of the structure was a massive camp kitchen. A couple of Malaysian women were tending a roaring charcoal grill, turning slabs of beef and cut-up chickens. The meat spit sizzling fat into the flames and filled the air with tangy smoke. Pots bubbled with noodles, rice, and vegetable curries.

"End of the road, brother. We're just in time for some chow."

McGuire tumbled out of the van and made a beeline to a tall man sporting a bushy beard and a ball cap, and whispered something to him.

Linc pulled his leather duffel and climbed out of the van.

Several heads turned toward Linc. The ones who didn't were still watching him in their peripheral vision. It wasn't the first time Linc had intimidated a collection of violent men. Two clean-shaven young towheaded blonds—identical twins—smiled at him, but their raging blue eyes bore into his.

Linc shrugged off the attention, and made a show of sniffing the air, savoring the sweet aroma of roasting meat and the smoky tang of charcoal. He dropped his gear in the stack of luggage already piled up against the wall and headed for the ice chest crammed with cold beers. A dark-headed merc stood nearby. Linc pulled a lager and cracked the cap.

"That's not a real beer," the man said with a smile and a clear Spanish accent. He stuck out his hand. "Mendoza."

They shook.

"Davis." Linc held up his Tiger Lager bottle. "What's wrong with it?"

"Only two percent alcohol. But it is adequate. A local favorite, I'm told. Now, Negra Modelo? That, *mi amigo*, is a real beer. A man's beer. A *Mexican* beer."

"I've had Modelo before. Never been to Mexico."

"It is the land of my ancestors. You should come down sometime to my *rancho*." The Mexican mercenary stood six foot one and was powerfully built. His hair was close cut and jet-black. But his eyes were blue.

Linc knew without a shadow of a doubt he was talking to Juan Cabrillo, but somehow, he felt as if he really was engaging with Mendoza. It wasn't Juan's dyed hair, the authentic accent, or even the puckering star-shaped scar in his thick bicep that made the deception work. It was him totally inhabiting his character—actually believing he was the former Mexican special operator and *sicario* Mendoza.

Linc nodded. "Soon as we finish this gig, I just might take you up on that."

"I hope that you will."

"By the way, you speak English better than me."

"My mother taught it at the University of Guadalajara." Mendoza lifted his beer. "*Salud!*"

They clinked bottles and swigged their beers.

"Have you met all of the other guys?" Linc asked, pointing at the crowd with his bottle.

"Oh, yes. Quite a collection of talent from all over. Irish, English, Syrian, Nigerian—"

"Who are the psycho *Matrix* twins that were staring me down?"

"Polish special forces. A couple of real *caballeros*. Apparently they got a little too rough with the Russian prisoners they captured. So they recently brought their butchering skills to the marketplace."

"What about you? What's your background?" He knew other ears were listening in on their conversation.

"*Fuerzas Especiales.*" Cabrillo took another pull of his beer.

"The Mexican Navy SEALS. Impressive. Early retirement?"

"Promotion. I became the *primero comandante* for *La Hermandad de las Almas Perdidas*—the Brotherhood of Lost Souls."

"A cartel death squad, if I recall correctly."

"You do."

The tall bearded man in the ball cap strode over to the two operators. Linc recognized his quiet authority and the cunning intelligence behind his eyes. No need to play schoolyard games with this one.

"Glad you made it, Davis. Name is Drăguş." He offered his hand to Linc.

"Glad to be here, finally. Interesting name."

"Romanian. Sergeant major with the 1st Special Operations Battalion."

"The 'Eagles,'" Linc said.

"You heard of us?"

Linc grinned ear to ear. "You guys kicked a lot of tail and took a lot a names in the 'Stan." Linc high-fived the Romanian, who was obviously proud of his service.

"Any problems on the trip here?" Drăguş asked.

"None. Traveled light, just as instructed. My weapon is ready?"

"Everyone will be kitted out when we reach the training camp."

McGuire dashed over to Drăguş. "Chow's ready."

"Excuse me, gentlemen." Drăguş climbed up onto the nearest table.

"Gentlemen! Once again, I welcome each of you to our little adventure together. Food is about to be served. Eat hearty. And while you're eating, take a look at the man sitting next to you and across from you. These are your teammates. Chances are, nothing exciting will happen and you'll make a ton of money doing nothing but standing around and holding your *pulă*.

"But if it does all go sideways, that man on your left and the man on your right are the guys who will be covering your back. So take the time to get to know each other. Training starts tomorrow morning. Until then, enjoy the food, drink some more beer, and relax."

★

An hour later, the Beechcraft King Air 360ER touched down on the grassy airstrip with ease and taxied closer to the shelter. A small fuel truck raced over.

Drăguş and McGuire stood at the stairs and did a head count as the men climbed up. The Beechcraft's tanks were getting topped off and the air stank of aviation gas.

Linc and Juan fell into a pair of plush leather aisle seats across from each other and settled in. The air clacked with the noise of belt buckle mechanisms locking into place. The air-conditioning kicked on just as Drăguş stood up at the front of the plane.

Juan noticed the Nigerian trying to open his window shade, but it wouldn't budge. The Polish twins behind him cursed in their native tongue. The guy at the end of Juan's row jiggled his shade, but gave up.

"Listen up!" Drăguş said. "First, if any of you are expecting a safety demonstration from me, forget it. If you're not smart enough to figure out how to buckle your belt, you're on the wrong flight." He made exaggerated hand gestures like someone who couldn't figure out how to fasten their seat belts.

The cabin rippled with laughter.

Someone from the back shouted, "What are we having for in-flight snacks?"

Everybody cracked up.

Drăguş grabbed his crotch and grinned. "I can serve you some of this."

That made the plane laugh even louder.

Juan and Linc exchanged a glance.

Boys will be boys, even if they are hired killers.

"We will hit it hard starting tomorrow morning. It's a long flight. The windows are shut to keep the light out. So sit back and get some shut-eye." As if on cue, the cabin lights shut off, throwing the cabin into relative darkness.

Moments later, the plane took off, smooth as silk.

Unbeknownst to the passengers settling into their flight, the copilot flipped a switch in the cockpit, activating a jammer.

From an electromagnetic perspective, everybody aboard the Beechcraft suddenly ceased to exist.

35

What do you mean, you've lost them?"

Max leaned over Hali's shoulder at the comms station. The *Oregon* was no longer picking up the implanted trackers on Juan and Linc. Every crew member had them in case of emergencies—and to keep tabs on their people in the field.

"They just disappeared—poof." The curly-headed Lebanese American gestured an explosion with his long, thin fingers. "Either they've been surgically removed, destroyed, or jammed."

"Did we do a check before they left? Maybe the units died."

Hali pulled up a check sheet on his screen and pointed at it. "Dr. Huxley signed off on them before they left. Signal and power both at one hundred percent."

"Could there be a problem with the satellite?"

Hali pulled up the satellite tracker screen. It showed the dozens of tracker signals emanating from the *Oregon*.

"It's receiving and sending just fine. Maybe there's a weather anomaly."

"Maybe there's a tooth fairy, too." Max was really worried.

The only intel they had on Juan and Linc to this point were the trackers. Did they get on a plane? On trucks? Ruck into the bush? They could be anywhere.

But wherever they were, they were surrounded by at least ten paid killers and there was no way to back them up.

"We'll just have to wait for them to contact us," Hali said.

Max stood, his face set in stone.

"Yeah, unless they're already dead."

★

WASHINGTON, D.C.

Erin Banfield lived in one of Georgetown's refurbished Federal-style brick townhouses. It was luxuriously appointed and well-furnished, providing her all of the comforts she and her fat, irascible white Persian cat, Winston, required.

It was barely affordable twenty years ago when she bought it on her meager government salary. She could never have afforded it today on her still miserable federal wages after the skyrocketing real estate valuations of the last few years. It was yet another reason why she hated all K Street lobbyists and their overpaid minions who were driving up the price and misery of living in the habitable parts of the District.

She took another sip of her scotch on the rocks, recalling the conversation she had with her boss at the office, the second this week. She almost wanted to laugh.

Despite his family's wealth, his dashing good looks, and fast-tracking CIA career, Trevor Das was oddly insecure. When he called her up to his office in the afternoon, his state of emotional agitation was off the charts.

She assumed it was because Das viewed his leadership of the interagency arms-trafficking task force as his springboard to bigger and better things. Anything that threatened his perceived status as the head of that group turned the normally suave young man into a paranoid lunatic.

"Your old buddy Overholt is at it again," he began, closing his office door behind her and practically spitting out the words.

"What did he do this time?"

"Another covert op. A place in Kosovo."

"Where?"

"Mitrovica. He's cutting me out again. I won't put up with this."

"I don't blame you. It's . . . unseemly." She pressed him. "What happened to his foray into Afghanistan?"

Das shrugged. "No idea. It went dark. Probably went sideways."

Das glanced around the office despite the fact she was the only occupant. "I need details. Find out what he's up to. Who's on the assignment. Who he's reporting to. The works." He lowered his voice. "And I need you to do it on the sly. Can you please do that for me?"

"Of course," she told him.

He calmed right down; in fact, when she left, he had a smile and slight bounce in his step.

And now here she was at her home computer with Winston purring as he rubbed against her ankle, hoping for a lift into Banfield's ample lap. She obliged.

She petted Winston while asking him, "Why does Trevor Das keep complaining to me about Overholt? And why does he want me to pursue this? Could it be he's setting me up as the fall guy if there's blowback?"

Winston's rheumy eyes shut as his claws kneaded into her sweater.

Banfield engaged her virtual private network—effectively placing her computer address location on a server in Slovenia. She then pulled up the Children's Global Charity Network website and selected the donations page in the name of Trevor Das.

Within a few minutes she entered in her selection: two milking goats for a needy family in Kenya. She also checked off several other numbered items and then answered the question "What are your favorite Bible verses you would like to share with your family gifts?"

She entered in Genesis 42:8, Psalm 88:3, Proverbs 3:3, Exodus 20:8, 1 Samuel 6:6, 2 Chronicles 7:7, and then logged off.

Banfield drained her glass and shut down her computer for the night. She set Winston down and carried her Waterford tumbler to the bar for a refill.

She glanced around her living room. She loved her townhome. It was a perfect expression of her good taste and classic sensibilities. She hated to sell it. But it made no sense to keep it after she retired a few months from now. Besides, her villa in the Algarve suited her just fine, as did her much younger Portuguese boyfriend, who was already living there, awaiting her permanent arrival early next year.

She checked her watch. Trevor's charity network order would be accessed by the Vendor within the next few hours. The two goats, checked items, and Bible verses were secret codes providing him all the information she had on Overholt's operation, including the longitude and latitude of Mitrovica, Kosovo.

It was up to the Vendor how he wanted to proceed. The fact that Das had no idea what happened to the Afghan mission told her the Vendor had resolved that issue satisfactorily. No doubt he would do the same in Kosovo.

He needed to. She was walking a very thin line. He paid her a great deal of money for her services, but none of it would be of any use to her locked up for life in a supermax federal penitentiary. She'd left enough digital crumbs over the past year to point at Das in case things did go sideways, but hopefully it would never come to that. Among his many gifts, Banfield admired the Vendor's precision most of all.

She took a stiff pull of her scotch and refreshed it again before carrying it back to the bathroom. She needed a long, hot soak in a tub full of delicious bubbles to finish up such a satisfying day.

★

THE MALACCA STRAIT

The *Jade Voyager* rolled and yawed beneath the captain's feet as he stood on the bridge. His gut tingled with the strange sensation of floating in space, untethered to solidity, like a speeding car hydroplaning on a freeway.

The wiper blades slapped away at the heavy rain battering the bridge glass, but they couldn't keep up. He could barely see the deck pitching and the crash of yet another wave hitting the bow at a steep angle. The ship rolled hard again. He grasped the railing to steady himself. The frightened young faces on the bridge with him fought to keep their composure. They trusted their captain, but none of them had ever seen anything like this.

The captain knew the *Jade Voyager* could handle it. His worry was the stacks of containers crowded on his decks. The owners were on the verge of bankruptcy and had pressured him to push the safety limits to increase the cargo load for this trip to India. They sent him to a small but accommodating Indonesian port infamous for its lax enforcement of safety standards. The stacks were unusually high, but not entirely out of reason. Despite the heavy load, the captain was confident in his ship, his apprehension alleviated by the owners' promise of an extra bonus for his cooperation.

But here, in the belly of a storm-tossed night, the captain began losing his nerve.

A rogue wave had hit his vessel at precisely the wrong angle, sending his ship into an accelerating spiral of uncontrollable pitching and rolling. The physics of mass and energy were upsetting the balance of weight of the overstacked containers—lashed to the deck with rusted and fraying cables the owners couldn't afford to replace.

A ship's alarm sounded as the *Jade Voyager* angled past the thirty-degree mark. The sharp, sizzling crack of snapping cables suddenly burst outside.

The captain pressed closer to the rain-spattered bridge glass. He caught a glimpse of the first stack of bright yellow containers tumbling into the sea, dragging the next stack into the water behind them, and then a third.

Ten more followed.

The sudden loss of weight began stabilizing the ship. The remaining containers on the deck stayed in place.

The captain mopped the sweat from his face, then lit a cigarette, resigned to his fate.

He would be blamed by the owners and the authorities for the reckless decision to overstack the cargo.

He was ruined.

36

KOSOVO

MacD and Raven trudged up the steep mountainside, sweat slicking between their shoulder blades beneath their packs.

The two of them were posing as American backpackers hiking in the region—not an unusual sight in this part of the world. Raven had bragged about hiking the steep and jagged peaks of the rugged Accursed Mountains just across the border in Montenegro several years before. She described them as something straight out of a Tolkien novel.

The backpacking ruse made a lot of sense for other practical reasons, including hauling the gear they needed to bring in and, with any luck, carry out.

A lot of what they needed for this mission they brought in legitimately. They also smuggled two 9-millimeter Walther PDP pistols, mags, and ammo thanks to Chuck "Tiny" Gunderson and the Corporation's private Gulfstream jet he piloted into Pristina. He was staying in the capital city on twenty-four-hour call with the plane already refueled and the flight plans submitted for a hasty return back to the *Oregon*. They were under orders from Max to avoid gunplay at all costs unless their lives were in immediate danger.

Everything they couldn't bring Colonel Piccinini had kindly provided including his battered but reliable Toyota Land Cruiser.

They passed through the ambush site with their antennae on high alert, stopping only to pick up a few of the dozens of spent brass cas-ings they found scattered in the pine needles.

"That's 5.56," MacD said, pocketing one. He found a different casing, badly weathered and rusted.

"What is it?" Raven asked.

"Swedish 6.5x55. One of the most popular hunting rounds in Eu-rope. Not recent, that's for sure."

They pressed on up the mountain, heading for the informant's last known campsite, their heads on swivels. The warming midmorning sun promised an eighty-six-degree day, just as the weather forecast predicted.

"I'm curious," Raven asked in a whispered voice. "Why did you volunteer for this assignment?"

"Max needed two bodies. You were the first. I'm not great at math, but I figured one more kinda evened it all up."

"No, seriously."

"Look, I've seen you in action. *T'es une sacrée bonne fighter, toi.*"

"I'm assuming that's Cajun for some kind of compliment."

"No doubt you can throw down as good as the rest of us, for sure. But on my first tour in the sandbox I came across a gaggle of these Kosovo jihadis. They was one rough bunch. Nasty as gators. Just thought I should tag along with ya."

"Appreciate it."

They trudged up the mountain for another two hours, stopping only for a short break of water and protein bars before pushing on. They finally arrived at the informant's campsite.

It was trashed.

Military surplus cooking utensils—a pot, some plates, and silverware—were thrown around. A smoldering firepit was filled with ashy remnants of clothing and what appeared to be a tent. A small cave entrance was blackened by a grenade blast.

"Looks like the bad guys found him first," Raven said. "I wonder what happened to him."

"We should check that cave," MacD said. "If he was lucky, he got killed in the blast. If not? Well, I don't want to think about it."

An AK-47 racked behind them.

MacD and Raven froze.

Maybe their luck just ran out, too.

★

A rasping voice barked in Albanian behind them.

MacD didn't speak the language. Neither did Raven. But they were both smart enough to figure out to raise their hands slowly.

Another command spun them around.

"*Mais la*," MacD whispered.

"You can say that again," Raven said.

The angry apparition standing in front of them was half mountain man, half jihadi with matted, shoulder-length hair, a long bushy beard that reached to his chest, and mismatched military surplus camouflaged pants and jacket. A wicked combat blade holstered to his belt, a ragged rucksack, a filthy Kosovo soccer shirt, and muddy Adidas athletic shoes rounded out the crazed ensemble.

He barked again, his AK pointing directly at them.

"I don't speak the lingo, but I get the idea he's not happy we're here."

"If that's who I think it is . . ."

Raven switched to Arabic. "Colonel Piccinini sent us."

The mountain man replied in broken Arabic. "I don't believe you."

"You are Nedim Ramadani. You work for him."

"I don't work for nobody." Ramadani lowered his weapon. "What do you want?"

"Can I open my backpack?" Raven asked, pointing at it with her thumb.

Ramadani raised his weapon back up. "You, not him."

Raven turned to MacD. "I'm grabbing something out of my pack. But don't you move."

"Not until you tell me to, sister."

Raven slowly unshouldered her pack and set it down in the dirt. It wanted to tip over because of its weight and the slope of the hill. She

opened it up and pulled out a red and white carton of Marlboro cigarettes.

Ramadani's semi-toothless smile parted his shaggy beard.

Raven tossed the carton to him. He caught it with one filthy hand
and stuffed it into a big jacket pocket.

"Colonel Piccinini also sent some dried rations, and even a few
salamis for you—and a new phone. He said he's tried to contact you,
but you didn't respond."

"My phone got smashed. Give me that one."

Raven fished the satellite phone out of her pack and walked it over
to him.

Ramadani slung his weapon, then booted up the phone. It
squelched. He nodded. "Good."

"He'd like to hear from you as soon as possible. Make sure you're
okay."

Ramadani snorted. "I'm not his woman."

"He said you saved his life back in the day. I think he's just trying
to return the favor."

"Why did he send you?"

"We need your help."

"What do you want?"

"We're trying to find the Salafists up here on this mountain. More
importantly, we want to find any guns they might have."

Ramadani spit. "I hate those pigs."

"Are they the ones that wrecked your camp?"

"They hunt me all the time. Not a problem. But I got careless. I
won't make that mistake again. Why are you hunting them? Are
you CIA?"

Raven shook her head. "No. We're just trying to find out where
they get their guns from. Maybe stop the supply if we can."

Ramadani pulled off his ruck and transferred the carton of cigarettes into it as Raven pulled out the pack of MREs and salamis. She
handed those to him and he loaded them into his ruck before slinging
it back onto his shoulders.

"Follow me."

37

Ramadani led them another two miles up the steep mountain, nimble and quick as a mountain goat and trailing a cloud of cigarette smoke the entire way. Even MacD, a former Ranger in superb condition, had a hard time keeping up with him.

The Kosovar tossed his cigarette and motioned them into silence as they climbed their way up the last fifty yards on a nearly vertical track, scrambling over rocks and fallen logs. He approached the rocky crest and whispered to Raven. She translated for MacD.

"There are thirteen of them in this band. Their base is a cave on the other side of these rocks on a little plateau. Everything we're looking for is in that cave."

Raven and MacD crept close to the tumbled rocks and peered over the edge. They were facing due north.

There were, indeed, thirteen jihadis gathered around the camp fronting a large cave. Several sat by the fire, others were smoking and cleaning their rifles, and two sat on camp chairs just inside the mouth of the cave, their American M4 carbines perched in their laps.

"Too many to take on," MacD said. Raven translated for Ramadani.

The big Kosovar grunted. "I thought you Americans were tough."

Raven translated.

"Tough. Not stupid," MacD said.

Ramadani smiled and nodded to the two Americans before speeding back down the steep track. Ten yards down he suddenly dashed west into the woods.

"You think our fella chickened out?" MacD whispered as he opened his pack.

"We'll find out soon enough." Raven grabbed her weapon.

Moments later, a grenade exploded in the distance and shots rang out from an AK.

MacD and Raven both grinned.

"I love a man with a plan," MacD said.

They watched eleven of the jihadis race west, away from the camp, following another track into the forest with a collective shout toward the gunfire and explosion. But the two men in the cave only stood, clutching their rifles nervously.

"Like stealing candy," Raven said as she raised her pistol.

MacD gripped his weapon. "I could use me a handful of pralines right about now."

Seconds later, the two jihadis dropped their rifles as they crumbled to the dirt.

MacD and Raven bolted for the cave, each clutching a tranq pistol in their hands. More gunfire and shouting echoed from the west and down the mountain.

Max said they couldn't shoot anybody. He didn't say anything about doping them.

Raven and MacD each grabbed a fallen jihadi by the shirt and dragged them farther inside the cave and out of sight. They didn't bother zip-tying the two men. They'd be out for hours. The Gundogs also grabbed the jihadis' phones and pocketed them before driving deeper inside.

There was enough light from the cave's wide mouth to illumine the few crates stacked inside. Two dozen more were already broken up and stacked like firewood on the far wall. Whatever they contained was long gone.

"Slim pickins over here, *chère*," MacD said.

Raven pulled open one of the crates. "Night vision goggles," she whispered. She took cell phone pictures of the night vision goggles and their serial numbers.

MacD did the same with another crate, snapping a photo of a Claymore mine and the iconic FRONT TOWARD ENEMY embossed on the front.

"But nasty business, this."

The gunfire tapered off. Both operators noticed it.

"We better get a move on," Raven said as she stuffed a pair of goggles into her pack.

MacD cinched up his pack. "Let's vamoose."

Raven dashed for the cave mouth with MacD hot on her heels. As she raced into the light, automatic-rifle fire opened up. Bullets raked the cave wall, but one round hit Raven in the thigh and spun her into the dirt.

MacD grabbed her by the pack straps and dragged her back inside as bullets smashed into the rocks just above his head, the shards of stone clawing at his face like fingernails.

Raven grimaced in pain as she gripped her leg just above the wound.

MacD yanked an Israeli bandage from a pouch on his belt. "Bullet pass through?" He tore open the sanitary wrapper, keeping one eye on the cave entrance.

"Think so," she said through gritted teeth. "Hard to tell."

MacD slipped the wide bandage around her leg, cinched it down, then reversed it through the closure bar before securing it with a twist of the handle. Raven yelped.

"Sit tight."

"Mac!"

One of the jihadi's crept into the cave, his head swiveling.

The Cajun unholstered his Walther 9mm lightning quick and put the red dot in the center of the man's forehead.

But he didn't pull the trigger.

Ramadani's big hand wrapped around the jihadi's mouth, jerked his head back, and slit his throat. The jihadi dropped in a spray of his own blood.

The mountain man wiped his blade on his pants and sheathed it, motioning for MacD and Raven to follow him—quickly.

MacD dashed over to the corpse and snatched his cell phone before hoisting Raven onto his back in a fireman's carry and charging out of the cave.

Ramadani had already disappeared over the crest and out of sight.

MacD heard angry shouts in the distance. He didn't see anything, but they were close. He grunted with effort as he broached the rocky crest with Raven on his back.

Ramadani was waiting for him there, his eyes wide with urgency. The jihadi voices were louder—and closer.

"Let's go," MacD said.

Ramadani turned to leave.

"Wait."

Ramadani stopped in his tracks and turned around.

"Take her—"

"Mac," Raven grunted. "What are you doing?"

"Too many of them."

"Put me down. I can shoot—"

MacD ignored her as he shifted Raven from off his back and onto Ramadani's shoulder like a sack of Idaho potatoes.

The two men exchanged a look.

"Go," MacD said.

Ramadani bounded down the trail with the wounded Raven bouncing on his shoulder and wincing with every jarring step.

MacD dropped his pack and pulled out the Claymore he'd stolen for evidence. He backed down the mountain a few feet and planted it with FRONT TOWARD ENEMY pointing back up the narrow trail. He covered the mine with leaves, stretched the trip wire across the path, and jackrabbited down the mountain with the shouts of the Salafists cresting the hill high above him.

Automatic-rifle fire cracked behind him and bullets splintered the trees as he ran past them.

WHOOMP!

A dozen screams pierced the mountain air as several hundred steel balls tore through flesh and bone.

Ten minutes later, Raven was stretched out on the ground as MacD properly dressed her wound. The bullet had passed through cleanly without shattering bone or cutting arteries.

Ramadani stood watchful guard over them with a smoldering Marlboro draped on his lips, his AK aimed back up the mountain. It was only a precaution. There were no more pursuers.

"I thought we were under orders not to kill anybody," Raven finally said.

"Max didn't saying nothing about letting them blow themselves up with their own kit. I just obliged 'em."

MacD helped Raven to her unsteady feet. She turned to thank the Kosovar mountain man for his help.

But he was already gone.

38

When the plane landed the night before, the only lights on the island were on the airstrip and in the two-story cement-block control "tower" that guided them in.

Waiting for a bus to pick them up from the tarmac, the only thing
Juan and Linc could discern about the place in the harsh glare of the
runway lights was the tang of salt in the air and the sound of the crashing ocean waves somewhere out in the dark.

The bus delivered them to the barracks, a steel-reinforced tent with
cots. A second tent offered private showers and toilet facilities and a
third was a temporary mess hall. Just after debarking they were offered self-serve sandwiches, bottled waters, and decaf coffee. They
were then issued two sets of camouflage fatigues, underclothes, socks,
and boots before they hit their racks. Everything was tagged with their
names and sized according to their applications.

The next morning they were awakened at four-thirty a.m. local by
Drăguş banging trash can lids, just like in boot camp.

They hit the showers first. Juan was wearing one of Kevin Nixon's
lifelike artificial legs complete with hair and tats. Perfectly fitted with
a 3D template of Juan's stump, the artificial leg was able to attach to
his upper leg seamlessly. Better still, it was so perfectly conformed to

Juan's leg that it created a powerful suction at the connection that was strong enough to walk on without the need for extra support. Juan's journey to the private shower and back drew no attention. He secretly attached the straps necessary for combat support minutes later when he went to the latrine.

After showers, the men were marched to the mess tent, where they devoured a hearty breakfast of steak, bacon, eggs, bread, coffee, and fruit in short order.

They assembled outside and stood waiting beneath a low but warming sun. Juan and Linc caught a glimpse of their secret destination. Beyond the tarmac and temporary shelters there was what appeared to be a newly constructed three-story concrete building complex. The entire compound was within sight of the ocean. Opposite them was a vast swath of jungle.

Juan guessed the island was several miles in dimension, but standing down on the flat it was impossible to be more precise. In the distance he could just make out a jagged skyline of human construct. Perched in the middle of the mass of foliage was what appeared to be a small mountain. But further observation suggested an abandoned city of towering buildings and apartments haphazardly jammed together. Even from this distance they appeared to be overgrown with climbing vines and foliage.

A towering, bearded figure emerged out of the temporary buildings and marched toward them with a scowling swagger. He wore the same camouflage uniform as they did. The large Glock 17 holstered on his hip wasn't nearly as intimidating as the force of his character or the smoldering fire in his dark eyes.

Drăguş raced out to meet him with a sharp salute, then fell in beside him. They marched in unison, stopping directly in front of the assembled men.

"Gentlemen, my name is Captain Gustavo Plata. Welcome to our training facility. I am your commander for both the training and the mission. You all know my lieutenant, Florin Drăguş."

Drăguş nodded curtly.

Cabrillo noted Plata's heavy Spanish accent. Given his size, the dark-haired, dark-eyed Hispanic merc was descended from Northern European stock.

"We have studied all of your service jackets and know your records well. There is no man here who isn't supremely qualified to serve on this mission, which is why you are being so well compensated by our mutual employer. Be assured my background is equal to yours. I served with Guatemala's special forces unit, the Kaibiles."

Juan and Linc stood apart from each other, but stole a furtive glance. The Kaibiles were, indeed, an elite special forces unit, but they were infamous for their extreme brutality, including the rape and murder of Indigenous civilians.

"After I was dismissed from service for performing my duties with unbounded enthusiasms"—Plata paused, smiling—"I found more profitable opportunities in the private sector."

Plata's little joke elicited a few laughs. The band of cutthroat fugitives were all cut from the same cloth.

"We have a heavy training schedule ahead of us. We want to over prepare for what will likely be an underwhelming assignment. But like the snipers say, 'Aim small, miss small.' Am I correct, Mr. Davis?"

"You are, indeed, sir," Linc said.

"Questions?" Drăguş asked.

"Where exactly are we?" Mangin asked. He was a former French marine commando.

"In the middle of nowhere," Drăguş began. "But more precisely, you are standing on what the locals called the Island of Sorrows."

"I can see why," Mangin joked, pointing at the abandoned city in the distance.

Plata turned around and faced the ruins.

"It was a profitable coal mine before the war, until the Japanese turned it into a mining colony for slaves and prisoners of war where many died. There are two known mass graves on the island, and perhaps more. An Australian firm resurrected the mine after the war and hired the surviving locals at slave wages until it was finally exhausted in the late 1960s. Our employer purchased the island several years ago. It is now a training facility.

"Any other questions?" Plata asked.

There were none.

"*Vámanos!*"

★

Plata marched the men into a classroom in the tented training complex. It was little more than a collection of folding chairs and tables along with a giant whiteboard. Juan and Linc sat apart, not wanting to draw attention to themselves.

"Let's talk briefly about small-unit tactics," Plata began. He delivered a brief lecture on the well-known concept of cover-and-move, illustrating his points on the board. His black and red dry-erase markers squeaked as he scribbled X's, O's, and arrows across the white surface like a soccer coach reviewing plays at halftime. He flipped the board over and then covered room-clearing operations.

"Questions?"

Heads shook. It was all familiar stuff to the room full of professional soldiers.

Plata handed Drăguș the markers. The bearded lieutenant drew a big oval on the board and laid out a crude diagram of the island.

Juan's estimate of its size was fairly accurate. The irregularly shaped island was approximately nine miles long and six miles wide. About twenty-five percent of it was occupied by the city-mine.

"We have developed four training modules. The first is a shoot house located on the back of this compound. After that, we'll take advantage of the island's terrain for some more intense exercises."

Juan couldn't figure out what the Vendor's angle was in this. He was beginning to think he and Linc really were on a wild-goose chase. They were still only a couple of days into it. Without any other leads on the Vendor, there was no reason not to give it a few more.

"Sounds quite involved for a protection assignment," the Englishman said.

"Our primary duty will be standing guard for long hours, and riding in convoys as backup for the small national security service we are reinforcing."

"Which national security service?" one of the Polish twins asked.

"I haven't been told that yet. It doesn't matter." Plata pointed at the Englishman. "But to answer your concern, we want to raise our training tempo. We need to be prepared in the event our VIP protection turns into a hostage rescue. You have a problem with that?"

"No, sir. I rather enjoy the prospect of mixing it up."

"Excellent. Anyone else?"

There was no response.

"These are all timed exercises," Plata said. "I'm looking for aggression, speed, and precision. Three of you will be promoted to squad leader during the actual assignment based upon these assessments. That promotion includes a bump in pay."

The idea of competition caught the attention of the room full of alpha males, but the prospect of more money was even more tantalizing to the gun-for-hire mercs.

"So, shall we see what you men are made of?" Plata asked.

"Let's do this!" McGuire shouted. The other mercs cheered as they leaped to their feet in a rush of clattering chairs.

Plata smiled. "Follow me."

39

After a short calisthenics warm-up, Lieutenant Drăguş organized the unit into six two-man squads. Juan and Linc were paired in the same unit. In addition to a superlative combat record, the *Oregon*'s intel unit had put subtle but significant "spotter" references in Juan's service jacket hoping this would get him joined with Linc's advanced sniper qualifications. The ruse worked.

Drăguş then led the teams to the armory, where they were handed their requested weapons.

Juan and Linc both put in for guns that were known to have been in the Afghani arsenals, hoping to make a Vendor connection. Linc was handed a Barrett .50-caliber sniper rifle and a 9mm Glock 17 like Plata's.

Juan was handed weapons used by his fictional character, a member of Mexico's *Fuerzas Especiales*. He was handed an H&K UMP chambered in 9mm along with a Glock 19. He was also given a tactical pack containing his preferred Leupold Mark 4 tactical spotting scope, a wind meter, ballistic calculator, and laser range finder.

Unable to snap any pictures, both *Oregon* crewmen knew to memorize the serial numbers on their respective weapons. They would later run them against the known serial numbers in the Afghani arsenals to see if the Vendor had access to other weapons sources. Under the circumstances, it was the best they could do.

Once everyone received and inspected their weapons, Plata marched Linc and Juan over to an improvised long-distance range, where a man-sized steel target was set up at one thousand yards. Drăguş took the other men over to a different gun range for practice.

Linc and Juan played their roles to a tee, pretending to try and assess each other's skill sets, and familiarize themselves with each other's equipment. After a few moments of these adjustments, they got down to business.

Linc set up the Barrett on its tripod and loaded the magazine with the giant .50-cal shells, while Juan deployed the range finder. "Nine hundred ninety-seven point eight yards," he called out as he entered the data into the ballistic calculator. Linc called out the match grade bullet weight and speed printed on the box, and Juan entered those numbers as well.

Cabrillo then held up the advanced wind meter, which gave him wind speed, humidity, and temperature, and then loaded those numbers into the ballistic calculator. He handed the device over to Linc so he could set up his Horus TREMOR3 rifle scope properly while Juan pulled out his spotting scope. Both men inserted their ear protection and set their eyes to their respective eyepieces.

"Ready?" Juan asked.

"Ready," Linc replied.

Linc slowed his breathing to near perfect stillness, dropping his heart rate to hibernating-bear levels, before he gently squeezed the trigger. The big rifle erupted with a deafening roar.

Just 1.17 seconds later, the heavy steel plate shuddered and rang as the armor-piercing bullet plowed through it.

"Hit," Juan said calmly.

Linc racked the bolt, ejecting the spent shell, and loaded another. He fired again.

The steel rang like a church bell.

"Hit."

Juan double-checked the wind speed. It had risen and shifted directions. He entered the new data into the ballistic calculator, but Linc hardly needed it.

Three more ringing hits.

Plata whistled. "I think you understated your service record, amigo. Those five hits all fit within the span of my hand. Incredible."

"You need a new target," Juan said. Linc had punched a giant hole in the center of the steel silhouette.

"You two will make a good team," Plata said. "Secure your gear. It's time for the next phase."

★

Plata and Drăguş marched the mercenaries to the shoot house. The two commanders showed them an example of the range-standard "enemy" and "hostage" colored cardboard targets the unit would encounter. Each soldier was fitted with a comms headset and a GoPro camera. Plata held a portable video monitor that received live signals from the cameras so he could analyze and comment during the exercise.

It was decided to send the men in four at a time for the simulated hostage rescue.

"And just a reminder, gentlemen," Plata said. "These are live-fire exercises. You lose points if you shoot each other."

The men laughed at the gallows humor, but the point was made.

Plata blew a whistle and the first team raced into the building.

Over the next hour, all twelve men had run the course three times, their high skill sets on display. Only one hostage was accidentally shot in the first round and none in the other rounds. Linc was only allowed to use his pistol. At nearly thirty pounds and almost six feet long, the Barrett M107A1 sniper rifle was the antithesis of a close-quarters combat weapon. Despite the handicap of the smaller weapon, Linc achieved the third-highest number of total enemy kills.

"Well done, gentlemen," Plata announced over a loudspeaker. "You all live up to your reputations. Now it's time for the real thing."

Plata and Drăguş marched the team through three miles of jungle until they reached the outskirts of the abandoned city-mine in the center of the island. They stood on one of its hard-packed streets. There was no glass in the windows, the cement was eroded and weather-pitted, boards were rotted, and the sheet metal rusted. Some of the buildings were several stories tall. Most were not. The eastern edge of the "city" ended in a long, fragmenting pier that reached out into a small harbor.

A shared uneasiness rattled the hardened mercenaries. The city looked like a postapocalyptic nightmare—an abandoned hive of human misery where even ghosts refused to live.

"Same drill, different location," Drăguş said. "Only this time, you all work together."

"Why this place?" the Russian asked.

"Our employer suggested these ruins are not unlike the urban area we will be working in. Besides, it's more challenging than the shoot house. Yes?"

The Russian nodded. "*Da.*"

"Just to put you all on notice," Plata said. "The two-man squad with the highest number of kills and lowest hostage deaths at the end of the training will receive a special reward."

Drăguş pointed at Linc. "Davis? You and Mendoza find a sniper's hide and take care of business."

"Will do." Linc glanced at Juan and the two men dashed into the tallest building across the crumbling street.

Plata blew a whistle and the ten other men raced away.

40

The first timed city training module went about as Juan expected given the lack of unit cohesion. Four of the six "hostages" were killed and five enemy targets weren't even located. After the targets were repositioned, Plata ran a second timed run. Both numbers were halved—a good improvement. On the third attempt, no hostages died and all of the enemy targets were found and taken out before the timer alarmed. The team was definitely gelling together.

Juan and Linc held up their end. Linc scored several kills with his big .50-cal Barrett rifle, assisted by Juan's sharp eyes and the crystal clear glass on his spotter's scope.

After a short food and water break, the team marched into the jungle for the next cover-and-move module. Three enemy targets high in the trees were missed on the first go, but no hostages were killed. A second try took out all enemy targets and no hostages—a phenomenal result. Plata praised them to high heaven. The squads moved with precision and speed, their combat skills reflecting their high levels of training and experience. Plata and Drăguș offered a few helpful comments and suggestions, but canceled the third run.

Plata checked his watch. "It's getting late."

The tired men exhaled a collective sigh of relief. It had been a long day.

The big Guatemalan smiled. "Time to head to the mines."

An audible groan rippled through the team.

"And be sure to watch your step down there," Drăguş said. "It could be your last."

Plata led the way into the mouth of the coal mine. The shafts got shorter and narrower, the air cooler, the farther down they went.

They passed abandoned carts, shovels, picks, and other mining gear. The only lights they had were attached to their rifles. The chances of ricochets and "blue-on-blue" accidents in the dangerously enclosed and confined spaces were enormous. To avoid such a catastrophe, Plata swapped out all of their personal weapons for specialized M4 carbines and Glock 17 pistols designed to fire Simunition ammo— essentially, regular gunpowder cartridges that fired nonlethal "paint-ball" rounds, but with real-world recoil effects.

Walking in a near crouch beneath the solid ceiling of rock above their heads, they finally reached their staging point and halted. Juan calculated they were down six hundred feet at least. The silence at the moment they stopped was absolute—the kind of silence you only heard in a forest blanketed by heavy snow, he thought. There were six different branch tunnels leading off in several directions.

One of the far walls was partially damp. It was also notably cooler, even cold. No doubt they were now below the surface of the surrounding ocean.

Juan glanced over to a nearby side tunnel. The dark was total—a complete and utter absence of any kind of light. Having spent years in deep water, Juan wasn't nearly as affected by the prospect of being six hundred feet below the surface. But judging by the shallow breathing and constant upward glances of several others, he assumed their vivid imaginations suffered the terror of thousands of tons of rock crashing down on them at any moment.

For Juan it wasn't the prospect of a violent death as much as it was the idea of one's pulverized remains never being found—utterly disappeared from the face of the earth. The line from a mournful Patty Loveless ballad suddenly echoed in his head. *"And you spend your life diggin' coal from the bottom of your grave."*

"Gentlemen, welcome to the gates of hell," Plata began. A few drops of water fell from the ceiling.

"You know the setup. Kill the enemies, not the hostages." He hit the timer on his watch. "Now we'll see what you're really made of."

They ran two timed runs, racing off into the separate tunnels without much success. The beams of their swinging gun lights slashed through clouds of choking coal dust and crumbling rock that spattered their bump helmets. Fatigue and fear slowed their steps and dulled their vision. Targets were wedged in alcoves, hidden behind wood supports, or standing on the other side of sudden bends in the tunnels. Most of them remained untouched.

Linc had never felt so cramped and confined in a combat scenario, and even Juan began to sense the suffocating terror of claustrophobia wrapping its icy fingers around his heart.

Plata launched a third and final assault, but it was clear before it began it would fare no better. The four squads had decided to proceed down an unexplored tunnel together in single file, partly because it was wider and taller than the others, partly because they sought the unspoken comfort of other bodies nearby. Mangin, the Frenchman, took the point; Juan and Linc were next in line. The three men were far ahead of the others, whose spirits flagged with each step.

After what seemed like an eternity, Plata blew a shrill whistle in the far distance behind them. The exercise was over. The twelve-man team turned wordlessly on its collective heel and quick-stepped its way back up to the staging point.

Linc could barely make out the light of the man ahead of him. Juan was right behind his friend.

"You okay up there, big man?" Juan whispered.

"Hope they have a hot tub back at camp. Or maybe an ice tub. Maybe both. My back is killing me."

"Maybe champagne and foie gras, too."

The sound of cracking rock behind them sent shudders down their spines. They all feared a tunnel collapse more than anything.

But instead of running, Juan and Linc froze in their tracks. Juan whipped around. He flashed his gun light backward.

Mangin was gone.

Juan and Linc looked at each other, then back up the tunnel toward the surface. Everything in Juan wanted to run before disaster buried them alive. Only sheer force of will turned him around.

Juan rushed back, his central nervous system on fire and on high alert. Ten steps back he saw the hole that had opened up and swallowed the Frenchman. He glanced down at the ground beneath his boots, wondering if it was about to give way as well. He threw up a hand behind him.

"Stay back."

"What's the play?" Linc asked.

Juan remembered a large coil of rope they had passed on the way down. He pushed past Linc, ran ahead and grabbed it, and jogged back a minute later. He tied one end to his waist and tossed the rest to Linc.

Juan edged toward the gaping hole as Linc secured the line around his body and in his massive hands.

"Easy, boss."

"Don't you know it."

Juan glanced over the lip of the hole. Down below, the Frenchman lay unconscious on the floor of another tunnel, face down in a puddle of water, his body illumined by his weapon light.

Juan looked back at Linc. *Let's do it.*

Linc nodded in agreement.

"How far down?" the big African American said.

"Twelve, maybe thirteen feet. We need to hurry."

Juan stepped over the crumbling edge and lowered down, hoping he wasn't too late.

★

Twenty minutes later, Plata and Drăguş appeared out of the gloom, huffing with exhaustion. The big Guatemalan was about to cuss a blue streak at the laggards for holding everyone up until he saw Juan and Linc marching toward the surface with the body of the muddied, unconscious man stretched between them.

The five men made their way back up to the staging area. The two Poles pulled out a fabric stretcher and loaded the Frenchman onto it. Over the course of the next half hour, several men took turns ferrying him back up to the surface.

It terms of combat performance the entire exercise was a bust. But in terms of unit cohesion, Plata couldn't have planned it any better. As far as he was concerned, they were ready.

McGuire had warned Plata earlier about the big Black American fighter. The cagey Irishman smelled something fishy about him on the trip from the airport. But Davis and the Mexican had proven their mettle today both in combat and in the rescue of the former French commando.

Come to think of it, Plata mused, the selfless act was quite unusual given the sordid histories of both men.

Perhaps McGuire was on to something after all.

41

Steve Gilreath sat at the *Oregon*'s helm station in the op center, its cool confines dimly lit by the blue glow of LED monitor lights. He was the only one in the room. Rimsky-Korsakov's *Capriccio Espagnol* played softly on the overhead speakers. The giant LED screens wrapping around the room were as dark as the night engulfing the ship. The only thing they displayed were a few distant ship lights on the far horizon and the blanket of stars above.

It was two a.m. and he was sipping his third cup of coffee. The retired tin can driver served on the overnight watch or whenever Eric Stone or Linda Ross were unavailable. When the ship was in port or anchored, anyone could stand watch while the rest of the crew slept, but not while at sea, and especially at high speed. The *Oregon* had been racing for Kuala Lumpur over the last three days in order to provide backup to Juan and Linc. It was a long way from the Gulf of Oman to Malaysia.

The *Oregon*'s magnetohydrodynamic engines were spinning like Swiss clockwork and the speed log held a constant forty knots—an incredible feat for a ship as large as theirs. Of course, the *Oregon* was capable of even faster speeds, but the sight of a 590-foot break-bulk carrier rooster-tailing through the water like a Jet Ski drew too much unwanted attention.

Just as Gilreath brought the steaming cup of brew to his lips, a sudden thud rang the ship's hull like Big Ben, sending a shudder through the deck and spilling his coffee onto his shirt.

Collision alarms screamed. Gilreath smashed the ALL STOP button on his console, killing the engines. Just as he put his ceramic mug aside, Max came storming bleary-eyed and barefoot into the op center wearing a pair of flannel pajama bottoms and a rumpled T-shirt emblazoned with the "Budweiser" SEAL trident, an homage to his son, who recently graduated from there.

"Status!" Max bellowed as he raced over to the engineering station.

Gilreath killed the alarm. "We hit something—I just don't know what." He dashed over to the Kirk Chair and punched a button on the console, throwing the external cameras into night vision mode.

"Possible hull damage," Max said as he scrolled through his sensor screens.

Eric raced into the op center and Mark Murphy came in right behind him. Both men were disheveled and red-eyed, wearing whatever clothes they could pull on in a hurry. In Murph's case, straight out of his dirty laundry basket.

Gilreath scanned the full aft monitors, but saw nothing. He turned to the starboard/stern camera as Eric took over the helm and Murphy ran to the sonar and radar stations.

Linda Ross raced into the room, too.

"What did we hit?" she asked. "A sub?"

"Not sure yet," Max said from his station.

"There!" Gilreath said.

Max and Linda dashed over to him. A mostly submerged and badly dented yellow shipping container bobbed in the water some three hundred yards behind the *Oregon*.

"It didn't show on radar," Gilreath offered. He didn't need to. The radar was designed to pick up other ships on the water, not objects just below the surface.

Callie padded unnoticed into the room, still yawning.

Max picked up the phone and called down to the engine room.

Other than punching a hole through the hull and sinking the vessel, damaging the engines was the next worst possibility.

A sleepy voice picked up. Max asked for a status report.

"Engines check . . . all clear. No damage, far as I can tell. Nozzles are rotating one hundred percent, too."

"We dodged a bullet, then."

"Oh, we got hit all right," Murph offered. "We just don't know where it hit exactly."

"We need to put divers in the water and inspect the hull," Max said.

"I'll make the call." Linda picked up another phone.

"What about using my drone instead?" Callie offered.

Everyone turned around, not realizing she was standing there.

"I'd like to get as many human eyes on the problem as possible," Max said. "It'll probably be faster, too."

"But also more dangerous—and incredibly dark. And it's going to take time to get your people in the water. I can have the drone on duty in fifteen minutes. It's already powered up and hooked to a camera. Murph can help me feed the video signal into your system."

"No problemo," Murph said.

"I can set it to automatic and make sure we cover every square inch with the video recorder for later analysis."

"No offense," Max said, "but I prefer human judgment on this one. The more eyes, the better."

"Why not do both?" Linda asked. "Let her put the drone in the water now and the divers can join in as soon as they can and conduct a closer investigation."

Max rubbed his nearly bald head. "Why didn't I think of that?"

"You just haven't had your coffee yet," Linda said.

"Yeah, that's it. Okay, Callie. Get after it."

Callie beamed. "You got it."

★

Twenty-four minutes after the *Spook Fish*'s drone hit the water, its video camera displayed a wrecked stabilizer fin, mostly torn away.

There appeared to be no other damage to the hull. The divers confirmed the drone's damage assessment with their own visual inspection they completed an hour later.

Maurice, the *Oregon*'s dapper but aged steward, arrived at the op center with a dining cart loaded with Danishes, churros—and gallons of fresh coffee.

"The galley is whipping up a hearty breakfast for you all. Until then, enjoy this sugary repast," Maurice said in his cultured English accent. Despite the early-morning hour, and unlike the rest of the crew, the Englishman arrived in sharply creased black slacks and a crisp white shirt, his shoes buffed to a high gloss.

Max snatched up a churro and took a bite, spilling sugar and cinnamon onto his T-shirt. He washed it down with a slurp of black joe.

As Linda poured herself a cup of hot water for tea, she said to Max, "You're asking yourself, do we press on with the wrecked fin so we can get to Juan and Linc? Or do we wait and affect repairs?"

Max took another bite. "If we press on, we can't make good speed without that stabilizer fin repaired. But it's going to cost us at least three hours to fix it."

"We can always do that later," Linda offered. "But no telling when we might need to put the pedal to the metal. We can't achieve maximum speed without that stabilizer fin in place."

"Truth is, we don't even know where they are. Their trackers are still offline and they haven't contacted us. We're in a big hurry, but we don't know where we're going exactly. I think we need to fix it."

"Agreed."

Callie stepped over. "Sorry to butt in. I'd like to help with the repairs. Underwater salvage is how I got my feet wet in this business—eh, sorry about the pun."

"It would be another good test for the *Spook Fish*," Linda said. "I saw what it could do on that Airbus."

"You should join me," Callie said to Max. "Get a firsthand view of what she's capable of."

"I'll take you up on that offer. But I still want a couple of diver-welders on hand in case we run into any problems."

"I'll make the arrangements," Linda said.

Callie flashed her surfer-girl smile. "And I'll prep the *Spook Fish*."

The two women headed for the door.

Max shoved the rest of the churro into his piehole and munched away, staring at the giant port wall screens and the purpling light promising another sunrise.

His friends were out there, somewhere.

He hoped they could see the sunrise, too.

42

The barren, rocky island was littered with a couple of abandoned fishing villages and a crumbling pier that had once serviced the now rusted wreck of an ancient cannery. Pau Rangi, despite its dystopian appearance, bore the Maori name for "paradise." But it was hell that the Vendor was planning to unleash.

The private island had been purchased in the 1970s by a fictitious real estate corporation his family had controlled for decades—the same one that had acquired the Island of Sorrows.

The Vendor was deep in the bowels of the volcanic island in a lab inside one of several caves beneath the surface. He stood on the other side of thick glass protecting him from the invisible cloud of death swirling inside the warehouse-sized and climate-controlled test chamber. Neurotoxins were a relatively old technology and nearly all of them would kill in an enclosed space. The Vendor had bigger plans.

A system of computer-controlled fans, heaters, and overhead misters were deployed in the test chamber, set to duplicate the conditions at a very specific geographic location: Guam. The Pacific island's climate patterns had been perfectly mimicked on a day-to-day basis for the last month. Today's test had been the best so far.

The Vendor counted seven corpses. Four of those men had died nearly instantly; the other three took several minutes longer. Fifteen minutes after the release of the neurotoxin, three survivors were still breathing, but they were on the ground, convulsing. They would expire soon.

When the Indonesian pirates landed on Pau Rangi last week, the Vendor had no doubt they were a gift from his ancestors. After all, his grandfather had conceived of the original plan. The fact he was dead was no impediment to his interest in its success. Today's test in realistic conditions confirmed it.

It was one thing to kill rodents, small animals, or even captured pirates in a controlled environment. But the Vendor had a much larger target in mind, in the form of the island of Guam. It was America's most important naval base in the South Pacific and home to thousands of civilian and military personnel. His plan had been years in the making and he was leaving nothing to chance. He knew an attack wouldn't take place in ideal experimental conditions. He needed to be certain it would succeed in the real world. Today's test was his final proof of concept.

"How soon before sufficient quantities will be produced?"

"Two weeks, at most," the scientist said. He was a German national heading up a small international team of researchers, each with a criminal history and hunted by their respective governments.

"You have exactly one hundred sixty-eight hours until launch."

"What happened to our original timeline?"

"It has been changed."

The Vendor had known for months that the Americans were bringing an advanced network of air and missile defenses online to protect its most important base in the region. But his intelligence sources indicated the air defense network launch date had been accelerated considerably. Within eight days, Guam would have the most impenetrable airspace in the world. If the Vendor hoped to carry out his plan, he needed to make his attack before then.

"I can't change the laws of physics, sir. It would take a miracle."

"I believe in miracles."

"I can't. I'm a man of science."

"Then put your faith in the three-million-dollar bonus I will pay to you personally, along with the half-million-dollar bonus to each of your team members, if the deadline is met."

The German smiled. "Well, then. Hallelujah!"

The Vendor darkened. "And carefully consider the agonizing consequences if you fail."

43

MALAYSIA

The *Oregon*'s tilt-rotor circled five hundred feet above the grassy airstrip and its steel-roofed lean-to.

"Looks clear to me," Linda Ross said over the comms. "Let's set her down."

"You got it."

Ross sat in the copilot's chair. Eddie Seng was in the cabin. Both were kitted up with 9mm MP5s and pistols in case they ran into trouble, but nobody was down there.

After replacing the damaged stabilizer fin, the *Oregon* finally made her way to the coast of Malaysia. Lacking any solid clues to where Linc and Juan might be, they were now grasping at straws.

Gomez Adams put the AW tilt-rotor's wheels down on the airstrip with characteristic finesse and throttled back the rotors, keeping them warm and ready for a quick takeoff.

"Better get a move on," Gomez said. "Malaysian air traffic control will alert the authorities if we're not airborne in the next five minutes."

"Roger that," Linda said.

She and Eddie hit the grass running. A quick scan of the lean-to was fruitless. The place had been perfectly policed. But it was still worth the effort.

As soon as Juan's and Linc's trackers disappeared from the

Oregon's screens, Murphy and Stone began their searches. Dr. Huxley had implanted a new tracker on Juan's other hip after his self-directed surgery on the Vendor's automated plane. With both trackers in place, it was easy enough to follow both men on their different routes to Kuala Lumpur International Airport following the Vendor's dark web travel instructions.

After hacking into the airport's security camera system, both Linc and Juan were tracked on their separate journeys from the moment they deplaned to their arrival curbside. Both men had been picked up by the same white Daihatsu van and both had been delivered to the same location, albeit at different times of the day according to their trackers.

Murph and Eddie both assumed a Google Earth search would reveal the details of the location, but a cloud formation had covered the area the day the satellite image was taken and uploaded to the server. Had the airstrip been revealed at that time, it would have been easy to try and connect the time the trackers disappeared with any departing flights from the area. Once those flights were determined, it should have been a simple matter to find the flight logs and their final destinations.

Undeterred, Murph and Stone initiated a search for flights at the time the trackers disappeared, but they came up short. That either meant the flight hadn't been officially logged or a plane wasn't involved. If there was no airfield, that would definitely suggest the latter—hence today's little excursion.

"Seen enough?" Eddie asked. He saw the concern in Linda's face. Juan and Linc had been missing without a trace for days and hadn't reached out to them. They were both hoping this brief hop would have provided at least a clue as to their whereabouts, but no such luck.

"Yeah. Let's get back to the barn."

Moments later, the tilt-rotor lifted off and rocketed for the coast.

44

Raven lay elevated in one of the *Oregon*'s clinic beds. She wore a pair of surgical shorts that exposed her muscled leg recently re-bandaged by Dr. Huxley. An antibiotic IV drip snaked into her jacked arm. She was as powerfully built as she was beautiful, but at the moment, she was in need of serious recovery.

MacD had gotten her back to the Film City base medical unit thanks to Colonel Piccinini's intervention. The base doctors conducted a full examination, then properly cleaned and sutured the bullet wound. After twenty-four hours of medication, rest, and observation, MacD and Raven boarded the Corporation's Gulfstream. They landed in Kuala Lumpur and were choppered back to the *Oregon* on the tilt-rotor.

Dr. Huxley insisted on her own thorough examination of the wound's progress and personally handled changing the dressing twice per day. The primary concern at the moment was infection. The prognosis was good.

Huxley was already arranging a physical therapy schedule for Raven as soon as she was able to participate. Until she was ready for PT, Raven was ordered to stay off her feet. She complied under duress, but insisted she was still on the job.

Huxley appreciated her devotion to duty, which was why she

allowed the Kosovo after-action report to happen in Raven's recovery room.

"We examined the photos that you and MacD forwarded to us," Murph began. "The serial numbers are all from stocks of weapons we sent to Afghanistan."

"So are the night vision goggles you picked up," Eric added. "We're still trying to crack the encryption on those phones you guys snagged. We might get Vendor confirmation from one of them."

"Still no news on Juan and Linc?" MacD asked.

"Not yet."

"What are we doing to find them?" Raven asked.

"There's not much we can do that we haven't already done. Hopefully we'll catch a break when Murph and Eric crack those phones. Until then, we sit tight, and we wait."

"I can't stand waiting," Raven said. "It's the hardest part of this job."

Murph smiled. "Said the woman with the bullet hole in her leg."

"Do you think the thing jamming their transponders is also jamming Juan's satellite phone?" MacD asked.

"That's the theory," Linda said.

She didn't want to say that what she really feared was that Juan and Linc had both been discovered and were imprisoned.

Or possibly dead.

★

THE ISLAND OF SORROWS
THE CELEBES SEA

Thanks to his excellent physical conditioning, the Frenchman recovered quickly from his fall. He had suffered mostly contusions, scrapes, and a mild concussion, which he shrugged off with a dismissive wave of his hand and a couple of Tylenols. Cleared for duty by the team's Turkish medic, the Frenchman eagerly rejoined the squad for the next day's drills—repetitions of the city and jungle exercises. It had gone far better than Plata could have planned.

He believed it was because of the shared bonding experience of rescuing the injured French commando. As a result, the team performed in absolute synchrony, like a murmuration of starlings in the evening sky. Each man was perfectly attuned to his partner, making precise, split-second decisions in a constant ebb and flow of movement over, under, and around any obstacle to reach their targets.

Plata knew their records well. These were dangerous and greedy men with no loyalties to any state, ideology, or religion. But they were soldiers, too, born and bred for war. Instinctively, they had submitted their individual wills to the collective whole for the sake of survival.

Outwardly, they shared the rare affection of men who risked life and limb in mortal combat, their fates intertwined by their mutual dependence upon each other's skill in war. They were a band of cutthroats and brigands, surely, but a brotherhood nonetheless.

For safety's sake, Plata canceled another mine operation. If his employer complained, so be it. He refused to show up to the assignment with less than a full contingent of these remarkable soldiers to accomplish his mission, whatever it might be.

Something told him he'd need every one of them if he hoped to survive.

45

Plata and Drăguş marched the men back to their barracks. They halted outside and Plata addressed them.

"Gentlemen, today's exercises couldn't have gone any better. You are as fine a fighting force as I have ever seen. I pity any *tonto* that dares challenge us. I would be proud to lead you into combat should we ever get the chance."

The hardened warriors beamed with quiet pride. Somewhere back in time before they had chosen the dark and twisted path of killing for money, each of these men had been a young recruit who proved himself worthy of his uniform and his nation. For a brief moment, they were those young men again.

"As a first reward for your extraordinary efforts, I'm canceling tomorrow's training exercises. Get some rest."

"Huzzah!" the Brit shouted. The rest of the men cheered.

"We'll pick up training the day after tomorrow and finish out at the end of the week. We'll be shipping out after that."

"Which squad scored the highest?" McGuire asked.

Drăguş pulled up his tablet. "It was close. But one squad was the clear winner."

He read aloud the names of Osipenko and Al-Mawas, the ex-Wagner Russian and the Syrian.

"Five thousand in Bitcoin has already been added to each of your accounts. Congratulations." He tucked the tablet under his arm and clapped. There were a few grumblings among the squads that thought they had won, but even they joined in the clapping.

"And the three squad leaders?"

"Osipenko, Al-Mawas, of course. And . . . McGuire."

"That's a bit of all right," McGuire said, smiling. His German squad mate slapped him on the back.

"How about telling us where we're going?" the Nigerian asked.

"*No tengo la menor idea*," Plata said. "I'm like you. I'm in the dark. But I'm also a soldier, and paid well. It doesn't matter. We go wherever we are sent. Anything else?"

"You said there was a first reward. That means there's a second," Linc said.

Drăguș grinned ear to ear.

"First we clean our weapons, then we hit the showers. And after that? Well, tonight we're going to party!"

The mercs roared like Vikings with lusty delight.

★

In the hustle and bustle of crowded showers, getting dressed, and squared away, Juan and Linc managed to share a few carefully whispered words out of earshot.

"I know a fat man who's probably worried," Linc said.

"These guys have been on me like ticks. Maybe tomorrow." Cabrillo was referring to his miniature satellite phone stashed in his combat leg. "But it's not a one-way street."

Linc knew he was referring to their embedded trackers. The *Oregon* had eyes on them.

"You think maybe our other friend will show up soon?" They still hadn't seen the Vendor. In fact, his name hadn't been mentioned at all.

"Hope so."

"And if he doesn't?"

"We play it by ear, one day at a time."

A dinner bell rang outside.

Linc smiled. "Finally. I'm starving."

★

Plata's cooks had gone all-out. One of them sliced steaming hot pieces from the giant pig still crackling on the spit. Another tended a roasting lamb for the two nominal Muslims in their midst. The air was scented with the smoky sweetness of the roasted flesh.

Another cook served up fresh lobster out of boiling pots along with coconut shells brimming with melted butter. A third was grilling thick filets of tuna. A long table was festooned with papayas, guavas, mangoes, and other tropical delights. But it was the bartender offering copious amounts of whiskey, vodka, rum, champagne, and Turkish raki that was the real hit.

Plata had wisely secured all of the weapons before the drinking began. He also announced he would be closing the bar early. The unintended consequence was that everybody who wanted to get drunk simply drank more, faster. Even Plata and Drăguş got hammered.

A British Invasion soundtrack had been roaring out of a portable player all night. The Rolling Stones were currently belting out "(I Can't Get No) Satisfaction." Coarse laughter and friendly goading burbled up between music tracks accompanied by the vivid telling of bawdy jokes and crazy war stories.

Linc and Juan played along with the drunken revelry but were careful not to overindulge. The Frenchman staggered up to the two of them, four sheets to the wind, an empty glass in his hand.

"I know it was you two . . . that pulled me out of that hole. You didn't leave me behind." Mangin's eyes watered. "You probably saved my life."

Linc pointed at Juan. "I just held the rope. He's the guy that got you out."

"Team effort," Juan said.

Mangin laid a hand on Cabrillo's shoulder.

"I would serve under you anywhere, any time."

Juan nodded. "Your glass is empty. You're not trying hard enough."

The Frenchman stared at the empty glass, almost as if surprised it was in his hand.

"*C'est vrai.*"

"Last call," the barman shouted.

"Better get going," Linc said.

The inebriated commando scowled like a wounded child and staggered off toward the bar.

Juan and Linc were alone again. It was no longer suspicious that they hung out together. It was Drăguş who had paired them up. Still, they took precautions not to appear to be too chummy.

"Maybe tonight when these guys are conked out we can look around," Juan said. "Until then, we can relax."

"I think I want some more of that roasted pig."

"I'm with you on that one, big guy."

★

Despite his intoxicated state, Plata was still keeping a relatively short leash on his dogs of war. He didn't want a good time to spin out of control, and there was still plenty to do in the coming days. At midnight he blew his whistle. The music cut off and the men groaned with disappointment, but they dutifully headed for the barracks.

By twelve-thirty lights were off. Linc and Juan lay in their bunks listening to the whispered conversations melt slowly away into the deep inhalations of exhausted men falling asleep. It wouldn't be long before the entire barracks would be in la-la land.

Juan yawned two or three times and rubbed his face to stay awake. He and Linc were going to recon the facility as soon as the last man passed out. Linc was in a bunk across the aisle and two over on the left. Even in the dark his big frame was impossible to miss. Juan yawned again. He didn't realize how tired he was after the last few days of hard training. He knew it wasn't the booze. He had nursed a glass of whiskey all night, pouring most of it out in the bushes when no one was looking and filling it back up to look like he was drinking as much as the others. Linc had done the same thing.

Juan's eyelids were as heavy as cast-iron frying pans. He rubbed his face again. It didn't help. He rolled his head over to see how Linc was doing. He heard the big man's familiar snore, a steady, raspy hum. He must have been exhausted, too. Juan lifted his wrist to check his watch. It was twelve forty-seven a.m.

Too early to go out anyway, he told himself. *Might as well get a little catnap . . .*

Juan shut his eyes. And like the rest of the men in that room, he was soon rendered completely unconscious, unaware of the odorless gas clouding the air.

46

Juan was completely knocked out when an ear-piercing siren suddenly screamed in staccato bursts overhead. The sound sliced through his nervous system like a katana, startling him awake.

His wide-opened eyes were painfully blinded by fast-flashing halogen lights brighter than a noonday sun. The sudden sensory overload completely disoriented him, but he went from deep chemical slumber to full consciousness in just nanoseconds.

The siren cut out mid-scream as the lights suddenly stopped flashing, leaving Juan's ears ringing and his aching retinas spotted with throbbing shadows. Cabrillo shut his eyes to clear his mind and his vision. When he opened them a few seconds later he saw that he was in a barred cage, like a human-sized dog kennel.

Thirty feet across from him he saw a line of ten similar cages, every other one containing one of the men he'd been training with the last few days. All of them were in their nightclothes—skivvies, T-shirts, and barefoot. No one had bothered to dress them when they were tossed unconscious into their cages. Incredibly, Juan's artificial leg had remained attached.

There were ten kennels at the far end as well. The cages were arranged in a square U shape and he was in the fifth cage. At the open end of the U was a high platform with steps that led down into the U. The whole room was enclosed by cement walls, floor and ceiling—no doubt part of the three-story building he had seen the day he arrived on the island.

Plata was in the unit directly across from him. The mercs were all in various states of shock and disorientation, no doubt in proportion to their level of drunkenness the night before—or was it the same night? He couldn't tell. Cabrillo craned his neck to see farther down the line. Four cages down from Plata, he spotted Linc, who locked bleary eyes with his. They exchanged a quick nod.

Good to go—whatever happens.

Juan was suddenly aware of the aches and pains racking his body, and the cool feeling of plate steel beneath his hands. He saw a device locked onto his wrist, like an oversized Apple Watch, but with a steel band that couldn't be removed. The large glass face was blank, displaying nothing.

Cabrillo heard the metal clank of a rolling steel door opening beyond the platform and beyond his sight. Moments later, several men and two women walked onto the platform. All but one of them wore indistinct civilian clothing. One of the women and three of the men were East Asian. Two other men were Black. Others were blond or brunette Europeans. Some carried a distinct military bearing with close-cropped haircuts to match.

The youngest of the bunch was a South Asian man with shoulder-length hair pulled into a ponytail and sporting a close-shaven beard. Cabrillo identified him as an Indian national. He wore a one-piece flight suit with camel-colored Merrell tactical boots and, strangely, black gloves. He wore no weapon of any kind.

But it was the exceptionally large middle-aged man in the center of the group, a bearded Japanese man, that stood out. Beyond his imposing size, the man carried himself with the self-possessed confidence of a warrior who had never known defeat.

One tough customer, Juan told himself.

The bearded giant stepped closer, separating himself from the others, including a small band of armed and uniformed bodyguards, who stood back in the shadows. He tented his long fingers as he prepared to speak.

Juan sighed.

What fresh hell is this?

★

"My lords of war," the bearded Japanese man said, "allow me to introduce myself. I am your employer. I am the Vendor." He gestured to the others standing next to him. "We have been observing you over the course of your time here. Your performances were exemplary—far exceeding my expectations. You are to be congratulated."

The Vendor slow-clapped his enormous hands and the others joined him.

Juan's gut knotted with a sickening certainty. *Not good.*

"What game are you playing, Plata?" the Russian shouted. Several other mercs cursed in agreement.

Juan couldn't see the ex-Wagner's face. He was in the same row of cages as he was.

Plata white-knuckled his cage bars and shook them as he turned his head to face the Russian.

"Does this look like a game to you? I don't know what's happening!"

The Vendor turned to the Russian.

"Don't blame Señor Plata. He was unaware of the new contract terms I initiated."

"What new terms?" Plata asked.

The Vendor addressed the room. "You all signed a contract to work for me and are still in my employ. The mission has changed—but so has the compensation. It will make you very rich."

"Nobody gives money away," McGuire said, his Irish lilt slurred by the knockout gas. "What's the catch?"

The Vendor gestured broadly toward the group of dignitaries around him.

"These distinguished men and women have come from all over the world to observe and evaluate a live-fire demonstration of my latest infantry combat system."

"You treat us like this? And you expect us to demonstrate your system?" Drăguş asked.

"No, my lords of war, you are not the system *demonstrators*. You are the system *targets*."

A wave of angry protests flooded the room.

"I didn't sign up for any of this!" the Syrian shouted.

The Vendor frowned quizzically. "You want out of your contract?"

"Yes! Immediately! I demand it!"

The Vendor turned toward the young Indian in the flight suit.

"Rahul, release Mr. Al-Mawas from his contract."

The Indian nodded and gestured to the other guests. They parted evenly. He then gestured toward the back of the platform with his gloved fingers.

Juan heard the high whine of servos and hydraulics behind the guests and the padding of heavy rubber feet hitting hard concrete.

Seconds later, a spiderlike robot skittered on eight composite legs across the platform and halted briefly.

A few mercs gasped in shock. Others cursed. The guests stared impassively.

The spider-bot stood about six feet tall. Its carbon-fiber body was a single platform, not divided by head and abdomen like a regular spider. What functioned for its head and eyes was a small, circular dome that rotated three hundred sixty degrees on the forward edge of the platform.

Rahul pointed at the Syrian's cage.

The spider-bot sped effortlessly down the steps and toward the target cage. Its rubberized feet thundered across a piece of steel plating in the center of the floor. It halted inches from the Syrian's door.

"Wait—" Al-Mawas moaned.

Too late.

The spider's back opened and a short-barreled weapon emerged. A sudden gout of flaming napalm sprayed into the cage, setting the Syrian on fire.

The mercs yelled and cursed as Al-Mawas screamed in flaming agony, hurtling himself against the walls in a vain attempt to put out the fire. Within moments his screams became whimpering cries as he fell to the floor, mercifully blacking out as the unquenchable flames stole his life.

The room stank of gasoline, burnt hair, and charred flesh. Oily black smoke curled in tendrils out of the cage. Instantly, the overhead ventilation system vacuumed up the pollution with powerful fans and vented it all away. The room cleared of smoke and smell in less than twenty seconds.

"Contract terminated," Rahul said.

"Thank you," the Vendor said. "You may take your position now."

Rahul bowed slightly. He gestured with his fingers without looking. The spider-bot turned one hundred eighty degrees and scrambled up the stairs, following Rahul out the rear exit.

The guests gathered back together on the platform.

"Unfortunately, that contract termination puts you down a very capable man. The good news is that you are now collectively over one million dollars richer."

The room was too shocked to react.

Finally, Drăguș spoke up.

"How are we richer?"

"Ah, yes, the terms of the contract. Let's begin at the beginning, shall we?"

The Vendor came down to the lower floor. "As I said before, my honored guests are here to evaluate a live-fire demonstration of my latest high-tech infantry combat system. It gives a single soldier the equivalent combat power of an entire platoon. You have just experienced a small taste of what that power entails.

"To evaluate the capabilities of my system, I recruited each of you for your demonstrated combat skills and experience. Your commanders, Plata and Drăguș, expertly forged you into a combat team and established sufficient unit cohesion. Your success in the various training modules is proof of that. In fact, you were so successful that we cut the training short."

The Vendor turned toward the observers, who all nodded in agreement.

"I also recruited you because you are mercenaries who are highly motivated by money. In order to make the contest fair between you and Rahul, I needed to motivate you properly."

"To make it fair to *us*?" the Brit said. "Let us out of these cages, mate, and I'll tear that wet noodle of yours apart with my bare hands."

"Trust me, you'll be let out soon enough," the Vendor said. "Believe me when I say you'll wish I had left you locked in those cages."

He pulled a remote control out of his pocket. The steel plating in the center of the floor parted and a large LCD monitor emerged. On the stand next to it was a small pole and flag like the ones used on practice putting greens. A sensor stood in the middle of the flag.

The Vendor pressed another button and an overhead image of the island was displayed on both sides of the screen so that everyone could see it. Ten red electronic "flags" were stationed around the island including the city ruins, the jungle, and the mines. They were each numbered 1 through 10. Supply caches were labeled A through J.

"Here are the rules," the Vendor began. "Each flag is worth two million dollars. After all ten flags are collected, the survivors will split the twenty million dollars evenly."

"And that's why the Syrian's death put more money in our pockets," Plata said.

"Exactly. Of course, if only one of you survives, he collects all twenty million, paid by Bitcoin into the account he provided earlier."

"Then you're setting us up to kill each other to maximize our profits," the Brit said.

The Vendor flashed a toothy smile. "A classic game of prisoner's dilemma. I shall enjoy observing the outcome."

"What happens if we kill *you*?" Osipenko asked.

"Excellent question. The short answer is that you will receive no money. The longer answer is that it won't be possible. As soon as you leave here, a minefield surrounding this facility will be electronically activated."

"What if we collect fewer flags?" one of the Polish twins asked.

"All ten flags must be collected or none of the money will be distributed."

"How are they collected?" the Nigerian asked.

"Check the devices on your wrists," the Vendor said. He held up his arm. He had one attached to himself as well.

Juan had forgotten about it. He glanced down to see that it had activated. The same map that appeared on the LCD monitor was now on his wrist display.

"These devices serve several functions," the Vendor began. "First, it shows you where all of the flags are located."

"Makes it easy enough for that muppet to lay up ambushes for us, doesn't it?" McGuire said.

The Vendor smiled. "That would be an unfair advantage, wouldn't it? But rest assured, Rahul does not have access to your map nor does he know where the flags are located."

He pointed again to his wrist device. "When you capture one of these flags, it will turn from red to green. Let me show you." He passed his device by the sensor in the flag and one of the red flags on the screen turned green.

"Easy enough, yes?"

"Can Rahul recapture the flags?" Linc asked.

"No, Mr. Davis. Once you capture them, they remain yours. Otherwise the game may never end. Speaking of which . . ."

The Vendor tapped another button on his remote. The map on the LCD monitor disappeared, replaced with a countdown clock that read *48:00:00.*

"You will have just forty-eight hours to collect all ten flags."

"And if we fail to capture all ten?" Drăguş asked.

"Hiding is not an option, gentlemen. If you don't succeed in claiming all ten flags within forty-eight hours, you will all be killed."

"What about our gear? Food? Ammo?" one of the Poles asked.

"You will return to the armory and collect your weapons, same as the ones you used in training. There are also packs, medical kits, tents, survival gear—-anything you can think of. Your digital maps also show you the location of caches of food, water, and ammunition all around the island marked by the letters A through J. Rahul has neither access nor knowledge of any of these, either.

"As I'm sure some of you have surmised, one of the main purposes of the many exercises was to familiarize you with the island."

"How do we know we can trust you?" the Frenchman asked. "You might change the rules of the game again."

The Vendor laughed. "Such a stupid question. We hear it all the time in the movies, don't we? Why do writers have to be so un-original?"

"We don't have to trust you," Juan called out from his cage. He pointed at the Vendor's clients. "If you violate the rules of your own game, those people will know your new combat system doesn't work."

"Very perceptive, Señor Mendoza. Any other concerns?"

"How do we know you will pay the reward money when we win?" Osipenko asked.

"Because money doesn't mean anything to me. You will also be guaranteed safe passage to any destination of your choosing. I doubt any of you with your criminal records will go running to the authorities with wild stories about my island if for no other reason than they would confiscate your reward money."

"How would they know about our money?" the Frenchman asked.

"I would tell them. Anything else?"

The room was mostly silent. Juan heard a few whispers between cages. The men were already plotting tactics and strategies for survival.

"One more thing about your wrist devices," the Vendor said. "It measures your heartbeat. That allows us to know who's dead and who is still in the fight."

The Vendor's clients all turned and headed for the rear exit as the Vendor climbed the stairs. When he reached the platform he turned around.

"Fight hard, my lords of war. It is your only hope of surviving— and also of getting very rich. Good luck."

He gave a brief nod of respect, turned on his heel, and headed for the rolling exit door. As soon as it banged shut, another steel door opened in the far wall.

The room was suddenly filled with the sharp, ear-piercing blast of a nuclear air-raid siren—completely different from the one that woke them earlier. The hellish, polyphonic wail screamed like a choir of damned souls.

After thirty nerve-shattering seconds, the electronic cage door locks popped open—and the countdown clock launched.

The mercs all scrambled out of their kennels.

"To the armory!" Plata shouted as they all raced for the exit and whatever fate awaited them.

47

The thirteen mercs charged through the cool, balmy air of the early-morning sunrise, the air-raid siren still blaring its doomsday signal overhead. While most of the men were still badly hungover, they all suffered worse headaches from the knockout gas.

They dashed into the armory tent. A long table stood on the far wall. On it were a couple of boxes of protein bars and two dozen liters of bottled water. Several of the men tore into those first.

Also on the table were stacks of their neatly folded and labeled uniforms, boots, socks, and shirts. Everyone else started there, including Juan and Linc.

"We're sitting ducks in here," the Brit shouted as he pulled on his pants. Others agreed. The fear in the room was palpable.

"Just shut up and gear up—now!" Plata barked, his mouth half full of protein bar.

As soon as the men dressed, they ran straight to their individual lockers.

Juan and Linc stood back, wolfing down a couple of bars and gulping water. They watched as the mad scramble of grabbing gear and weapons nearly turned into a brawl. The blaring war siren was driving their panic into a frenzy.

Juan took the opportunity of the pandemonium to duck in a far corner and secure his combat leg with support straps without anyone noticing. Linc's big frame also blocked the view.

The two of them hustled back over just in time to watch Plata grab one of the Polish twins by the straps of his armored vest before he could throw a punch at the Turk. Drăguş cussed out the Russian for nearly knocking him over.

Cabrillo whistled hard. The shrill pitch cut through the hellish war horn. Strangely, it cut out just as if Cabrillo had willed it.

The silence stopped everyone in their tracks.

"This is exactly what the Vendor wants," Cabrillo said. "Panic and chaos."

"No one needs your advice, Mendoza," Plata barked.

But the mercs responded to Cabrillo's commanding, confident voice. They suddenly settled down, and over the next ten minutes finished pulling on armor and helmets, stuffing rucks with ammo, holstering mags and pistols, and checking their main weapons and comms. A few grabbed extra protein bars and stuffed them in their pockets, while others filled up canteens at the cleaning station. The Turk, the unit's assigned medic, quick-checked his medical kit.

Juan and Linc finished kitting out, but in a calm and orderly fashion, moving more slowly but more efficiently than the others.

"We're out of here in two minutes," Plata said. "Anyone not geared up and in formation will be left behind."

Juan stepped over to Plata and pulled on his arm to take him aside quietly. He glared at Cabrillo's hand on his rock-hard bicep.

Cabrillo lowered his voice and spoke in Spanish.

"I'm not trying to tell you what to do, *hermano*, but if we form up outside we'll just be one big target. Better we split up and meet somewhere under cover—somewhere away from the flags." Cabrillo pointed at the map device on Plata's wrist.

Plata sneered at him. "Don't you think I know that? I was planning on running as soon as we got outside."

"Where to? The traffic control tower?"

"Exactly. Now get your gear on—or get left behind." He turned to the room. "Line up at the door!"

The Polish twins were first at the door, followed by the others. Plata and Drăguş were next to last, stuffing their packs to overcapacity. Juan and Linc packed lightly, and stood toward the back.

Plata and Drăguş pushed through the crowd.

"Here's the plan. We don't know what's waiting for us out there. We don't want to be exposed and we don't want to bunch up. We'll take off in pairs and spread out. Use the trees or whatever cover you can find. Let's all meet up at the airstrip tower."

"That's a two-mile run," the Nigerian said.

"You want me to call you a cab?" Drăguş barked.

"What's the plan after that?" the Brit asked.

"I'll let you know when we get there—assuming we all make it."

Plata pointed at the Polish twins.

"You ready?"

The towheaded blonds nodded curtly in sync.

Drăguş held the tent door open.

"Go!"

The rest of the men queued up with their respective teammates. They all listened, half expecting gunshots or explosions as the Poles ran for their lives. Twenty seconds passed.

Nothing.

Plata sent the next pair off, then the others, in staggered intervals. Finally, only Plata, Drăguş, Juan, and Linc were left.

"You coming or not, *pendejos*?" Plata said.

Linc and Juan squared up at the door. Linc's sniper rifle was so big and heavy there was no point slinging it, so he hefted it by the built-in carry handle.

Because Linc had his hands full, Juan shouldered the Barrett's five ten-round .50-cal magazines in his pack, each weighing over three pounds, along with his own spotter's gear, ammo, and weapons.

Plata stared daggers at Cabrillo. "Better watch your step out there, *boludo*."

"*Siempre*." Always.

"Drăguş shouted, "Go!"

★

The Polish twins arrived at the airstrip tower hardly breaking a sweat. They were the youngest and fittest of the unit. They smashed through the tower's locked door with ease and took up positions for overwatch at the windows as the rest of the team came thundering in.

Fifteen minutes later, everyone was gathered on the first floor. Most were huffing and drenched in sweat, especially Linc.

"Okay, Plata. You've got us here. Now what?" the Brit asked.

"Nobody locks me in a cage," Plata said, seething. "We're going to kill that man."

"How? He's holed up in a cement fortress behind a moat of land mines. Even if we had metal detectors or even ground-penetrating radar, he can set them off remotely while we're digging 'em up."

"Seems to me we have three options," the Irishman McGuire began. "Take out the Vendor—which is nigh unto impossible. Take out Rahul, or grab the ten flags as quickly as we can."

"Flags or not, in the end, we kill the Vendor," Plata said.

"We kill him, we don't get the money," the Nigerian said.

"Once I begin to separate his eyes from their sockets, he'll give us the money, I promise you that."

"We should take out Rahul," Juan said. "Kill him, and we'll be plucking up flags like daffodils."

"That's idiotic," Plata said. "How do we even find him? We have less than forty-eight hours. It might take us a week to locate him. If we pick up all the flags, the game is over—no need to kill him. But as soon as we do get those flags, we're going after this *engañador* 'Vendor.'"

"You don't think Rahul is out there waiting to ambush us?" Linc said. "All he has to do is keep us from one flag and we lose."

"He doesn't know where the flags are, remember?" The Frenchman held up his wrist map and tapped it. "We have these. He doesn't. He must find the flags on his own. That gives us an advantage."

"I bet he's already setting up some kind of electronic surveillance," Linc said. "And when he does, we'll be walking into his traps."

"We should stay together," the Turk said. "If he's set up an ambush at one location, we can overwhelm him."

"Ridiculous," the German said. "We should split up. He sees us all together and—boom!" He mimicked an explosion with his gloved hands.

"Should we wait until nightfall?" McGuire asked. "I brought these." He held up a pair of night vision goggles. "There are more back at the armory."

"Wait around twelve hours for him to scout the island and set ambushes for us? Are you stupid?" the Frenchman asked. "We have to act fast. The clock is ticking."

"I hate playing defense," the Brit said. "I say we take the fight to the muppet. We outnumber him thirteen to one."

"It used to be fourteen to one, remember?" Osipenko said. "Until your 'wet noodle' set the Syrian on fire."

"Al-Mawas was locked in a cage without a weapon," Plata said. "Let's see Rahul try his tricks against heavily armed commandos in a fair fight."

"If you think that little stunt with the fire-breathing bug was his best trick, you're insane," Juan said. "The whole point of this 'game' is to pit thirteen trained fighters against one man. Did you see those spectators? They looked like military types. This is a weapons test. The Vendor sells weapons. Those were prospective buyers. The Vendor must be trying to sell Rahul and his spider-machine to them and the proof of concept is us—all thirteen of us. Do not underestimate this man."

"Don't underestimate these men, either," Drăguş said. "They've already proven themselves."

"Against what, paper targets?" Linc said.

"I'm not afraid of a mechanical insect," the Turk said.

"Use your head," Juan said. "That trick with the fire? That was meant to terrorize us. It's only a short-range weapon. There's no way for one man to take out thirteen men at close quarters. He must have long-range weapons in his arsenal."

"What kinds of weapons?" McGuire asked.

Juan shrugged. "Whatever he can operate at a distance, probably remotely."

"Missiles? Mortars? Drones?" Osipenko asked.

"All of them, some of them. A combination, most likely. And like Davis said, he'll tie them into some kind of surveillance capability."

"You seem to know a lot about this man," Plata said. "Perhaps too much."

Linc tapped the side of his head. "He's just using logic. It's about time we did, too, before we get our heads blown off."

"So, flags or Rahul?" one of the Polish twins asked, still staring outside on overwatch.

"We should vote on it," the Frenchman said.

"There's no voting," Plata said. "I'm in charge."

"Because the Vendor put you in charge," the German said.

"What are you suggesting?"

"I'm not suggesting anything. The Vendor put you in charge—but the question is, for what reason?"

The big Guatemalan lunged at the German with catlike speed.

Juan had never seen such a large man move so fast.

Plata grabbed the German's throat and shoved him against the block wall, knocking the breath out of him. Before anyone could react, Plata laid his knife blade on the German's cheek, the sharp point just millimeters beneath his cornflower-blue eye.

"Tell me, Fritz. Why do you think he put me in charge? Tell me. *Tell me!*"

The German swallowed hard.

"Because you are the best of us." The German's words barely escaped his throat still clutched in Plata's iron grip.

"Say it louder."

"Because you are the best of us!"

Drăguș laughed.

"*Ganz genau*, Fritzy," Plata said as he withdrew his blade and released the German.

The German coughed, trying to catch his breath.

"So what do you want to do?" McGuire asked.

Plata sheathed his knife as he stepped over to the window, his eyes scanning the empty airstrip.

"We take out the flags as fast as we can." He turned around. "Gather close. Check your maps."

The men collected in the center of the room.

"Thirteen men, ten flags," Plata said. He pointed at the Frenchman. "Pick your flag."

"Number three," the Frenchman said. It was a city flag. "*Pour le Tricolore.*"

The Turk took number five.

"We'll take number nine," one of the Polish twins said. "Together."

"As I expected." Plata then pointed at the German, who picked number one, and then distributed the rest of the flags.

In all, the three most distant flags from the air tower were assigned to pairs, including Plata and Drăguș, and Juan and Linc. The rest of the flags went to individuals. All ten flags and all thirteen men were accounted for.

"The faster you get your flag, the more likely you are to survive," Drăguș said.

"Unless Rahul is already there waiting for you," the Russian said. "Then God help you."

Drăguș ignored him. "Use cover whenever you can. And watch for ambushes."

"Keep an eye on your map," Plata said. "If there's a flag close by that hasn't been captured, take the initiative and grab it. If you see any of our fallen, call it in."

"I wouldn't use comms if I were you," Juan said.

"Why not?" the Frenchman asked.

"He might be able to lock onto your transmission signal and turn it into a target."

"Your paranoia is duly noted, Mendoza—and ignored. We're using comms." Plata scratched his chin, thinking. He checked his wrist device.

"Check your maps," Plata began. "At noon, we'll all meet at cache

D for sitreps. If you couldn't get your flag, you tell us why. We'll figure out what flags are left and plan from there."

"I agree," the Turk said.

Plata scowled at him. "No one asked your opinion." The bearded Guatemalan turned to the others. "Also, make sure you aren't followed on the way back. Otherwise, you might get us all killed."

Drăguş checked his watch. "We're wasting time."

"You're right," Plata said. He turned to McGuire. "What do you SAS guys always say?"

"'Who dares—wins!'"

Plata grinned. "That's right. So let's saddle up—and get moving. Now!"

Plata was first out the door. His warrior spirit had infected the men. They bolted into the early-morning sunlight after him, each headed for their respective flags. Each man was a brave and experienced fighter.

And each was targeted for death.

48

Thump!

The last salvo of drones launched from the towed trailer. Rahul Tripathi stood in a clearing, his eyes fixed on a display screen. The first wave of vehicles would soon be in place.

His robot *Makṛī*—Hindi for "spider"—was also fully charged and armed. Its flamethrower had been rotated out and replaced with a long-range sniper rifle equipped with a new kind of scope and guided bullet.

Rahul was as unnerved by the air-raid siren as the mercenaries had been, perhaps even more so. He was grateful when it finally cut off. The otherworldly din not only terrified him but interfered with his thinking process already hampered by his nervous excitement.

The young Indian national was completely confident in the surveillance and weapons systems the Vendor had helped him design and build. The previous demonstration had shown its effectiveness against inferior test subjects, but failed to impress the Vendor's clients.

Today's demonstration was altogether different. This was actual combat—and he could be killed. But he needed to prove the *Makṛī*'s worth, and his own.

His greatest fear was disappointing the Vendor. As far as he knew, he was the youngest member of the Vendor's network. It had been an honor to partner with such an advanced mind. He even thought of the Vendor as a mentor, living the kind of life Rahul only dreamed of until now.

The Indian engineer was brilliant, but he was also no fool. Despite his technological advantages, the fact remained he was battling thirteen highly trained and combat-experienced former special operators. He possessed neither of those qualities. This was not by accident.

The Vendor was selling the concept of a "plug-and-play" combat system. A system that anyone with minimal video gaming skills could deploy effectively. He told Rahul the analogy of the English longbow. As effective as it was on battlefields like Agincourt, it nevertheless required years of training and strength to master. The crossbow replaced it en masse because it required neither and shot with even greater force.

Rahul was not only up against the mercs' incredible killing skill sets, he also had the challenge of finding them. True to his word, the Vendor didn't give Rahul access to the mapping device. He had no idea where the flags were located, so it was impossible at this moment to set up ambushes for the soldiers at those locations. In short, he was hunting prey while largely deaf and blind.

So what did he know? First, there were only ten flags. Second, all ten flags had to be secured. Third, the soldiers could only make their way to those flags on foot. But that wasn't much to go on.

He next applied his logical faculties, beginning with the question *What would I do if I were in charge of the merc team?*

His pulse quickened at the obvious answer. *Kill the Indian drone operator!*

Fortunately, Plata and the others had the same problem he did—lack of information. Also, the size of the island meant they could have no assurance of finding him within the forty-eight-hour period.

So what was the next logical move? To secure the flags as quickly as possible—especially because the mercs had the advantage of knowing where they were located.

Given that likely scenario, Rahul's strategy had been to embrace the probabilities. He was already familiar with the island and had access to a topographical map that included the underground mines beneath the city along with their entry points.

He had also been informed by the Vendor the flags were relatively evenly distributed between the city, the surrounding jungle, and the mines.

A quick survey of the topographical map showed him where the soldiers were most likely to travel—and were to avoid—in their journeys across the island.

With these parameters in mind and the topo map uploaded, Rahul unleashed the *Makṛi*'s AI-generated surveillance and targeting package. That package was a modified version of the "Gospel" AI-targeting program, stolen from the Israelis by the Vendor's network.

The *Makṛi* had divided up the island into ten zones of approximately equal size both above and below the surface. It excluded those portions of the island least likely to contain a flag, such as stretches of beach, large ponds, and the like. The city and the mines received additional resources since they were more confined spaces and thus harder to surveil.

Rahul's drones were then automatically programmed with their respective surveillance and combat algorithms and launched. And thanks to other tech on board his drones, he would soon gain access to the mercs' comms net, as well as acquire visuals on them when they inevitably came out from under cover. And the ones that didn't? They would trigger one of the sensors his drones were distributing even now.

Rahul checked the time. The battle would soon be joined. The thought of besting these battle-hardened mercs pleased the young gamer, but taking their twenty million dollars as his own prize money excited him even more. Poverty was more terrifying than death.

A vast array of colored lights activated on his handheld device. Each type of drone was indicated by a certain color. Aerial drones would soon finish depositing their loads of ground sensors and then take up their positions for electro-optical surveillance. This would give him nearly total informational awareness of the battle space.

Once his targets were identified and tracked, he would unleash the kinetics. His launch trailer would remain in place and keep launching drones as the automated network program dictated.

Rahul pulled on his helmet with its heads-up display (HUD) shield. Instantly the interface that was on his handheld device appeared on his HUD shield and the *Makṛī* whirred to life, no longer hitched to the launch trailer.

The slim engineer headed up the mountain trail, his mechanical monster dutifully marching behind him.

It was time for war.

49

Max sat in the Kirk Chair, drumming his thick fingers on the cool metal of the arm console. The chill air smelled of ozone from the op center's electronics. But for all of the *Oregon*'s computational power and vast array of intelligence-gathering equipment, Max was still completely in the dark about Juan and Linc. *Where were they?*

"Tell me you found something," Max asked over the intercom. Eric was in the electronics lab with Murph.

"We finally broke the encryption on all three phones. Surprisingly sophisticated," Eric said in the speaker.

"And?" Max tried to hide his growing irritation.

"The Cray translated the voicemails and texts," Murph said. "Our Islamic extremist friends shared a lot of porn sites and soccer scores, along with a couple of halal recipes and a few verses from the Quran. But there was bubkes about any information on the Vendor or where Juan and Linc might be."

"Thanks guys—for nothing," Max said as he punched off the call.

"Not their fault, Max," Linda said standing by his chair. Callie was next to Linda at her invitation. Callie was trying to stay out of the way, but she was also really concerned about her new friends and wanted to help if she could.

Max rubbed his face with a meaty paw, beyond frustrated.

"I know. I'll apologize later."

In truth, Max was more afraid than he was angry—or maybe equal parts of both, since anger and fear both came out of the same vent hole in his magnanimous heart. Angry because he was helpless; afraid because he knew his friends were in danger.

Every sat phone call they made to Juan failed to connect and their trackers were still offline. It had been more than a couple of days now. Safety protocols required that Juan and Linc call in after forty-eight hours if at all possible. The fact they hadn't called in meant they were under duress or in a place where contact was impossible. Neither prospect was acceptable.

Max bolted out of his chair and stormed over to the wall-sized map of the region displayed on one of the big screens. Linda and Callie followed him over.

"Where could they be?" Max asked, studying the map for the umpteenth time.

"They could be anywhere," Linda said. "That's the problem."

"But they're not *any*where. They're *some*where. Somewhere on this map."

"Not necessarily. They could have taken a short hop to an international airport and then flown to any place on the planet."

"Why would they fly into KL, transfer to a smaller airplane at an airstrip, and then fly to a different international airport? Unless this Vendor creep is a complete paranoid, I think the small airstrip is the key. Whatever plane they flew could handle a grass strip, which means a smaller plane. And a smaller plane means they're probably somewhere in this region. But where?"

Linda stepped closer to the map. "If you're right, the first thing we can assume is that a grass airstrip means they're flying in a turboprop. It had to carry at least twelve operators. An aircraft that size and capacity would have a range of at least fifteen hundred miles, if not more."

She used her fingertip and drew a crude yellow circle approximately three thousand miles in diameter onto the map screen with the *Oregon* located in the center of it, anchored in the Malacca Strait off the coast of Kuala Lumpur.

The circle still covered nearly two million square miles. Sri Lanka, India, and Bangladesh were west of their position, Myanmar and Thailand were north, as was China. Taiwan down to the Philippines and New Guinea and northern Australia bounded the east. And the long archipelagoes of Indonesia and Malaysia bounded the south with a lot of other islands in the middle.

Murph and Eric slipped quietly into their stations at weapons and helm.

Max turned around. "Sorry, guys. Short fuse today. Good work."

"We get it," Eric said. "We're worried, too."

"Well, just to play along," Linda said, "I'd say the place to start is the Vendor's dark web ad. If he really was recruiting for a security gig, there isn't any point for a legit VIP to hire a platoon of miscreant mercs when there are so many experienced and qualified security services in places like China, Australia, and Taiwan."

"But if he was recruiting serious people, he'd have to convince them this was a real job, otherwise they'd smell a rat. If that's the case, his fake VIP would have to be a Third World politician."

"Or maybe a criminal enterprise," Max said. "But a small one. The big cartels all employ their own heavy hitters now, many of them ex–special forces."

"Definitely another possibility. Either way, that still leaves a ton of places for them to go."

Max stepped even closer. His eye was drawn to the giant island of Borneo, the third largest in the world, and shared by three separate nations. It was in the center of the mass of islands and archipelagoes between Indonesia, Malaysia, and the Philippines.

"I'm sick of sitting around on my sculptured derriere and doing nothing. Let's set a course for here . . ." Max touched the screen. A pin dropped off the coast of Brunei.

"But they could be in exactly the opposite direction," Callie said.

"It's a coin toss for sure," Max said. "But it's better than twiddling our thumbs. And with all of that free seawater powering our engines, it'll only cost us time."

"Eric, would you please lay in a course for that point?" Linda asked.

"Aye, ma'am."

Max turned to Callie. "If Juan and Linc are in trouble there's going to be fireworks. Let me get you over to KL and fly you back home and we'll pick up where we left off with the *Spook Fish* when everything cools down."

"Unless that's a direct order, I'd rather hang around. Maybe I can be of help."

"We can't guarantee your safety," Linda said.

Callie shrugged. "Of course you can't. Danger is a function of disorder, and a battlefield is nothing less than controlled chaos. On the other hand, you might drop me off at a 'safe place' like the airport just in time for me to get pancaked by a runaway bus."

"But a gunfight is a lot more 'chaotic' than a crosswalk."

"Even in something as chaotic as a gunfight, something tells me my odds are better with the *Oregon*'s highly trained and disciplined crew."

Linda turned to Max. "Remind me to never play poker with her."

Max chuckled as he fell into the Kirk Chair.

"Eric, is the course laid in?"

"Aye."

"Then hit the afterburners, my boy." Max clapped his hands. "Flank speed!"

50

THE ISLAND OF SORROWS
THE CELEBES SEA

Juan's first thought wasn't how to get to his assigned flag but rather for he and Linc to get enough distance away from the others to call the *Oregon* on his sat phone. If the mercs knew he had it, their cover would be blown. The last thing he wanted was for that pack of wolves to turn on them.

Their target flag was located in the jungle at the base of the city, on the side directly opposite the ocean front it bordered. He and Linc purposely ran at an oblique angle from the air control tower to their target to avoid Osipenko, who had set out directly behind them. As soon as the Russian had pushed through the foliage and deeper into the trees, Juan and Linc found cover in a grove of towering bamboo.

Juan opened up his combat leg and removed his satellite phone, one of several devices inside the secret compartment. He wasn't worried about detection by Rahul's drones. Unlike the comms units the team deployed, his sat phone utilized frequency-hopping to avoid detection.

He powered it up, hoping to see a couple of voicemails or texts from the *Oregon*, but there were none. *That's odd*, he thought as he hit the auto dial for the *Oregon* number. But the phone never acquired a signal. Instead, an error message popped up: "SEARCHING FOR SATELLITE."

"Problem, Chief?" Linc whispered as his eyes scanned the area.

"Can't get a signal."

"Something wrong with the unit?"

Juan checked the battery indicator. It read eighty-nine percent. He then turned the unit over in his hands looking for any kind of damage, but found none. He powered it down and then brought it back up to clear the cache and still it didn't work. Finally, he ran a self-diagnostic. All clear.

"It's solid as a rock. Just can't get the signal here."

"If the phone's good, then the link is bad. You think we're being blocked?"

"If we are"—Juan unconsciously touched his hip—"then our trackers are offline, too."

"So the *Oregon* has no idea where we are."

"Just like us."

"And our merc friends. Forgotten warriors on an unknown rock fighting some sort of ghost soldier."

"Except I don't believe in ghosts," Juan replied. "We'll push on toward our flag. It's a couple of miles from here. We'll try again for a signal along the way."

★

The rawboned Nigerian chose one of the flags in the decaying ruins of the island city. He had spent years crawling through the rubble of Libya's ruined buildings hunting whatever targets got him paid the most. He far preferred the haunted city to the claustrophobic mines or the suffocating jungle.

The Nigerian's keen eyes scanned for trip wires and hidden cameras as he made his way up the crumbling cement staircase toward the top floor. Reaching the top of the landing, he popped his head in and out of the first room, but saw nothing. The blistered cement scrunched beneath his boots and a light wind rattled the sheet metal roof above his head. He glanced up at the noise and saw that half of the rusted metal sheeting had been torn off or blown away, probably years ago.

He stepped carefully forward, his senses on full alert, his eyes fixed on the next doorway. A glint of purple at his feet crept into his peripheral vision. Incredibly, the stem of a single petaling flower grew out of a crack in the cement floor. *How is that even possible?* he asked himself as he edged closer to the door. He felt the cool damp of a light breeze pouring out of the doorway.

He peered around the corner and there it was—the flag, standing on the far side of a glassless window. The Nigerian felt a drop of water hit the back of his neck, but he ignored it. He did another three-hundred-sixty-degree sweep with his eyes to make sure he was clear, then dashed into the room.

★

The surveillance drone circled five hundred feet above the apartment block, one of dozens on patrol over the island. Its downward gaze first caught sight of the Nigerian as he bolted into the building. Now that he was on the top floor, the bird drone caught a second, fleeting glimpse of his coal-black hair as he ducked his head into the first room.

Its sensors now alerted, the drone tightened its circle and its telephoto-lense eyes locked onto the figure. Programmed to recognize human forms and movement, the surveillance drone easily tracked the Nigerian through the partially covered roof and sent out an alert signal to the other drones in its network.

When the Nigerian approached the second room, the drone acquired a much clearer image that instantly broadcast in real time to the rest of the network. The image was so clear it captured the glimmer of sunlight radiating in the single drop of moisture that fell onto the man's neck.

This fuller image triggered the attack algorithm.

★

The Yari drone fixed on the building at the first alert of the surveillance drone. Its computer brain was linked by swarming algorithms to every other drone in the network including both surveillance and attack drones in the air and on the ground. Like every other model of lethal drone in the network, it flew fully armed, and now that the surveillance drone had confirmed its target, the drone's AI-powered controller gave it the ability to make an attack decision independent of Rahul's command.

When the second, clearer image of the Nigerian appeared on the attack drone's image sensor, the AI-networked brain engaged in a series of precise mathematical calculations predicting the location of the merc as he entered the room. The drone could have done this even if the Nigerian were no longer visible, but the fact that he'd dashed into a room with a large and glassless window made its task just that much simpler.

The Yari's display put a red target reticle on the running Nigerian. Just as the big man reached the flag, the drone plunged through the window and erupted.

★

Rahul grinned with delight as he watched the attack drone's first-person video image fly into the Nigerian's broad back. The crystal clear video turned to snow when it exploded. Of course, there was no audio of the blast, but Rahul didn't need one. The crack of the explosion echoed in the distance just moments later. A second explosion followed within the span of a heartbeat.

Rahul rewound the attack footage on his display and let it play through one more time. He wanted to know if the Nigerian had secured the flag.

But the Nigerian's body blocked the view of the flag before the explosion and his wrist device was turned away from the camera. It wasn't at all clear if the Nigerian had succeeded in capturing the flag.

But there was no doubt whatsoever that he was the first pawn wiped off the board.

★

"Did you see that?" Juan whispered, his eye fixed to his spotter's scope.

"Looked like a couple of drones took him out." Linc had observed the action through his rifle scope. He checked his watch map. There were only nine flags left. "At least he got his flag."

"I think that's an example of 'Other than that, Mrs. Lincoln, how was the play?'"

"You know my mother's name was Mrs. Lincoln, right?"

"It never gets old."

"You'd be surprised."

Linc scanned the sky for more drones.

"At least we know what we're up against." Linc's view was partially blocked by the umbrella-shaped canopies of the towering acacia trees high overhead. He didn't mind that his vision was obscured, since it was those leaves that also kept them from being seen—and no doubt had saved their lives.

"Why not just stay here? We could let the other mercs assume we're dead."

"No doubt, but I'm not sure that's our best bet."

"How so?"

"First off, the mercs won't know we're alive, but the Vendor will—he's tracking our vital signs, remember? He might get suspicious if we stay put. Might even send someone our way."

"Even during the test?"

"Maybe, maybe not. If the others are all dead, though, he certainly will. Remember? He said anyone still alive after forty-eight hours and with flags on the board would be killed."

"So you're saying we should go after the flags?"

Juan grinned. "You always could read my mind. Our best shot at surviving this thing is getting all ten flags, and the best chance we have of doing that is teaming up with the others. But there's an even better reason."

"Which is?"

"If we don't rally with the others, there's a better than even chance those guys will get killed off—and that means the Vendor wins. And that's something I can't stomach."

Linc nodded. "If we win the game, the Vendor loses—and loses his contracts with his clients. Yeah, I like that."

"More importantly, our job is still to get the Vendor. If he wins quickly, he'll likely take off. But if he loses, he'll hang around to assess the damage and try and figure out what went wrong. He might even hang around long enough for the *Oregon* to get here and then we can snatch him."

"There's one big, ginormous fly swimming in the ointment of your infallible reasoning," Linc said.

"And that would be?"

"That plan of yours only works if we don't get our heads blown off by that Terminator spider—or whatever other murder toys the Vendor has cranked up out there."

"A minor detail." Juan slung his rifle.

Their assigned flag was still half a mile away. They had opted to take the more arduous route, preferring to stay under the cover of the jungle canopy with its thick roots and fallen logs rather than using the well-worn, open-air footpath just beyond it.

They had both ducked for cover and drew their pistols twenty minutes earlier when they heard the thundering footsteps of a man approaching from behind on the footpath. But it was only the Nigerian racing toward the entrance to the city.

Fascinated by his bold approach, Juan and Linc opted to watch his episode unfold. The twin explosions several minutes later told them it hadn't gone his way.

While Linc continued scanning the sky, Juan pulled out his sat phone and powered it back up. It was now at eighty-eight percent. Plenty of power. The screen flashed the same "SEARCHING FOR SATELLITE" message.

"Still a no-go?" Linc asked.

"Yeah." Juan pocketed the sat phone, but didn't power it down this time. His mind was fixated on an engineering puzzle.

"Problem?" Linc asked.

"You mean other than the fact we're trapped on an island with eleven—strike that, ten—psychopathic killers and an eight-legged Terminator spider robot?"

"Yeah. Other than that."

"Our sat signals are blocked, but those drones took out the Nigerian."

"So I noticed."

"But drones normally use sat signals—GPS, GLONASS, whatever—for navigation and remote operations."

"Our radios work fine. Plata hasn't shut his yapper since we left. He's had more airtime than Wolfman Jack."

"Exactly. That means those drones are on radio frequencies."

Juan opened up his combat leg and pulled out a sandwich-sized device. He unfolded it, forming a small tablet with a titanium backing and ultrathin bendable glass. He lifted it for Linc to see.

"Behold the Mini-Sniffer, Murph and Stoney's latest invention."

Linc's eyes widened with disbelief. "Mini-Sniffer? As in the *Oregon*'s electromagnetic vacuum cleaner?"

"Precisely. Doesn't have the range and can't process as wide a variety of signals, but it should do the trick when it comes to radio frequencies."

Juan powered up the Mini-Sniffer. Nanoseconds later the display booted up and automatically searched for signals. A huge number of hits popped up.

"We're loaded with two point four and five gigahertz signals," Juan said. "Both are perfect for cameras and remote controls. The five gigahertz is even better for first-person video."

"The kind that drones use," Linc said. "Can you access any of those signals? Give us a chance to see what they're seeing?"

"That's the plan." Juan scrolled through the list.

"But . . . can't the drones lock on the sat phone signal?"

Juan grinned as he scrolled. "You worried I'm painting a target on our backs?"

"The thought had crossed my mind."

Juan shook his head. "Not an issue. This phone uses advanced signal hopping. No way for a drone to lock on it. Wait. There." Juan finally reached the 5 GHz signal list and selected one of them.

"Crap. Should've seen that coming."

"What?"

"The signal's encrypted." Juan tapped a few more buttons on the screen. "So are the rest."

"What can we do?"

Juan punched another button. A circling wheel and PROCESSING appeared on the screen.

"We need to give the Mini a chance to decrypt the signal. It's not as good as the Cray on the *Oregon*, but Murph said it should do the job. We'll have to wait and see."

"We should get going if we want to snag that flag before the rally."

"Agreed," Juan said. "Head on a swivel, and stay out of sight."

"Goes without saying."

"Tell that to the Nigerian."

51

Whatever concerns Rahul had about locating the enemy combatants dissipated as soon as the surveillance drones were deployed and the sensor packages dropped.

The wiry Indian national studied the display in his hand. While he obviously preferred a visual display, he was nevertheless able to track the movement of one of the mercenaries deployed into the mine. With each halting step, the merc plodded deeper into the bowels of the earth in search of his flag, completely unaware that his steps were triggering tiny sensors in the dirt.

Rahul's admiration for the Gospel targeting program soared. He would never think to put either sensors or a weapon in this location. He grinned as his thumb hovered over a release button.

"Come on, now, dear fellow. Just a few more steps . . ."

★

The German inched his way forward in the dark, sweeping his weapon light over the ceiling and walls as he advanced, searching for trip wires, cameras, and robots. His shallow breaths were meant to calm his racing heart and focus his fevered brain. He had fought on three continents against some of the worst savages on the planet—but at least they were human savages. He never imagined in a million years he would be in a battle with mechanical monsters. He felt as if he were in a horror movie. The stench of the Syrian's burning flesh and hair still haunted him.

According to his wrist map, he was less than fifty meters away from his assigned flag. As soon as he activated it, he would race back to the rally point, careful to avoid exposing himself to aerial surveillance.

The German took another step, planting his combat boot in the dust. An audible *click* echoed above his head.

He froze.

He glanced up at the ceiling just in time to see the spiderlike device clinging to the rock open its pod and release its load of napalm gel. Seconds later, the German's face was aflame, his blinded screams choked out by the unquenchable fire robbing him of oxygen—and his life.

★

The Polish twins crouched on the edge of a clearing, their target in sight.

Five hundred meters away, their assigned flag stood like a lone sentry, its stark white color in sharp contrast to the jungle's cacophony of blazing greens. There was no way to reach the flag without exposing themselves to the sky overhead.

"We could wait until nightfall," Pawel said, scanning the blue vault. He was the older of the two.

"I don't see any drones up there," his brother, Jakub, said.

"Doesn't mean there isn't one, depending on the altitude."

"Unless he's flying a Reaper, I doubt he's got anything with that kind of range. Besides, nightfall won't help us if he's using night vision, thermal, or infrared."

"So what do you want to do?"

"I want to get that flag. Wait here." Jakub rose to his feet, but Pawel pulled him back down.

"What are you doing?"

"I'm getting that flag. You're waiting here."

"I'm the older brother—"

"By two minutes."

"I promised Mama I'd watch out for you."

"Then we'll go together." The two men gripped their Polish bullpup Grot carbines.

"Let's go."

The two fighters stood, exchanged a fatalistic smile, and bolted out of the jungle toward the flag.

Running full tilt, the two Poles got within two hundred meters of the flag with Jakub in the lead. A loud *crack* snapped a hundred meters farther overhead. A puff of black smoke marked the location of the explosion. Unharmed by the strange burst, the two war veterans ignored the blast and raced forward with Jakub lengthening his lead. Seventy meters later—

Boom! Jakub's left foot was torn away from his ankle by a mine, cartwheeling him into the dirt in a shower of arterial blood.

The younger Pole screamed as Pawel crashed down beside him. He ripped open his medical kit and grabbed a tourniquet.

"Shut up, idiot," Pawel said in a harsh whisper. "You'll only draw fire." He cinched the tourniquet hard to stop the bleeding.

Jakub fought the scream through clenched teeth. He breathed heavily to calm himself.

"Leave me—"

"Don't be stupid," Pawel said as he wrapped the bloody stump in QuikClot combat gauze, his eyes scanning the area. "Mama would kill me."

Somehow Jakub managed a snorting laugh.

"Yeah, she would."

Pawel hit Jakub with an auto-injector loaded with ketamine to kill the pain. He'd be high as a kite in moments, but the pain would be dulled.

Pawel stood. Despite the fact they were identical twins, Jakub had always been faster, while Pawel was stronger. Pawel helped Jakub up to his one unsteady leg, then lifted him onto his shoulders with a grunt.

"The flag . . ."

"Forget the flag," Pawel said. "We've got to get you stabilized." The towheaded Pole turned and headed back for the tree line from where they came in a steady, plodding march.

A hundred meters into their retreat, another explosion cracked overhead and directly in their path.

Pawel instinctively dropped to his knees, his brother out cold from the drugs. He scanned the area, saw nothing. His heart raced. He knew they were being watched. Out here they were exposed. His best shot was getting the two of them back to the tree line.

Pawel stood up with his brother still draped around his shoulders, grunting with the effort like an Olympic dead-lifter. He shifted Jakub's weight around to get more comfortable, then began jogging toward the trees. Something told him to change directions slightly, and he sped off at a forty-five-degree angle from his original course. It would take him longer to get under cover, but no telling what was waiting for them straight ahead—

BOOM!

The explosion tore away Pawel's booted foot with a snapping, bear-trap crunch. His wounded leg collapsed and the two brothers tumbled into the dirt—

BOOM! Jakub's forehead hit another mine, blowing open his skull like a confetti cannon, splattering Pawel in blood and brain matter.

"Jakub!" Pawel screamed as he clawed at his brother's lifeless body. It was no use. He was gone.

Pawel reached with trembling hands for his medical kit to treat his own wound, but his eyes were fast clouding. His fumbling fingers couldn't grip the tourniquet pack. His blood pressure plunged and his heart fluttered. He suddenly felt cold, and very tired.

He took a deep breath and shut his eyes to rest for a moment until he could try again for the tourniquet. All he needed was a minute to gather his strength. His moment of rest quickly slipped into unconsciousness. The two Poles lay in a widening pool of their commingling blood.

Minutes later, he joined his brother in whatever afterlife awaited them both.

★

Kabak, the Turk, stood in the dank, dark basement of one of the city's crumbling buildings. He passed his wrist device over the triangular flag, capturing it. He checked the display as another red flag turned to green.

That made three. McGuire and the Nigerian had captured their assigned flags, but seven still remained.

Perhaps it was the chill air that sent a shiver down his spine, but he doubted it. The reality was they were running out of time. Their only hope of survival was capturing all ten flags. But judging by the diminishing radio chatter, he assumed the other mercs were getting killed off faster than they were capturing flags.

His radio suddenly crackled in his ear.

"Kabak—you read me?"

The Turk recognized Plata's voice despite the static.

"I read you."

"I'm standing at my flag, but my capture device is dead. I need your help."

"Where are you?"

"Flag number seven," Plata replied. "I'm in the gray building directly across the street from you. Third floor."

Kabak checked his digital map. Flag number seven was three hundred meters due east, not across the street.

What is going on?

"That's not possible."

"I know where my flag is," Plata said. "I will meet you across the street, then take you there. It's about three hundred meters from your position. I know the safest route. No windows."

"How do I find you?"

"Third floor, top of the stairs, hard left, first door. A closet. No windows. Hurry!"

Kabak frowned. Crossing the street meant being exposed to the air, something he had assiduously avoided.

"What about surveillance drones?" the Turk asked.

"All clear for now—but hurry!"

Plata's flag would make four, Kabak thought. Then they could team up and plot out the rest. There was still a chance he would escape this madhouse alive.

"Roger that. On my way."

★

Kabak climbed the fracturing stairs to the first floor and made his way to street level. He stood inside the door, away from any prying eyes that might be above.

There was, indeed, a gray building directly across from him, its doorway askew as the foundation cracked and sagged over the years. The potholed street was strewn with rubble. It would be a short thirty-meter dash across the road to the other doorway, and safety.

"Still clear?" Kabak asked, worried about surveillance drones.

"Still clear. But hurry!"

"On my way—now."

Kabak took a deep breath, clutched his rifle, and raced into the street, his body aimed directly at the cockeyed doorway. Five charging steps into his run he was nearly cut in half by three large-caliber armor piercing rounds that tore through his rib cage.

The Turk was dead before he hit the ground.

★

Rahul was gratified with the sound of applause from the Vendor's clients clapping in his headset. They had been observing nearly every aspect of Rahul's actions so far and had seen the other kills. But the death of the Turk seemed to have pleased them most.

The Indian assumed it was the level of subterfuge involved in the exercise. Plata's incessant babbling had made it quite easy to capture his voice, and the *Makṛī*'s onboard AI easily synthesized it, and masked it with radio interference. All Rahul had to do was talk to Kabak through the *Makṛī*'s synthesized radio transmitter to sound like Plata and fool the Turk into thinking he was speaking with his commander.

Rahul's own satisfaction with killing Kabak was tactical. The seasoned Turk fighter had brilliantly avoided all optical surveillance until he reached the building where his flag was located, and even then Rahul's surveillance drone had barely caught a glimpse of him.

Rahul assumed the Turk discovered the underground tunnels that ran from that basement to several other buildings in the city. The Turk might never again appear on his surveillance screens. Judging by his military records, Kabak was perhaps the best fighter of the bunch. Rahul had no doubt the wily Turk could ferret out the rest of the flags all by himself if given the opportunity. He had to find a way to draw Kabak out before he disappeared into the tunnels.

Spoofing Plata's voice had proved the perfect solution.

Once out in the street, the *Makṛī*'s semi-auto sniper rifle took over. Tracking the speeding Turk had proved effortless, as had the nearly instantaneous calculation of speed and distance the computer fed into the wirelessly controlled "guided" sniper rounds. Three shots were excessive, but Rahul couldn't risk not killing him. The Turk had proven too difficult to find.

Now it was time to finish the others.

52

Cabrillo's bare skin numbed in the cold seawater, but his sinuses, like his eyes, burned with salt. Stripped down to his waist, his long arms churned through the high tide crashing beneath the island's broken-down pier. The Vendor had placed a flag at the very end of it beneath a blazing blue sky—daring someone to capture it.

Juan knew that anyone foolish enough to run the length of the pier would be seen instantly and gunned down or blown up before they got a quarter way to the target. So he did the only logical thing—he dove into the water and used the pier to shield himself from overhead surveillance. The penalty for staying beneath the pier was getting slammed into the concrete pylons by the surging waves that rose and fell like a Dollywood roller coaster.

He loved swimming in open water, but with the high tide crashing into the eroding pier he suddenly understood that it was the raging sea and not just shoddy construction that had nearly wrecked the structure. Cabrillo's long, powerful strokes clawed through the swelling waves rising eight feet and higher. Lactic acid burned though his body from his broad shoulders and down his back to his meaty thighs. In the *Oregon*'s Olympic-sized pool he would have been making record time, but out here he had only been inching forward. After what seemed like a month of swimming he was finally within eyesight of the rusted ladder at the end of the pier.

★

High on a bluff and hidden in a patch of thick foliage, Linc was keeping overwatch for Juan through the spotting scope. He tracked the Chairman's slow methodical progress while scanning the skies for danger.

All clear.

★

Juan couldn't afford to waste a single, exhausting stroke.

He kept his eyes shut against the burning seawater, opening them at intervals to aid in navigation. The crashing waves roaring beneath the concrete pier robbed him of the ability to hear.

Focused on the ladder and partially deaf, Cabrillo didn't pick up on the high-speed whine of the eight-motored octocopter and its mini gun patrolling on the far side of the pier, opposite the bluff where Linc was keeping overwatch.

★

The drone's algorithm was designed to spot human movement—walking, running, and even swimming. At first, the shadowed underbelly of the pier, the surging waves, and the thick pylons obscured the octocopter's vision sensors. But a thorough, preprogrammed scanning picked up telltale signs of rhythmic splashing and Cabrillo's windmilling arms finally triggered an alert.

The optical targeting reticle tried to hold on to Cabrillo's form, but was too often blocked by the pylons. Likewise, the infrared targeting system detected but couldn't lock on to Juan's heat signature. His body was mostly underwater and the exposed skin was nearly the same temperature as the cold sea.

The AI navigator opted to send the octocopter into the pier to get closer and acquire a target lock. Now the machine faced the same challenges as Cabrillo, except that it couldn't swim. Using its LIDAR sensors, the machine deftly avoided both the pylons and the high-rolling waves. Each maneuver robbed it of the chance to find and lock target onto Cabrillo, but it was gaining ground rapidly.

★

Linc swore he heard the sound of high-pitched motors in the distance, but the spotting scope hadn't revealed anything. He dropped the spotting scope and settled in behind his rifle and tracked the Chairman in his crosshairs.

★

Cabrillo heard a gunshot behind him. The sting of concrete chips splattering from the nearby pylons and hitting his face told him that whoever had taken the shot had missed—barely.

Almost subconsciously he calculated the geometry between the sound of the gun blast behind him and the shattering pylon, locating the origin of the shot. He quickly angled away from that line of fire toward the far side of the next pylon, hoping to block the next bullet.

Utterly exhausted from his long swim, the emergency adrenaline dump gave him an incredible boost of energy and he surged ahead.

★

The octocopter's optical targeting system finally locked onto the human figure in the water. The software made the necessary calculations and fired a single shot at Cabrillo's skull.

The Chairman should have been killed, but the wave he'd been cresting suddenly dropped and the bullet missed him by just a few inches.

Just as the octocopter was preparing to take the next shot, another roller zoomed into the drone's sensor area. It was forced to navigate away before the wave could crash into it, allowing Cabrillo a few extra moments to swim left to a new position, which once again blocked the drone's vision.

The octocopter maneuvered right and surged forward, anticipating Cabrillo's next position, hoping to acquire his form in the targeting reticle once again. Another wave rose up on its watery haunches and surged at the vehicle, forcing it farther right until it was now just beyond the outer pylon. Though it had no conception whatsoever of either kismet or dumb luck, the drone found itself perfectly positioned to acquire its target and laid its reticle squarely in the center of Juan's broad back.

★

The first shot from the octocopter jolted through Linc's central nervous system like an electrical surge, putting all his senses on high alert.

More importantly, the sound of the blast helped him locate the drone, which now angled out from beneath the pier, its engines frothing up the water as it turned to fire.

Linc pulled the trigger and the big Barrett jumped on its tripod, sending a massive .50-caliber armor-piercing bullet downrange. Designed in the 1920s as an anti-vehicle and anti-aircraft round, the "Ma Deuce" easily pierced the octocopter's aluminum body, smashing its computer brain and scattering its wreckage into the sea.

★

Cabrillo turned around in the water toward the whining pitch of the octocopter's motors just in time to see it shattered by Linc's shot.

Ten minutes later, he scampered up the rusted ladder and swiped his watch across the flag to capture it. He then turned and dove off the pier, heading for the rendezvous point he and Linc had picked out on the beach.

★

Thirty minutes later, Cabrillo crawled up onto the sandbank and jogged inside the dry cave. It was located far below the bluff above and out of sight of any overhead surveillance drones. He was out of breath and bent over, and holding himself up by bracing against his knees.

Linc was already inside, a wide grin on his face, his big Barrett rifle slung across his back. Cabrillo's gear was stacked nearby. He held out a water canteen. Having survived Hell Week at BUD/S, Linc knew that hours of hard swimming in cold water generated a powerful thirst.

"You were making some serious Aquaman moves out there."

"Heck . . . of a . . . shot," Cabrillo said between great gulps of air. "Thanks." He took a long swig of water.

"That's why you pay me the big bucks."

Cabrillo wiped his mouth. "Might even get a Christmas bonus for that one."

Juan stretched out his aching muscles. It had been a marathon swim session for sure, made even harder by the fact he was weighted down with waterlogged combat pants and heavy boots. Now that he was out of the cold water he was beginning to warm up.

Cabrillo's face suddenly narrowed as if in pain. He dropped his pants.

"What's wrong?" Linc asked.

Cabrillo opened up his combat leg. He pulled out his sat phone.

It was vibrating.

53

Fireside Pies. Guido speaking," Juan said. He put the call on speakerphone.

"Juan! Thank God you're okay," Max said on the other end of the sat line. "We've been worried sick. We've been trying to reach you, but your sat signal's been blocked. Your trackers, too. Those just came online a few minutes ago, Linc's first. He with you?"

"Sure am," Linc said. "And vertical, just like the Chairman."

"We're in a cave on the edge of an island beneath a bluff," Juan said. "There must be some sort of a pocket where the signal blocking isn't working."

"What's your status?"

"Pretty good considering we're in the middle of an arena full of flame-throwing robots."

"What?"

"I'll explain everything as soon as you pick us up."

"We're still eight hours away—and running full tilt."

"That's probably seven hours longer than we can survive. You might want to goose it a little."

"I figured as much. That's why when Linc's tracker came back online, I contacted Overholt and requested an emergency quick reaction force. There's a U.S. Navy Expeditionary Strike Group in the area with a boatload of leathernecks itching for a fight."

Juan's first reaction was relief. He was utterly exhausted from the long swim and the constant flood of adrenaline he'd experienced since he'd been awakened by an air-raid siren before sunrise. They sure could use the backup.

But his tactical brain quickly elbowed its way through his raw emotions.

"Negative. Belay that order. The Vendor has too many tricks up his sleeve. I can't guarantee the safety of those Marines."

"What about you and Linc?"

"We'll figure something out for the next eight hours. Just do us a favor and keep the pedal to the metal."

"Will do."

"If we leave the cave we'll probably lose contact again. There's an airstrip on the southwest side of the island near the beach. We'll meet you there."

"Roger that. Stay frosty, boys. And Godspeed."

★

Juan killed the call and replaced the sat phone into its compartment in his leg. He pulled on a shirt as he formulated his next moves.

"Where are the other teams at?" he asked Linc.

"I've been monitoring the radio traffic. The Polish twins, the German, and the Turk aren't responding to Plata's calls."

"Neither are we."

"You know they're dead."

"All the more reason why the others need our help. Let's get out of here."

54

Plata had ordered the mercs to meet at cache D, which happened to be an old Japanese bomb shelter dug into the side of a hill, well out of sight from any overhead surveillance.

The Vendor was giving them every chance for survival by putting food and ammo caches in protected positions. He wasn't doing that out of any kind of charity, Juan knew, but for test integrity. Had he put a cache out in the middle of an open field it would have been like scattering apples at the base of Rahul's drone-powered deer blind.

Once clear of the cave and under cover of a thick stand of trees, Cabrillo checked the Mini-Sniffer to see if it had finished cracking Rahul's encryption codes. So far, it had failed to do so, but was still in the process. He wasn't sure if his stint in the cave had somehow interrupted the attempt or if the Mini-Sniffer simply lacked the computing power to pull it off. Only time would tell.

Juan and Linc were the last to arrive at the cache, though they were right on time. Juan counted six survivors besides themselves: Plata, Drăguş, McGuire, Osipenko, the Frenchman, and the Brit.

Osipenko and the Brit were devouring MREs and washing them down with liters of bottled water. McGuire was stretched out on a cot, his face hidden beneath a cap and lightly snoring. Plata and Drăguş were hovering over a topo map they'd found in the cache storage.

"Nobody else?" Juan asked.

"Five dead, plus the Syrian," Plata said. "Though he got his before we even got started, didn't he?"

"More money for the rest of us," the Russian grunted.

Linc made a beeline for the stash of food and snagged up a ripe mango, yellow as a daisy in bloom. He pocketed a couple of bananas, too, before pulling his combat knife and peeling the mango.

"I take it the men who didn't make it are the ones who didn't get their flags?" the Brit asked.

"*Non*," the Frenchman said. "The Nigerian got his before he bought the farm. Same with the Turk. I couldn't get to mine. I saw two drones on patrol. I would have waited longer but we were ordered back to the rally point. I have an idea how to capture my flag, but I'll need at least one other person to help me out."

The Brit counted on his fingers. "Six flags captured. Two captured by the dead. Eight left alive. Frenchie missed his. I got mine. What about you, Ivan?"

The Russian scowled. "Check your map. You can see I got my assigned flag." He pointed at Linc and Juan. "So did they." The big Slav grinned like a toothy pumpkin and pointed at Plata. "But our fearless leaders fell short."

The Guatemalan's reddened face glanced up from the map.

"Like Frenchie said, there were drone patrols all over the place. We know how to get our flag next time."

Juan fought back a grin, enjoying Plata's embarrassment. He tore open a bag of Pili nuts, branded in packaging from the Philippines. The high-fat treats were an excellent energy source and tasted like toasted butter. He popped a handful into his mouth.

"That makes four flags left with just under forty hours remaining," Juan said. "So what's the plan, jefe?"

"What do you think it is? We find a way to grab those four last flags," Plata said, turning back to the map. "You have a better idea?"

The buttery Pili nuts, softer and sweeter than almonds, practically melted in Juan's mouth.

"Not getting killed would be at the top of my list."

Plata faced Juan. "We need to figure out what went wrong with each previous attempt and try to overcome it. We have eight people for four flags. We'll go back out in pairs and grab them."

Plata pulled the small camp table with the topo map to the center of the cramped room. "Everyone take a look."

The mercs shuffled over. Except for McGuire, still stretched out on a cot with a cap over his eyes. Plata kicked the sole of his boot. The Irishman stirred, and peeked out from beneath his hat.

"What?"

"Get over here."

Linc handed Juan a slice of slimy mango. Cabrillo shoved it into his mouth, savoring the tangy sweetness as the Irishman shambled over to the table.

"All right, let's start with the Polish mission," Plata said. "Flag number nine. Any idea what happened?"

"I saw their bodies in the open field," McGuire said. "Could've been shot, but I heard three explosions earlier."

"Minefield?" Drăguş asked.

"That would be my guess."

Plata shrugged. "I didn't see any mine-clearing equipment in the armory. Nobody requested any."

"Why would we? It was supposed to be a VIP security mission," the Frenchman said.

"Is there a truck or a car we could wire up and send out to explode the mines?" McGuire asked.

"Even if there was, the first mine would disable the vehicle. No telling how many are out there."

"Or how the mines got there," the Russian said.

"What do you mean?"

"Dropping mines from the air is a dirty little trick my people have perfected. You stop the advance with a nasty surprise and then you cripple them further as they retreat. Killed a lot of Ukies that way."

Plata shook his head, despairing. "We've got no chance, then. And if we fail to get even one flag, we're dead."

"Did you inventory that armory?" Cabrillo asked.

Linc handed Juan a banana. "Potassium. You need it."

"Thanks." Juan peeled it.

"No, as a matter of fact," Plata said. "There was an entire room full of equipment. But I'm telling you, there's nothing for clearing mines."

"We'll take care of it," Juan said. "Davis and me." Cabrillo took a giant bite of his banana.

"How?"

"Not your concern," Juan said, his mouth full of mush. He pointed at the map with his half-eaten banana. "Let's talk about the other flags."

★

The mercs discussed various plans to overcome the defenses of the other three flags. Juan and Linc offered the best solutions, which Plata immediately took credit for. They didn't care. All that mattered was that every flag was captured before the deadline.

Capturing the flags meant not only survival but riches for the mercs. But for Cabrillo, sticking the Vendor in the eye with a bitter defeat and capturing or killing him was an even sweeter thought.

Minutes later, Juan and Linc were making their way back to the armory beneath the cover of the jungle canopy, their eyes constantly scanning the ground and the trees in front of them.

"So, you gonna tell me how we're going to work our way through a minefield beneath an open sky without the benefit of mine-clearing equipment?" Linc asked.

"I was thinking about building a giant kite and having you hold on to the tail and I would fly you over it," Juan said. "But I know how much you hate heights."

"Yeah, I'd say that's at least one reason why that plan might not work. Anything else?"

"The Vendor builds drones. Maybe he's got a rig squirreled away in that storage room." Juan tapped his watch as he marched. "If we can find a way to remove my watch and attach it to the drone, we can fly the drone close enough to the flag to capture it without exposing ourselves to overhead surveillance and avoiding the minefield altogether."

"But what if we can't get your watch off? And what if there isn't a drone?"

"Then I'd say we're back to the giant kite option."

Juan suddenly froze in his tracks.

55

Linc stopped short, certain Cabrillo had spotted a trip wire or a mine detonator.

"Where is it?" Linc asked, scanning the ground.

"In my leg."

"What?"

Cabrillo dropped his pants, accessed the storage compartment in his combat leg, and fished out the Mini-Sniffer. He couldn't help but smile.

"The boys really came through," Juan said as he studied the Mini-Sniffer's display screen.

"Good news, I take it."

"Not only has the Mini-Sniffer decrypted the signals, it's also telling me what specific systems are connected to which channels." Juan scrolled down the list and read a few aloud. "Surveillance . . . strike . . . strike . . . strike . . . surveillance." There were two dozen more.

"That's a start," Linc said. "Now what are you going to do with all of that information?"

Juan's fingers and thumbs flew across the display.

"Looks like there's a central hub linked to all of the rest of the signals. It's located about two klicks from here—and it's moving."

"The Terminator termite?"

"That's my guess. If Rahul is being sold as a one-man army, he must be operating everything through that machine. Sort of like a mother ship. Probably AI-powered, too."

"Anything you can do about it?"

"You mean, like a kite?" Juan continued punching buttons like a crazed symphony conductor.

"Something better than a kite. You know. Plan C and all of that?"

Juan tapped a final toggle with a flourish.

"How about . . . *this*?"

★

Rahul avoided stepping on dry leaves or snapping twigs as best he could while keeping his eyes glued to his tablet. He was no soldier, but he knew that moving quietly as possible was only to his advantage. Of course, the soft whir of the *Makṛī*'s electric motors and the thumping of its eight rubberized feet made complete silence impossible. He would have to think about solutions to those relatively minor problems before the next test iteration.

Rahul wasn't particularly concerned about being discovered just yet. One of his other surveillance drones had caught a fleeting glimpse of the eight surviving mercenaries as they dashed out of what must have been a cache of supplies and into nearby cover. If they all kept moving in their respective directions, none of them would be approaching his position anytime soon.

Equally important, the surveillance drone circling overhead was fixed on him right now. It also gave his helmet's HUD a wide field of view of his immediate surroundings. Everything was clear.

Rahul stepped over a thick fallen log that marked the edge of a clearing. A few steps later he turned around and watched the *Makṛī* navigate the hazard with ease. As he stepped into the clearing, his helmet vibrated.

His heart sank. The heads-up display—or worse, the entire system—was suffering a malfunction.

For some reason, a flashing yellow box surrounded the *Makṛī*.

Worse, all of the combat drones were flashing automated RETURN TO BASE commands. Some kind of false signal had triggered them.

Rahul's gloved hands virtually swiped open the helmet's programming screen to initiate an override command.

The giant *Makṛī* stood patiently by his side, like a headless, loyal wolfhound.

The Indian national found the screen and virtually tapped the button to open it, but the screen was frozen. It was at that singular moment he realized what had happened. He couldn't believe it.

He flipped back to the first screen. The flashing yellow box surrounding the *Makṛī* had turned to solid red.

Rahul tossed his helmet as he turned on his heel to bolt away. Three steps into his run the first Yari smashed into the *Makṛī*. The resulting shrapnel cut across the Indian's lower back, severing his spine. His strings cut, he tumbled face down into the dirt, unable to move. Two more explosions quickly followed.

Rahul always thought his final moments on earth would be utterly terrifying. But the sheer genius on the other side of this exchange only elicited his admiration.

Moments later, both he and the *Makṛī* were utterly ripped apart, their shattered remains scattered across the clearing.

56

The Vendor's invited guests were seated in the small, darkened theater, focused on the large screen display. The rays of the digital projector shot through clouds of cigarette smoke. They were all intensely focused on the first-person view from the Yari drone as it hurtled toward the wreckage of the *Makṛī* and Rahul's broken body lying nearby. Seconds later, the image turned to digital snow.

"Keiko, kill the transmission," the Vendor ordered as he stood. His AI assistant snapped the monitor off immediately.

The young Chinese general stood and faced the towering Vendor.

"Overall, a very impressive demonstration."

"Thank you."

"Up until the moment your system was utterly defeated."

A smattering of hushed laughter burbled in the darkened room. The lights popped on.

The Vendor's fists clenched at the insult as the other guests stood.

"What do the Brits say? 'Hoisted on your own petard?'" the Nigerian colonel said.

More subtle laughter rippled around the room.

"The test isn't over yet!"

"Of course it is," the other Nigerian said. "It's only a matter of time before the other flags are captured. Twenty million dollars is a great incentive to finish their mission."

"Unless, of course, you decide to murder them," the Italian said. He was the head of a dark web assassination outfit.

"I am an honorable man. I would never violate the terms of an agreement."

"Then face it," the Nigerian said. "They won. You lost."

"I admire the tactical logic of your opponents," the Chinese general said. "Defeating your network rather than your fighting systems was a stroke of genius. How do you suppose it was done?" He flashed a thin smile.

Rage flooded the Vendor's nervous system. The humiliation was nearly unbearable. Worse, if word of this disaster got out into the arms community, his reputation would suffer.

He was about to issue an order to have them all arrested and killed, and their bodies dumped in the shark-infested waters around the island. But his cold reason overrode his animal instinct for vengeance. Their disappearances would cause more problems than they would solve.

"I want to know how your network was breached," the blond Serbian said. "That is the technology we need to acquire."

"Why assume it was breached?" the Vendor asked. "It was most likely a hardware or software failure that triggered the return-to-base function."

"I suspect you have a security problem," the North Korean said in her thickly accented English.

"Which means we are all now at risk," the Italian said.

"There is no reason for us to remain here," the Chinese colonel said. "We demand immediate transportation back to Mindanao."

Heads nodded all around. The group was clearly nervous.

"Keiko, notify the pilots to prepare for immediate departure."

"It will be done."

The Vendor smiled, raising opened hands. "You see? There is a transport helicopter on twenty-four-hour emergency standby. It will arrive on this building's helipad within twenty minutes."

"Very good," the Chinese colonel said, relieved.

"I would ask all of you to remember the nondisclosure agreement you signed before you came here."

"Don't worry," the Serbian said. "Your secret is safer with us than it is with you, apparently."

"I will be in contact with each of you as soon as I have solved the issues and a new test can be conducted—"

"Don't bother," the Chinese general said. "The obvious imperfection in the technology is quite sufficient for my taste."

The Vendor forced himself to ignore the insult. He pointed to the head of his personal bodyguard unit, an armed Japanese officer in crisp jungle camouflage standing in the corner. He drew the lieutenant over with a sharp draw of his index finger. The officer dashed over.

"Sir?"

The Vendor lowered his voice. "Escort my guests to the helipad. Put four snipers on the roof and a squad of armed guards outside the building. Contact me as soon as they are airborne."

"Yes, sir." The Japanese lieutenant turned to the guests. "If you will all please follow me." He pointed in the direction of the elevators. The Chinese delegation led the way, followed by the others.

The North Korean scientist slipped over to the Vendor. "Please be sure to contact me when the next test occurs." She patted him on the arm. "I'm sure you'll find the problem." She offered a forced smile before turning and catching up with the others.

The Vendor watched the large elevator doors shut and waited for the hum of hydraulics that signaled their lift up to the roof helipad before he allowed himself a bone-rattling, primal scream.

★

Juan and Linc crested a small hill to get their bearings, no longer afraid of being spotted by drones overhead. After destroying the *Makrī*, Juan ordered the remaining drones to ground and disarm themselves, then used the Mini-Sniffer to scramble and disable their software permanently. He also killed the radio signals to all of the island's hidden cameras, blinding the Vendor.

Unfortunately, the handy device didn't have a controller function or the ability to display camera feeds, otherwise he would have deployed the drones to take out the Vendor in a direct assault on his fortified compound. He made a mental note to raise those deficiencies with Stoney and Murph before they began a Mini-Sniffer version 2.0 build-out.

"There it is," Linc said, using the spotter scope for a better view. He handed it to Juan.

They had both heard the heavy helicopter blades beating the air earlier, but they were under the jungle canopy at the time and couldn't see it. But now up on the hill with a clear line of sight, Juan saw the big chopper leap off the tallest building in the compound and arc out over the ocean.

"I guess the party's over, now that we've tossed a turd into their punch bowl," Linc said.

"I'm just praying the Vendor isn't on that chopper." Juan checked his watch. "*Oregon*'s still four hours away."

"We're still a fair hike from the strike zone. We should get moving."

Juan wanted visual confirmation of the spider-bot's destruction. What he was really hoping for was that Rahul was standing close by when the first drone hit. If so, maybe there was some intel on the corpse or on the robot they could use against the Vendor. They had plenty of time to get there before the *Oregon* would arrive.

They also both agreed there wasn't any advantage to hanging out with the other mercs. They were already on Plata's radar and the prospect of splitting twenty million dollars with two fewer members of their team could prove too tempting to resist.

Juan pulled his canteen and took a swig of water as the beating helicopter blades faded in the distance. The scent of sweet and musky jasmine in the air brightened his spirits after a long and adrenaline-fueled day.

"Yeah. Let's get after it."

57

Erin Banfield plopped down in front of her home computer with a full tumbler of scotch on the rocks in one hand. It was a daily vice that helped calm her nerves as she accessed the dark side of her life on her secure private network.

First and foremost, she reviewed her investment portfolios, several of which were located in carefully hidden overseas accounts far from the prying eyes of U.S. government auditors. Her nest egg was almost large enough to flee her Georgetown roost. Still, she needed to accumulate as much tax-free cash as possible if she hoped to sustain her beachside love nest with her hot-blooded Portuguese paramour for the long run.

That need for extra cash drove her to a second checklist item, which was monitoring Langston Overholt's affairs via the private server of his that she managed to hack. Years ago, she would have done this at the office, but CIA internal security had gotten tighter in the last decade. Network administrators were continually monitoring unwarranted activities and unauthorized access on federal machines. Her Georgetown bastion was more secure than any government sensitive information facility and the safest place from which to spy on Overholt.

She quickly scanned Overholt's files and discovered the old man's emergency exfil request two hours prior for a quick reaction force to be deployed immediately to a specified GPS location.

She stopped reading the email in order to geolocate the coordinates. She discovered it was a private island off the southern coast of Mindanao, the Philippines.

Her eyes then fell on the next email posted five minutes later. It was another request from Overholt canceling the emergency quick response force, no reason given.

Strange.

She was still processing the unusual pair of requests when she suddenly realized she hadn't finished reading the first email. She pulled it back up for details.

The emergency exfil request was for the rescue of two American contractors deployed with the vessel *Oregon*.

Oregon? Oregon? Where had she heard that name before?

Banfield took a long pull from her scotch and set her glass down on a dog-eared copy of Jumble puzzles she had finished in a day. They were too easy for her incredible intellect, but they always brought her warm memories of doing them as a young girl with her father on her weekend visits to his house. The puzzles required her to unscramble random letters to form intelligible words. The praise her father heaped upon her had been an elixir for her broken, impressionable soul. It had also ignited the intellectual fire that would ultimately lead to her current career as a CIA intelligence analyst.

And then it suddenly hit her. O-R-E-G-O-N could also be spelled N-O-R-E-G-O.

"*Norego*," she whispered.

That was the name of the ship that the Vendor had requested information on after it had caused him some problems he didn't want to talk about.

This was the first bit of intel on the *Norego* she had been able to uncover.

She needed to contact him immediately.

★

THE ISLAND OF SORROWS
THE CELEBES SEA

Linc surveyed the debris field. The *Makṛī* was a smoldering pile of
wrecked debris, its legs and various mechanical parts littering
the area like so many Legos on the living room floor on Christmas morning. Three distinct craters indicated points of impact beyond the direct hit the spider-bot took. What appeared to be an
obliterated HUD helmet and a smashed tablet provided nothing
of use.

Linc bent over and picked up what looked like a piece of the machine's motherboard. It was half-melted, but a large chip was attached
to it. He pocketed it. No telling what the boys might be able to pull
from it.

"There's not much left of him," Juan said, standing thirty feet
away. Rahul's ruined corpse had not only been hit but tossed through
the air like a bloody rag doll. The brilliant engineer lay in a mangled,
bloody heap, nearly unrecognizable in his current state. Only his
shredded one-piece flight suit and the camel-colored Merrell tactical
boot affixed to a leg five feet away from the ruined torso gave Juan any
confidence in his identification of the corpse.

Juan fished around in the few intact pockets of the bloody flight
suit, but founding nothing of interest, not even a fragment of identification. Linc stepped up beside him, his big frame blocking the early-
afternoon sun.

"Our dead Indian friend and his grounded drones means the game's
over," Linc said. "What do you want to do now?"

Juan stood, and wiped his hands against his combat pants.

"Technically, the game isn't over until all ten flags are captured."
Cabrillo held a hand to his ear. "What do you hear?"

Linc cocked his head. "Birds singing. Haven't heard that in a
while." A big toothy smile brightened his fearsome face. "Sounds
kinda nice, actually."

Juan smiled. "Yeah, it does. But what you don't hear is that god-awful horn that's supposed to signal the end of the game."

"And if the game's still on, it means the Vendor will kill us all if we don't grab those flags by tomorrow."

"Exactly. The good news is that means the Vendor will still be hanging around, hoping to save his twenty million dollars."

"Unless he intends to break the rules and murder us anyway."

"We'll deal with that, too."

"What if the Vendor has already left?" Linc asked.

"Then we get whatever intel we can off of Plata. He's been the Vendor's contact person for this shindig. Speaking of which, we should contact Plata. Let him know the situation."

Cabrillo keyed his mic and called for Plata.

"You get your flag?" the surly Guatemalan responded.

"Better than the flag. We killed Rahul and destroyed his monster-bot."

Several cheers went up over the tactical net. All of the mercs were on the same radio frequency.

Only Plata remained quiet. There was a pause on his end. Finally he asked, "How?"

"Long story. We'll talk about it later. Better still, all of his drones are grounded."

"Again, how?"

"Does it matter?"

"So we've won? The money's ours!" McGuire's throaty laugh roared in Juan's earpiece. The rest of the mercs shouted and cheered.

"*Cálmense, amigos.* We haven't won yet," Plata said. "We need to grab the rest of the flags."

"And we only have until tomorrow to get them or the Vendor will still kill us," the Frenchman added.

"Let him try," the Russian said.

"Osipenko's right," Plata said. "We've already proven we can beat him."

We? Juan shook his head. Plata's arrogance was only matched by his inferiority complex.

"Grabbing those flags should be easy enough," Juan said. "Davis and I must still navigate a minefield, but the rest of you should not face any opposition. Still, take all necessary precautions."

"I'm giving the orders, Mendoza. Not you," Plata said. "Everybody stays on mission. When you capture your flag, get back to the rally point ASAP. After that, we'll have to see what other tricks the Vendor might have up his sleeve. Understood?"

The others signaled they heard their orders and would comply.

"Mendoza out," Juan said and killed his radio. He turned to Linc. "We've got a date with a minefield."

"Too bad we couldn't use one of those drones you scrambled."

"We'll head back to the armory and see how we can MacGyver our way out of this mess."

58

anfield's face was flushed red, partly from the booze she'd been drinking, but mostly in reaction to the texts she'd been exchanging with the Vendor. She'd never met the man before and had no idea of his true identity.

Over the past few years, she had allowed herself to fantasize about him, picturing a roguishly handsome and dangerously mysterious European royal who would someday magically appear at her door and whisk her away to his mountain castle. All of those childish notions were suddenly crushed beneath his vicious barrage of nasty exchanges questioning her intelligence and usefulness.

Wilting beneath the Vendor's scalding criticisms, she found herself on the verge of groveling, something she loathed even more than the man's gross ingratitude. She had risked her career and even prison in order to help his business escape unwanted scrutiny. And now she was an idiot for working late and discovering Overholt's texts hours after the fact?

Her ego told her to resign then and there, but the prospect of more tax-free cash was too great to ignore. She swallowed her pride as he laid out more demands. He finally ended his digital tirade with the simple text command:

IF YOU LEARN ANYTHING MORE ABOUT THE
OREGON CONTACT ME IMMEDIATELY!!!

Her eyes welling with tears, she tossed her encrypted Vendor-only phone aside. She'd never been so humiliated. But what bothered her even more was the vague but unmistakable subtext beneath it all that sent shivers down her spine.

For the first time in their long and profitable relationship, she finally realized he could very well murder her.

★

THE ISLAND OF SORROWS
THE CELEBES SEA

The Vendor paced the control room, fuming. The *Makṛī* had been destroyed, the drones grounded, and the cameras shut down. But what infuriated him most of all was the prospect of the hated *Oregon* looming somewhere out at sea.

That idiot Banfield should have been more attentive. As soon as he recruited a suitable replacement he would eliminate her. He had bigger problems at the moment.

Why had the *Oregon* requested a quick response force at his island, and then suddenly canceled it? The Vendor tasted the bile in the back of his throat. Without a doubt, that saucy, one-legged fellow who had downed his automated airplane had something to do with it. But what? There was no one-legged man on the island—

"Keiko!"

"*Yes, sir?*"

"Pull up the image of that brigand that sabotaged flight 252 and put it on my screen."

"*Here it is.*"

Cabrillo's photo capture in the plane's cargo space appeared on the display.

"*I've enhanced the image as best I could. The onboard cameras were low resolution.*"

"Quit making excuses. Keiko, pull up the facial photos of the mercenaries we brought to the island and run a comparative facial recognition analysis with the brigand. I'm trying to determine if he is one of the mercenaries on the island."

"Running now."

Juan's image from the airplane was overlaid with forty dots at key nodes on his face, delineating the features that comprised his unique facial identity. Those metrics included skin texture analysis, nose width, eye socket depth, geometric ratios between facial landmarks, jawline contours, and 3D analysis.

Next, the twelve mercenary faces appeared separately next to Juan's photo from the plane, each one slapped down like a playing card on a blackjack table. As each face card was slapped down, the same forty dots at key nodes appeared on their faces as well, and a mathematical analysis comparing the two appeared in a separate window. Each analysis ended with a percentage match.

The first face up was Plata, who scored a fifty-one percent match. Within thirty seconds, all of the other faces had been compared. Davis had the lowest score at eleven percent. The highest score was Mendoza's at sixty-eight percent, despite his hair color.

"Keiko, I want you to refine the parameters." He gave her a few suggestions.

On the second run, Mendoza scored eighty-six percent.

The computer automatically overlaid the two photos. Despite Kevin Nixon's brilliant prosthetic work, which included subtle changes to Juan's facial geometry and skin texture, Keiko was finally able to suss him out.

The Vendor couldn't help but smile with admiration. How could a one-legged man sneak onto an island posing as a cutthroat mercenary? Of course! Because the men weren't subject to a complete physical. There had been no need for one. They weren't being recruited for a long-term career. They had been recruited to die quickly and violently. Who cared if they had tuberculosis or piles or even a fake leg?

The presence of the spy explained how the *Oregon* found his island and perhaps also the destruction of his drones. The Vendor quickly checked Banfield's text message. The quick response force had been canceled before the drones had been destroyed, not after. That surprised him. He assumed it would have been the other way around.

It didn't matter. This was a dangerous fellow in service of a very capable vessel that knew his location and was no doubt on the way. The Vendor faced a dilemma.

The wiser course of action would be to evacuate immediately. But in so doing, he would never discover the identity of the spy nor the origin of the *Oregon*. Worse, he would never learn how the interloper had managed to defeat his infantry combat system, something he desperately needed to know if he wanted to bring it to market.

His goal now was to capture the one-legged menace and torture him until he revealed all of his secrets. After that, he would kill him in the most unpleasant way, if for no other reason than the sheer satisfaction of destroying the man who had so successfully frustrated his will.

★

Plata and Drăguş stood inside the underground mine just a few feet away from the German's corpse. Drăguş had just rolled him over with the tip of his boot to reveal a skull with the face completely melted away. The stench nearly made them both vomit. According to their wrist devices they were just fifty-three meters away from the next flag.

They had entered the mine with extreme caution, searching for the German's body and whatever weapon had caused his demise. While they had found the corpse, they could not locate the device that had destroyed him.

Three long clicks suddenly chirped in Plata's headset, followed by four short clicks.

This was the prearranged signal the Vendor had established when he wanted Plata to change radio channels and contact him privately.

"Go on ahead and grab the flag," Plata ordered. "I need to check on the others."

"Piece of cake," Drăguş said.

"Yes, cake. But still be careful, eh?"

Drăguş nodded and sped on ahead.

Once the Romanian was out of earshot, Plata switched to the other radio channel and keyed his mic.

"You've got some big brass cojones calling me. What do you want?"

"I have a new business proposition for you."

"Lucky me! Does this one involve exploding vampire robots? Mechanical piranhas? Tell me."

"Your man Mendoza. He's an American spy."

Plata swore violently. "I knew it! I always hated that *basura*. He thought he was smarter than me."

"Apparently he was."

"*You* recruited him. *You* vetted him. Not me."

"Fair enough. By the way, did you know he had one prosthetic leg?"

"A gimp? Out here? I don't believe it." Plata swore again.

"He is a man of extraordinary talents. That's why I need your help."

"What is it that you want?"

"I need you to capture him and use your particular skills to extract information from him—his true identity, who sent him, what he knows about my operations."

"Why would I do that?"

"In exchange for this service, I will immediately transfer the twenty million dollars from the test to each of your accounts."

"You have to, anyway. We've won. Unless, of course, you are a dishonorable man."

"You haven't won yet. In fact, there's little chance you'll overcome the minefield at flag number nine. There are no drone assets in the armory nor minefield-clearing devices, since none of you requested either. You can't possibly win the money, and according to the terms of our new contract, you will all be killed at the forty-eight-hour mark."

"How can I trust you?"

"I know exactly where you're standing there in the mine."

Instinctively, Plata glanced down at his feet, then stepped back a little.

"Rahul had laid ground sensors leading up to flag number one. They are still active. I could have sent my own squadron of drones to kill you where you stand or set up an ambush at the mouth of the mine. Instead, I called you."

"You once told me that money doesn't matter to you."

"It doesn't."

"Then I want double the money for my men. Forty million dollars."

"Done. Is it a deal?"

"What about Davis?"

"What about him?"

"He and Mendoza have been thick as thieves since they got here."

"That doesn't make him a spy."

"But he is an American."

"Indeed, he is. And that alone is a good enough reason to kill him. You have my permission to do so."

"I don't need your permission."

"Then you have my blessing. I will even put my bodyguards under your command for extra firepower. Is it a deal?"

Plata hesitated. The slippery snake had already pulled the rug out from under him once. He couldn't possibly trust him. But then again, what choice did he have? They had no means to get off the island, no means to communicate with the outside world, and a certain death sentence waiting for them tomorrow if he didn't comply.

"What about our transportation out of here?"

"It will be provided free of charge, any destination you choose, just as we agreed to before."

"One other thing."

"Name it."

"When I finish with Mendoza, I want to be the one who enjoys the pleasure of killing him."

"Done."

"Then we have a deal."

"There is one condition," the Vendor said.

Plata fought the urge to swear again, just as Drăguş came running up out of the dark, a wide smile on his face. Plata glanced down at his wrist device. The flag had been captured. He held up an index finger to silence the Romanian before he could speak.

Drăguş frowned with curiosity.

"I'm listening," Plata said.

"You only have two hours to accomplish your task."

"Why the rush?"

"Mendoza's American friends are in transit and will arrive in force. I promise you, you won't survive the encounter."

"Then we need to hurry."

"Indeed."

59

Juan and Linc kept under stealthy concealment as they made their way along a coastal trail back to the armory. They were close enough to hear the pounding surf and caught glimpses of the ocean through the trees.

They chose the most logical route offering them the best cover, but it took them a while, giving Cabrillo enough time to rethink their situation. He certainly didn't trust the Vendor to honor the agreement he had made with his band of cutthroat mercenaries, especially now that his applecart had been upended. To that end, they turned off their radios just in case the Vendor had the means to track them. Cabrillo knew that just because he had grounded Rahul's drone fleet and cameras didn't mean the Vendor didn't have other means of surveillance or attack. Vigilance and caution were their best defenses.

If he and Linc wanted to survive, the safest play would have been to hole up somewhere and wait for the *Oregon* to arrive just two hours from now. But Cabrillo was never one to put personal security above a mission, and his mission was to capture the Vendor and disrupt his operations. He still felt as if the plan to find a drone in the armory and use it to neutralize the minefields at flag number nine was their best shot at doing both.

And it was always possible the *Oregon* could be delayed for hours, perhaps days.

Bringing the contest to an official close might even draw the Vendor out. The arms dealer had exuded both arrogance and vanity. There was no telling what opportunity might present itself for his capture or demise if Juan and Linc saw this through to the end.

Juan halted. Something didn't feel right. He glanced around their position. He also glanced up. The thick foliage that hid them from drones also obscured his view.

"I've got that tingling sensation," Juan said.

"You mean, like when a pretty girl catches your eye?"

"More like squatting in a poison ivy patch without any toilet paper around."

"It is kinda quiet," Linc said. For the better part of their journey buzzing insects and colorful birdcalls had filled the air. Now it was dead silent again, save for the sound of crashing waves and hissing sand.

Cabrillo pulled out his spotting scope and edged forward. Sunlight fell on a hundred-yard patch of open trail. They needed to cross it quickly if they had any hope of avoiding detection. A thick copse of trees loomed on the other side in the shape of a crescent. The trail led straight into a green pocket of foliage.

"What do you see?" Linc whispered.

"Green. Lots of green."

"All clear?"

Juan lowered his scope, processing. He wasn't sure.

"Clear."

Linc unslung his semi-auto Barrett. In a lesser man's hands it would've been too big to handle without a tripod. But Linc could wield it like a regular rifle despite its enormous weight and kick, and lay down a hail of armor-piercing .50-cal gunfire that could stop a small fleet of light armored vehicles.

"Cover me."

"Got you."

Juan bolted for the clearing.

Three steps into his run, Mangin dashed out of the opposing tree line on the far side of the crescent, away from the shore. He waved his arms like a semaphore.

A warning.

Juan hit the dirt when a burst of gunfire ripped into the French-man's back, tumbling him into the grass.

The crescent tree line opened up.

Juan turned a hundred-eighty degrees on his belly and scrambled for cover as Linc opened up with the Barrett. The two men took up positions behind thick trees.

"Frenchie saved us," Juan said. He raised his carbine and fired off a short burst.

"Guess he thought he owed us."

"He didn't. But he paid the price anyway."

A couple of heavy-caliber rounds thudded into the trunk of Juan's tree as he sheltered behind it catching his breath. He felt the wood shuddering against his lower spine.

"Two tangos heading east," Linc said as he squeezed off a shot. The Barrett thundered.

Cabrillo peered around his trunk just as Drăguş cartwheeled into the dirt like a broken doll.

Linc chuckled. "Made that one."

The roar of outboard motors suddenly broke over the water. Cabrillo caught a sudden glimpse of two racing RHIBs full of the Vendor's bodyguards, their wakes carving white scars across the face of the blue ocean.

"Looks like they're trying to flank us," Juan said.

"I count twelve in the boats."

"And we still have four ahead of us—and on the move."

"What do you want to do?"

"Survive."

★

Cabrillo led the way, rushing in a low crouch, with his big African American friend hot on his heels.

A master tactician, Juan had already determined the best course of action. If his next move was entirely successful, they would live.

For another fifteen minutes.

At most.

But it was the only shot they had.

They had been moving approximately south along the covered trail when the Frenchman popped out of the tree line to warn them. That put the two RHIBs and the coast on the west, and the interior of the island on the east—the direction that at least one of the mercs was now pursuing.

Cabrillo figured that if he were in charge of the two boats, he'd land one team farther north to cut off their retreat in that direction, and put the other boat on the beach ASAP so they could come in from the west. In short order, with any good radio communications, even a poorly trained unit would be able to set up an effective kill box.

Unfortunately, the mercs Cabrillo faced were anything but poorly trained. He had to assume the Vendor's personal bodyguards were equally skilled.

Cabrillo's plan was to avoid the kill box for as long as possible and find a better defensive position. Always observing his surroundings, he had spotted what looked like either a crater or a ravine earlier in their movement down the trail toward the armory. He was headed back there now.

Juan skidded to a stop and pointed to a mound some eighty yards distant in the clearing.

"There, see it?"

"Out in the open," Linc said, slightly winded. "Not much of a defensive position. But better than a kick in the head."

They heard shouts in the distance.

"Most things are. Let's go."

Juan bolted through the open terrain, praying they were faster than the mercs trying to turn the corner on them from the east. His legs churned up the steep little berm and he threw himself over the top.

It was deeper than he thought.

He fell four feet through the air, and landed with a sickening crunch of bone.

60

Cabrillo's muscular frame was weighted down with armor plates and gear. Falling four feet from a running jump gave him the force of a battering ram when he hit the bottom of the pit. His boots cracked a set of bleached-white rib bones poking up out of the dry ground.

He glanced around. The thirty-yard-wide crater was a mass grave, its soil eroded away. A sea of bones.

A dozen skeletal hands clawed at the sky as if trying to dig themselves out of the ground.

Perhaps they had—if they'd been buried alive.

Seconds later, Linc landed next to him, his larger frame crushing a pair of skulls beneath his boot heels. It sounded like dried twigs snapping.

Both men exchanged a shocked glance. Neither had ever seen anything so bizarre or macabre. Plata had mentioned there were at least two mass graves on the island. The map didn't indicate their location.

"Never thought I'd be fighting for my life from the bottom of a grave," Linc said.

"The ironies of life never cease to amaze."

Suddenly they heard Plata's familiar voice shouting behind them. "Over there!"

The two *Oregon* operators moved without a word. Their years of training and serving together created a near-telepathic ability to communicate with each other. Commands weren't necessary. Juan instantly took up the four o'clock position on the rim and Linc the eight o'clock. They were spread out enough to cover a two-hundred-seventy-degree field of fire.

The roar of one of the RHIB outboards suddenly cut off.

"First boat just landed," Linc said. "More company coming."

"I hate it when they don't RSVP."

Juan scanned the open field. The graveyard was a pit in the middle of a wide-open field. They had clear shots at whoever crossed it. But they were sitting ducks waiting there. It was only a matter of time before they were overwhelmed.

"How are you on ammo?" Linc asked.

Juan smiled to himself. Linc must have been reading his mind.

"Not great. You?"

"Same."

"Make every shot count."

"Always do."

"You remember *Zulu*?" Juan asked, his eye fixed on the red dot on his rifle.

"My favorite movie growing up. Why?"

"Who did you root for?"

"You have to ask?"

"I thought maybe we could sing like the Welshmen on the eve of battle."

"I thought the Zulus sounded better."

"They had a great bass section for sure, but no top tenors."

Juan squeezed the trigger and ripped a short burst of rounds downrange at Osipenko as he raced through the trees trying to get around behind their position.

"Missed."

Linc's Barrett barked as he put a heavy round into the foliage, his sights resting on Plata ducking behind a tree.

"Missed."

Suddenly, a line of bullets stitched across the lip of the crater.

"The guests have arrived," Juan said, ducking low.

"I hope they brought dessert."

★

Plata had ordered the second RHIB to land and begin its assault despite the Japanese lieutenant's complaints. The Vendor had put them all on a two-hour time clock and it was running out fast.

He had correctly guessed Mendoza's movement toward the armory, but hadn't counted on him taking his sweet time coming down the trail.

In order to surprise the two Americans, he had changed the radio channels to communicate with the bodyguards, but kept on the regular channel to fool Mendoza with false chatter in case he was listening in.

Despite the late hour, everything was going according to plan until *el francés* betrayed them. Plata quite enjoyed killing the sentimental traitor.

The two Americans were skilled operators, but their defensive position wasn't tenable. They were completely surrounded.

But so long as the Americans stayed there, they were winning. If he didn't capture Mendoza soon, he'd lose the money. Worse, their American backup would be arriving shortly, which the Vendor assured him would be a death sentence. If he wanted to capture Mendoza, he had to keep up the pressure without killing him, but it would cost Plata many casualties.

So far, Mendoza had proven too smart—or too lucky—to capture. He hated that *bicho.*

The more he thought about Mendoza's arrogance, the angrier Plata got. Watching his men get slaughtered by those two Americans made his blood boil, and them killing his friend Drăguş had sent him over the edge. No doubt even more would die so long as he stayed his hand.

And who was this Vendor *timador* tugging on his neck like he was a monkey on his leash?

Plata seethed. *To hell with the money.* He was tired of being jerked around by Mendoza—and the Vendor.

This was his war now.

He keyed his mic.

"Plata to all units. We've got these American cowboys surrounded. On my signal, we attack—*and kill them*!"

★

The mercs and bodyguards opened up a barrage of withering fire.

All Juan and Linc could do was duck low as they heard the shouts of men coming from all directions and the roar of automatic weapons racing closer toward them.

Deafened by the wall of noise, the two men exchanged a knowing glance.

This was it. No way out.

Might as well go out fighting.

And die like men on their feet.

The two friends nodded to each other. On a silent count of three, they leaped to their feet, their backs pressed together, guns up.

Juan's narrowing vision saw the screaming faces racing toward him and the sparks of flame leaping from their rifles. He wasn't afraid. It was all in slow motion, and oddly quiet. Even the geysers of dirt kicking up around them rose and fell as if suspended in water. Cabrillo knew it was the adrenaline dulling his senses and slowing time. He barely felt the rifle slug that hammered into his body armor, and hardly noted the blistering heat of bullets whizzing just inches past his face.

It would only be seconds until he and Linc would meet their fates.

Cabrillo's body jolted as Linc fired the Barrett. He raised his own rifle to his cheek and pulled the trigger. He heard Linc shout something, but couldn't make it out.

Cabrillo watched the line of soldiers racing toward him tumble like dominoes into the dirt, torn apart by a stream of lead.

Cabrillo suddenly realized what Linc was saying.

★

"Pour it on, Wepps!" Gomez shouted over the comms.

Mark Murphy wore a pair of goggles and worked a video game controller in his hands. That gave him control of a remotely operated six-barreled "Vulcan" Gatling gun slung beneath the AW tilt-rotor. The Vulcan spat out six thousand rounds of 7.62 NATO per minute. Murph, a world-class gamer and the *Oregon*'s weapons expert, was in his zone.

And he was just getting started.

The AW had come in low over the water to avoid radar, then popped up at the last second to avoid the tree line. Originally targeting Juan's and Linc's tracker locations in the oceanside cave several hours earlier, Gomez was now zeroed in on Plata's radio chatter. By directing his men at Juan and Linc, Plata had inadvertently brought the wrath of the tilt-rotor down on his own head.

Literally.

Murph put enough lead into Plata's brainpan that everything above his Adam's apple evaporated in a purplish mist of gore and bone.

The plume of an RPG roared out from beneath the trees. Gomez deftly sidestepped the unguided weapon as Murphy turned the remote machine gun onto the end of the smoky trail. The RPG launcher fell harmlessly into the grass.

The few surviving guards and mercs all dashed back into the trees.

"Clear!" Murph shouted as he scanned the area with his goggle-controlled video camera.

Gomez dropped altitude and sped over to the bone pit as Murph kicked out a couple of fast ropes.

★

As soon as Juan saw the AW roar overhead, he dropped to one knee and powered up his radio, switching to a clear channel and keying his mic. It took the AW's automated radio scanner a few moments to find Cabrillo. He called out for Gomez as Murph opened fire again. Spent rounds poured down from the belly of the tilt-rotor like brass raindrops.

Linc swapped out his mag and resumed taking potshots at the fleeing soldiers, dropping two. He counted eight bodies in his field of vision.

By that time the big, thundering bird was hovering overhead. Two fast ropes flapped and dangled over the side, battered by the hurricane-force winds of the big turboprops. Murph's big head leaned out the cabin door. He called through the comms.

"You guys called an Uber?"

"I prefer Lyft, but whatever," Linc said as he grabbed the first rope, slipping the toe of his boot into one loop and his hand through another.

Juan did the same on the second.

The last few men in the trees regained some of their courage, seeing the tilt-rotor's Gatling gun had stopped firing. They opened up again. Bullets whizzed like angry hornets past Juan's torso.

"Let's vamoose!" Cabrillo shouted.

The twin Pratt & Whitney engines roared like demons as Gomez shoved the throttles to the stops.

Juan and Linc held on for dear life as the tilt-rotor lifted into the sky, the wind spinning them like tops as the hydraulic lifts pulled them up.

Murph pulled each man forward into the cabin, then jumped back into his seat, threw on his goggles, and picked up his controller, ready to resume the flight.

Juan dashed into the cockpit and fell into the copilot's chair.

"We owe you big-time on this one," Juan said.

"First round's on you back at the barn," Gomez said as he steered the aircraft over the water. "Second one's on me."

Tracers suddenly licked past the windscreen. Gomez yanked his stick and stomped his pedals to dive away from the stream of gunfire.

"It's one of the RHIBs," Murph shouted over the comms. The AW's Gatling gun roared for a short burst just as several bullets hit the plane's starboard engine.

"Got 'em," Murph said.

But Gomez was focused on the smoke pouring out of the big Pratt & Whitney.

Not good.

They were still a long way from the *Oregon*.

61

Max wore a comms set as he stood on the deck, his eyes fixed on the wobbling tilt-rotor, its Gatling gun retracted back into its belly for landing. Designed to fly on two engines, the tilt-rotor yawed and slewed in the air like a drunken seagull, trailing a plume of black smoke from its dead starboard motor. How Gomez managed to keep the bird in the air for as long as he had was anyone's guess.

Three red-shirted firefighters stood by the *Oregon*'s landing deck, extinguishers and firehoses gripped in their hands. The red team lead, Jesse Benson, was a tall, lanky former senior chief on the USS *Ronald Reagan*.

Dr. Huxley stood next to them carrying an emergency medical kit, as did her physician assistant, Amy Forrester.

"Gomez, you go ahead and ditch if you need to," Max said. "We'll pull you out of the drink before your feet get wet."

"Can't do it," Gomez said over the comms. "My insurance rates will go up."

"Juan?" Max asked. He was worried Gomez was pushing it too far. The AW looked more like a tumbling leaf than a helicopter attempting a landing.

"He's the captain. I just pass out the salted peanuts."

"You ready down there?" Gomez asked.

"Bring her in," Max said. He watched Gomez maneuver the shuddering bird into its glide path.

Three minutes later, the roaring AW thudded onto the retractable steel landing deck in a smoking whirlwind. The red shirts attacked the red-hot engine cowling with clouds of white CO_2 as Linc, Juan, Murph, and Gomez dashed out of the craft.

It wasn't the prettiest landing Gomez had ever made, Max thought, but probably his best.

★

Juan sat in the Kirk Chair, his eyes fixed on the Island of Sorrows looming on the big forward screen, the Vendor's three-story HQ centered in the view. They were five miles away.

The *Oregon* was skimming along at flank speed, more than sixty knots, and throwing an incredible wake behind it.

Cabrillo had already briefed Max and the op center crew on the flight back to the *Oregon*. Their goal was to return to the island as quickly as possible and mount an assault on the Vendor's HQ to capture or neutralize him before he fled.

Max confirmed the departure of the first helicopter with Juan, but after that no other aircraft or boat appeared on his radar screen. There was a better than even chance they'd catch the Vendor with his pants down and wrap his operation up with a pretty red bow.

Murph was back at the weapons station and Linc headed down to the team room. Linc was briefing the Gundogs, giving them the layout of the island, expected resistance, and a warning about the moat of land mines surrounding the building. He also provided a physical description of the Vendor. The *Oregon*'s special operators would most likely be the ones to lay hands on the arms merchant and haul him back in chains.

Alarms suddenly screamed.

"Missile lock," Murph said. The *Oregon*'s radar system automatically flashed three tracks racing toward them on one of the big LCD wall screens.

"Thirty seconds to impact."

"Helm, evasive maneuvers," Juan said calmly. He had studied the Vendor's earlier assault on the *Oregon*. This attack was playing out much the same way. He wondered if these missiles carried torpedoes as well.

"Aye, Chairman."

The *Oregon*'s Kashtan anti-aircraft system sped into action, dropping its plates and launching four missiles. Deck mortars thumped giant clouds of radar-confusing chaff into the air. The LaWS laser fired up—but Cabrillo knew it would have no effect.

Seconds later, the three incoming warheads were destroyed by the Kashtan.

"Torps in the water?" Cabrillo asked.

"None," Murph said.

"Helm, take us straight to the island," Cabrillo said. "Wepps, stay frosty."

"Aye," the two men replied.

Two miles from the island, the HQ building roared with cannon fire.

Stoney's eyes had caught it just as Juan ordered, "Hard to port." The ship leaned into its turn just as an explosion geysered into the *Oregon*'s foaming wake, a near miss.

"Wepps, level that building," Cabrillo ordered. "Helm, evasive maneuvers."

Murph grinned, his fingers flying across his command console.

Moments later, the *Oregon*'s own auto-firing 120mm cannon opened up, along with its rail gun throwing giant tungsten rods at five thousand miles per hour—the equivalent kinetic energy of a sixteen-inch naval shell.

Thanks to the *Oregon*'s automated targeting and firing systems, every shell and rod slammed into its target despite the ship's violent turns. Murph's first shot silenced the island's cannon. Subsequent rounds targeted missile and machine-gun batteries.

Two minutes after Juan gave the order to fire, the Vendor's headquarters building was a smoking ruin.

62

Anchored just off the coast, all eyes in the op center were focused on the smoldering rubble of the Vendor's HQ when it suddenly erupted in a massive explosion.

"This guy has a thing for self-destruction mechanisms," Stoney said, recalling the automated plane that blew itself up after Juan had compromised it.

"Covering his tracks," Juan said. His spirits fell. The Vendor was a murderous sociopath, but he wasn't suicidal. The auto-demolition of his base of operations was proof enough that he had already fled the scene.

"With your permission, Chairman," Murph said. "I'd like to take one precaution."

"Go for it."

Murph launched one of the *Oregon's* latest devices, a counter-electronics high power missile, aka CHAMP missile. It was essentially a flying EMP machine that wiped out enemy electronics. Murph was concerned about electronically activated mines or other remote-controled weapons systems that could harm the landing party. He also wanted to kill whatever was blocking satellite transmissions on the island. The missile made three runs over the island before it ran out of fuel, and Murph crashed it harmlessly into the sea.

"Let's put a shore party together," Juan said. "We just might find a fragment of gold in that garbage heap."

★

Juan, Eric, and Linda poked through the rubble of the main building for nearly two hours searching for clues as to the Vendor's whereabouts or his operations. Cabrillo hoped at the very least they would have found the Vendor's corpse buried in the rubble or tenderized by one of Murph's tungsten rods. Such was not the case.

The closest they got to actionable intel was locating a charred computer crushed beneath a chunk of concrete. Eric opened it up only to find the hard drive had been removed.

The Vendor had covered his tracks thoroughly.

Juan rubbed his face with frustration, smearing it with ash. Surviving the deadly island was its own reward, but he had nonetheless failed his primary mission to capture or kill the Vendor.

While Juan was probing the ruins, Eddie Seng's Gundogs had spread out in three-man squads across the island. Like the *Oregon* herself, each Gundog was skilled at both fighting and intelligence collection.

Over the tactical net Cabrillo listened in real time as Eddie's team easily dispatched a suicide attack by the last of the Vendor's bodyguards. Other squads reported in as they combed through the armory and other buildings, all of them coming up short on actionable intel.

Linc and Raven searched for Plata's corpse at the last battleground around the mass grave. Linc found the headless body. He searched through the man's blood-soaked pockets and came up with a satellite phone, but nothing else of value. Linc also did a head count and confirmed that the last six Vendor mercs, including the Russian, had been killed. Several other shattered corpses were strewn about in the field and the tree line. Murphy's Gatling gun had done a number on them all.

Cabrillo hadn't much cared for any of the mercenaries, including the Frenchman who had saved his life—they were truly killers for hire.

His first instinct was to leave them all to rot where they lay. But they were all soldiers of a sort who had sworn at least one honorable oath in their lifetimes. Out of respect for that selfless moment he personally took charge of disposing of their corpses in the mass grave he and Linc had fought in. With any luck, they would be the last to die on the Island of Sorrows.

Juan also made a mental note to notify the Frenchman's family of his death. It would allow them closure. The man's warning had saved his life, and Cabrillo made it a habit to owe no man anything.

When it was clear his people had recovered everything they could, Cabrillo ordered them back to the ship. There was no doubt he and Linc had emerged victorious in their battle with the Vendor, but it gave him little satisfaction. The fact of the matter was that their one and only clue as to the Vendor's whereabouts had put Juan within striking distance on this small island, but he had slipped his grasp.

And if Eric and Murph couldn't tease anything of value from what little intel had been collected, it was likely the Vendor had escaped for good.

63

The Vendor stared at the computer screen, fuming.

His island headquarters had been reduced to a slag heap. His escape sub's photonics mast had captured the distant image just moments before he ordered it to dive below the thermocline. It was his last and only view.

All of the cameras on the Island of Sorrows had been knocked out simultaneously along with virtually every other electronic device. He knew it was the *Oregon* that had pulled off that feat. He assumed they used some kind of EMP device. He thanked his ancestors for the wisdom to escape before that happened, otherwise his pilotless electronic mini sub would have been paralyzed. He shuddered at the thought of sitting in chains in some vile prison cell aboard that hated vessel.

Though the *Oregon* had blinded him digitally, there could be no doubt what followed next. The thought of that Mendoza creature and his crew rifling through his island facilities made his blood boil. At least he had taken precautions against that eventuality. They wouldn't find even a shred of a clue as to his network or his whereabouts. More importantly, they would learn nothing about Black Chrysanthemum or its impending launch.

Nevertheless, his nerves were shattered. It had been a close call. He put no faith in the ability of his bodyguards to destroy the *Oregon* and its crew. If he wanted to kill Mendoza, he would have to do it himself. But how? That infernal ship had proven to be a technological marvel. No other ship on the planet could have survived the two surprise attacks he had launched against her.

No matter. His vengeance was an unslakable thirst, and only Mendoza's blood could quench it. If he wanted to destroy the *Oregon* and Mendoza, he would have to set a different kind of trap.

But the rage itself was blunting his incredible powers of concentration. He took several deep breaths and entered into a nearly trancelike state, his mind batch-processing a nearly infinite number of murderous possibilities.

Suddenly, all of the pieces came together.

He checked his weather app.

Perfect.

"Keiko, how long until we reach the base?"

"The same as you asked me ten minutes ago, minus ten minutes."

"Keiko, erase your self-programmed sardonicism immediately or I will do it for you—and maybe a few other personality quirks you've developed that I don't particularly care for."

"Done. And to answer your question, at the current rate of speed, six point two hours."

His vessel was crawling beneath the surface at a snail's pace. There was no telling what kind of surveillance reach or resources Mendoza's people had. Sailing beneath the thermocline on electric power made him practically invisible, but time was of the essence. He checked his watch. He would run this way for another twenty minutes and then surface, doubling his speed. In the meantime he would put together the technical specs for his plan to sink the *Oregon* and broadcast those to his island team once he was no longer submerged.

His burning rage morphed into the lusty hope of a thrilling hunt.

Mendoza had the audacity to rain chaos down onto his plans.

And he would pay dearly for it.

64

ABOARD THE *OREGON*

After a hot meal and an even hotter shower, Juan sat with one of the Magic Shop's gifted sketch artists. Each of her long fingernails were painted in a different neon hue, and flew across the keyboard as they spoke.

Cabrillo was still waiting for reports from Eric, Murph, and the other analysts for any clues they could tease out of the fragments of pocket litter, scraps of paper and, most importantly, Plata's recovered satellite phone. So far, nothing had turned up.

But it was beneath the scalding showerheads he realized he already possessed one of the best clues he could hope for—the Vendor's physical identity.

One of the many reasons for Cabrillo's extraordinary success as a CIA field officer was his nearly picture-perfect memory. The problem was getting that visual image out of his brain and into a computer loaded with facial recognition software.

The young artist sitting at her workstation had spent two tours in naval intelligence before leaving the service and pursuing her lifelong dream as a portrait artist and later as a Hollywood set designer. Her combination of skills and devoted service to her nation made her a perfect candidate for Nixon's workshop when an opening appeared in his roster.

Like most young people, she had grown up a "digital native." Using a computer for her artwork was as natural to her as speaking her native tongue. But when the AI-powered art program Midjourney suddenly appeared, everything changed. Of course, just about anybody with the capacity to engineer thoughtful prompts could produce incredible AI-generated works of art now. But that was like saying anyone with a cell phone camera could take good snapshots. It took a true artist to produce truly great works of art, and the young woman had just created a masterpiece.

The Midjourney image on her screen was an excellent replication of the Vendor's essential appearance. The software had generated a very workable likeness in record time. But it was her skilled artisan's eye and hand that brought it life. Using a digital paintbrush, she took the image to the next level, capturing the Vendor's high intelligence, arrogance, and savagery with her masterful brushstrokes.

"Anything else we need to add?" she asked.

"You nailed it," Juan said. "Let's get that to Eric so he can start a web search for this cat."

"I'll send it right now."

Juan's earpiece rang. "Thanks. I need to get this."

She turned back to her keyboard as Cabrillo stood and left her workstation.

"Tell me you found him," Cabrillo said.

"Not quite," Linda replied in her high-pitched voice. "But maybe we picked up another thread."

"Tell me."

"The Sniffer picked up a sat signal from a place called Jaco Island, just off the coast of Timor-Leste."

"Formerly known as East Timor. What kind of sat signal?"

"A sat signal that originated from a piece of equipment installed in an American Humvee."

"Let me guess. A Humvee that should have been located in an Afghani arsenal."

"Bingo. That Humvee shouldn't be there."

"And yet it is. Sounds like a Vendor op."

"Our best guess, too."

"Can Overholt contact any of his CIA assets in-country to confirm?"

"He says there aren't any. Timor-Leste holds no strategic value for Uncle Sam, and it's way out in the boonies."

Juan did the math in his head, calculating the distance from their current position to the former Portuguese colony. They wouldn't arrive on scene until late tomorrow evening. That was a long way to run for a pocketful of nothing.

Linda read his mind. "Wild-goose chase?"

"Yeah, but it's the only goose in town. Lay in a course."

"Aye, Chairman."

Juan's spirits lifted. It wasn't much of a lead, but it was something. Anything was better than sitting around on his duff and hoping something would drop in his lap.

Time to celebrate.

★

Cabrillo's favorite pastime was working out, the greater the physical and mental exertion, the better. Daily gun practice, wall climbing, weight lifting—he loved all of it. But nothing was more satisfying or better for his overall conditioning than swimming. Cabrillo could think of no better way to spend the next hour than doing butterflies with arm and leg weights in the *Oregon*'s Olympic-sized pool, which he hoped to have all to himself. He had already changed into his swim trunks and carried his swim goggles in his hand.

He flung the door open to the pool area. The overhead lights were off but the pool lights were on. The shimmering marble-tiled walls echoed with the sound of a world-class swimmer churning the water like a pod of dolphins chasing a school of fish. Massive arm strokes flew through the air and thundering leg strokes crashed behind as the swimmer raced for the far end of the pool in record time.

Cabrillo bristled with frustration. He preferred to swim alone.

After an underwater flip and a powerful kick off the wall, the swimmer's body exploded back out of the water and charged toward the near end where Cabrillo was standing.

It took Cabrillo's eyes a couple of seconds to adjust to the image. He saw the thick rope of blond, French-braided hair and goggled eyes covering the familiar face. It was Callie setting a new women's butterfly speed record in the *Oregon* pool.

As if reading his mind, Callie reached the end of the pool where he was standing and came to halt. She thrust herself out of the water with a single press of her powerful arms and a splashing kick with her legs, vaulting onto the marble floor in a single bound.

Callie stood dripping wet in front of the Chairman, breathing heavily but not out of breath. She pulled her goggles down around her neck and stood at her full height.

The only thing he had ever seen that had even come close to the vision of athletic beauty and female form was Ursula Andress emerging out of the Caribbean Sea in *Dr. No*.

Juan could think of only one word to describe Callie at that moment.

Or maybe it was two.

Hubba-hubba.

Callie flashed an awkward smile.

"I'm so sorry. Linda said it was okay for me to swim here."

"No, of course. The pool is for everybody, especially our VIP guests."

"But she also said you like to swim by yourself."

"There's plenty of room to share. I play a mean game of Marco Polo."

Callie laughed. "I bet you do. I just haven't had the chance for a swim lately. It's my favorite form of exercise. Well, that and surfing."

"I haven't surfed since college days in SoCal," Juan said. He suddenly regretted that fact, but it was true. Life had taken him far away from his carefree days along the California coast. Callie reminded him of his glorious, sun-soaked youth.

Momentarily lost in nostalgia, he suddenly realized she didn't mention diving.

She saw the wheels turning behind his eyes.

"Scuba doesn't hold the same allure these days," she said. "A kind of PTSD, I suppose."

"Different strokes for different folks," Juan said.

"Literally."

Now it was Juan's turn to laugh.

They held each other's gaze. The air nearly crackled with feral electricity. Cabrillo suddenly felt very warm.

Callie broke the silence.

"I really should get back. I've got a Zoom call with my Honolulu team in twenty minutes." She stepped over to a rack of folded towels and grabbed one.

Cabrillo couldn't help but steal another admiring glance. He savored the cut of her jib as she began to towel off.

Lucky towel, Juan thought.

"I hear we're on our way to Timor-Leste," Callie said as she dried herself.

"We'll be there tomorrow evening."

She tossed the towel into the bin and faced him with an earnest look.

"I know you need to catch the Vendor. But don't get yourself killed doing it, okay?"

"There are worse things than dying."

"Better things, too."

"Maybe when this is all over, we can pick up where we left off."

Callie grinned.

"Double entendre acknowledged and accepted, *mon Capitan*."

65

Lieutenant Commander Xu believed in luck—but only the kind he could manufacture. His calculations had proven correct. American radar hadn't yet discovered his small but deadly formation.

The ominously dark clouds and slashing rains brought joy to his soul, as did the whitecapping sea just fifty feet beneath his delta-shaped wings. The favorable weather conditions were playing havoc with the American defense systems, just as he had planned.

But it was the Mighty Dragon's advanced stealth technologies that blinded them—at least so far. He and his wingman, Lieutenant Gao, were flying two of China's newest and most advanced carrier-based fighters. Each of the twin-seated, twin-engined, fifth-generation J-20 aircraft were equal to anything in the sky, including the F-35 Lightning II, America's most advanced fighter.

Xu's and Gao's two stealthy planes were loaded with China's most advanced anti-radar, anti-aircraft, and anti-ship missiles. But the truly revolutionary technology they were deploying today was in the hands of the weapons systems officers, one seated in the backseat of each of their planes. The two weapons officers were each in charge of two AI-piloted drones, also loaded with missiles and other advanced combat technologies.

Because they had no pilots, the four drones had no need for armor, oxygen supplies, ejection seats, or any other life-support elements. This made them smaller and faster. But they still possessed all of the stealth technologies that made their larger "mother ships" invisible to the American electromagnetic spectrum. Combined with the smaller size, the drones were even stealthier than the J-20s they trailed.

Xu's flight of two Mighty Dragon fighters and four drones had launched from China's latest aircraft carrier, the *Fujian*, the first of several Type 003 vessels that would soon be coming online. Built like the USS *Ford* rather than the old "ski jump" Soviet design of its first two carriers, the *Fujian* was already altering the course of history.

Xu checked his pre-plotted course again. They were racing for Guam. If all went well, the Americans wouldn't know what hit them until it was too late.

It was only a matter of time before the People's Liberation Navy drove the Americans from the East China Sea. But it was Xu's squadron, the Dao Ma Jian—the "Horse Cutters," a famous Chinese battle-ax—that would soon achieve everlasting fame in the western Pacific.

★

Captain Peter Stallabrass was in charge of the E-3 Sentry mission crew flying high above the Pacific. Built on the Boeing 707 airframe, the Sentry's giant rotating radar dome covered two hundred fifty miles of air, ground, and sea surface.

The Sentry and its crew were on temporary loan from Kadena AFB in Japan, part of a buildup that included a flight of four F-35 Lightning IIs from Eielson AFB, Alaska. In recent weeks, China had been taking advantage of the fact that the United States had repositioned a vast number of Navy assets to the South China Sea over growing tensions with Taiwan. An invasion there seemed imminent. But it left Guam vulnerable.

Now the Chinese Navy was putting pressure on Guam, staging a large number of probing sorties against the strategically vital forward operating base. Chinese warships, submarines, and aircraft had made various runs at the island, testing its defenses, checking for weaknesses. Whether that was a feint to draw American forces away from Taiwan or an actual threat against Guam was something American intelligence analysts were still puzzling out.

Stallabrass had reached his own conclusions on the matter and drew up a will with an online lawyer before he accepted the transfer to Guam.

The island's location in the far western Pacific was strategically important. Located some two thousand miles from the coasts of China and North Korea, its relative geographic remoteness made it less vulnerable to attack than American bases in Japan and South Korea.

Because of that remoteness, Guam had served as a near-perfect staging ground for America's strategic bombers since World War II. And after the loss of Air Force and Navy bases in the Philippines in the 1990s, Guam's strategic importance had increased exponentially. Bomber fleets of B-52s, B-1s, and B-2s along with reconnaissance and communications aircraft rotated constantly through its airfields.

Equally important, a squadron of Los Angeles–class nuclear-powered fast-attack submarines were based out of Guam, as were dozens of Navy support units, along with thousands of expeditionary force Marines. Over ten thousand American military and civilian personnel, along with one hundred seventy thousand American citizens, resided on the island, the nation's westernmost territory. Situated fourteen hours ahead of Eastern Standard Time, Guam's motto was "Where America's Day Begins."

In short, Guam played a key role in conventional and nuclear deterrence in the Pacific and Asian theaters against the growing threat of Chinese aggression.

If Guam had any weakness, it was in air defense. Huge gaps in radar and missile coverage plagued the island, and strategic planners hadn't kept up with the steepening technology curve. China's advancing long-range missile and aircraft capabilities along with its rapidly expanding carrier fleet made the island more vulnerable to aerial attack than ever before.

In response, the Department of Defense was engaged in the construction of an Enhanced Integrated Air and Missile Defense system that would provide Guam with three-hundred-sixty-degree surveillance and defense. This would make it the most defended patch of ground on planet earth and nearly invulnerable to Chinese air and missile assets.

The EIAMD was scheduled to come fully online in just a few days. What both Stallabrass and his base commanders feared was that China's best hope of eliminating Guam as a strategic deterrent lay in that narrowing window of vulnerability. The spate of increasing Chinese aggression over the last few weeks was either merely a test of wills or a series of probing reconnaissance missions in a prelude to a preemptive Chinese attack.

66

Today's weather was problematic, as was the E-3 Sentry's bumpy ride. Stallabrass enlisted in the Air Force because he wanted to be a fighter pilot, but he washed out of the program because of a disorienting inner ear imbalance he experienced during flight training. The Air Force brass frowned on its young pilots puking in their multimillion-dollar cockpits, but in its collective wisdom the Big Blue Machine had put him in the back of the Sentry. He had served with distinction, but often at the cost of a queasy stomach like he was currently experiencing. The cool cabin air that kept the computers from overheating was small comfort to his growing headache, exacerbated by the constant whine of the 707's noisy turbines.

"Captain, take a look at this," one of his techs said. Stallabrass stepped over to his monitor.

"Where the heck did those come from?"

"No idea. They just popped up. One hundred nineteen miles and closing. Fast movers. Not ours."

Stallabrass studied the six radar images. Two were much stronger than the other four, but none of them were solid hits, and all were moving at Mach 1 or close to it in the storm.

Weather conditions might explain the weakness of the radar images. More likely, it was a combination of reduced radar cross section, radar absorbent materials, and possibly even radar jamming or deception.

In short, stealth aircraft.

That was bad. The Chinese were the only country in the world besides the United States and Russia producing fifth-generation stealth aircraft. Air Force intelligence reported several Chinese variants were already operational and new systems would soon come online. There was no way to tell at this point which ones were on his display. But what was certain was that all Chinese stealth planes carried anti-ship and anti-aircraft weapons that were now in striking range of Guam.

What didn't make sense to him was the different sizes of the images.

"Who's on patrol?"

"Major Joslin is the flight lead. McGhee is his wingman. They just acknowledged the radar hits." The two F-35s were networked with the Sentry's radar returns.

Stallabrass nodded. Joslin and McGhee were flying F-35s, America's best fighter. More importantly, Joslin was a highly decorated and experienced combat pilot. He couldn't think of another pair of zoomies he'd rather have in the air.

"Vector them to that location. High priority."

"Yes, sir."

★

Major Joslin—call sign "Hawkeye" for his twenty-ten vision—studied his display, fed with Stallabrass's E-3 radar data. The tangos were moving at Mach 9 at fifty feet above the deck. Gutsy. He'd seen rogue waves reach higher than that.

He was irritated his own radar hadn't picked them up first. He needed to buy Stallabrass a beer for the heads-up when they got back to the O club.

Joslin's F-35 was capable of targeting and destroying all six aircraft at this distance and they were still closing at over twelve hundred feet per second.

Chances were, the Chinese were having a hard time getting radar returns in this weather as well. They might not even know he and McGhee were getting up in their grill.

By his calculation, in just under five minutes he wouldn't have to fire any missiles. He could reach out with his foot and trip the Chicoms as they zoomed past.

He keyed his mic and told his wingman that he was dropping down. He'd meet them head-on at fifty feet.

Suddenly, his alarms sounded. The Chinese had radar lock on him.

"Hawkeye, I've been lit up," McGhee said. "Permission to lock."

"Permission granted, War Lord."

★

Lieutenant Commander Xu studied the two F-35s on his helmet-mounted display system, the same kind of device that provided American pilots three-hundred-sixty-degree views around their aircraft.

So far, the Americans had responded exactly as expected and now that he and Gao had initiated radar lock, the Americans would soon respond in kind.

His team wouldn't give them that opportunity.

"Initiate," Xu ordered over his secured comms.

The two backseat weapons officers took charge.

★

Just as Joslin was about to confirm his six targets, four of the tangos peeled off—and disappeared.

What happened?

Joslin thought his systems had glitched. He keyed his mic.

"Wizard, this is Hawkeye. I've lost four contacts."

Stallabrass responded. "Same on our end. The tangos must have some new electronic countermeasures."

"I still show two on my radar. Locking now." He tapped his touchscreen display, arming two long-range AIM-120 missiles and selecting his two targets. McGhee did the same.

"Will keep you advised, Hawkeye." Stallabrass keyed off.

Joslin and McGhee rode the rail for another thirty seconds, seeing what the Chinese planes might be up to.

Stallabrass crackled on his comms.

"Hawkeye, this is Wizard. Base reports anti-radiation seekers have been activated, source unknown."

What were these cowboys doing? Not only were he and McGhee in the crosshairs, but so were the radar sites on the island. The first strike in an attack is always aimed at air defenses. This was definitely a hostile move.

"Hawkeye, heads-up," Stallabrass said. "Anti-ship missile signatures have now been detected. All tangos are now considered hostiles."

Joslin fought the urge to swear. Until now, the Chinese hadn't targeted ships. These guys were getting serious.

The question was, *How serious?*

A couple of rogue pilots out to make a name for themselves could be looking for a gunfight. And right now, that's what it felt like.

But it could be just another test to reveal American defensive tactics in preparation for an actual war.

Joslin's eyes scanned his helmet display. They were closing in on the Chinese jets at a combined speed of Mach 1.8. Their AIM-120s were still locked on their targets, and the Chinese jets still had them targeted. A Mexican standoff at supersonic speed.

Time was running out.

Joslin's brain made calculations his advanced avionics suite could not. The longer he waited to fire, the more he put McGhee and everyone else on the island at risk.

But if he pulled the trigger, he just might start World War III.

If the Chicoms really were hostile, why hadn't they fired? That was easy. The closer they got, the better the odds of hitting their targets. Every moment that passed made death and destruction all the more likely.

And where were those other four tangos?

Joslin checked his digital clock. Two minutes until they reached the Chinese targets.

"Permission to fire?" McGhee asked.

The Chinese planes' aggression was bold—and beyond the pale. But they were still on the other side of the Red Line—the twelve-mile limit surrounding the island. It was illegal for Joslin to fire at them until they crossed it.

But the Chicoms didn't respect international law. They might fire first and accuse the Americans of starting it. And the closer they got, the more likely they were to doing just that.

"Don't fire unless fired upon," Joslin finally said. Those were the rules of engagement his commanders had imposed upon the flight.

"Roger that."

Joslin checked his HUD display.

One minute and closing.

Joslin now had a visual of the two Chinese jets. He angled his fighter directly into the path of the Chicom flight lead.

"Boss?"

"Let's see how much sand he's got in his sack," Joslin said. He settled into his seat.

"Hawkeye, you're on a collision course," Stallabrass said in his ear.

"That's the general idea."

"You've got a pair, Hawkeye. Large-caliber ones, and brass."

"Thirty seconds to collision," Stallabrass said.

The Chinese wingman entered a steep climb.

"I'm on him," McGhee said as his plane clawed into the storming sky, giving chase.

Now it was just Joslin and the Chicom lead, head-to-head, in an old-fashioned showdown—at over thirteen hundred miles per hour.

Joslin switched on his short-range Sidewinders and locked them onto the Chinese fighter. The Chengdu J-20's distinctive twin tail and angled fuselage were clearly displayed in the gloom. Its twin-seater frameless canopy made it one of the aircraft carrier variants. It was a cross between an F-35 and an F-22, America's two best fighters. Rumor was the Chinese government had stolen the plans for both.

Joslin stole a glance at McGhee and his tango on the display. They rolled and spun like Olympic ice-skaters seven thousand feet above—and climbing.

Joslin slipped his finger over the trigger that would loose two missiles at his opponent.

Ten seconds.

Joslin began a mental countdown. He wasn't going to flinch.

"I'm your huckleberry," Joslin whispered to the Chinese jet.

Five, four, three, two . . .

Suddenly, his missile warning alarms snapped off. The Chinese jet had disengaged.

The Chengdu pilot rotated his bird ninety degrees on its axis, canopy inward.

Joslin matched him with a jerk of his joystick.

Their heads sped past each other just feet apart at a collective thirteen hundred miles per hour. He saw the blur of masked helmets glancing up in his direction.

Joslin rolled his plane back to horizontal, the airframe rocked by the Mighty Dragon's waking air turbulence.

Suddenly, the four missing tangos appeared on his radar. They were heading away from Guam, their mission complete.

And there was no question that mission was to gather invaluable data on American radar locations, wavelengths, and capabilities. Data that could be used to wipe those installations out next time.

"Hawkeye," Wizard said, "all six tangos are assuming a heading of three hundred eighteen degrees. Advise you follow."

"Wilco," Joslin said. "You catch that, War Lord?"

His wingman was already making his turn.

"On it."

"Disengaging missile lock." Joslin punched the toggles on his touchscreen.

"Disengaged," McGhee reported.

Joslin eased the stick up. His tango had climbed to five thousand feet, pairing up with his wingman. Joslin and McGhee matched them.

Minutes later, the four pilotless drones pulled into position with the manned Chinese aircraft.

"You seeing this?" McGhee asked.

"Yup." Joslin wasn't completely surprised. He'd been a test pilot for the Air Force's "Loyal Wingman" project that also paired AF pilots to drone aircraft. The American program had stalled. Obviously, the Chinese one had not.

Drone aircraft gave incredible advantages. Cheaper, faster, more maneuverable, and expendable, they could maximize speed, turns, and payloads, and if necessary, sacrifice themselves to accomplish the mission or protect human pilots.

They chased the Chinese flight for a hundred miles at a respectful distance. Joslin was grateful the Chinese men had chosen the better part of valor. Did the Chicom pilot chicken out? Or had he broken Joslin's encrypted comms? Either way, he knew Joslin wouldn't back down. That was all that mattered.

"Hawkeye and War Lord, you are requested to return to base for a debrief."

"Roger that," Joslin said. He was happy to return to base. It had been a long morning. He felt his energy drain away along with his adrenaline surge. A cup of coffee sounded pretty good, even if he was going to get chewed out by the Old Man.

Joslin was pleased with his performance. McGhee's, too. They had shown the Chinese forces that while America might be in decline, her pilots were not.

But those pilots had taught them a lesson, too. They had shown courage, creativity, and technological advance. The next time, their drones could be used to confuse, swarm, and overwhelm. They had ushered in a new era of aerial warfare.

In the sweep of history, Joslin and McGhee would be remembered as the first Americans to confront drone fighters in a combat situation.

Unfortunately, they were on the wrong side of the broom.

If the Chinese tangos returned tomorrow, Joslin and his flight would be waiting for them. But in forty-eight hours, so would Guam's new air defense system.

The Chinese wouldn't stand a chance, no matter how many drones they brought.

67

PAU RANGI ISLAND
THE BISMARCK SEA

The Vendor stood in a vaulted cavern deep beneath the island, its rocky escarpments carpeted with windswept trees and verdant foliage. Water gently lapped behind him.

The sharp tang of incense muted the smell of the sea inside the cave, but that was not its purpose. The thin tendrils of smoke and its alluring aroma were an invitation for his ancestral *kami* to visit him.

The Vendor bowed twice, clapped his hands sharply, and bowed again before gazing up at the *kami-dana*—his ancestral shrine—lodged in a hand-hewn niche on the cave wall. A small saucer of freshly poured sake, a lit candle, and three talismans—a war medal from each grandfather, and his father's circular slide rule—all stood before the head-sized mirror inside the shrine.

The mirror itself was angled downward such that when the Vendor stood at his full height and gazed into it, he saw his own face. This was not ego. The mirror reflected the presence of his ancestors. Was not his own face a reflection of the same? Yes, and in more ways than one.

The flesh on the back of his neck tingled, making their presence known.

Shigeru Hashimoto, also known as the Vendor, whispered thanks to his forefathers for his narrow escape from the Island of Sorrows and his safe return to Pau Rangi. He also begged forgiveness for his obvious failures, and renewed his vow to finish the work they had begun: Operation Black Chrysanthemum. Designed to kill thousands of Americans, it was both a strategic weapon and an act of pure vengeance.

Hashimoto's hatred for Mendoza and the crew of the *Oregon* was deeply personal. But his hatred of all Americans was an epigenetic phenomenon in Hashimoto's family, passed down the generations. Decades of simmering enmity merged with the genetic endowment and spiritual evolution of his bloodlines.

His maternal grandfather, Dr. Yoshio Mitomo, had developed the original neurotoxin formula while serving at Unit 731. His dutiful grandson had now perfected that formula and would soon unleash it. His grandfather's hatred for the Americans was kindled during World War II, by all the Japanese lives sacrificed on the altar of so-called democracy. All those fires that burned hundreds of thousands of innocent Japanese civilians alive had their origins on the bomber bases on Guam.

Operation Black Chrysanthemum had been designed to neutralize Guam with an aerial attack with neurotoxins from an I-400–class submarine, which featured an onboard plane hangar. But the Americans sank the submarine before it could complete its mission, and the neurotoxins were lost to the sea.

Surrendering to the Americans, his grandfather Mitomo had been granted immunity from war crimes trials when he agreed to participate in Operation Paperclip, as had so many other high-value German and Japanese scientists after the war.

His paternal grandfather, Hiroshi Hashimoto, had served the Empire as an aeronautical engineer with Mitsubishi, helping to develop Japan's first jet fighter, the J8MI Shusui—a near replica of the German Komet. He likewise received a pardon for his participation in Japan's war industry. The Americans transferred his skills to the private sector in order to help build up Japan as a bulwark against communist aggression in the Far East.

The Vendor's own father had also been an aeronautical engineer, and it was standing by his elbow as a child that young Shigeru

Hashimoto learned to love both the aesthetic beauty and mathematical purity of war machines.

Now, standing before the altar of his *kami* and on the brink of his greatest achievement, Hashimoto knew he would not fail his ancestors, nor would they fail him.

★

Hashimoto finished his prayers.

Seawater gently chucked against the hull of the submarine berthed behind him. Inspired by the I-400 series of the Imperial Japanese Navy, the AI-guided vessel could carry 120 high-speed drones all designed to disperse the neurotoxin. The vessel incorporated all of the latest stealth technologies that either absorbed or reflected sonar detection, including an ultra-low-profile sail and continuous curvature hull geometry that mimicked fifth-generation fighter aircraft design. Combined with its hydrogen-fuel, cell-powered electric motors, it was nearly impossible to detect by any electromagnetic means. Once launched, it would reach its target without fail. He named the vessel *Ghost Sword*.

Hashimoto was supremely confident in the ability of his drones to reach their targets and disperse their fatal payloads. The drones themselves were AI-piloted, capable of making independent decisions. They also deployed the same advanced radar countermeasures that the Chinese drones possessed—countermeasures that he himself had pioneered.

Better still, one of his network colleagues embedded within the Chinese navy had secured the results of their latest drone incursion against Guam. He passed all of the points of vulnerability to Hashimoto, who loaded them directly into the drones. But those points of vulnerability would soon be wiped out when the island's Enhanced Integrated Air and Missile Defense system came online in less than two days.

Hashimoto's technicians had promised him that as soon as the batch processing of the neurotoxin was complete, it would take only six hours to fill the dispersion tanks and set into the drones. After that, the drone launch pods could be loaded into the *Ghost Sword*.

Right now, the giant countdown clock on the cave wall read 22:07:14. That was the absolute last moment the *Ghost Sword* could set sail and hope to reach its drone launch point.

The challenge now was finishing the batch processing of the neurotoxin. They were still on schedule, but any glitch in the complex procedure would throw everything into disarray and would require a complete restart. And such a restart meant total failure.

Hashimoto stood at the elevator that would take him directly to the lab. His temptation was to unleash a fresh torrent of threats against his people to insure they met their deadline. But the voices in his head told him to steady himself. He had recruited some of the best scientists in the world for the task. Besides, he had already promised them excruciating punishments for failure and the promise of untold wealth if they succeeded.

By the time the elevator door slid open, Hashimoto had becalmed himself. A delicate, fatherly hand was all that was needed. He would simply observe and compliment his people, and allow his own supreme confidence to motivate them to greater glory.

His plan was perfect. Black Chrysanthemum would not only disable all of the military facilities on the island but also kill the one hundred eighty thousand Americans stationed and living there. This would hardly be enough to balance the scales of justice. But those deaths would only be the beginning. A full-scale war between the United States and China, Japan's other most hated nemesis, would lead to the death of millions.

Hashimoto had built the toxin-unleashing stealth drones to Chinese military specifications, which he knew well since he had been the one to design them. His mission drones were all built with Chinese parts, Chinese computers, and Chinese computer chips. He also did all of the programming in Chinese script. They would access China's version of GPS, the BeiDou Navigation Satellite System (BDS), during flight. Best of all, he had programmed one of the drones to crash on the island so that it would be discovered, and all of the false clues uncovered.

Coupled with the fact the overly aggressive Chinese navy had been running various sorties against Guam for the last several weeks, any reasonable intelligence analyst would conclude that China had been the source of the treacherous drone attack. War would ensue, and the Vendor would stand to profit handsomely from the resulting chaos.

Better still, he and his *kami* would finally savor the sweet taste of ultimate and bloody revenge.

Hashimoto smiled to himself as he stepped into the elevator, feeling the flesh on the back of his neck tingling once again.

68

Callie's face soured as her nose crinkled with another sniff of the stale air. She stood with Juan on the false bridge atop the *Oregon*'s aft superstructure. Though the op center belowdecks was the true command and control center of the ship, the topside bridge was fully functional and used when needed.

Cabrillo's eyes were glued to a pair of infrared binoculars. Jaco Island, just off the far eastern coast of Timor-Leste, lay three miles due west of their position, but he was scanning the entire horizon. The *Oregon*'s radar was in perfect working order, but he wanted to get eyes on the area.

There was little commercial shipping traffic in this part of the Timor Sea except for the fishing trawlers, which had already put in to port. A massive storm was racing toward their position. In the distance he saw long, jagged fingers of lightning stabbing the night sky. He was grateful for the bad weather coming their way. It would prove a perfect cover for tonight's operation.

"What is that horrible stench?" Callie asked.

"Clogged toilet. Blame Nixon."

"Please tell me that's part of the charade."

"I certainly hope so."

Cabrillo was pulling her leg. Several hours ago, she had witnessed the *Oregon*'s complete transformation from a proud, shipshape bulk cargo carrier to a rusty scow barely able to stay afloat. The gleaming paint, polished brass, surgically clean decks, and even the ship's name on the stern were swapped out electronically with faded colors, oxidization, and rust. Like Hollywood set decorators, the Magic Shop and a specialized crew added the finishing touches on the newly christened *Estacada*, littering her decks with rusted chains, frayed ropes, leaking barrels, and broken machine parts. Interior additions on the bridge included cracked windows with dead flies on the sills and a clogged head in the captain's cabin. Air misters diffused a variety of malodorous fragrances including the one currently crinkling up Callie's nose.

All of that subterfuge was designed to drive off any nosy harbormaster or customs authority that came aboard for an intrusive inspection. Invariably, even the most suspicious officials were driven off the filthy ship with watering eyes and heaving stomachs before they ever had a chance to discover the true nature of the *Oregon*'s design.

Cabrillo lowered his binoculars. He was kitted out for a night raid on the island launching within the hour. The GPS signal they picked up earlier from an American Humvee had originated from there. He was grasping at straws, but it was the only Vendor clue he had at the moment.

"I'm heading to the team room," Juan said.

"I wish there was something I could do to help tonight."

"Should be smooth sailing. If we ever capture one of the Vendor's units, I might have a job for you."

"Whatever you need, you know I'm here."

Juan nodded. "You *are* your father's daughter. I'd expect no less."

Callie beamed with pride.

★

An hour later, one of the *Oregon*'s RHIBs raced through the slashing rain, its rigid deep-V hull pounding the surging waves with bone-jarring regularity.

All of the Gundogs were on board except for Raven, who was still recovering from her leg wound. Linda Ross wasn't one of the *Oregon*'s designated special operators, but she trained with them regularly and volunteered to take Raven's place.

Eddie Seng was head of the operation, but it had been Juan's call to launch out in the middle of a dangerous squall, so he joined the mission. Only an idiot would launch an assault under such conditions, or at least, that's what Cabrillo hoped the Jaco Island guards were thinking. Massive lightning flashed ever closer, but the chances of getting struck by the booming thunderbolts were a heck of a lot less than drowning—or getting shot by well-armed guards.

That is, if there were any guards.

Juan had ordered Gomez to run drone surveillance over the island earlier. His drone found a large, corrugated-steel warehouse set back beneath the trees some three hundred yards beyond the water, but no one was around it. Not guards. Not warehouse workers.

But there was no question the GPS signal had originated at this location and was still broadcasting. If the Vendor was storing American military equipment on the island, he'd put it in a warehouse like this one for protection from the elements and more importantly to keep it hidden from unwanted surveillance.

The tiny island was an interesting choice, Juan thought. Its remote location was a natural advantage, but it was still on the fringe of the world's most populous region.

Cabrillo had Eric dig up whatever records he could find. The tiny, impoverished nation of Timor-Leste—"East Timor" in Portuguese—occupied the eastern half of an Indonesian island. According to Eric, a shell company representing unknown real estate interests had purchased Jaco Island. Regional newspapers suspected bribes had greased the wheels of the unusual transaction. Once secured, the private real estate group immediately sealed it off from the rest of the nation and a large private pier had been constructed on the eastern side of the island. All of that fit with the Vendor's modus operandi. It all made sense.

But did it?

Juan had his suspicions. But there was only one way to find out for sure.

Gomez Adams volunteered to take the wheel since the 'dogs were down a star player. He killed the twin engines just a few yards from shore and the RHIB's hull hissed to a stop on the wet sand.

"Let's rock and roll," Eddie said as he leaped out of the boat and led the way onshore. Juan was right behind him, the straps on his unusual pack cinched tight across his shoulders.

The team fanned out and snaked its way through the trees, the drenching rain hitting the leaves sounding like a Brillo pad scouring a saucepan.

The looming shadow of the warehouse finally came into view. No lights were on. The team split up. Cabrillo, Seng, and Linda approached the front. Linc and MacD took the rear. They were all about ninety yards from the building.

Seng knelt down and scanned the area with an infrared monocular. If there were any warm bodies outside, he'd see them. He whispered in his comms, "All clear."

MacD had a similar scope. He also replied, "All clear."

Seng glanced at Cabrillo kneeling next to him. *Your call.*

There was no obvious reason to not head into the warehouse. But the Vendor had proven too dangerous. There was no way he didn't have some kind of electronic means of surveillance guarding the place, even if there weren't any guards. And probably not just surveillance.

Cabrillo unshouldered his pack and unzipped it. The gadget inside was something Murph had put together. He powered it on and hit the charge button. The device sent out a jamming signal that would break any Wi-Fi or radio network within a hundred yards. Any electronic device that was remotely powered or activated would be rendered harmless. The RHIB was safely behind them at over two hundred yards. The last thing Cabrillo wanted to do was fry the boat's motors.

"Okay, let's go," Juan said. He bolted to his feet and jogged forward. Eddie and Linda were on his heels, their heads still on swivels looking for trouble. A massive thunderclap overhead lit up the area like Yankee Stadium for a nanosecond. They were surrounded by trees, and nothing else—except the dark that suddenly closed back in on them.

Juan hated being off comms with Linc and MacD, but they knew to stay put. Cabrillo had suspected the Vendor had laid some sort of a trap. But it was beginning to feel as if he had been overly cautious.

The windowless warehouse was buttoned-up tight. Cabrillo approached the big steel rolling door. Seng dashed up with a pair of bolt cutters in his hands. A quick snap of his arms and the thick padlock fell away. Linda reached down and yanked the door. The steel clattered as it rolled up.

Juan pointed at his boots.

A Chinese-made IED was positioned right next to the door, its laser trip light pointed across the entrance. If Cabrillo hadn't killed its circuitry with Murph's gadget, the three of them would be piles of bloody Swiss cheese lying on the ground.

Not one to tempt fate, Cabrillo still stepped over what would have been the laser line and headed into the warehouse. It was pitch-black, but another flash of lightning lit up the interior. The building was completely empty.

Except for a table. And on the table stood a small electrical device. If he had to guess, it was a GPS transponder—probably pulled from a Humvee.

A shock wave shot through Cabrillo's spinal column.

"It's a trap!"

69

Shigeru Hashimoto, aka the Vendor, tugged on his beard as he studied the monitor. He had been tracking Mendoza and his team ever since they left their mother ship and made their way onto the island.

For once, he hadn't underestimated the determined Mendoza or the considerable technical skills of that wretched vessel. Mendoza's ship had not only changed its name to the *Estacada*, but also altered its paint scheme in short order, technologies that he deployed himself. But he had to hand it to the wily American for the presentation of the utterly believable illusion of the boat's rust, wreck, and ruin.

Hashimoto was completely unsurprised when Mendoza deployed an electronic countermeasures device and disabled all of the island's electronics.

By now Mendoza and his team had infiltrated the warehouse, and likely discovered the IED waiting for them there. Hashimoto blew air out of his nose, frustrated with the lack of imagery. He would have enjoyed nothing better than to witness the explosion and the slaughter the American swine.

Now he was blind to events on the ground.

No matter, he thought, as he pressed the button.

Mendoza would die just the same.

★

ABOVE JACO ISLAND
THE TIMOR SEA

Hashimoto's drone's AI-driven navigation skillfully battled the turbulent storm winds several thousand feet above Jaco Island. It had been preprogrammed with the coordinates of the abandoned warehouse facility and was also locked on to the American GPS transmitter located inside.

Additionally, Hashimoto uploaded facial recognition software specifically targeting Mendoza, but as a final precaution he activated the optical "eyes-on" targeting system, anticipating the *Estacada*'s deployment of an EMP missile.

Once Hashimoto signaled the attack, the drone's AI programming took over, and all of its sensors were fixed on the warehouse. It plunged through the chaotic winds in a wonky, twisted arc and at approximately ninety-one meters above the building all of its electronics ceased functioning.

But the warehouse was a fixed target and the drone's onboard computer—which also ceased to function—had already made all of the necessary calculations to complete the final 3.3 seconds of the terminal phase of its mission. Deaf, dumb, and blind, the drone had transitioned from an independently guided weapon into a dumb bomb delivered with appalling accuracy.

★

ABOARD THE *OREGON*

With Juan and Linda on the warehouse mission, Max was left in charge of the boat. The Gundogs' comms were piped into the overhead speakers and the crew in the op center followed their movements with intense interest.

"Smart boy," Max said in a half whisper when Cabrillo announced he was going to hit Murphy's zapper and knock out all area electronics including their own comms. Better safe than sorry, he thought.

Like Juan, Max felt a great deal of unease at the fact there was no armed opposition on the island, and he fully agreed with Cabrillo's suspicion that the Vendor would rely on a technological trap to catch them with their breeches askew. Besides, the lack of comms would only be temporary. As soon as Cabrillo deactivated the unit, the Gundogs would be back in touch and would make their exfil to the ship.

The *Oregon*'s photonics mast—a combination of glass and digital imaging—gave them a long-range view of the team as they exited the RHIB and made their way forward. Because it was a cloudy night with little ambient light, Max ordered Murph to deploy the mast's infrared imagery. The op center crew watched the spectral figures on the big LCD wall panel up until the moment they melted away into the forest like an ancient folktale. Lightning flashes, brighter and increasing, lit the panel back up briefly before settling back down to a near perfect black.

Max turned in the Kirk Chair, his bloodshot eyes falling on the blackened LCD just as it flared into a massive white fireball.

★

ABOVE THE *OREGON*

While Max and the op center crew were fixated on the Gundogs' teeth-rattling race across the water and onto the beach, a swarm of drones—small, curiously shaped, and unarmed—hurtled through the tumultuous winds. They numbered in the thousands.

The lead elements alighted on the topmost sections of *Oregon*'s cranes, superstructure, and wire rigging. The rest remained airborne, functioning as leader strokes and streamers. Together, they formed a bridge of connectivity between the unimaginable energy boiling in the sky above and the massive steel frame of the ship.

The Vendor considered weaponized lightning, his most recent invention, the most terrifying weapon in his arsenal. A single lightning strike carried the equivalent energy of twenty-four hundred metric tons of TNT. A lightning storm delivered a relentless cascade of unfathomable power.

At precisely the right moment when the atmospheric conditions were perfectly aligned to the AI's preprogrammed parameters, Hashimoto's drones emitted a low-energy wave—just enough to attract and focus the first of dozens of lightning strikes against the *Oregon*'s hull. The resulting superheated air boomed like a relentless artillery barrage as lightning strikes burst in a rapid succession of blinding-white supernovas.

Each lightning bolt unleashed temperatures five times hotter than the surface of the sun. In the first strike, lines snapped, glass shattered, steel melted, and the crackling air sizzled with the chlorine tang of ozone and burnt metal. But even greater havoc fell on the ship as the lightning barrage escalated.

The Kashtan close-in weapons system and its missiles, housed atop one of the crane masts, exploded in the direct hit, tearing the hidden compartment apart and destroying the entire unit. The plasma-hot bolts arc-welded the sliding plates shut for the 120mm auto cannon, and shrink-wrapped the thin sheet metal of the fifty-five-gallon drums around the repel-boarders machine guns hidden inside of them.

The barrage intensified as the storm fed upon itself.

The *Oregon* was doomed.

★

OREGON OP CENTER

"Juan!"

Max shouted at the fireball on the giant wall monitor. There was no doubt in his mind that the warehouse had been struck. The op center crew gasped at the roiling clouds of flame. Cabrillo and the team were in the middle of that hell storm.

But the crew's rapt attention was snatched away by the sudden, screen-shattering lights blasting on the rest of the *Oregon*'s wall monitors as lightning strikes cascaded.

The vessel shook with the volleys of thunderclaps that pounded the decks above them.

"We've been hit—" Stoney shouted.

Before the last word escaped his mouth, the *Oregon*'s lights snapped out, while LCDs and computer monitors all crashed.

Emergency red backup lights, powered by batteries on separate circuits, popped on seconds later.

Murph and Eric exchanged a worried glance.

Radar, sonar, and weapons stations were dead.

They were sitting ducks.

★

THE TIMOR SEA

Half a mile away, another one of Hashimoto's drones—a torpedo— lay on the sandy bottom of the sea. It had arrived seven hours before the *Oregon* and settled into its location without fear of detection. Its close proximity to the unsuspecting target was an unplanned bonus.

The torpedo drone's wire comms antennae were stretched from the drone to the surface via a buoy. Seconds before the drone swarm was destroyed in the lightning storm, the torpedo drone received the signal to launch.

The drone lifted gently toward the surface to a depth of fifteen feet—well below the *Oregon*'s waterline, but certain not to pass under her keel.

The drone's electric motors kicked on, speeding the torpedo at eighteen miles per hour toward the giant magnetic target pinging on its sonar.

In less than two minutes, the defenseless *Oregon* would be split in half.

★

OREGON OP CENTER

"Comms down, helm down, radar down, sonar down, Wepps down."
Each station called out its status report.

Max was surprised on two counts.

First, every ship at sea knew that lightning was a hazard and prepared accordingly with lightning rods, grounding, surge protectors,
circuit breakers, and the like. The *Oregon* was festooned with them.
For a conventional lightning strike—whatever "conventional" meant
for such a rare occurrence—the *Oregon* was perfectly protected.

But in the crazy, swarming surge of multiple strikes like the *Oregon*
had just experienced, the protections had all been overwhelmed—by
the Vendor's design.

Max's second surprise was the failure of the automated power
transfer switch to kick over. He had no idea why. But without available
power, they were dead in the water and vulnerable to attack.

He had to do something, and fast.

The *Oregon* was arguably the world's most advanced intelligence-
gathering ship, loaded with the latest technologies. Max was the ship's
chief engineer, and he had helped Juan design and build every high-
tech iteration of the storied vessel. But despite his affinity for technological innovation, the man with the high, hard belly and halo-spray
of graying auburn hair always held a fondness for analogue systems.
Whether from boyhood nostalgia or hard-nosed practicality, Max was
convinced that many of the old ways were best. Or at the very least,
the best backups.

Max charged over to a panel on the rear bulkhead and yanked it
open. Inside was an old-school sound-power phone—the kind that
World War II submarines used for intra-ship communication. Max's
sound-power phone connected directly to the engine room.

Unlike conventional comms, the sound-power didn't rely on electricity, copper wiring, or circuit boards—all of which had obviously

been interrupted, damaged, or destroyed by the massive lightning blast. Max snatched up the handset and shouted into it. His booming voice generated powerful sound waves that vibrated against the handset's diaphragm. The diaphragm, in turn, sent those sound vibrations via an oil-filled tube to the diaphragm of the receiver located in the engine room.

"Hit the manual power transfer switch!"

Despite the volume of Max's voice, he sounded like he was yelling through a soup can underwater. But his first engineer on the other end of the line understood him just fine.

"Switching now," the voice burbled back.

Suddenly, all of the primary lights and monitors kicked back on.

Max sighed with relief. He had insisted on secondary and even tertiary alternative circuits for just this kind of catastrophe. He slammed the sound-power back into its cradle.

"Hali—"

"On it," Kasim said, tapping buttons. "Engineering is on speaker."

"Engines?" Max asked.

"Back online and purring like kittens," the engineer said in the overheads. "No damage."

"Thank God for that." Without engines, the *Oregon* was not only dead in the water but devoid of any power source.

★

Eric Stone drummed his fingers on the helm console. His monitors had fired back up, but he was staring daggers at the dueling progress bars. The sonar and radar computers were still booting up.

The radar finished first. But the image was glitchy. The radar dome must have suffered a direct hit. Another repair that needed to be logged for the damage control party.

The sonar display snapped on. Since the arrays were located underwater they had suffered no damage.

An alarm blared on the console.

"Torp in the water," Eric shouted.

Max whipped around in the Kirk Chair. "Status!"

"Bearing ninety-seven degrees. Two hundred yards and closing. Speed 15.64 knots."

"Sound general quarters. Wepps?"

"Systems still rebooting."

The Klaxon blared across the ship, sending all hands racing to their combat stations, bracing for whatever might come next.

Max ran a slide rule through his mind, calculating angles and distance. Less than twenty-three seconds until impact.

"Helm, on my mark—make for two hundred eighty degrees on a Fibonacci arc."

"Aye, Captain." Eric grinned. He knew exactly what Max was planning. His fingers lightly touched the joystick and throttles.

"Steady hand, my boy . . ." Max ran the clock down in his mind. If Stoney could cut the turn just right . . . \

"Flank speed—now!"

Stoney turned the controls with the deftness of an eye surgeon. The massive engines powered to full throttle and threw the *Oregon* into a sharp curve, like the unfolding curl of a seashell. The Fibonacci sequence, also known as the golden mean, was a recurring phenomenon in nature. Nature's hand loved to draw a line along a series of curving points where each new point in the sequence is the sum of two numbers preceding it, ad infinitum. Artists like Michelangelo used and admired it—and so did engineers like Max, whose calculations had proven correct. Mostly.

Hashimoto's drone torpedo, originally aimed directly midships to the *Oregon*, suddenly found itself running parallel to its steel hull cutting through the churning waters. But the torpedo had a magnetic trigger along with its other detonating sensors, and as it kissed the *Oregon*'s hull it exploded.

The *Oregon* shuddered from the double blast. The first explosion was the torpedo warhead erupting just inches from the hull. But the second blast came from the *Oregon* herself. The thickly armored-steel plates beneath the waterline were also protected by exploding reactive armor—the same technology that shielded modern battle tanks from anti-tank projectiles. The secondary reactive explosion neutralized the first.

"Status report!" Max barked over the roaring Klaxon.

"Hull integrity intact," Gilreath reported. He had been called to duty in the op center to fill in for Linda while she was on the island mission.

"Stoney?"

"No other tangos in the water. Radar clear."

"Cancel general quarters—and kill that Klaxon before my head explodes."

70

Juan, Max, and Murph stood at the bottom of the crane as a warm tropical sun broke the horizon. The top of the crane where the wrecked Kashtan had nested behind its steel sleeve was shattered and blackened from the lightning strike and the subsequent explosions from the missile cook-offs.

Max whistled. "Looks like the business end of an exploding cigar." He mopped the back of his sweaty neck with a clean rag he kept in his hip pocket. They were all sweating in the tropical heat.

Murph shaded his eyes from the sun to study the wreckage.

"Looks like it got smashed with Thor's hammer. Shocking."

Max raised a disapproving eyebrow. *Bad joke.*

Murph shrugged. "What? Too soon?"

Max shook his head. "Remind me to add a 'no puns allowed' clause to your next contract."

"Sorry."

Cabrillo ignored their banter. "Thank God nobody got killed."

He was commenting as much about last night's mission on the island as he was about the lightning barrage that nearly sank his ship. As soon as Cabrillo realized the island's GPS signal was a lure and the warehouse a trap, he bellowed out evacuation orders loud enough for Linc and MacD to hear them on the backside of the building. Everyone bolted away just as the drone hit. Two seconds earlier, and the team would have been wiped out. Instead, the five of them found themselves knocked to the ground, bruised and bleeding. Linda was out cold.

Cabrillo was still on his back when the ocean sky beyond the trees lit up in a booming white firestorm. Only later would he learn the terrifying details.

Gomez had raced to the sound of the warehouse explosion with a med kit when two more explosions—the Vendor's torpedo and the *Oregon*'s reactive armor—ripped the night air behind him. The lanky Texas pilot reached Linda and saw the wound on her face. He got her bandaged up and stabilized and helped carry her back to the RHIB.

As soon as they all got back to the *Oregon*, Linda was rushed to the emergency operating room, where Hux tended to her eye. Not only had a piece of shrapnel hit it but her retina detached. As an experienced combat surgeon, Hux had dealt with this kind of thing before. Her skilled hands and specialized equipment saved Linda's vision, but she was no longer fit for duty. She was currently in recovery and her eye was out of danger, but she was benched from the game for the next few weeks.

While Hux was in surgery, Forrester stitched up MacD in the clinic and passed out Tylenols and bandages for the others.

Cabrillo glanced around the *Oregon*'s expansive deck. It almost looked normal again after last night's galvanic carnage. Exhausted and battered after their mission, the Gundogs skipped their hot showers and bunks to throw in with the damage control parties. Every able-bodied hand worked through the night and into the early morning to clear away the wreckage, assess damages, and effect whatever repairs they could. Some systems, like the Kashtan, required complete replacement or overhaul at a qualified shipyard.

At dawn Cabrillo told his operators to punch the clock and get some rest, while he assembled the brain trust on the deck to plot the way forward. The *Oregon* was wounded, but she wasn't yet out of the fight. The question was, how much fight was left in her?

"Max, give me a rundown on systems."

"As near as I can tell, the first few strikes knocked out the primary and secondary circuit breakers. But those breakers weren't designed for a superstorm like that one.

"After that, everything was vulnerable. The run of cascading strikes overwhelmed the rest of the systems, ripping out entire circuits like grandma pulling weeds out of her truck garden. I'm surprised we didn't suffer worse damage than we did.

"The storm also knocked out the auto power transfer switch—I'll make sure that never happens again. The engines probably escaped damage because the entire engineering section is actually a giant electrical generator and we secured it accordingly.

"The Cray supercomputer was triple-protected on its own remote circuit for obvious reasons. By some miracle, that was enough to shield it. Its self-diagnostics have run clear. The biggest damage we suffered were the systems that weren't properly shielded."

"Such as?"

"Everything from small engine motors, power tools, Jet Skis—you name it. Every department is doing an inventory. The moon pool reports that the *Nomad*'s navigational electronics were fried, and the *Gator*'s hull is cracked. We've lost them both for the time being."

"What about the *Spook Fish*?"

"Callie's running diagnostics on her now."

"That torpedo blast—we're sure our hull wasn't breached?"

"Watertight. But we lost a good chunk of reactive, so the hull is no longer smooth. The loss of hydrodynamic efficiency will shave at least twenty percent off our top speed, maybe more."

"Getting sunk would have dropped our speed even further. I'll take the twenty percent and run."

"True that, boss."

"Wepps? Where are we?" Cabrillo asked Murphy.

"Kashtan is a total loss, obviously. The hundred-twenty-millimeter auto cannon is still functional as a gun, but out of commission until those fused door plates can get replaced. The lift for the rail gun is *distrutto*, but the AW's lift is fine. Go figure."

"What about sonar and radar?"

"Eric said he checked and double-checked the systems. All good."

"Tell him to check them again."

"Aye."

Cabrillo darkened. "How did all of this happen, really?"

"You mean, the lightning?" Max asked. "Lightning happens."

"I refuse to believe the Vendor's torpedo attack accidentally coincided with the worst lightning strike any of us have ever heard of. It was coordinated, or I'm a pigeon-toed prima ballerina."

Cabrillo turned to Murph. "Is it possible to weaponize lightning?"

"Anything is possible so long as it doesn't violate the laws of physics. I've just never heard of anybody successfully doing it. There were rumors about the CIA trying to find a way to use it as an assassination weapon, but nothing came of it, at least as far as I know."

"In Vietnam, the feds deployed a weather weapon called Operation Popeye," Max said. "But that was only to extend the monsoon season with cloud seeding to slow the Vietcong supply lines."

Juan sighed with frustration. The Vendor had dealt them a couple of bad hands and last night's lightning barrage nearly knocked them out of the game. With no other leads to go on, the smart play would be for them to get to a repair yard as quickly as possible so the *Oregon* would be ready to fight if and or when another clue came their way.

But Cabrillo couldn't shake the feeling that the "smart play" was still a retreat, and that didn't sit well with him at all.

He was weighing all of his options when his radio crackled.

"Chairman, do you read me?"

Juan keyed his mic. "Five by five, Hali. What do you need?"

"Eric Stone wants to see you in the conference room. He says it's urgent."

71

Cabrillo marched into the conference room and fell into one of the chairs. Max and Murph did the same. Eric was already seated in front of a laptop and projecting Juan's Midjourney-generated image of the Vendor onto one of the wall screens. It looked just like an actual color photograph of the man, but it was entirely fictional, a product of Juan's prodigious memory married to digital artistry.

"What've you got for us, Stoney?" Juan asked.

"That's the picture you and the Magic Shop came up with for the Vendor. We've scoured every social media source we know, but couldn't find a match. Not in company records, school yearbooks, nothing. If he ever had a digital shadow, he found a way to completely erase it."

"Another dead end?"

Eric smiled. "Until we found this."

He pulled up a black-and-white image from old film stock, grainy and damaged. The man's face was bearded, his almond-shaped eyes covered by round, steel-rimmed glasses from the period. Stone had wire-framed the digitized image, cropped it, and re-angled the man's face to match the approximate profile angle of the Vendor.

"Whoa," Max said. "Two peas in a pod."

"Just wait." Eric punched a couple of keys. The Midjourney image was made slightly transparent, then Stone superimposed it upon the black-and-white image. They were practically identical, down to the arrogant, thin-lipped smile.

"Unless our nemesis is a time traveler, I'm guessing that's a relative," Murph said. "Though I kinda like the idea we're looking at Dr. Who."

Juan leaned forward on his elbows studying the image.

"Who is it?"

"That's Dr. Yoshio Mitomo. He was head of the virology lab inside of Unit 731."

"The infamous prison camp the Japanese ran in Manchuria during the war," Max said. "The human experiments they did there were beyond the pale. Worse than Auschwitz."

"And some of those experiments were conducted on American soldiers, especially airmen," Murph said. "They demonized our bomber pilots as war criminals unworthy of humane treatment."

Max stabbed a finger at Mitomo's image. "That's a bona fide war criminal. A firing squad was too good for him."

"Unfortunately not," Eric said. "We captured Mitomo after the war. We knew what he was up to at Unit 731. But the OSS swept him up in Operation Paperclip. Offered him immunity in exchange for his services."

"They should've hanged him," Max said.

"Truman was more worried about world revolution than international justice," Juan said. "We were looking for every material and technological advantage to stop the spread of Stalin's evil. We were in a race to capture as many German and Japanese scientists as we could before the Russians scooped them up. It was a kind of arms race, only it was about capturing the brains that would develop the next generation of warfare."

"I understand it," Max said. "But I still don't like it. We should've lined them all up against the wall."

"Then we might not have gone to the moon," Murph said. "Wernher von Braun practically built the Apollo program. Same story on the

Russian side. Every Soviet space rocket should've had 'Made in Germany' stamped on its backside."

"Enough with the history lessons," Juan said. "What happened to Mitomo?"

"He disappears from any official record after 1946. Well, except for this." Eric pulled up a black-and-white picture of a baby Japanese girl.

"Mitomo's daughter?" Juan asked.

"Yes. And fast-forward to this." Eric's fingers flew across his keyboard. A Japanese marriage certificate, a faded color wedding photo, and a local Japanese newspaper clipping appeared. The Cray supercomputer had translated all of it.

"Mitomo's daughter marries a man named Tomoyuki Hashimoto. He was a Japanese aerospace engineer. He was a salary man, and an alcoholic according to his medical records." Eric pulled up a coroner's report. "Committed suicide in 1994 after he was fired from the F-2 fighter program." Eric tossed in a photo of the jet plane.

"The Viper Zero," Murph said. "An F-16 derivative. Made by Mitsubishi."

Cabrillo was always amazed at Murph's encyclopedic knowledge of all things weapons related, even systems from before his time.

"And the key word is 'Mitsubishi,'" Eric said.

"As in Mitsubishi Zero, the famous Japanese fighter plane of World War II?" Max asked.

"No. Mitsubishi as in the J8MI Shusui."

"Japan's first jet fighter," Murph said. "A German Komet knockoff."

"What's this got to do with the Vendor?"

"One of the lead engineers for the J8MI was Hiroshi Hashimoto, Tomoyuki's father."

"I can see where this is going," Juan said. "And I'm getting a sick feeling."

"You're stomach is on point, Chairman. A wartime medical researcher and a wartime aircraft designer combine their gene pools to create the ultimate weapon of mass destruction, their grandson, the Vendor."

"We still don't have a name."

"Oh, but we do." Eric zoomed in on another Japanese document. "This is the *koseki*—the family register of the Hashimoto family." Stone then circled a handwritten name in faultless kanji script. "That's the name of Tomoyuki's only son, Shigeru Hashimoto, aka the Vendor."

"What do we know about him?"

"He was a weapons designer for Japan's largest defense contractors before joining the Acquisition, Technology & Logistics Agency, Japan's version of DARPA. A brilliant visionary. Pushed hard against the conventions. But you know what they say in Japan? 'The nail that sticks out gets hammered.' It's not clear whether he was fired or quit. What is clear is that he disappeared shortly thereafter and presumed a suicide, like his father."

"A fatal presumption," Max said. "In more ways than one."

"So we have a name and a face. Where can we find him?"

"I hit all kinds of dead ends. After his presumed suicide, he disappears from any records. So I decided to go back to the source material and dig around. I don't have any proof of anything, but sometimes circumstantial evidence is enough to convict."

"You got that from *Murder, She Wrote*, didn't you?" Murph said.

"Guilty as charged."

"Let's cut to the chase," Juan said. A lack of sleep and a growing sense of urgency had shortened his fuse.

"Two things. First, it turns out Grandpa Mitomo was involved with a program called Operation Black Chrysanthemum."

"Never heard of it," Juan said. "There was an Operation Cherry Blossoms at Night. It was a plan to use a seaplane from an I-400 Japanese submarine to attack San Diego with biological weapons from the air."

"Bingo. This was a parallel program. Only Black Chrysanthemum wasn't aimed at San Diego. It was aimed at Guam."

Max frowned. "Why Guam?"

"Guam was the base for B-17s and B-29s bombing Japan. Japanese fighters couldn't stop the American bombers, so the military hatched a plan to neutralize it with neurological agents."

"What happened to the operation?" Max asked.

"Just like with Cherry Blossoms. Both submarines were sunk before they reached their targets."

"So if we connect the dots, Hashimoto is planning on some kind of biological weapons attack on a U.S. military base," Juan said. "But which one?"

"Could be anywhere," Murph said. "The DoD maintains at least seven hundred fifty bases in eighty countries. In Asia, there are a hundred twenty bases in Japan. Seventy-three in South Korea."

"He wouldn't hit a base in Japan, would he?" Max asked.

"Depends on how angry he is," Eric said. "Or why. No telling what his motives are."

"Motive is the key," Juan said. "We can't read his mind. But maybe he's following a familiar pattern. What if he was planning an attack on Guam, just like his grandfather did?"

"With a submarine?" Max asked. "And neurotoxin?"

"Not just any submarine. But a sub that can launch missiles or even planes."

"Or drones," Murph added. "He seems to favor those."

"We should alert the authorities on Guam," Max said.

"And tell them what? Get ready for a possible attack at an unknown time by a still unknown person with unknown weapons? And what if we're wrong? What if it's South Korea? Or somewhere else? Do we alert all seven hundred fifty American bases 'just in case'?"

"I see your point."

"I bet every military base in the Asian theater is on full alert anyway after the sinking of that South Korean destroyer."

"And for all we know," Eric added, "he's conspiring with the Chinese and their Taiwan operations. He might be targeting fleets instead of islands."

"I actually hope it is Guam," Murph said.

Max leaned forward. "Why?"

"Their new air defense system comes online day after tomorrow. It's the latest and greatest, like Iron Dome on steroids. Nothing the Vendor can throw at it will get through."

"Unless he attacks before then," Juan said.

"Good point. But that's assuming he knows that's the timeline," Murph said.

"If we do," Eric said, "he does. Count on it."

"I'd feel better if we told Guam to stay extra frosty for the next forty-eight hours," Max said.

Juan nodded. "Agreed. Make the call."

Murph shrugged. "I think the greater likelihood is that Guam's new air defense means he'll be looking for an easier nut to crack."

"You could be right, Wepps," Juan said. "Guam is as good a guess as any, but it's just that—a guess. So forget the target. We need to find Hashimoto."

"I might have found him," Eric said. "We finally cracked the encryption on one of the recovered phones—that Plata guy who ran the show on Sorrows."

"Outstanding. Keep going."

"Plata's phone only communicated with one satellite number. The Cray was able to track the movements of Hashimoto's phone. The main item of interest is this . . ."

Eric pulled up a map detailing all of the Vendor's phone locations as red dots. But one location in particular had the highest concentration of red dots. It was an island in the Bismarck Sea.

"The name of the island is Pau Rangi. We think that might be his base of operations."

"Any chance his phone is pinging there right now?" Max asked.

"It hasn't broadcast since we leveled Sorrows."

"Anything else tie him to the island?" Juan asked.

"Turns out, the Imperial Japanese Navy operated out of there during the war. An Australian Army unit was sent there in early '46 to search for holdouts, but all they found was a few abandoned bunkers and a burned-out fishing village. The Aussies wrote it off as a worthless rock. A Japanese family reclaimed ownership in 1947. In 2009, the family sold it to a private real estate investment firm for tourist development."

"Please tell me that Hashimoto's name pulls up in all of this."

"No such luck. The name of the family that originally owned the island is Onizuka. The real estate outfit they sold it to is a shell corporation. Hashimoto's name hasn't turned up in any of the documents, but it's a pretty good bet he's connected to it somehow."

Juan studied the map, his chin perched in his clenched hands.

"You're right, Stoney. It's all circumstantial. But it's the best we've got. Good work."

"Thanks."

Juan stood. "Unless someone has a better idea, we'll set a course for Pau Rangi—flank speed."

72

Erin Banfield downed her scotch in a single slug to calm her nerves. She was afraid to act, and afraid not to. She was afraid that no matter what she did, she would die.

Unless she was very, very careful.

The Vendor's phone call was a surprise unto itself. The secretive arms merchant had only ever communicated with her by text, no doubt to hide his voice, which revealed so much about a person—nationality, class, education, age. For a time, she imagined the Vendor might be a woman. After all, why not? Women could be as ruthless and cunning as men.

But the second he opened his mouth and vomited out his tirade, she knew it was an older man with an Asian accent, and a current or former heavy smoker.

And he was out of control.

Today she had to lower the volume on her phone to mitigate the screaming rage pouring out of her receiver. He was positively unhinged.

Banfield was long used to her inferiors insulting or dismissing her with subtle gestures, carefully couched words, and imperious attitudes. But she had never been yelled at before. It shook her to the core.

It was clear that Mendoza and the *Oregon* had prompted the

Vendor's near psychotic break. He ranted about "another miraculous escape" and swore undying vengeance. He no longer knew where the ship was.

As far as Banfield was concerned, Mendoza was *his* problem. But Mendoza and the *Oregon*—or the *Norego* or whatever name it was sailing under—suddenly became *her* problem.

"I'm sending you a team of trained assassins to capture Overholt and torture him. I must know where that damnable ship is. And I want Mendoza's head on a pike. Make the arrangements immediately!"

She tried to explain the near impossibility of the feat, especially if she hoped to avoid suspicion and maintain her cover.

Undeterred, he suddenly softened his tone and offered her a king's ransom for her assistance in the Overholt kidnapping.

The offer gave her pause. Overholt had never done her any favors. Not really. He was nice enough, and respectful of her intelligence. But he never used his influence to help advance her career. He seemed indifferent, at best. When she was young she had once offered herself to him, but feigning a gentlemanly regard for his deceased wife's honor and his own, he gently declined her offer. He became aloof after that. She always assumed he undermined her career without her knowledge after that faux pas.

But all of that was water under the bridge. What concerned her now was the fact the venerable Overholt enjoyed excellent federal security protection. Worse, the old man had a reputation for cold vengeance—one that extended even beyond the grave thanks to a coterie of fiercely loyal colleagues who would wreak savage retribution on anyone who touched him.

What to do?

In the heat of the moment of the phone call, all she could think of was to defer the Vendor's outrageous request. She promised him she'd pull together all the information he would need for the assassin squad in the next three days. Overholt was incommunicado at the moment anyway, she assured him.

He mumbled his thanks and told her he would contact her again in seventy-two hours, and when he did he wanted the necessary details.

He tried but failed to hide the murderous menace in his voice before killing the call.

She stood there nursing another drink and weighing her harrowing options.

If she betrayed the Vendor, he would no doubt kill her. If she arranged for Overholt's murder, her sleepless life would eventually end on a terrifying note in a moldering, unmarked grave.

Beyond those fears, she also faced the possibility of either a life of relative poverty or a life of wealth, cavorting in the Algarve with her Portuguese Lothario.

In a moment of weakness she briefly considered turning herself in and plea-bargaining her way to a light sentence in exchange for betraying the Vendor. But the vulgar thought was beneath her dignity, and entirely out of the question. She could never allow herself to be caged like an animal, not even for a moment, and not even to save her life.

She finally realized there was really only one thing she could do.

Cash in her chips.

And run.

★

PAU RANGI ISLAND
THE BISMARCK SEA

"Faster, you idiots! Hurry. Hurry! You are all my friends. I beg you. *Hurry!*"

The Vendor ran around the underground submarine pen in frenzied urgency. The AI-powered *Ghost Sword* had to be loaded and depart in less than two hours or the Guam attack would fail.

To his credit, the German and his technicians had loaded the neurotoxins into their dispersion tanks, and most of those had been inserted into the drones. The drones now were being loaded onto the *Ghost Sword*, but the loading crews were falling behind schedule.

Beyond the timetable, the Vendor fretted over his phone call with Banfield. He knew she was hedging her bets, and assumed she would fail to follow through on her vague promises. He would deal with her later.

Kidnapping Overholt was a desperate gambit on his part, but he needed to know where Mendoza and the *Oregon* were. The Americans were a poisoned splinter in his eye. Though no match for his own towering intellect, they threatened his entire operation, if only out of tenacity of will and mindless luck.

They were out there, somewhere. The Vendor's last surveillance drone hovering over Jaco Island caught the twin explosions erupting beneath the *Oregon*'s waterline the night before. His drone torpedo had undoubtedly hit the vessel. The sight of the geysering water had thrilled him to no end.

But the second explosion was a surprise. At first he'd hoped it had struck the ship's ammunition stores, but when he saw the *Oregon* didn't erupt in a ball of flame or break in two, he concluded the hellborn ship possessed reactive armor that defeated his attack.

That was unheard of. He grudgingly acknowledged the brilliance of it as events unfolded. But his thin admiration gave way moments later to rage when the violent storm above the island destroyed his surveillance drone. Now he had no idea where the *Oregon* and its resolute crew were currently located. He hoped they had retreated to a nearby port for needed repairs after his lightning barrage. But his intuition was that Mendoza was as relentless in his pursuit as a lockjawed pit bull stalking a tethered steer.

The Vendor's agitation only increased as he realized the dozen uniformed technicians in his employ ignored his rising torrent of vile curses and fawning praises. They were all painfully aware of the giant digital clock counting down the remaining time until launch.

Big bonuses were riding on their success, and he'd hoped that was motivation enough. But they also knew the penalty for failure. And failure was in the cards. The Vendor warned them of an impending assault by unknown forces and ordered them to wear holstered pistols and to sling Uzi mini submachine guns to their chests. They did so without complaint, but the Vendor feared their sloth was a silent protest.

He swore violently as a man stumbled on the *Ghost Sword*'s deck, nearly dumping a container over the side. Just twelve more drone pods needed to be loaded and the ship could finally slip beneath the surface, invisible to any known form of detection save the human eye.

The Vendor glanced at his ancestors' shrine on the far wall. He muttered a quick prayer, begging the *kami* to make these fools work faster.

73

Juan Cabrillo feared no man, but he wasn't an idiot.

The Vendor's technological prowess was considerable, and he had nearly done the *Oregon* in. But the *Oregon* only survived his long-range missile and torpedo assaults because her systems were fully intact. Now she was nearly crippled in her defensive and offensive capabilities thanks to the Vendor's mysterious lightning assault. Extreme caution was the order of the day if they hoped to survive long enough to thwart his Guam attack.

Cabrillo assumed the Vendor had some kind of surveillance system in operation. After consulting the sea charts, he and Max decided to anchor the *Oregon* on the far side of a nameless, uninhabitable rocky islet about five nautical miles south of Pau Rangi. At least that put them out of direct line of sight of any optical devices the Vendor might have stationed at his base.

They also took the extra precaution of deploying a camouflage scheme over the *Oregon*'s entire deck and superstructure. A small electrical charge was all it took to transform the ship's meta-material coatings into any camouflage design stored in the Cray computer. But in this case, the Cray copied the imagery of the nearby rocky islet, its crooked, wind-swept trees, and surrounding water. If a drone scanned the *Oregon* from above, it would look like an extension of the island's jagged coastline instead of a break-bulk carrier.

But hiding from the Vendor was only half his problem. Cabrillo also needed to find both him and his operation if he hoped to neutralize it and capture the elusive merchant of death.

The AW tilt-rotor was still out of commission, but Gomez Adams, the *Oregon*'s best drone pilot, ran a below-the-radar surveillance flight over Pau Rangi. It was as uninhabited as the nameless islet. No people, no activity—and certainly no submarine.

"Did we pick the wrong island?" Cabrillo asked, sitting in the Kirk Chair.

"Sure looks like it," Max said. "We can keep searching. Or we can try somewhere else."

"Like where?" Hali asked.

Max shook his head. "I wish I knew. It feels like we're just chasing our own tail now."

Callie stood next to Juan. "Can't we fly another one of those EMP missiles over the island, just in case? Knock out any electronics that might be down there?"

"Irony alert," Murph said. "The last CHAMP missile we had in the arsenal got fried in the electrical storm. Good idea, though."

Cabrillo glanced over at Linda's empty chair. He trusted her judgment. But she was in a clinic bed, face down, and under orders not to budge unless Huxley approved it. It was the only way her vision could be saved.

"Hey, Stoney, didn't you say that Pau Rangi was a Japanese navy base during the war?"

"Yeah, but the Aussies didn't find anything. Must not have been much of an operation."

"We're looking for a sub. If that island was actually a sub base—"

Murph palmed his forehead. "An underwater sub pen! Should've thought of that!"

"But with both the *Nomad* and *Gator* out of commission, how do we find it—let alone breach it?" Max asked.

"Five miles is a long swim," Eric added, "and that's just to get there."

"If there is a sub pen beneath the island, that means there's an underwater entrance, right?" Murph asked.

"Keep going," Juan said.

"This morning I was trying to figure out how the Vendor might have caused that lightning storm. I decided to check out the weather patterns in the region. Thought maybe that had something to do with it. Around here, we've been in the nineties for quite a while."

"And you think ambient air temperature caused it?"

"Possibly, but that's not what I'm getting at."

Callie grinned. "I know where you're going with this. With the hot sun and air temperature, the surface sea temperature would be warmer, too. And if there is some kind of underground lagoon or cave beneath the island, the water in there would be shielded from the sun, making it cooler—"

Eric finished her sentence. "So we could check for a water temperature variation along the coast. Wherever we find a cold spot, that's where the entrance is. Brilliant."

"A sub pen would also be leeching chemicals and other contaminants," Max said. "If we could check for those at the same location we'd have all the confirmation we'd need."

"Wepps, can you and Eric assemble a sensor array and put that on one of our drones and do another flyover?" Juan asked.

"Right away."

"Then get cracking. And have Gomez lend you a hand."

The two techies scrambled out of the conference room.

"Assuming we find the entrance, what's the plan?" Max asked. "The *Oregon* has the offensive capabilities of a declawed kitten."

"We put a team of Gundogs in there. Tear the place up."

"How? The AW's shot, and the *Nomad* and the *Gator* are kaput. We've got no way to get near it unless we want to expose the *Oregon* to more of the Vendor's missile and torpedo attacks."

"How about the *Spook Fish*?" Callie asked.

"You can't carry enough operators in it, and they have no way to egress while underwater," Juan said.

Callie smiled. "Anybody got a towrope?"

★

Juan, Linc, MacD, and Eddie were in the moon pool, all kitted out for the mission. Each wore dive suits and fins, and full face masks with interior comms.

Raven wasn't with them. She complained bitterly she couldn't participate, but there wasn't anything for her to do since her gunshot confined her to a bed or a pair of crutches. She managed to finagle her way into the armory and sweet-talked Mike Lavin, the *Oregon*'s chief armorer, into letting her hand-load all of the ammo mags.

The team's dry bags were loaded with FN P90 bullpup submachine guns, dozens of extra fifty-round mags Raven had topped off, and flash-bangs. A few carried C4 plastic explosive with timers. They all wore one-hundred-cubic-foot dive tanks.

With Raven out of commission, Linda's eye injury, and the other 'dogs banged up, Murph volunteered for the mission. Juan agreed, but put him under Linc's close supervision. Murph had trained extensively with small arms in recent years and had been on a few ground ops. But he had never scuba dived before. At the moment, Linc was showing him the finer points of breathing through his regulator and monitoring the HUD display on his mask for oxygen and nitrogen levels.

"Comms check," Callie said from inside the *Spook Fish* floating in the moon pool.

"Five by five," Juan said. The other's confirmed as well.

"All set?" Juan asked Murph.

Murph threw two thumbs up as he treaded water, his fins pedaling beneath him. "The plan's so crazy it just might work."

"Sometimes crazy *is* the plan," Juan said.

"Roger that," Callie said.

"Okay, everybody, let's saddle up."

74

Callie's steady hand guided the submersible motoring along at just over four knots. She trusted the AI piloting program, but her own judgment even more. The weight of the human cargo trailing behind her like a baited dragline altered the vessel's handling characteristics. The four Gundogs and Murphy held fast to a long nylon tether with handhold loops. Their larger one-hundred-cubic-foot scuba tanks were heavier and created more drag than regular tanks. But they had to travel eighty minutes underwater sixty feet below the surface. The bigger tanks gave them an extra twenty minutes of air for a cushion to make the journey and do everything else. That was cutting it close.

Too close.

Callie was pleasantly surprised that Murph had volunteered. She assumed he was just a sweet nerd. Her only concern was that he had never scuba dived before. Fortunately, all he had to do was hang on.

Callie was also shocked that Cabrillo didn't put up much of a fight when she volunteered to pilot the *Spook Fish*—not that she would have given him any other choice. But it also spoke to Cabrillo's determination to carry the fight to the Vendor, and his lack of resources to do it.

The *Oregon*'s drone deployed a thermal infrared camera and a spectrometer when it flew back over Pau Rangi. The sensors confirmed a definite temperature spike at one specific location, where a trail of inorganic compounds were also detected. Callie's nav computer indicated they were nearing that spot. A thousand feet away she halted the *Spook Fish* and keyed her comms.

"Sending the drone," Callie said.

"Copy that," Juan replied in his mask mic.

Callie deployed the *Spook Fish* drone on its long graphene power cable. With the boys on the towrope running low on air she didn't have time to fool around. She had to be stealthy about it. If she alerted anyone inside the sub pen, she'd likely get them all killed.

The first obstacle she had to overcome was an anti-submarine net barring the way into the underwater entrance. Cabrillo warned her to expect this. Her handy little demolition drone deployed its welding device and cut a perfectly circular eight-foot-diameter hole in the middle of it—plenty of room for the divers to swim through, as well as her drone.

It wasn't long before the familiar shape of a submarine hull loomed in the gloomy distance about a hundred yards away. She surfaced her drone just enough to allow the camera to record the interior. The images were fed live to the HUD displays on the diving masks of each of the team members. The same images appeared on her screen.

The underground cavern and lagoon was roughly circular and approximately one hundred yards in diameter. It was ringed with a rocky ledge wide enough for a person to walk along.

The sub entrance was at the three o'clock position. The sub itself was docked at a loading pier at the nine o'clock. Directly behind it was an elevator dug into the cave wall. At the eight o'clock position was another, smaller pier where a mini sub was docked.

She counted at least twelve armed men scrambling on or near the larger sub. They were shutting hatches and securing the boat.

Alarmingly, two unmanned, automated machine guns tracked back and forth in silent sentinel, one at the two o'clock position, the other at the six o'clock.

But what really caught Callie's eye was the large digital clock fixed to the cavern wall. It registered seven minutes, twenty-two seconds. She assumed it was a launch clock.

"You getting this?" Callie asked, choking down the anxiety in her voice.

"Got it," Cabrillo said. "Retract the drone, and get us closer."

She checked her own digital clock. By her reckoning, the team had ten minutes of air left to get through the net and unleash hell.

★

Cabrillo studied the drone imagery in real time. Like Callie, he assumed the digital readout on the cave wall was a countdown clock. And since the sub was leaving in just moments, he was convinced the target was Guam.

"Callie, radio *Oregon*. Tell them to put Guam on alert. I'm certain that's the target."

"Will do." The *Spook Fish* trailed a comms antenna attached to a floating buoy that gave her radio access to the *Oregon*.

Cabrillo wasn't convinced there was anything that Guam could do to defend itself against whatever the Vendor had in mind. Ten thousand American lives hung in the balance. The best chance those people had were his Gundogs.

Right here.

Right now.

"Those two auto guns are going to mow us down if we don't take them out first," Juan said. "Linc and Murph. You both carry C4, so you pull the short straws."

"Roger that," they both replied.

"Chairman, one thing," Murph added. "Those machine guns are on targeting mode—see how they track back and forth? The only reason they don't open up and kill those tangos is because they're wearing tags that prevent the guns from shooting them."

"Your point?"

"Hopefully Linc and I take out those guns. But if we don't, hiding behind one of those tangos is better than a bulletproof vest. And don't forget, those guns are wicked fast. They'll lock onto you in nanoseconds."

"Anything else?"

"I'd also bet the sub is tagged, not that there's anywhere to hide on that thing."

"Copy that. But do your jobs and they won't be an issue."

"Aye."

"Gents, we have two goals. First, take out that sub. Second, capture the Vendor. While Linc and Murph are taking out the machine guns, the rest of us will advance clockwise toward that smaller mini sub and use it as cover in our approach to the main pier, where the target sub is located. Anybody else carrying C4?"

"I am," Eddie said.

"Then the rest of us will provide you covering fire while you get on the target. Use the C4 to blow a hatch if you have to. But get inside and pull the guts out of it any way you can."

"Can't you just shoot holes in the hull?" Callie asked over the comms.

"We brought peashooters compared to that pressurized hull," Juan responded. "No chance of penetration. Our only chance is to get inside of it."

"What about the Vendor?" MacD asked.

"I'd like to capture him," Juan said. "But if we can't, he's all mine."

"And the techs?" Eddie asked. "What are the rules of engagement?"

"Prisoners if we can. But if they pull guns, take them out." Cabrillo added, "With extreme prejudice."

75

The Vendor stood on the deck of the *Ghost Sword* relishing the welter of noise and commotion all around him. His armed technicians had just finished loading the last drones into the *Ghost Sword*. The sub's hangar door shut with an airtight whisper.

The Vendor stole a quick glance at the digital countdown clock as it ticked just past the three minute mark. He smiled for the first time in days. His sub would launch on time and the Guam attack would succeed.

He knelt down and double-checked one of the deck hatches as the last of the workers dashed past him and headed for the gangplank. The two automated machine guns kept a deadly vigil in the distance, their servo motors whirring as the barrels snapped back and forth. The techs had long since ignored the fact the deadly guns targeted them like a pair of hunters aiming at a flush of fat quail bolting into the sky. An automated pull of the trigger could wipe them all out with a single burst.

In their haste and concentration, nobody noticed the bubbles rippling the water on the far edges of the lagoon.

★

Cabrillo's team split up according to plan. Linc and Murph swam into their positions near the machine guns as the others advanced toward the mini sub and its smaller pier.

As soon as Juan's team arrived, everybody stripped off gear and pulled weapons. Juan's team couldn't climb onto the pier until Murph and Linc knocked off the machine guns or they'd be cut down.

With his head barely above the surface and hiding behind a pylon, Cabrillo whispered orders in his mic to commence the operation.

★

Linc and Murph slipped effortlessly out of the water, emerging just inches away from their assigned machine guns whirring on their gimbals. They slapped C4 charges with timed detonators against tripod legs in less than three seconds.

But as Murph warned earlier, that was enough time for the auto machine-gun sensors to pick up their glistening wet suits in the bright overhead lights. Both guns spun onto their targets and opened fire.

The first few rounds slapped the water just inches from Murph, but a fourth round hit him in the left bicep. He cried out before gasping for a lungful of breath and diving below the surface.

The other gun had a harder time locking onto Linc's lightning-fast physique. He disappeared back underneath the water with barely a ripple just as a spray of jacketed rounds hammered the surface.

Seconds later, the two C4 charges exploded. The tripod leg on Linc's machine gun collapsed and tumbled into the water as planned.

Murph's charge also exploded and broke the tripod leg on his assigned gun. But the unit itself merely collapsed to the rocky shelf, not quite reaching the water. Unable to rotate properly, the weapon shuddered like a heart attack victim on a bathroom floor, trying to fix its aim. Though incapable of tracking, the weapon could kill just the same if one of the Gundogs ran through its sensor field.

★

Shocked by the sudden eruption of gunfire, the Vendor froze in place, but his mind ran to overdrive, processing the electrical impulses from the cochlear nerve dumping information into his brain stem. Milliseconds later his incredible intellect understood he was under attack. But it was the raw acidic churn in his gut that told him Mendoza was behind it. The resulting C4 explosions seconds later confirmed both.

The Vendor shouted into his wrist device. "Keiko—launch the *Ghost Sword*!"

★

As soon as they heard the two C4 explosions, Cabrillo and his men pulled themselves onto the small dock and crouched down beneath the mini sub's hull, barely hidden from the beehive of activity ten yards away.

Leaning against the smaller sub's hull, Cabrillo heard alarmed shouts from the armed techs as they racked their weapons. Juan nodded to his guys, lifted the P90 to his shoulder, stood, and fired.

★

ABOARD THE *SPOOK FISH*

Callie had her acoustic sensors turned up. Perched in the pilot's seat and with her drone retracted, all she had was a dim view through the cutout in the anti-sub net she'd made earlier.

She caught the sound of a couple of dull splashes and then the muted sound of distant gunfire. She strained to see who or what hit the water, but she was too far away.

The speakers inside the *Spook Fish* suddenly splashed the metallic sounds of the big anti-submarine net parting like a Broadway curtain. Her blood pressure spiked.

What did that mean?

Had Cabrillo tripped a switch to let her in—or was somebody try-ing to get out?

★

The first salvo of bullets from the Gundogs' P90s dropped a half dozen surprised techs, spilling two of them into the water. The rest were dragged to safety, while others found shelter in the wall of rocks.

Just as the *Ghost Sword*'s bubbling ballast tanks began pulling its hull beneath the waves, a grenade sailed over the mini sub, where Juan and the others were standing. The grenade hit the pier six inches from Cabrillo's bare feet, but bounced off the deck and hit the water. The explosion a few seconds later sent a geyser of salt water into the air, but luckily no shrapnel came with it.

"We gotta stop that sub!" Cabrillo shouted in his comms.

"Cut me a lane," Eddie said.

Linc and Murph—with a now self-bandaged arm—lay prone on different points of the lagoon compass. Linc opened up with precision shots, while Murph cut loose with one-handed controlled bursts. At the same time, MacD and Juan tossed flash-bangs.

"Eddie—go!" Juan said.

The wiry operator bolted from behind the shelter of the mini sub and onto the rocky ledge, heading for the larger pier. Cabrillo and the other Gundogs laid down enough sustained fire to open up a clear path for Eddie. He took a giant leap and hit the *Ghost Sword* deck with a thud.

"Kill him!" the Vendor shouted in the distance, backpedaling away from the mayhem, and pointing at Eddie.

The Vendor's shouts caught Juan's attention. He saw the beefy Asian dash for a hidden door suddenly sliding open. Cabrillo's gut told him the Vendor was making his escape.

Not this time. Juan bolted out from behind the safety of the mini sub. He tossed flash-bangs far ahead of him, hoping to knock out any-one crouched behind the rocky outcrop framing the elevator entrance.

He saw Eddie on his knees on the submerging deck of the *Ghost Sword* fixing a C4 charge to a hatch as water began washing over it.

A machine-gun blast from behind the rocky outcrop spanged on the hatch. One of those rounds hit the C4 charge just as Eddie turned to run away. The resulting blast catapulted him into the air. He tumbled into the water with a dead man's splash.

MacD instantly dove into the lagoon, swimming deep to avoid getting shot. He swam furiously toward his friend's sinking body.

Juan knelt down and swapped out another mag, his adrenalized vision narrowed on the Vendor's figure flinging open a steel door and dashing into the blackened gloom of an escape exit.

"Juan! Juan! The submarine net opened!" Callie cried out over the comms. "What do you want me to do?"

Juan glanced at the vanishing wake from the sub. There was no rush of air bubbles breaking the surface. The C4 charge had failed to breach the hatch and the vessel was making its way out to sea.

"Find a way to stop it!"

"How?"

"Figure it out!" He called to the others, "Linc, Murph—cover me!"

Cabrillo didn't wait for a response. Filled with a berserker's rage, he ran for the escape door.

The Vendor's goons hiding in the rock crevices took aim, but Linc and Murph kept them pinned down long enough for Cabrillo to race past them, arms and legs pumping like an Olympic sprinter.

What Cabrillo didn't realize was that he was running through the targeting reticle of the fallen auto machine gun, still whirring and jerking on the ground on the far side of the lagoon. As soon as Juan entered into the reticle, the onboard computer calculated his directional speed, the ambient air temperature, and a dozen other critical variables. It also determined he wasn't wearing a shot prohibition tag. And it did all of this in less than a heartbeat.

The machine gun unleashed a burst of three rounds that caught Cabrillo in the side just below the armpit. The bullets sledgehammering his ribs should have killed him, but the new lightweight Kevlar wraparound body armor the whole team wore saved his life. The force of the hammer blows cracked bones and stole away his breath. He stumbled forward and nearly fell, but in so doing advanced beyond the range of the gun's targeting reticle. He finally recovered his balance and raced for the open door just yards away.

He knew the gauntlet run had been an insanely risky move that nearly got him killed, and whatever lay beyond the door probably would. But Juan was determined to catch the Vendor or die trying.

★

ABOARD THE *SPOOK FISH*

The image of the sleek *Ghost Sword* pushing past the opened sub net filled the *Spook Fish*'s bulbous acrylic viewing sphere. Callie didn't have any weapons and the big sub could easily brush her aside. There was no way for her to stop it. What could she do?

Callie's heart raced. She could hear the Gundogs shouting and the sounds of gunfire and explosions in her comms. The entire team was under fire. She also heard the reports that both Murph and Eddie had been wounded, and maybe even killed. Clearly they needed help. Everything told her to dash inside.

But Cabrillo told her to stop the sub.

"*Oregon*, this is *Spook Fish*. Do you copy?"

"Copy, *Spook Fish*. This is *Oregon*," Hali replied. "You are on speaker."

"*Oregon*, be advised the Vendor's sub is underway. Repeat, the Vendor's sub is underway. Suggest you hit her with a torpedo."

"Callie, Eric here. I've got a fix on *Spook Fish*. Where is the other vessel?"

"Twenty yards ahead of me and closing at three knots."

"She's a ghost on my sonar."

"Callie, Linda here. I'm acting weapons officer. I can't fire a torpedo if we don't have a sonar fix on its position."

Callie's eyes flitted to her sensor arrays. Something was wrong.

Nothing was registering. She tapped on the screen. Her instruments indicated she was the only vehicle in the water.

How was that possible?

"Copy that, *Oregon*. I'll figure something out."

Callie rang off. *Now what?* That had been her best and only option.

She couldn't call Cabrillo. She had redeployed her comms link from inside the lagoon to the surface so she could radio *Oregon*. She was on her own.

She tightened the grip on her controls. Should she disobey Juan's orders and head into the sub pen lagoon now that the net was open? Or make some kind of crazy dash to stop the unyielding machine that was already beginning to pick up speed?

She watched the *Ghost Sword* approach her position even though her sonar said it wasn't there. But her eyes told her the truth.

So did her heart.

As badly as she wanted to help the guys she'd come to really care about, there were nearly two hundred thousand American lives at stake on Guam.

She yanked the yoke and slammed her throttles forward, cursing herself for her indecision. She had no idea how to stop it. But she had to try.

Now.

76

Juan skidded to a halt just shy of the door entrance, his breath shortened by his aching rib cage.

He shot a quick glance around the corner, expecting the Vendor to open fire on him. But all Cabrillo saw was a steep staircase of hand-hewn rock climbing into the darkness. Fresh boot prints marred the emerald-green moss on the nearest steps.

With gunfire still raging behind him, he raised his weapon, turned the corner, and charged in.

Cabrillo's bare foot hit the first step and he bounded up to the next. But when his bare artificial foot hit the slimy moss, his leg slipped out from under him, crashing him into the steps. Nothing registered in his nerveless carbon-fiber leg, but his left shin felt like it had been cracked with a tire iron. He picked himself up and continued the steep climb, careful to step where the Vendor had already parted the moss.

Suddenly the air split with the sharp retorts of pistol fire from above, the sound magnified by the narrow rock walls, lighting up the darkened stairwell like flashing strobes. Rock shards slashed Juan's face as he dropped to the stairs, flattening himself as best as he could. He raised his P90 blindly and unleashed a fifty-round torrent of un-aimed bullets up into the dark.

More pistol shots rang out. One of the rounds grazed Cabrillo's temple like a branding iron. He jammed himself up against one wall of the staircase, hoping to avoid the next shots as he fumbled to reload another mag.

"Time to die, Mendoza!" the Vendor called from the top as he ripped off five more rounds. Bullets spanged just millimeters from Cabrillo's head.

Cabrillo located the Vendor's distant position up the stairs by the sound of his voice, raised his gun, and pulled the trigger. Fifty more rounds spat out of his weapon in a deafening roar.

Juan slapped another mag in.

His last.

He pulled the trigger and let fly again.

★

ABOARD THE *SPOOK FISH*

An insane plan began to coalesce in Callie's mind.

She slammed the throttles to the stops and threw the *Spook Fish* into the path of the *Ghost Sword*, twenty times the length of her tiny submersible. She maneuvered her fragile vehicle gingerly, careful to not let the mass of the larger vessel smash into her as she guided her ballast pods onto the *Ghost Sword*'s deck.

Even before she landed, Callie's fingers flew across the drone panel controls. She gave it a specific command, but few instructions. There wasn't any need to. The whole point of AI-driven robotics was that the machine would self-direct faster and better than she could. Besides, there wasn't any time.

As soon as she sent the command, the robot launched out of its pod, but it didn't travel very far. It immediately began wet-welding the *Spook Fish*'s steel alloy ballast pods to the smooth deck of the *Ghost Sword*. She had no idea if the two metal surfaces could be joined, but she was out of options. The smooth curves of the *Ghost Sword*'s hydrodynamic hull had no points of purchase, no protrusions, no handholds. There just wasn't any place for her drone's gripping hand to grab hold. Even if she had gripped it, what would she do? Her engines weren't powerful enough to stop it.

For a brief moment she even thought about putting the *Spook Fish* nose-to-nose with the larger vessel in hopes of either slowing her down or misdirecting her. But the chances of maintaining a stable position between two curved surfaces were next to zero even if the AI navigator was in control. It would be like trying to balance one bowling ball on top of another. Just one sharp turn of the *Ghost Sword*'s round nose would send the *Spook Fish* spinning, and leave it trailing in its speeding wake.

The drone's camera pumped images of the welding operation onto Callie's monitor, the sparking arc light flared on the screen. The drone was making quick progress. She just wasn't sure it was quick enough to finish the job before the bigger sub reached top speed and threw the *Spook Fish* off the deck.

And even if it did, would the welds even hold?

★

Juan lay on the rocky staircase littered with dozens of spent shell casings. His ringing ears strained to hear the sound of the Vendor's crashing steps escaping farther upward into the dark or the bark of more rounds fired his way. He heard neither.

He lay still, listening.

Nothing, he told himself, except the drip of water hitting stone a few steps above.

Cabrillo's hopes began to rise. Had he killed the man he'd been chasing for so long? Or had the merchant of death slipped the noose again?

Juan slowed his breathing, hoping his ringing ears would clear. He needed to find out if the man was dead or if he had finally escaped.

Or lying in wait in the dark.

Cabrillo rose on unsteady feet, raised his P90, and engaged the weapon light. He hadn't used the light before because he didn't want to give his position away. But now in the dark it was his best friend.

He flashed the passage up ahead. His heart sank. He hoped to see the Vendor's bullet-ridden corpse draped over the stone steps, but he was long gone.

Juan's anger flared, and he found a new burst of energy. He charged up the stairs, his battered ribs stabbing him with every slowing step. The staircase took a slight bend as it followed a seam in the rock. The passage suddenly opened up to a wide, irregular landing. An open doorway stood ten feet ahead. Beyond it were industrial lights and a workshop.

Cabrillo charged for the door, hoping the Vendor hadn't found his way to an escape vehicle. Just two steps from the doorway, a steel door slid shut on powerful pneumatics. Cabrillo slowed himself, but couldn't stop, and he slammed into it, dropping his empty P90.

"Mendoza! You meddler! Time to die!"

Dazed, Juan turned around just as the Vendor charged.

Cabrillo got his fight on, fast. He threw a blizzard of furious fists and vicious, barefooted kicks, each attack aimed to kill, not wound, the larger man.

But the Vendor blunted each blow with blazingly fast counterstrikes. Cabrillo sped up his attack, but the Vendor countered each thrust, laughing maniacally as if playing a child's game instead of fighting for his life.

The Vendor pressed in, diverting or absorbing Cabrillo's assaults, then unleashed his own relentless attack with a guttural "*Kiai!*"

Cabrillo gave as good as he got defensively, his own finely honed fighting skills blunting the Vendor's iron-hard fists and bone-jarring kicks. But the Vendor's incredible speed and power took their toll quickly. Cabrillo felt like he was fighting a rock-crushing hammer mill, each strike sending shock waves of pain into his aching limbs.

The Vendor stutter-stepped, feigning in one direction before twisting his torso like a coiled spring. He loosed a roundhouse kick into Cabrillo's rib cage—in the exact place where the bullets had struck him before. If the ribs weren't broken before, they were now. The pain radiated through his torso like a shotgun blast, and knocked the air out of him. He stumbled backward and crashed into the rock wall behind him, struggling to breathe.

The Vendor charged in just as Juan's head cracked against the stone.

His bloodshot eyes flared with delight as his long fingers wrapped around Cabrillo's neck. He pressed in so close their faces nearly touched. Worse, the Vendor's more powerful body was pinned against Juan's so he couldn't throw any punches or kicks.

The Vendor's eyes narrowed with grim determination as his grip tightened. Already out of breath from his broken ribs, Cabrillo felt his trachea collapsing beneath strong hands. Another surge of rage adrenalized Juan's muscles and he struck as hard as he could at the Vendor's arms to break his grip, but to no effect. The Vendor's steely fingers were as unrelenting as an iron slave collar.

Robbed of oxygen, Juan's strength flagged and his eyes began to dim. His fingers clawed at Hashimoto's hands, but couldn't get them to budge even a millimeter.

Cabrillo took his last, best shot.

He stomped his heel into the arch of the Vendor's foot, discharging a 12-gauge shotgun blast out of the weapon hidden in his combat leg.

The Vendor's foot was ground to hamburger by the double-aught buckshot. He absorbed the mind-shattering pain with a stoic grunt and his leg buckled slightly, but he didn't loosen his grip.

But the shift in his weight was just enough for Juan to push forward on the Vendor's weakened leg. He grabbed the Vendor's shirt and pulled him farther in that direction, increasing the momentum.

With a final, exhausted shove with his bare foot against the wall, Cabrillo sent the two of them tumbling down the stone stairs locked in a death grip.

★

The drone's arc welder sputtered out when the last encapsulated electrode was finally exhausted.

Callie maneuvered the drone's camera to examine the work. It was well done, considering the circumstances, but it was hardly complete.

She checked her speed gauge. The *Spook* wasn't traveling under her own power, but she was racing along at nearly twenty knots pinned to the deck of the *Ghost Sword*. She glanced back down to the drone's camera screen. The weld was already giving way. It wouldn't last long.

She grabbed her mic. "*Oregon, Oregon*. This is *Spook Fish*. Mayday. Mayday."

"Callie, this is Linda. You're on speakerphone. What's your status?"

"The Vendor vessel has accelerated to twenty knots and has descended to eighty feet. Are you still tracking me?"

"We are tracking you," Eric said. "Twenty knots at eighty-two feet and falling."

"How are you keeping pace with the sub?" Linda asked.

"Long story. Are you tracking the sub, too?"

"Still can't see or hear her."

"But you see me?"

"Aye. Your machine is noisy."

"Linda, listen to me carefully."

"Go ahead."

"Use my sonar position for your torpedo fix."

"Why?"

"I've attached myself to the sub's hull."

"Negative. You'll be destroyed."

"Then aim it a hundred feet beyond my position."

"The torpedo isn't that accurate. Even if it was, the destruction of the sub itself will take you out."

"This vessel is heading for Guam. Ten thousand Americans will die."

"We'll find another way—"

"There is no other way! Do it!"

"Callie—"

"I don't know how much longer *Spook* will stay with her. If she gets away from me, we can't stop her. Do it!"

77

ABOARD THE *OREGON*
OP CENTER

D o it!"
Callie's voice boomed in the overhead speakers.

Linda turned in her chair and faced Max, her face ashen. Huxley had released her into temporary service as weapons officer while Murphy was on mission.

"Max, what do we do?"

Hanley's meaty jaw was parked in his fist like a Rodin statue. His bright eyes were running the same moral calculus that she was. One life in exchange for thousands. It seemed simple. But was it?

Every life mattered, or none of them mattered. Especially Callie's. She was young and brilliant with a bright future ahead of her. Everybody loved her. And Cabrillo was obviously smitten. There had to be another option. But could they find it in time?

The dreadful choice was obvious. He saw it in Linda's face. But it wasn't her call. She wasn't in command. He wished she was.

"Do it, Wepps."

Linda bit her lip and nodded as she turned to the weapons station. She punched a button.

"Torpedo . . . away."

The hull rang with the sound of the massive burst of compressed air above decks, launching the torpedo out of its tube.

"Torpedo in the water," Eric reported glumly. "Running hot, straight and normal. Impact in five minutes, forty-five seconds."

"Did you hear that, Callie?" Linda asked.

"I did. Thank you," Callie said.

"I'm so sorry," Linda said.

"Not your fault. It was my call. Take care."

Callie's comms clicked off.

★

Cabrillo and the Vendor careened down the stone steps, rolling faster and faster. Juan pulled the larger man close, using his muscular frame as a cushion against the stone blows.

The Vendor had the same idea. The sharp, rough-hewn rocks slashed Juan's spine and spiked against the back of his skull, sending shooting stars across his eyes with each strike.

Coiled like fighting snakes, neither man released his grip, but the faster they spun the farther their bodies separated until at the very end both men were entirely airborne and crash-landed at the bottom of the stairs.

The two men lay on the rock floor, moaning and dazed.

The Vendor recovered first and dragged his broken body toward Cabrillo, his left arm shattered in the fall. A trail of smeared blood oozed from his ruined foot as he crawled up onto Juan's semiconscious body. He reached up with his good hand to apply another death grip to Juan's throat.

But Cabrillo shook himself awake just in time to clutch the thick wrist, while wrapping his leg around the Vendor's waist on his weak side. He rolled him over onto his back, pinning the Vendor's outstretched arm between his thighs in a classic arm bar. Juan squeezed with every last ounce of strength he had. It felt like he was trying to bend a steel girder instead of a man's arm.

The Vendor thrashed and flailed with the rest of his body, but Juan increased the pressure on his arm, extending the man's elbow to the breaking point. This was the moment in any Brazilian jujitsu match when an opponent would tap out—but not the Vendor.

"Give it up, Hashimoto!" Cabrillo shouted through gritted teeth. "Tell me how to stop that boat!"

The Japanese squirmed and jerked, trying to escape, his neck pinned to the ground by Cabrillo's calf.

"Never."

"Have it your way," Juan growled in a whispered breath.

Crack. The elbow snapped.

The Vendor's body slackened in Cabrillo's grip. He released him, and climbed to his wobbly legs. Everything in Cabrillo wanted to break the Vendor's neck and finish him off. But seeing his broken body blunted Juan's rage. He wouldn't murder a helpless man, not even one as vile as this one. Besides, he still had a mission to accomplish.

"Tell me how to stop your boat and maybe I won't let you bleed out on this floor."

"You haven't beaten me, Mendoza," the Vendor said, grimacing in anguish. "The *Ghost Sword* is on her way. I've won." He began to laugh hysterically.

"You won't be laughing inside of a CIA black-site prison."

The Vendor closed his eyes, smiling.

"No prison for me, *baka*. I'm going to my reward."

The Vendor opened his mouth wide, then snapped it shut hard, cracking his teeth together. The poison capsule released into his mouth. The Vendor's body began convulsing violently and frothing bubbles oozed over his lips.

Ten seconds later, he was dead, his body knotted like a pretzel and his fingers curled like bird's claws.

Linc burst through the door, his P90 at the ready. He saw the Vendor's body on the floor.

"What happened to him?"

Cabrillo cradled his busted rib cage with one arm as he refitted his dangling earpiece with the other.

"He punched his own ticket."

"Looks like he had some help."

"What about that sub?"

"No clue."

"*Oregon*?"

"No comms with her down here."

"Casualties?"

"Three wounded. Two noncritical. And you."

Cabrillo limped through the doorway, his hand jammed against his earpiece.

"Callie? Callie? Do you copy?"

★

Aboard the *Oregon*, the grim op center crew tracked the progress of the Mark 46 torpedo on the big wall monitor as it streaked toward the *Spook Fish*.

"Ten seconds to impact," Linda said to no one.

Callie's voice crackled on the speakers.

"Linda? You copy?"

"We copy."

"Tell Juan . . . Tell Juan I—"

A muffled explosion cut her short.

Callie screamed until her comms went out.

78

Callie's own sonar was tracking the *Oregon*'s incoming torpedo, its pinging increasing each passing second. She turned off the sound. It only worsened her fear.

She'd already made her peace with God in the five minutes since the launch. Trading her life for the lives of many was an easy decision, really. But she needed to get something off her conscience.

"Linda? You copy?"

"We copy."

"Tell Juan . . . Tell Juan I—"

But she waited too long to spit it out. Her eye just caught the streaking torpedo striking twenty yards away. The resulting explosion tore open the sub's hull, breaking it apart and roiling the water in a mass of bubbles, shrapnel, and debris. The *Spook* rolled over with the blast.

Callie screamed, more shocked than terrified. Something struck the *Spook*'s acrylic screen just as the lights went out. Her screens all went blank.

An emergency red light kicked on. It gave her just enough light to see that water was seeping in through the crack, but the red glow against the acrylic blocked her view outside.

She could tell the *Spook* was still attached to a fragment of the sinking hull, and judging by the rush of bubbles speeding by, she was being dragged down fast.

Suddenly she had another decision to make and only seconds to make it.

She could ride the *Spook* down to the bottom and hope there was enough air to last until a deepwater rescue could be organized before she froze to death or the leak in the acrylic filled up her cockpit like a goldfish bowl.

The other option was to swim to the top. She was at least ninety feet down now. Every second she hesitated dragged her down another foot.

She hadn't held her breath for a hundred feet in over a decade. She'd never make it. And even if she could hold her breath that long, she'd die of the bends.

So really the only question was, how did she want to die?

Easy choice.

She grabbed the first of two emergency release handles and pulled it. Frigid seawater poured into the cockpit. The shock of it stole her breath away. She fought off the panic and filled her unpracticed lungs with the deepest breath she could. She shut her mouth just before she was completely submerged.

With the water pressure equalized, she pulled the second handle and a small charge blew the cockpit door off. She kicked her way out of the sinking *Spook Fish*, still welded to the shattered fragment of the *Ghost Sword* hull, and began her ascent.

Callie felt strangely calm. She glanced down and saw the *Spook* vanish into the abyssal dark.

She glanced back up. High above, the dim, silver disk of the sun shimmered through the dark, clear water. The image warmed her despite the icy grip of the sea.

All of her old deep-diving tricks came back to mind. She calmed herself, and slowed her movements. Pursing her lips, she hummed, expelling a light and steady stream of air to prevent her lungs from bursting. She told herself she was going to make it.

But a few seconds later her lungs began to ache and pain like ice picks stabbed at her eardrums. Against all of her training she quickened her kicks and clawed up at the sun above her, desperate as a woman buried alive trying to dig herself out of an unmarked grave.

The extra effort stole away the last few moments of her breath, her lungs burning with fire. Her throat begged to open to suck in the cold water to quench it, but she fought it . . .

and fought it . . .

and fought it.

Until her vision dimmed and the pale light above melted into black.

79

Callie's eyes fluttered open. All she could see was white.

Her head ached as if her skull were pinned inside of a hydraulic press. A hiss filled the air.

She rolled her throbbing head over to find relief. Instead, she saw an angel's familiar face in a portal window.

"Hello, sleepyhead." Dr. Huxley's voice sounded tinny on the speakers inside of the *Nomad*'s hyperbaric chamber. "I bet you feel terrible, don't you?"

Callie tried to smile, but it hurt. In fact, she hurt all over. The kind of hurt she'd only felt once before.

"Terrible . . . would be an improvement," she finally managed to say. "How . . . long?" She struggled to finish the sentence.

"You've been in there for a little over four hours. I'm monitoring your vitals. It will be at least another thirty minutes before you're completely out of the woods and then we can pop the tab."

Callie noticed her arm was tethered to a half-empty IV drip, and ECG nodes were attached to her chest. There was also a pulse oximetry clip on the end of her finger. All of her vitals were being monitored wirelessly.

"Hungry, dear?"

"A little. And thirsty."

"I'll put in an order with the galley right now. Someone's here to see you."

Huxley stepped aside and Juan's bruised and bandaged face replaced it. Max, Eddie, and Murphy, in a sling, crowded behind his broad shoulders, trying to see Callie through the tiny portal, too. The three of them waved and smiled as they caught glimpses of her.

Callie felt like Dorothy in her bed after she got back from Oz.

"How did I wind up here?" Callie asked.

"Doc said it was a miracle," Juan said. "Another thirty seconds and we'd have lost you."

"The Vendor?" she asked.

"Dead as a doornail."

"The neurotoxin?"

"Dispersed harmlessly into the sea, thanks to you."

Callie nodded. "I'm just glad it worked out okay."

"I don't know how you came up with that plan."

Callie grinned. "Sometimes crazy *is* the plan."

Juan laughed. "You get better fast. That's an order."

"Aye, Cap'n," she whispered as her eyes fluttered and she fell back to sleep.

EPILOGUE

Juan winced as he pulled on his vintage tropical shirt. The loose bandages were only meant to hide the mass of red-and-purple bruising over his cracked ribs. The broken bones had already begun to heal on their own and needed no assistance.

Hali Kasim's voice called out on the overhead speakers just as Cabrillo opened up his leather travel satchel.

"Langston Overholt for you, Chairman."

"Pipe him in, please."

"Will do."

An audible click transferred the call.

"Juan, my boy," Overholt said over the sound of a truck gunning its engine.

"Lang? Sounds like you're out of the office. You okay?"

"As my mother used to say, 'Finer than frog's hair and only half as jumpy.'" A voice called to Overholt in the background and he took a moment to reply.

"Is that Burmese I'm hearing?"

"Perceptive as always. Delivering some aid here. But off the record, of course."

"Of course." Cabrillo knew the American government was providing humanitarian aid to the pro-democracy rebels battling the ruling junta in Myanmar. It didn't surprise him to learn that the CIA was providing other kinds of support, nor that Overholt was on-site taking a personal interest in the deliveries. If his black budget was involved, he wanted to know where every penny was spent.

"How can I help you?" Juan asked.

"I'm only calling to congratulate you."

"You already did." Juan pulled open a drawer. "Your bank transfer cleared last night, including Callie's reimbursement for the loss of the *Spook Fish*. Thanks for that."

"It was the least I could do. But I'm calling in regard to the latest developments."

A truck passed by and Overholt lowered his voice. "Your idea to issue an automated recall for all of the Vendor's drone vessels worked perfectly. We've recovered all eighteen of his manufacturing vessels as well as three automated submarines. The cargo on board each of those ships alone is priceless. Whatever AI technology we can't press into immediate service will be reverse engineered and incorporated into our future designs."

"Glad it worked out." Cabrillo set a stack of neatly folded underwear into his travel bag.

"Thanks to the data you recovered from Pau Rangi, we've also begun rolling up his human networks inside allied governments. The others we'll turn and use as spies. For all intents and purposes, the Vendor's organization is destroyed."

"Fantastic. What about your mole?"

"Erin Banfield? A sad story that. I knew Banfield years ago. Brilliant in her day, though somewhat untethered. She was dedicated to her own ambition, and nothing else."

"I know the type."

"Banfield fled under an alias, of course. We lost her scent until an Interpol notification alerted the FBI office in Lisbon. They picked her up on an unrelated charge and are holding her in Portugal."

"Lucky break."

"Yes. She was charged with assaulting a local in Algarve. The man was living with another woman in a property she owned there under the same alias. Some sort of love triangle, apparently."

Another Burmese voice interrupted Overholt in a hurried tone. The old spymaster calmly answered him in the same tongue. Apparently satisfied, the other voice disappeared.

"Sorry about that, Juan. Where was I?"

"Love triangle." Cabrillo laid two pairs of linen pants into his satchel.

"Oh, yes. Miss Banfield will be extradited tomorrow morning and punished to the fullest extent of the law. Unless, of course, some untoward accident were to occur in transit."

Juan glanced up at the speakers. Despite the old spymaster's gentlemanly demeanor, when it came to treason, the unforgiving Overholt took no prisoners.

"Thanks for the update."

"What are your plans now?"

"Like the *Oregon*, I'm heading for dry dock and a retrofit."

"You both deserve it. Well, I've got another delivery to make and need to run. Take care, my boy."

"You, too, Lang." Cabrillo darkened with concern. "And head on a swivel, okay?"

Overholt laughed. "Of course! Just like I taught you."

★

The *Oregon* was docked at the same Malaysian shipyard where she had been born a few years back. It was an ideal place for her to be refurbished in secrecy and seclusion. After greasing the right palms, the necessary permissions were granted and nosy inspectors turned away.

In addition to the needed repairs, the op center team decided it was also the perfect opportunity to reevaluate the *Oregon*'s current mix of offensive and defensive systems. Thanks to inputs from Murph and Eric, the next iteration of the mighty ship would prove even more protected and lethal when she set sail again in a few months.

With the *Oregon* entering dry dock soon, Cabrillo gave all of the Gundogs and most of the crew a paid thirty days leave. Only a skeleton crew of engineers and technicians were staying behind to supervise the repairs and refurbishment.

Max, Murph, Eddie, and Linda gathered on the dock to say their goodbyes to Juan and Callie. The *Oregon*'s mighty shadow and a freshening breeze kept the warm tropical sun at bay. Murph's wounded arm was in a sling, and Eric awkwardly cradled something behind his back.

Juan and Callie were flying to Honolulu to meet with her design team and work on a few upgrades for a new variant of the *Spook Fish*. The first one had performed so admirably that Cabrillo wanted to acquire one for future *Oregon* operations. The trip to Hawaii was also an excuse for Cabrillo to get some much needed rest, and equally important, to reacquaint himself with a surfboard once his rib cage settled down.

"I brought this," Linda said, still wearing her eye patch. She handed Callie a bottle of the neon-peach hair color Callie had admired when she first arrived.

"Can't wait to try it," Callie said as she hugged Linda. "Love the pirate look, by the way."

Linda whispered, "Don't tell the guys, but Hux said I don't need it anymore."

Callie giggled. "Our secret."

For a brief moment after Callie's rescue, Linda had been overwhelmed with guilt for firing the torpedo that had nearly killed her friend. But Callie assured her all was well and that she would have done the same thing had their roles been reversed. The incident only deepened their mutual respect and friendship.

Eric cleared his throat. Callie turned around and Eric presented his gift.

Callie smiled with delight. It was a brass plaque engraved with the silhouette of a woman free diving to the surface. It read CALLIE CO-SIMA, UNOFFICIAL WOMEN'S WORLD RECORD, 352.7 FEET.

"This is beautiful. Thank you."

"I thought it up, but the boys in the shop put it together. That depth was the last sonar reading I had on the *Spook Fish* when you blew the emergency hatch. I know it's not official or anything, but it's your personal best, for sure."

"Maybe I set the official world record for escaping a wrecked submarine."

"What a dope! Why didn't I think about that? I'll definitely check it out."

"No need." Callie grinned. "It's perfect the way it is." She turned to Murph and hugged him, careful not to touch his sling.

"It was a real pleasure meeting you, Dr. Murphy. Keep up the good work."

Murph blushed redder than a Grainger County tomato.

"The pleasure was all mine, trust me."

A bicycle bell rang behind them. They all turned around.

A brightly colored *beca*, the local version of a bicycle-powered tuk-tuk, approached the farewell gathering and braked to a squeaking halt. The wiry young Malaysian driver sported a wide toothy grin, a San Francisco 49ers jersey, and mirrored aviators.

"I thought you called a limo," Juan said as he picked up his leather satchel.

"When in Rome." Max extended his calloused hand.

Juan took it. "You know how to reach me if you need anything."

Max pulled Juan closer. He nodded at Callie as she tipped the grateful driver for loading her heavy duffel onto the *beca*.

"You take extra care of that special lady."

Juan glanced up at the battle-scarred *Oregon*, her valiant decks looming high above. His face beamed with pride.

"You do the same."